Praise for *The Cottingley Secret*

"*The Cottingley Secret* tells the tale of two girls who somehow convince the world that magic exists. An artful weaving of old legends with new realities, this tale invites the reader to wonder: could it be true?"
—Kate Alcott, *New York Times* bestselling author of *The Dressmaker*

"There is real magic in these pages. And beauty. And heart."
—Nicole Mary Kelby, author of *The Pink Suit*

"I adored *The Cottingley Secret,* which shifts between a bookstore in present-day Ireland and an actual account from the World War I era of two girls who claimed to have seen fairies—and captured them on film. Gaynor has penned in majestic prose an enchanting and enthralling tale of childhood magic, forgotten dreams, and finding the parts of ourselves we thought were lost forever."
—Pam Jenoff, *New York Times* bestselling author of *The Orphan's Tale*

"Richly imagined and terrifically enchanting, Hazel Gaynor's *The Cottingley Secret* is an enthralling tale where memories serve as lifelines for the living, and the unseen is made real. Reading this novel is akin to finding hidden treasure—each character, a friend; each chapter, a revelation."
—Ami McKay, author of *The Witches of New York*

Praise for *The Girl from The Savoy*

"Hazel Gaynor captures both the heartache and hope of England between the wars in this richly imagined novel peopled with unforgettable characters, impossible ambitions, and unexpected twists of fate. Once begun, I dare you to put it down."
—Kathleen Tessaro, *New York Times* bestselling author

"A disarmingly charming story of a young woman determined to make her dreams a reality. *The Girl from The Savoy* is as sweet as a love song, as energetic as a tap dance, and full of dazzling details about life in London after the disasters of the Great War. I won't soon forget Dolly Lane and her rise from loneliness and hardship to the glitter of stardom."

—Jeanne Mackin, author of *The Beautiful American*

"Hazel Gaynor's artistry as a storyteller shimmers like satin in *The Girl from The Savoy*. Evocative, transportive, and redemptive, this is an enchanting gem of story."

—Susan Meissner, author of *Secrets of a Charmed Life*

"Gaynor struts her historical stuff once again in her latest novel, set in 1920s London. . . . Gaynor's latest quickly and completely takes readers into the exciting world of London between the wars. This story of loss and longing and of the power of ambition and dreams to carry us forward is filled with rich period details and unforgettable characters."   —*Booklist*

Praise for *The Girl Who Came Home*

"*The Girl Who Came Home* follows on the centenary remembrance of the *Titanic* in 2012. Is the world ready for yet another account of this tragedy? With this novel, the answer is a resounding yes."

—*New York Journal of Books*

"Readers will enjoy this lovely, heartfelt story."

—*RT Book Reviews* (4 stars)

"A phenomenal book that is a must read!"   —Examiner.com

the
COTTINGLEY
SECRET

Also by Hazel Gaynor

The Girl from The Savoy
A Memory of Violets
The Girl Who Came Home

WILLIAM MORROW
An Imprint of HarperCollins*Publishers*

the
COTTINGLEY
SECRET

HAZEL GAYNOR

PUBLISHERS
Since 1817

P.S.™ is a trademark of HarperCollins Publishers.

HarperCollins books may be purchased for educational, business, or sales promotional use. For information, please email the Special Markets Department at SPsales@harpercollins.com.

FIRST EDITION

Designed by Diahann Sturge
Part title art © Fona/Shutterstock, Inc.

Library of Congress Cataloging-in-Publication Data has been applied for.

ISBN 978-0-06-249984-4
ISBN 978-0-06-269048-7 (library edition)

17 18 19 20 21   LSC   10 9 8 7 6 5 4 3 2

For Frances and Christine, and everyone who believes.
And in memory of Nana Aelish Gaynor, who
left us on January 13th, 2017.

If the confidence of children can be gained, and they are led to speak freely, it is surprising how many claim to have seen fairies.
—SIR ARTHUR CONAN DOYLE

Those who don't believe in magic will never find it.
—ROALD DAHL

the
COTTINGLEY
SECRET

Prologue

Cottingley, Yorkshire. August 1921.

*F*airies will not be rushed. I know this now; know I must be patient.

Stiff and still in my favorite seat, formed from the natural bend in the bough of a willow tree, I am wildly alert, detecting every shifting shape and shadow; every snap and crack of twig. I dangle my bare feet in the beck, enjoying the cool rush of the water as it finds a natural course between my toes. I imagine that if I sat here for a hundred years, the water would smooth and round them, like the pebbles I collect from the riverbed and keep in my pockets.

In the distance I can see Mr. Gardner, the man they sent from London, with his round spectacles and bow tie and endless questions. He peers around the trunk of an oak tree, watches for a moment, and scribbles his observations in his notebook. I know what he writes: remarks about the weather, our precise location, the peculiar sense of something different in the air.

Elsie stands on the riverbank beside me, her camera ready. "Can't you 'tice them?" she urges. "Say some secret words?"

I shrug. "They're here, Elsie. I can feel them." But like the soft breath of wind that brushes against my skin, the things we feel cannot always be seen.

I know that the best time to see them is in that perfect hour before sunset when the sun sinks low on the horizon like a ripe peach and sends shafts of gold bursting through the trees. The "in between," I call it. No longer day, not yet night; some other place and time when magic hangs in the air and the light plays tricks on the eye. You might easily miss the flash of violet and emerald, but I—according to my teacher, Mrs. Hogan—am "a curiously observant child." I see their misty forms among the flowers and leaves. I know my patience will be rewarded if I watch and listen, if I believe.

Tired of waiting, Elsie takes her camera and returns to the house, where Aunt Polly is waiting to hear if we managed any new photographs. The others soon follow: Mr. Gardner, the newspaper reporters, the "fairy hunters" who come to snoop and trample all over the wildflowers and spoil things. My little friends won't appear just to please these onlookers. They move according to the patterns and rhythms of nature, not the whims of so-called experts from London. Fairies, I understand. These men, I do not.

Glad to be alone again, I watch the pond skaters and dragonflies, listen to the steady giggle of the water, sense the prickle of anticipation all around me. The sun dazzles on the water and I squint to shield my eyes as the heat at the back of my neck makes me drowsy and tugs at my eyelids, heavy with the desire to sleep.

I press my palms against the bark, smoothed from decades of weather and countless children who have sat here. How many of them have seen, I wonder? How many of them have known?

I wait and I wait, whispering the words from my picture book: "'There shall be no veil between them, / Though her head be old and wise. / You shall know that she has seen them, / By the glory in her eyes.'"

And then . . .

The lightest ringing at my ears. The slightest movement of fern and leaf.

My heart flutters. My eyes widen with excitement.

A flash of vibrant emerald. Another of softest lavender-blue.

I lean forward. Draw in my breath. Don't make a sound.

They are here.

Part One
The Bottom of the Garden

It all started with the very best of intentions ...
—FRANCES GRIFFITHS

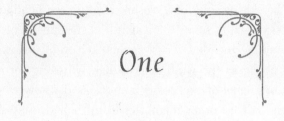

One

Ireland. Present day.

Olivia Kavanagh didn't believe in happy endings. Life hadn't worked out that way for her so far. At thirty-five, she had almost stopped believing it ever would. Almost, but not entirely, because there were moments—flashes—when she remembered who she used to be: someone who thought anything was possible; someone who believed in everything.

Often it was her dreams that transported her back to happier times, flickering sepia visions played out like a silent movie reel. Sometimes it was a remembered fragment of a favorite bedtime story—the *púca* and the *sídhe,* the Good People of Irish folklore who'd crept from the torch-lit pages of her books to inhabit the wildest places of her imagination. And on special days, her memories were stirred by the familiar refrain of a song her mammy used to sing to her, madly operatic and wonderfully silly. She would hear the voice on the wind, a faint whisper at first and then louder: *"There are fairies at the bottom of our garden! / It's not so very, very far away; / You pass the gardener's shed and you just keep straight ahead— / I do so hope they've really come to stay.*" It was always a welcome burst of light among the shadows that clouded Olivia's heart.

She heard the song now as she stood on the headland, face tipped skyward to savor the warmth of the sun on her cheeks and the tangerine glow it cast against her eyelids. Rowdy gulls circled above as the wind sang to her, whistling through the stubby branches of the gorse that released its sweet coconut scent and stirred other memories from their drowsy slumber: picnics between rain showers, leaning into the wind and pretending to fly, laughter, love. She wrapped her arms around herself, embracing all these simple joys she'd once known. Like other children collected pebbles and shells from the beach, Olivia collected memories of her childhood, filling an imaginary bucket with the best of times. Yet she would gladly have emptied it for one more of her mammy's special hugs, one more encouraging smile, one more whispered *"I love you, Livvy."* Those particular memories were her greatest treasures.

Opening her eyes, she absorbed the familiar view: the chameleon sea, green then gray then blue; the distant peaks of the Wicklow Mountains; the rhododendrons below, painting the headland in a parade of purple and pink. She made a frame with her thumbs and forefingers, squinting through it to find the best light and angle and composition. Something else she'd stopped doing and couldn't remember why. Her camera, like so many passions she'd once held, lay idle in a box beneath the bed. Where had she gone—that creative, independent woman? Where was she?

Determined not to let her mind stray to thoughts of Jack and the wedding plans she was drowning in, nor to the painful secret that pricked at her conscience like a splinter, she focused, kept her thoughts only of now, of *this* moment. The breeze tugged at her sleeve, encouraging her to do what she'd come here for. She inhaled—a deep, moment-defining breath—exhaled, unzipped her backpack, and removed the heavy package.

FOR OLIVIA KAVANAGH. TO BE OPENED ONLY
AT THE TOP OF HOWTH HEAD.

So deliberate and precise. Just like him.

Opening the package, she removed a folded sheet of writing paper. It flapped frantically in the breeze, a fledgling eager to test its wings. Her fingers grasped it tightly as she turned her back to the wind, sat on a slab of granite rock, and began to read.

23rd June 2014

My dearest Olivia Mae,

They tell me I should put my affairs in order now that your dear Nana has gone into the nursing home, and as a result, I am writing the saddest of good-byes to you although I will actually see you on Sunday. Such are the curiosities that accompany the later years of one's life.

I cannot bear the thought of you reading this letter alone in the stuffy solicitor's office I have the misfortune to find myself in now, so I hope—when the time comes—you follow the instructions, choose a nice bright day, and enjoy your walk. You always loved it up here with the wind blowing and the secret tunnels through the rhododendron bushes that open up into such breathtaking views. You loved the romance of the place where Joyce set Molly Bloom's proposal scene: ". . . the sun

*shines for you he said the day we were lying among the rhodo-
dendrons on Howth head in the grey tweed suit and his straw
hat the day I got him to propose to me. . . ."* You once said you
felt closer to your Mammy when you were up high, which is
why I brought you here, so you could read the letter together.

I know this will come as a surprise, but I have left you the
bookshop in my will. Something Old (and Hemingway the
cat, if he'll have you) is now yours, my dear girl. You always
said it was a special place, that there was something magical
about all those old books on my dusty shelves. Well, now the
magic is all yours and I leave it gladly in your care. Don't
be too alarmed. I know this will pose something of a logisti-
cal problem with you living in London, but a dear friend of
mine—Henry Blake—and a clever nephew of his have agreed
to be on hand, should you run into any difficulties (such as interfering old crows like Nora Plunkett. She is best ignored, by
the way, but if you have the misfortune to run into her, please
be sure to pass on my disregards).

I have also left you something I hope will be of interest.
It is a memoir of sorts—a fascinating story. It was given to
your Nana many years ago. She passed it on to your mother.
I would have mentioned it to you sooner, only I'd forgotten all
about it until I rediscovered it recently. You know my views on
stories choosing the right readers at the right time, and now
is not the right time. When you read this letter, it will be.
Consider it a project in distraction, if you like. Your Nana had
some other things connected to the events related in the memoir,
but I can't remember what, or where, they are. Have a good
rummage around and you'll hopefully find them.

So now, my dear, I must say good-bye—and look forward
to seeing you on Sunday!

I suppose I should leave you with some words of wisdom, but find myself lacking when the moment demands. All I will ask of you is to remember that you can do anything if you believe in yourself. You don't need anybody's permission to live the life you desire, Olivia. You need only the permission of your heart.

All my love to you,
Pappy
x

PS The shop key is enclosed.

Olivia had always found good-byes and endings difficult, but this was the hardest of all. Harder than the wake, or the removal, or the funeral mass she'd endured in the past week. She read the letter again, then once more, her heart aching with grief for the dear grandfather she'd lost, and glowing with pride to know he had entrusted her with his beloved bookshop.

With salt tears stinging her wind-reddened cheeks, she took a heavy document from the package: hundreds of typed pages, bound together by a violet ribbon. The title page read, "Notes on a Fairy Tale, by Frances Griffiths," the thin pages crackling satisfyingly as Olivia flicked through them, the fanned paper blowing against her face like a long sigh released. Her bookbinder's instincts sensed a forgotten story in need of care and attention, her thoughts turning to sheet leather and awls, paper drills, seam stitching, and gold embossing—the familiar tools of her trade.

Untying the ribbon, she turned the page and read the opening lines.

In some ways, my story has many beginnings, but I suppose I should start on the April evening when I arrived in the Yorkshire village of Cottingley. That was when I first met Cousin Elsie, first heard the waterfall, and first became enchanted by the little stream at the bottom of the garden. So much has happened since, so many words and pages written about those summers and the things we saw, or didn't, depending on whose version of events you believe. Even now, as I start to put my story into words, I'm not quite sure how it ends. Perhaps that will be for others to decide. For now, all I can do is write it down as I remember it . . .

Olivia's interest was already captured. Cottingley was where her Nana had grown up.

With the wind tugging impatiently at the edge of the pages, she read on . . .

NOTES ON A FAIRY TALE
Cottingley, Yorkshire. April 1917.

An emerald locomotive delivered me to my new life in Yorkshire that cold April night. It had a brass plate, number 5318, and raced along the tracks, eating up the passing blur of green fields and soot-black towns, rocking me from side to side as I whispered the final words of the book I was reading. "'But remember always, as I told you at first, that this is all a fairy tale, and only fun and pretense; and, therefore, you are not to believe a word of it, even if it is true.'"

I remember blinking back tears that sent the letters swimming about on the page until I was sure they would fall off the edge. I'd read *The Water Babies* a dozen times, and I cried every time I reached the end. But my tears that day weren't just for the water babies and Tom, nor for the end of the story. My tears were for the end of so much more: my beautiful home in Cape Town, long walks by the ocean, seashells clacking in my pockets, rose-pink sunsets, my father's hand in mine. That I was hurtling toward a new home in a strange country only made everything worse.

Mummy stirred in the seat beside me and opened a sleepy eye. "What are you saying, Frances? What is it now?"

"Nothing, Mummy. I'm reading. Go back to sleep."

I watched her as she yawned, shifted in her seat, and drifted back to sleep. She looked different since we'd arrived in England, changed by the long journey across the ocean, travel-crumpled and gray-faced; colorless, almost. All the lovely color of our life had started to fade away when we'd said good-bye to Daddy in Plymouth. Even the drab khaki of his British Army uniform was reduced to shades of black and white in the portrait he'd had taken on the promenade and pressed into my hands before heading off to join his battalion and "do his bit."

I took the photograph from my pocket as the locomotive rattled along. I didn't like photographs, didn't trust the darkrooms and the mystical procedures required to make them, and I especially didn't like the photograph of Daddy. He was so much more than the serious-looking man staring back at me from the posed portrait. Daddy was loud and boisterous. His laughter boomed like cannon fire. His chin was bristly when he kissed me good-night. His arms comforted me like nothing else could. It made me anxious to look at him so stiff and still, like a corpse. I placed the photograph inside my book for safekeeping as the train slowed, creaked alongside a platform, and shuddered to a halt.

Mummy sat up with a start. "Why have we stopped? Where are we, Frances?"

I rubbed at the misted glass with my coat sleeve and read the station sign. "Bingley." My heart lurched. After weeks of traveling, we had reached our destination. All I wanted to do was turn around and go straight back.

"Bingley! That's our stop!" Mummy jumped up, retrieving our discarded hats and gloves and chivying me to do the same, quickly, as quickly as I could. "Have you got everything, Frances? Hold the door, please! Your hat? Rosebud? Your case?"

I said I had. It didn't take long to gather up two books and my rag doll. There hadn't been time to bring much more.

A round-faced woman reached up to the luggage rack to lift down my small traveling case. When I thanked her she looked at me as if she'd seen a ghost.

"Well, you're certainly not from 'round here. Where you from then? Australia?"

"South Africa."

"You're a *long* way from home. At least you won't be bothered by lions in Bingley, eh. Although I'd tek lions over some Yorkshire folk any day o't week."

The woman laughed at this and I said thank you again, hardly able to understand what she'd said at all.

Half a dozen people alighted at Bingley. One by one we stepped reluctantly out of the cozy carriage onto the cold station platform, where a ruddy-cheeked porter with saggy jowls rushed about, looking important. He spoke with the same accent as the woman on the train, and said something about being *nithered* as he helped sleep-dazed passengers with their luggage. I thought it clever of Daddy to have sent on our heavy portmanteau from Plymouth. I was weary enough of my small case as it was, and could tell from the violet shadows beneath Mummy's eyes that she, too, was exhausted from our long journey, although she would never admit it and hadn't complained once all the way from Cape Town. Mummy didn't like to complain. "There's always a silver lining," she said. "If you look hard enough." As I traipsed along behind, following her out of the smoke-filled station into dark, unfriendly streets, I doubted there was a silver lining in Bingley, no matter how hard I might look.

"Uncle Arthur'll be here soon to collect us," Mummy said, clapping her hands together and stamping her feet.

"He'll be driving one of Mr. Briggs's fancy motorcars, no doubt."

"Who is Mr. Briggs?"

"The boss. Your Uncle Arthur works for him at Cottingley Manor, looking after his motorcars. Wealthiest man in Cottingley. You're to mind your manners when you're introduced to him."

I assured her I would and stared numbly at the narrow street of terraced houses in front of me. Blackened windows obscured any sign of life inside. The street lamps also stood black and lightless. It was all so unwelcoming. Nothing about it said *Welcome to Yorkshire, Frances*. Nothing about it said *home*.

I don't know what I'd expected of Yorkshire, but somehow I wasn't surprised that my first reaction was one of enormous disappointment. The air was bitterly cold, the streets were dull and dark, and the people spoke in accents I couldn't understand. Yorkshire had none of the color I'd known in Cape Town—the vivid pinks and purples of the freesias and arum lilies in the flower sellers' baskets. Yorkshire had none of the fragrant floral perfume, or the tang of salt in the air from the ocean. My greatest disappointment was discovering the true identity of the dirty gray lumps heaped up beside the station walls.

Mummy laughed when I asked her what they were. "It's snow, Frances! Mucky old Yorkshire snow. What did you think it was? Suet dumplings?"

I didn't know what suet dumplings were and had only seen the pure white snow of my picture books. What I saw in front of me wasn't like that. This was dirty snow. Old snow. Disappointing gray Yorkshire snow to match the gray Yorkshire sky and gray Yorkshire walls and gray Yorkshire stone on gray Yorkshire houses. I bent down to scrape a ball of the snow into my hands and threw it immediately down again. It was so cold it burned.

"I don't like Yorkshire snow," I said, kicking crossly at it with the toe of my boot. "And I don't like Yorkshire." I folded my arms across my chest, crumpled my face into a furious scowl, and didn't even try to stop my bottom lip from sticking out, even though I knew Mummy didn't like to see me sulk.

She placed her hands on her hips and raised an eyebrow. "I see. Well, that's as may be, Frances Mary Griffiths, but you'll have to learn to like Yorkshire—snow and all— because this is where we live now. This is our home, and the sooner you get used to the idea, the better."

There was a sharpness to her voice that I didn't care for. A sharpness caused by the exhaustion and emotion of the long journey from Cape Town, by the worry of watching a dear husband and father go off to fight in a dreadful war that had already robbed hundreds of thousands of wives and children of their loved ones. Hot tears pricked my eyes, but I refused to let them fall. I muttered an apology and stared hard at my boots, shoving my hands deep into my pockets, glad of the heavy wool coat Mummy had made especially for the inclement weather she knew would await us in England. We stood in silence. The mist of our breaths mingled with the ribbons of smoke that crept from tall chimney pots on the houses across the road.

"I know it's all happened very quickly, love," Mummy said, her voice softening as she bent down so that her eyes were level with mine. She had pretty eyes. Blue-gray, like the dolphins I would sometimes see in the harbor back home. "But you'll soon think of Yorkshire as home. I promise." Her face relaxed into a weary smile as she grasped my hands in hers.

Much as I longed to believe her reassurances, I knew she was putting on one of her Brave Faces. Three weeks at sea, sailing toward an unfamiliar country and closer to the front line of war, had unsettled us all. I'd known about the plans to leave Cape Town so that Daddy could join the British Army in France, but still our sudden departure had come as a surprise. As the mighty *Galway Castle* had carried us across the heaving ocean, Daddy had explained that our departure was confirmed only the night before we set sail. "You have to be brave, Frances. We all do. Promise me you'll be brave." Looking deep into his eyes, I'd promised as solemnly as I could, but standing in the dark Yorkshire streets, I didn't feel brave at all.

"But I don't have any friends here, Mummy. And I miss Daddy."

There. I'd said it. The secret thoughts I'd carried with me for weeks had been spoken out loud, my whispered words snatched away by the frigid air that set my teeth chattering and my body shaking. I'd never been good at keeping secrets, and this one was too big to keep wrapped up inside me any longer. My Daddy had gone to war. I had left the only home and friends I'd ever known. I felt very lost and very afraid.

Mummy fussed at me, brushing the tears from my cheeks and tugging at my black fur hat, pulling it down to cover the pink tips of my frozen ears. I could see the glisten of tears in her eyes.

"Your father will be back soon. When the war's over. And you'll make new friends. Once you get settled into school and you and Cousin Elsie get to know each other, you'll forget all about Cape Town. You'll forget you ever lived anywhere other than Cottingley!" She smiled her special *we have to be brave* smile and wrapped her arms around me, pulling my woolen scarf close around my neck so that it tickled my chin. "Everywhere feels strange when it's dark and cold. You'll like it much more in the summer with the heather bursting out all over the moors." She squeezed my hands tightly as she spoke, as if to make absolutely certain of it. "Things'll get better, love. I promise."

And right there, in the dark unfamiliar streets of Bingley, the distant promise of summer became something of a talisman to me. By the summer, Yorkshire would feel like home, and I wouldn't miss Daddy or my friends in South Africa or the sight of the whales blowing out at sea. By the summer, the war would be over and everything would be perfect again. Holding my mother's hands, I thought of the words inscribed inside *Princess Mary's Gift Book*—the book of fairy stories I'd brought with me. "It is only by believing in magic that we can ever hope to find it." I had to believe in better times ahead, even though it felt impossible right now.

Mummy suggested we sing something while we waited for Uncle Arthur. "It'll cheer us up," she said. "And warm us up too." I loved it when Mummy sang. Nellie Melba was her favorite. "I'll start and you join in when you're ready."

Amid the murky darkness, the first verse of "Lo, Here the Gentle Lark" sounded so lovely and bright. I joined in with the chorus and our song left the narrow street, soaring over the rooftops and church spires and chimneys. I imagined that somewhere, out there in the dark, Daddy might hear us, and that he would be cheered by it too.

We sang until a motorcar pulled up at the top of the street and a tall man emerged from the driver's seat.

Mummy grabbed hold of my arm. "Look, Frances! It's Uncle Arthur." There was a new energy to her voice, a new purpose to her stride as she broke into a funny sort of trot and set off up the hill. "You'll like him. Come on!"

Clutching Rosebud tightly to my chest, I picked up the small traveling case I'd carried halfway around the world and trudged up the hill after her, hoping all my disappointment and worry would slip away into the gaps between the cobbles that threatened to trip me up with every weary step.

NOTES ON A FAIRY TALE
Cottingley, Yorkshire. April 1917.

If I hadn't been so cold, I might have laughed at Uncle Arthur standing beside the car, waving his arms wildly around his head like sails on a flour mill.

"You made it, then!" His voice was like a bass drum, reverberating off the terraced houses. I'd never heard anything quite like it. "Annie Griffiths—back in Cottingley! Well, I never."

Mummy grasped hold of Uncle Arthur's hands, her knuckles turning white with the effort, as if she would never let go. "Back in Cottingley, Arthur!" she said. "Who'd have believed it, eh? I thought we'd never get here. All those hours on the train from Plymouth felt longer than all the weeks at sea. Didn't they, Frances?"

I nodded and wondered why Mummy's voice had gone all up-and-downy as I stared at this man called Uncle Arthur who smelled of motor oil and pipe tobacco and was all broad smiles and firm handshakes. He wore dark gray woolen trousers and a gray woolen jacket and removed a funny-looking flat cap from his head, revealing erratic strands of wispy black hair and great bushy eyebrows flecked with gray, like his mustache. I thought it strange that he had so much hair on his face and so little on his head, as if everything had grown in the wrong place. I wobbled slightly as I gazed up at him, still unbalanced by the pitch and roll of the ocean, and was glad when he stooped down to my height, peering at me with kind amber eyes.

"Bah 'eck. Is this really our Frances?" I tried to smile, but my face was too cold. "What's up? Cat got your tongue?"

Mummy placed a reassuring arm around my shoulder
and excused my silence. "Don't mind her, Arthur. She's
worn out, poor thing. She'll come 'round."

"Suppose it's a bit of an ordeal, all that time at sea.
Never did care for it. Makes me go green at the gills. Good
to be back on dry land, is it?" I nodded again, mesmerized
by Uncle Arthur's eyebrows, which wriggled about like
great fat caterpillars when he spoke. "You'll be right after
a good feed and a decent night's sleep."

He stood upright and lowered his voice as he addressed
my mother. "Missing her father, is she?"

"She is. They're very close. She dotes on him, and him
on her."

Uncle Arthur declared the war to be a funny old business, and they both looked sad and shook their heads before Uncle Arthur turned to speak to me again.

"You were nowt but a bairn last time I saw you, Frances. You're almost as big as our Elsie now! Must be all that
sunshine, eh?"

His accent was so thick, I imagined you could slice it
and put butter on it. He had a funny habit of twisting his
cap between his fingers as he spoke, as if he were wringing out a dishcloth. As I watched him do this, I noticed his
hands were enormous. I tried not to stare because I knew
it was poor manners, but I stared anyway as Mummy chattered on beside me.

"It's strange to be back in Yorkshire, Arthur. I hadn't
realized how much I'd missed it. There's something in the
air, something that gets to you. You know?" She patted her
chest, and Uncle Arthur nodded to indicate that he understood. "For all the time we've been in Cape Town, now that

I'm back it's like I've never been away. I can't wait to see our Polly! How's she keeping?"

And with that, Mummy burst into tears. I stood awkwardly at her side, wishing she would stop. I'd seen her cry only once before—the previous day when we'd said goodbye to Daddy. It was as if by finally arriving in Yorkshire, all the emotion of our journey had to somehow escape from her, like a kettle singing on the stove. Except it wasn't steam coming out of Mummy. It was great fat tears that only came faster when Uncle Arthur put his hand on her shoulder to comfort her.

"Now, now, Annie. We'll have none of that. Can't have you arriving at your sister's all red-eyed and rotten-looking. She'll have you put straight to bed with a dose of castor oil." He took a striped handkerchief from his pocket and passed it to her before busying himself with our luggage. "Polly hasn't sat down since we got the telegram yesterday evening to say you'd landed in Plymouth. Never seen the house so clean." He peered over the top of the car. "Don't tell her I said that!"

Mummy laughed through her tears and promised she wouldn't.

"Don't mind me, Frances," she said, noticing my discomfort. "I'm just relieved to be here. I'll be right after a cup of tea."

I hoped so. I wasn't sure how long I could keep being brave if Mummy kept bursting into tears like that.

The wind tugged impatiently at my skirts and the hem of my coat, and I was glad when Uncle Arthur suggested I jump into the car and Mummy tucked a warm blanket over my knees. I placed Rosebud and my books on top of the blanket, turning the pages of *Princess Mary's Gift Book,* lingering over the illustrations that accompanied my favorite poem, "A Spell for a Fairy," and whispering the familiar lines of verse. "'There shall be no veil between them, / Though her head be old and wise. / You shall know that she has seen them, / By the glory in her eyes.'"

After a few minutes of huffing and puffing and what sounded like Yorkshire cursing, Uncle Arthur climbed into the driver's seat. He rubbed his hands together briskly, blowing on them for warmth as he declared himself nithered. When I asked what *nithered* meant, Mummy laughed and explained that *nithered* was a Yorkshire way of saying you were really cold. I tucked Rosebud beneath the blankets to stop her being nithered too.

"We'll have you back at the house in no time, Frances, love. You'll be better after a bit o' scran. Your Aunt Polly has stew and suet dumplings ready." Uncle Arthur had to shout to make himself heard above the noise of the engine. "Hope you're hungry. She's made enough to feed Kitchener's Army!" I thought of the mottled gray snow outside the station and hoped that Aunt Polly's suet dumplings would look more appetizing. "And our Elsie'll just be home from work," he continued. "She's all talk of her cousin from South Africa. Says she can hardly remember you. She's not a bad lass, our Elsie. Daft as a brush, mind, but not a bad lass."

He chuckled in a funny way that made me smile.

I didn't remember Cousin Elsie and was intrigued to meet her. Mummy had talked about her all the way here during the long sea crossing. It had been Cousin Elsie this and Cousin Elsie that. I imagined her to look like Alice from *Alice's Adventures in Wonderland* and that being six-teen—a full seven years older than me—she would tell me lots of clever things. I worried she wouldn't like sharing her bedroom with me, let alone her bed, but that was to be the arrangement. I'd worried about it all the way from Cape Town and worried about it now while Uncle Arthur crunched the gears as the motorcar struggled up the steep, narrow streets.

While Mummy and Uncle Arthur talked about boring grown-up things, I pressed my nose to the window, follow-ing the threads of smoke that wound their way from chim-ney pots on gray houses. Despite the gathering gloom, no light shone from the windows, and the street lamps stood lifeless, like fire irons. It had been the same in Plymouth. "Blackout," Daddy had explained. "So the enemy can't find us with their zeppelins." I didn't like to think about the enemy. War had felt far away in South Africa. Now it felt dangerously close. I thought about Daddy's portrait tucked inside the pages of my book and prayed for his safety.

After a short distance, the smoky gray town gave way to the dip and rise of valleys and rolling hills, field after field crisscrossed with undulating lines of low stone walls that stretched all the way to the horizon. Bracken and gorse covered the landscape, silvered by moonlight.

"God's own country," Uncle Arthur announced as the car struggled up another steep incline. "That's what York-shire folk call Yorkshire."

I said I could understand why, what with it being so high up and so close to heaven. Mummy turned to me and said I was a good girl and why didn't I shut my eyes now and try to sleep.

The motion of the car and the steady hum of the engine soon conspired to lull me into a travel-weary sleep. With my arms wrapped around Rosebud, I dreamed of heather-topped hills and sleepy valleys and a pretty woodland stream where dragonflies danced across the water as I sat down among the ferns and the meadowsweet, waiting for the summer to find me.

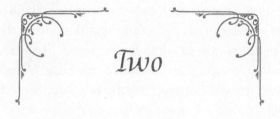

Two

Ireland. Present day.

Afraid the pages would be blown away by the wind, Olivia tied the ribbon around them and returned the document to her backpack to continue reading later. As she did, a gust of wind snatched Pappy's letter from her hand, sending it tumbling away among the scree and rocks.

Scrambling to her feet, she rushed after it, grasping at handfuls of air as the paper skittered past her feet, snagging momentarily on a distant gorse bush until another strong gust wrenched it free and sent it rushing over the cliff edge. She gasped as it took flight, joining the gulls to soar high above the sunlit sea toward England and Yorkshire, where Pappy had first met his beloved Martha. As she watched it shrink to a distant dot, Olivia thought of Pappy's last words to her: *"You need only the permission of your heart."* Her heart wanted everything she saw in front of her now: space to walk and to think, crisp natural light, fresh sea air, possibility. Pappy was right. She *didn't* need anybody's permission. Perhaps—and her stomach lurched as the thought developed from a murky seed of doubt to one of increasing certainty—she didn't have to marry Jack.

And there he was, back in her thoughts. Jack Oliver. The man she was due to marry in three months, despite the doubts that kept her awake at night and dragged like lead weights on the ivory lace train she regretted choosing. "A bad case of the jitters. Totally normal," her friends said, prescribing an antidote of gin and shopping when she'd confessed to her uncertainty. But it went deeper than the jitters. Far deeper. And then there was the letter she'd received three weeks ago. The letter she hadn't told Jack about. The letter that confirmed what she'd feared, and cast the greatest doubt of all in her mind.

Her breathing quickened as the audaciousness and then the conviction of her thoughts bubbled up inside her. What if she called the wedding off? Adrenaline rushed along her skin in goose bumps, like a child anticipating something forbidden about to be done.

She couldn't.

Could she?

Life was all about the wedding lately—endless decisions about chair covers and dessert wine and other things the guests would never notice. But what if she didn't *have* to make those decisions? What if she stayed in Ireland and took care of Nana and managed the bookshop? What if she made a life *here*, in Howth, the quiet harbor town she'd grown up in where people moved with the ebb and flow of the tide rather than an unreliable tube service?

As she turned the bookshop key over in her hand, it struck Olivia that in answering the wedding planner's questions, she'd ignored the most important questions of all: Was she happy?

Did she really want to go through with this? What alternative future might she find if she dared to look?

On impulse, she took off her engagement ring and pushed it deep into the corner of her skirt pocket. Her hand looked strange without its glittering diamond solitaire, better for its absence. She'd never liked it, or the way it caught on her favorite jumpers and trapped dough between the prongs when she made bread. She'd have happily worn one of her mam's vintage costume rings, bursting with character and story, but vintage wasn't Jack's style. Diamonds were Jack's style, and as he'd reminded her, they are, after all, a girl's best friend.

Just not this girl's.

Holding the bookshop key, she began to walk down the slippery scree of the headland, following the trail that descended through the candy-colored rhododendrons, stooping beneath the dark tunnels formed from their gnarled roots and branches. She walked through the golf course and on into the village, the wind pushing always at her back as the words of Frances Griffiths's memoir whispered to her and the melody of a much-loved song played at her ears and memories of happier times flickered through her mind. As she walked, she thought about the determined, inquisitive little girl she'd once been and the determined, optimistic woman she'd always imagined she would become.

She was sure she was still in there somewhere, among all the doubt and uncertainty.

She just had to find a way to believe in her again.

HOWTH VILLAGE SPARKLED beneath the extravagant May sun, tempting people outside with their coffee, despite the cool edge to the breeze. Olivia loved these spring days, before the arrival of summer's tourists and wasps. These were days for eating the first ice cream of the year and for blustery strolls along the harbor wall. She watched a young couple buy fish heads to throw to the seals in the harbor, drawing laughter from the gathered crowd as the seals barked their encouragement.

At the café on the corner, she ordered a latte and gave her name as Liv. While she waited, she caught her reflection in the mirror behind the counter, hardly recognizing herself without her curtain of long auburn curls to hide behind. She touched her fingertips self-consciously to the nape of her neck, wondering what Jack would say about her pixie cut. He'd always preferred her hair long. Said it was more feminine. She hadn't planned such a drastic change, especially not on the morning of Pappy's funeral, but she'd heard "Moon River" on the radio in the hairdresser's and remembered Pappy saying her mother used to look like Audrey Hepburn in *Roman Holiday*.

"Latte for Liv."

Olivia took the cup from the server, smiling as she saw what he'd written in black marker on the side. *Live*. It shouted at her like an urgent instruction. *Live! You must live!* The irony was not lost on her.

Leaving the café, she put her head down against the brisk wind and turned up Abbey Street, past the rainbow-colored terraces and the old abbey ruins, past the pub and the church. Poignant memories and half-remembered stories were waiting around every corner: awkward teenage kisses here, exam sorrows drowned there, the doleful chimes of the church bells as she'd wondered how she would ever learn to tie her shoelaces properly without her Mammy to show her.

As she walked, the familiar voices of doubt and insecurity surfaced. *What are you thinking? You don't know the first thing about running a bookshop. You can't call off the wedding.* But another—more hopeful—voice chimed in. *It'll be all right, Liv. This is a good thing. A fresh start. You need only the permission of your heart.*

She carried her doubt and determination along like awkward shopping bags, one in each hand, banging against her shins with every step. Only when she reached the top of the cobbled lane did her internal chatter shush, and her breath caught in her chest as she read the sign on the wall to her right. *Little Lane. Lána Beaga.*

She walked on, the cobbles familiar beneath her boots as she passed the thatched cottages: a bakery, a florist, a gift shop, a vintage clothing shop, and, at the end of the lane, the bookshop.

❧ Something Old ❧

It was like looking at a dear old friend, and her heart soared at the sight of it: whitewashed brick walls, two stories, four sash windows, an arched doorway, a rusting cartwheel leaning against the wall. The paintwork was chipped, the windows were dulled with rain spatters, the window boxes bloomed with weeds, and discarded flyers for harbor tours huddled apologetically in the doorway, but it was beautiful to Olivia. So many fragments of her life were anchored to this place, the safe haven where she'd sheltered among the magical places of other people's imaginations when the awful truth of her reality was too much to bear. Books were Olivia's salvation once upon a time. She hoped, with all her heart, they would be again.

The faded old sign above the door swayed in the wind on wrought-iron brackets, creaking a feeble *Hello, Liv.*

A smile curled at the edges of her lips. "Hello, Shop."

She remembered running curious fingertips over the em-

bossed lettering and fancy gilded flourishes of the old Gaelic
script. She remembered the comforting warmth of Nana's
hand in hers as they'd watched Pappy hang the new sign,
dressed for the occasion in his best three-piece suit. His dream
come true. His very own shop for rare and secondhand books.
"Special and much-loved," as he preferred to call them. *"Like my
Martha."*

Nana had worn her favorite blue coat, her red hair whipping
around her face like flames as she'd nagged at Pappy to move
the sign to the left a bit and to the right a bit until he lost his
temper and told her it'd have to shaggin' well do. He wasn't
really annoyed. He adored his Martha too much to ever be
properly annoyed with her. In any event, Nana had told him
to do it himself so, and they'd left him to it while they bought
cream cakes and red lemonade from the bakery.

The sign had hung there ever since. Lopsided. Perfect. Blackened now with decades of grime and dust, and yet still Olivia
sensed it: the suggestion of something magical in that ancient
lettering, the promise of wonderful things behind that old black
door. She took the key from her pocket and faltered. The thought
of Pappy not being inside was unbearable.

"You won't sell many books standing there gawping at the
place."

Olivia turned to see Nora Plunkett standing behind her,
arms folded in defiance, her face creased into her trademark
scowl. Nora Plunkett was the self-appointed, self-important secretary of the local Society of Shopkeepers and always looked
like she'd come prepared for an argument. She was a thorn in
the side of several shop owners on Little Lane, not least because
she refused to let anyone lease the cottage beside Something

Old. It had once been her husband's furniture shop but had stood empty for years.

"Hello, Nora." Olivia didn't have the emotional capacity to bother with Nora's spite today.

Nora sensed Olivia's defenses were down. "I hope you've come to give this place a good tidying up. Weeds and rubbish in the doorway won't tempt many customers." She cut Olivia off as she began to speak. "I'm surprised to see you're still in Ireland. I'd have thought you'd be back to London and planning your wedding now that Cormac's been laid to rest."

She at least had the decency to cross herself as she said this.

Olivia looked up at the shop sign, drawing strength from its familiarity before turning her gaze on her inquisitor. "Didn't you know, Nora? The shop's mine now."

A look of surprise. "Cormac left you this old place?"

"Yes. He left me this lovely, fabulous old place."

Nora tutted. "Should have given it up when Martha went doolally. Bit off more than he could chew if you ask me."

Nobody *was* asking her. People rarely did, but she offered her poisonous opinions anyway. There were so many things Olivia wanted to say to the interfering old cow, but she chose her words carefully, as Pappy had always reminded her to.

"First of all, my Nana is not *doolally*. She has Alzheimer's. It's a medical condition, and it's bloody awful. I wouldn't wish it on my worst enemy." She hoped her pointed stare drove her point home. "And second, my grandfather—God rest him—would never have given up on this shop." She felt an overwhelming surge of affection for the old place with its chipped paintwork and weeds. "And neither will I."

Nora harrumphed and folded her arms even tighter across

her chest. "How will you manage to run a bookshop all the way from London?"

And there they were, all the dull practicalities, waiting to trip her up. What about money? What about her car and her job? What about the invitations and the church and the deposit on the country house they'd booked for the reception? How could she ever unpick the tangled threads of her life in London?

Olivia took a deep breath, drawing courage from Nora's spiteful disapproval. "I'm staying in Ireland for a while, to sort things out."

Nora glanced at Olivia's left hand and raised her eyebrows meaningfully. "I take it your fiancé won't be joining you while you 'sort things out'?"

Olivia bristled. What business was it of Nora's, anyway? "No, actually. He won't. This is something I'll be doing on my own." It felt reckless and liberating to say it out loud. "So now there's something to gossip about with your friends. I'd say you'd be able to get some mileage out of that until Christmas, at least."

Before Nora could reply, and with her heart galloping in her chest, Olivia turned the key in the lock and stepped inside the bookshop, leaving Nora Plunkett alone on the cobbled lane to wrestle with her conscience. Assuming she had one.

THE SHOP BELL jangled above Olivia's head as she kicked aside the junk mail and closed the door behind her. The bell rang again before falling into a respectful silence.

It was like stepping back into her childhood.

The mellow scent of Pappy's pipe tobacco still lingered in the air, as if he'd just popped out the back to put the kettle on. Olivia imagined him pottering about, dressed to the nines, a bow tie or a cravat at his neck, a silk handkerchief in his top pocket, his fingertips conducting the air as he hummed along to a sweeping aria playing on his ancient radio, that knowing twinkle in his eyes, silver-gray, like moonlight. Pappy was like someone from another time or place. Nana used to say it was as if the stories on the shelves had become part of him, so that it was impossible to know where the bookshop stopped and he began. Olivia thought of his tartan slippers and his habit of closing the shop on a whim, because it was a lovely Tuesday afternoon, or because his favorite concert series was playing on the radio and he didn't want to be interrupted. He was one of a kind.

Was.

The awful reality of his absence hit her, ripping through the shop like a brick through glass, sending broken memories of happier times skittering across the creaky floorboards to hide in dark grief-stricken corners. He wasn't there, and yet he was everywhere: in every cracked spine, on every dusty shelf, in the warped glass at the windows and the mustard-yellow walls. Something Old wasn't just a bookshop. It was him—Pappy—in bricks and mortar, leather and paper. He'd loved this place so much, and Olivia knew she must now love it for him.

"I miss you, Pappy." Her voice was a whisper, her words rushing away to hide between the rows of thick encyclopedic volumes and slim clothbound novels. "I miss you so much."

Her eyes flickered around the dimly lit room. Every surface was covered with books, every shelf buckling beneath the weight of them. Teetering piles of recently donated books leaned against walls and table legs: the discarded spoils from house clearances waiting for rare treasures to be found. Some had toppled over, left where they fell, like a Neolithic monument. Olivia walked up and down the shelves, running her fingertips along the ridged spines. Layer by layer, the shop had grown over the decades. Like ancient rock, each newly added section held the story of a specific time in her life: Irish Poets was secondary school. Myths and Fables was graduation. British Classics was art college. Children's Books was London. Pappy had been working on a new section, Fairy Tales and Folklore. The shelves gaped with empty spaces. The job incomplete. Olivia's to finish.

Stepping over threadbare rugs with treacherous curls at the corners, she walked over to the old oak desk and put down her coffee, her fingertips tracing the stories that had been told here, captured forever in the grain. She pictured the three of them sitting around the desk to celebrate the infamous wonky sign-hanging. They'd laughed as they slurped red lemonade from Nana's best china teacups and sent bubbles up their noses. It was the first time Olivia had laughed since the accident. Everyone noticed, but nobody remarked on it, afraid to break the rare spell of happiness.

The silence of the shop grew heavy with expectation. Like a bored child waiting for ideas from a parent, Olivia sensed that it was waiting for her to tell it what to do next.

"What should I do, Pappy?"

The wind whistled through the letterbox, rattling the window frames, replying with her echo. *What should I do? What should I do?*

She finished her coffee and switched on the radio. Classical music blared out: Lyric FM. Pappy refused to listen to anything else, declaring other stations an insult to his ears. She was glad for the symphony that filled the impatient silence of the shop, glad for the dramatic crescendos and decrescendos that infused everything with a rich melody of possibility. She sat down in the Queen Anne chair and, for want of anything better to do, began to empty the desk drawers.

The first was full of boring-looking accounts and serious-looking business correspondence. Bills for rent and bills for the nursing home. She scribbled the name Henry Blake onto a scrap of paper and put it in her cardigan pocket. Whoever this colleague of Pappy's was, she had a feeling she would need his help sooner rather than later.

The second drawer contained the heavy old ledgers in which Pappy had diligently cataloged all the books, stubbornly refusing to embrace any new technology and insisting that the old ways were the best. She thumbed through the pages and pages of entries. All of them would have to be transferred onto a website if she was to have any hope of connecting with a wider range of collectors and buyers. It was a daunting task, but at least it was something practical she could do.

The third drawer—the last—refused to open at first. Olivia tugged at the handle, jiggling it from side to side until the drawer eventually gave way to reveal a tan leather briefcase, battered and mildewed. She lifted it out, brushed off a thick layer of dust, unbuckled the rusted straps, and folded back the soft leather flap. A sweet, musty smell bloomed around her, the scent of lost secrets and stories to be told. Inside the briefcase were a large hardback book and a manila folder full of yellowing newspaper articles. Olivia lifted everything out onto the desk to take a closer look.

The book was a children's picture book called *Princess Mary's Gift Book*. The binding was still mostly intact, and despite a little foxing on the frontispiece and flyleaf, it was in good condition. On the title page an inscription read, "To Frances. Happy Christmas, 1914. From Mummy and Daddy. 'It is only by believing in magic that we can ever hope to find it.'" Olivia turned the pages carefully, savoring the delicious old-book smell of leather and vanilla and imagination. The book naturally fell open at a poem called "A Spell for a Fairy" by Alfred Noyes, beautifully illustrated with pencil sketches of ethereal young girls in flowing dresses. Tucked into the seam between the last two pages of the poem was an old sepia photograph. It was a strange image, nothing but a jumble of shapes among long grass. On the back, in neat script, were the words "To Ellen. The fifth photograph. Real fairies! From Frances."

Putting the book and photograph to one side, Olivia picked up the manila file next and took out several yellowed pages from a publication called *The Strand Magazine,* dated November 1920 and March 1921. The headlines grabbed her attention:

FAIRIES PHOTOGRAPHED
AN EPOCH-MAKING EVENT DESCRIBED BY
A. CONAN DOYLE

and

THE EVIDENCE FOR FAIRIES
BY
A. CONAN DOYLE
WITH NEW FAIRY PHOTOGRAPHS

She was surprised to discover Arthur Conan Doyle had written about fairies, but the articles interested her. She scanned over the first one, stopping at a paragraph halfway down the page: "It was about the month of May in this year that I received a letter from Miss Felicia Scatcherd, so well known in several departments of human thought, to the effect that two photographs of fairies had been taken in the North of England under circumstances which seemed to put fraud out of the question." But it was when she turned to the second page that Olivia's hands stilled and the shop fell extraordinarily quiet. The page carried a black-and-white photograph of a little girl, a garland of flowers on her head, a slight smile at her lips as she watched a group of fairies dancing in front of her. The caption beneath it read:

ALICE AND THE FAIRIES.

Alice standing behind the banks of the beck, with fairies dancing before her. She is looking across at her playmate Iris, to intimate that the time had come to take the photograph. (An untouched enlargement from the original negative.)

Olivia's hand rose instinctively to her heart. She knew this photograph. Like a fossil in rock, the image of the girl and the fairies was imprinted forever on her mind, part of a forgotten story she had always sensed was somehow linked to the unwritten pages of her own. The sight of it sent her thoughts rushing back over the years as painful memories pushed forward, forcing her to remember.

SHE'D FOUND THE photograph at the bottom of her mammy's jewelry box and was instantly enchanted by the picture of the girl watching the fairies. She asked her mother about it while she was getting ready to go out.

"Ah, now, that's a very interesting story, Olivia. Far too interesting to tell you in a hurry." Her face was alight with secrets as she pressed the silver photo frame into Olivia's hands. "You take care of it. I'll tell you all about it in the morning."

She remembered that her mother's hands were cool in hers. She remembered the sweet marzipan scent of her hand cream, the rattle of the hooks as she drew the curtains, the tickle of hair against her cheek as she bent down to kiss her good-night and tuck her in. She remembered the smooth edges of the silver photo frame as she'd held it beneath the tight cocoon of sheets and blankets. She remembered small details like this.

It was her mammy's birthday. She was going out for the evening with friends and had never looked more beautiful to Olivia.

"Are they real, Mammy?" she'd whispered as her mother made to leave the room. "The fairies?"

The light caught the silver in her mother's earrings, making them shimmer as she turned in the doorway. "Anything can be real if you believe it is." A smile played at her lips as she blew a kiss. "Sleep tight, love. Nana and Pappy are in the sitting room. Be good for them. No messing, now. I'll see you in the morning and I'll tell you all about the photograph then. Fairies don't like to be rushed. We'll have more time tomorrow."

As her mother pulled the bedroom door softly closed behind her, something nagged at Olivia, a sense of foreboding she was too young to understand. Her stomach churned in knots of worry. Her skin prickled with a silent dread. She desperately—irrationally—didn't want her mammy to leave. She sat up in bed to call after her, but didn't want to make her cross and spoil her special evening, so she lay back down under the covers, clutching the photograph in her hands, first wondering and then dreaming about the little girl and the fairies.

AS THE FINAL chords of a Beethoven symphony danced around the bookshop, Olivia put down the article. She thought of Pappy's letter and the document in the package: "*. . . It is a memoir of sorts—a fascinating story. . . . You know my views on stories choosing the right readers at the right time. . . . Consider it a project in distraction. . . .*"

Taking the thick bundle of paper from her backpack, she untied the violet ribbon, settled back in the chair, and continued reading . . .

NOTES ON A FAIRY TALE
Cottingley, Yorkshire. April 1917.

I woke up to my mother gently shaking my shoulder.

"Wake up, Frances, love. We're here."

I opened a sleepy eye, forgetting for a moment where *here* was. There had been so many *here*s recently, new ports and towns to wake up in.

I sat up, stretched, rescued Rosebud from the floor, and clambered out of the car. The cold air nipped at my cheeks and crept into my bones so that I was sure I would never be warm again. A bitter smell of chimney smoke and damp wool settled on my skin and made me cough.

Mummy rubbed my back—for reassurance or to help the cough, I wasn't sure. "There it is, Frances," she whispered. "Number 31, Main Street. Just as I remember it." She fussed at the creases in her skirts before moistening the corner of a handkerchief and rubbing at a sooty mark on my cheek. I squirmed and batted her hand away. "Well," she prompted, "what do you think of your new home?"

The house stood at the top of a steep hill, at the end of a row of seven or so terraced houses bunched together like books on a shelf, with Number 31 the bookend propping them up. They were all the same simple shape: a narrow doorway in the middle, two lace-curtained sash windows at the bottom, two at the top, and a black gate and railing separating the small front garden from the street. I didn't think much of my new home, but I knew better than to say so.

"It looks nice, Mummy. Which is my bedroom?"

"You mean *Elsie's* bedroom. You're not to think of it

as yours, Frances. We're to remember that this isn't our house. That we're guests." She glanced at the house. "I think Elsie's bedroom's at the back. It looks out over the garden."

But I wasn't listening. My attention had strayed toward the dark space that lay beyond the row of houses and continued on beyond the crest of the hill.

"What's up there?" I asked.

Mummy's gaze followed mine. "Nothing much. Cottingley Woods and the glen that cuts through them. There's a small stream down there. A beck, the locals call it. Nothing for little girls to be troubling themselves with, anyway."

"I'm not little. I'm nine and a half."

I sensed Mummy stiffen beside me. "That's as may be, Frances. Still, you're not to be going there."

"Why not?"

"Because it's dangerous beside the water. And you'll muddy your new boots. That's why. Now, stop mithering."

There was something Mummy wasn't telling me. I wanted to know more about the woods and the glen and the beck, but my thoughts were interrupted by squeals of delight as Aunt Polly appeared at the front door.

Mummy grabbed my hand. "Eee! There's our Polly now! Come on, Frances."

I followed my mother up the short garden path, turning, just once, to look back at the dark space beyond the house. Mummy's words of caution only made it more appealing, but as I reached the front door, my curiosity was smothered by lavender-scented folds of soft green fabric as Aunt Polly scooped me up in a great big hug.

"Well, look at you, Frances Griffiths! All grown-up!"

She placed her hands on my frozen cheeks. Her palms were as rough as old calico but toasty warm. "And a real bonny lass too. Just like our Annie was at your age. Just the same."

Aunt Polly's voice was all singsong and merry. It reminded me of the birds I would hear in the evening through my bedroom window. I couldn't take my eyes off her—my aunt, my mother's sister—admiring her lovely smile and her thick auburn hair piled up in fashionable puffs around her face. I forgot all about forbidden woods and rivers and gray Yorkshire snow and stepped inside.

The narrow hallway was filled with tears of joy and *eeh*s and *ahh*s while Uncle Arthur carried in the luggage, declared himself jiggered, and closed the door behind him with a thud. I flinched at the sound. Everything I'd known was on the other side of that door, and wherever he was, I knew my poor Daddy wouldn't have a front door to close behind him, however jiggered he might be.

Aunt Polly bundled coats and hats under and over her arms until she resembled a farmer's scarecrow. "Our Elsie's ever so keen to meet you, Frances," she chirped, taking hold of my hand and leading me into a pleasant little room to the left of the hallway. "Come on through, love. There's no need to be shy."

There was no time to be shy. I was deposited on a rug in the middle of the room, like a museum exhibit declared open for inspection. In front of me, beside a crackling fire, stood a pretty girl whose eyes reflected the tawny glow of the flames and sparkled with mischief.

"Now, Frances," Aunt Polly announced. "This is your

cousin, Elsie. Elsie, this is Frances. Your cousin, all the way from South Africa."

Elsie was tall for sixteen, almost as tall as the ferns precariously balanced on high plant stands on either side of the chimney breast. I admired her pretty lace blouse with a cameo brooch at the collar, and her fashionable bottle-green skirt that skimmed her ankles. I hadn't expected her to look quite so grown-up. She had the same rich auburn hair as her mother, and the same beguiling smile. Even if she didn't look anything like Alice in Wonderland, she looked ever so friendly.

"Hello, Frances. I like your ribbons."

I'd chosen the violet ribbons for my hair especially that morning, keen to make a good impression on my Yorkshire relations. The color reminded me of summer evenings in Cape Town. I blushed at Elsie's compliment and muttered a thank-you.

"D'you want to see our bedroom?" she asked.

I turned to Mummy, who was hovering in the doorway with Aunt Polly, their arms linked together as they looked on in silent maternal delight. She nodded in encouragement and mouthed, *Yes, please.*

"Yes. Please."

Aunt Polly beamed. "Go along, then. Off you go. Tea in ten minutes, mind, so don't be getting settled into any of those daft games of yours, Elsie Wright."

Elsie said she wouldn't, and as we walked out of the room she whispered to me, "Don't mind her. We'll have plenty of daft games."

"What games?" I asked.

"Pretend expeditions. Like Shackleton at the South Pole. Do you know about him?" I nodded. Daddy had told me all about the polar explorers. "Sometimes I'm so far away I don't make it back in time for tea. Then Mummy gets vexed."

I giggled as I followed Elsie's black boots.

"And don't slouch, Elsie," Aunt Polly called after us. "Walk tall."

Elsie tutted, and held her head up and her shoulders back, making herself even taller. Daddy said good posture was the sign of someone who knew their own mind. I copied as I followed Elsie up the creaky stairs to the bedroom we were to share at the top of the house.

"It'll be a bit poky, what with there being two of us in it," she said, stooping to avoid a beam as we entered a small bedroom. "But I suppose we'll make do."

As she walked over to a narrow window that looked out onto the garden below, it struck me that Elsie wasn't the sturdy Yorkshire lass I'd imagined. Being so tall and slim, she was a rather dainty girl. She gave the impression that there was too much life inside her, fighting to find a way out through the long teenage limbs she couldn't quite control. She wasn't entirely unlike Alice, after all.

As Elsie chattered on about it probably being too cold to play out tomorrow and perhaps we could play rummy instead, I looked around the room. The narrow bed took up most of the space. A wardrobe stood under the eaves on one side. An oak chest sat at the foot of the bed and a ewer and basin stood on a washstand behind the door.

"We're to share the bed," Elsie said as she noticed me taking in my surroundings, unaware that I'd been thinking of little else for the past few weeks. "So if you've cold toes, keep them to yourself, and I promise I'll try not to snore. You can keep the chamber pot on your side if you like." She glanced at Rosebud, who I was still holding in my hands. "Who's this, then?"

My cheeks flushed. "Rosebud."

"Suppose she'll want to share the bed an' all?"

I stared hard at my feet, certain that Elsie was too old for dolls and must think me a silly little girl. "She's a favorite."

Elsie placed her hand on my shoulder. "I'm only teasing. You'd best get used to being teased if you're to live here. Daddy's always teasing me." She took one of Rosebud's floppy hands in her fingertips and shook it. "Very pleased to make your acquaintance, Miss Rosebud."

I giggled at Elsie's put-on accent. "You sound like I imagine Queen Mary to sound."

"Well, I *am* terribly posh. I hope you have a very pleasant stay, Miss Rosebud." She placed Rosebud on the pillow, tucking her in beneath the counterpane. "See? She likes it here. She's asleep already."

Elsie's kindness was a balm to my troubled mind. She was a bright splash of color in Yorkshire's palette of gray. Perhaps with Elsie, it wouldn't be so bad living here, after all.

"What else did you bring?" she asked.

"Just Rosebud. And two books. *The Water Babies* and a picture book. We didn't have room for anything else. Only our clothes."

"*The Water Babies* makes me sad."

"Me too. I'll show you the picture book if you like.

It's ever so nice. *Princess Mary's Gift Book*. It was sold as a fund-raiser for the war effort. It has lovely pictures and . . ."

Elsie laughed and grabbed my hands. "Stop blethering on, will you! I can't understand half of what you're saying, anyway. You talk funny."

"So do you. What's blethering?"

"Talking too much! You can show me the book later, and I'll show you my watercolors."

I'd always been a dreadful artist and admired anyone who could paint or draw with any skill. "What do you paint?"

"Scenery around Cottingley, mostly. And fairies." She saw the reaction on my face and grinned all the way up to her eyes. Something about her smile made my skin burst out into goose bumps.

"Why fairies?" I asked.

"Why not? Everyone loves fairies." She stood up and walked over to the doorway. "Come on. I'll show you the lavvy. You must be bursting."

I followed Elsie back downstairs, through a small scullery, down narrow steps that led to the cellar, and out through the cellar door to the outhouse. I didn't like being in there in the dark and told Elsie I was too nithered to go and would use the pot instead.

Over tea, I tried to follow the conversation, but kept losing it among the unfamiliar accents and funny words. Everything was new and peculiar—the taste of the water, the smell of the smoke from the fire, the prayer Aunt Polly said before we ate—but I felt warm and comfortable and there was a lot to be said for that after weeks at sea. I spoke only when spoken to and did my best to remember my manners, needing to be prompted only once by Mummy to say thank you. There was plenty of laughter around the table that evening, and although I wished Daddy could be with us and that I could have second helpings of Aunt Polly's delicious stew and dumplings, I remembered what Mummy had told me about war rations and tried to be grateful for what I'd had.

At bedtime, Elsie and I sat up for a while in our night-dresses and nightcaps while I showed her the photograph of Daddy, and she told me about her job as a "spotter" at Gunston's photographers in Bradford, where she filled in the holes in the gelatin on the photographic plates. "Otherwise you get black spots on the finished print," she explained. I thought her clever to know so much about it, but she said it was boring work, and she wished she'd been clever like me and had stayed on at school. She took out her paintings, which she kept in an old biscuit tin beneath the bed. They were very good: scenes of the village and landscapes of the hills around. I especially liked her paintings of fairies dancing beside a woodland stream.

"How do you make them look so lifelike?" I asked.

"It's to do with shading, mostly, adding shadow and light so they look less flat on the page. The rest is imagination."

After I'd admired them, I showed her *Princess Mary's Gift Book*. "You'll think the stories a bit babyish, I expect," I said. "But the pictures are nice."

I turned the pages by candlelight, showing Elsie my favorite illustrations from the Alfred Noyes poem "A Spell for a Fairy." I'd read the words so often I knew them by heart and recited the poem all the way to the end. "'You shall hear a sound like thunder, / And a veil shall be withdrawn, / When her eyes grow wide with wonder, / On that hill-top, in that dawn.'"

Elsie liked the illustrations and said I read very well, which made me feel proud and grown-up.

After she'd blown out the candle, we whispered a while in the dark, each too conscious of the other to relax into sleep. Elsie fidgeted beside me while I tried to keep my frozen toes away from hers until they'd warmed up on the stone hot water bottle at the foot of the bed. The room was coal-black, and strange creaks and cracks disturbed me.

I tried to go to sleep, but the wind whistled in the eaves, and there was another sound: a faint rumbling that set my mind racing.

"What's that noise, Elsie?"

Elsie rolled onto her back. "What noise?"

"That. Listen."

Elsie sat up, straining to hear. "That's the waterfall at the beck. It'll be full at the moment, with the late snow and the thaw." She lay back down again and yawned, a misty breath caught in the sliver of moonlight that slipped through the window. "Try to sleep, Frances. It's late."

My thoughts returned to the forbidden space beyond the house. Cottingley Woods, Mummy had said, and the glen that cuts through them. *"Nothing for little girls to be troubling themselves with. . . . It's dangerous. . . . And you'll muddy your new boots."* "Mummy said I wasn't to be going there. That it's dangerous."

Elsie didn't say anything.

"Is it?" I tensed my legs and gripped Rosebud tightly in my arms as the darkness intensified around me.

"Well, there *are* stories."

My eyes widened. "What stories?"

"Local folklore mostly—and then there's the Hogan girl."

"Who's the Hogan girl?"

"She went missing last year. Wandered off in the middle of the night and never came back. Sleepwalking, they reckon, although some people have other explanations."

"Like what?" I was terrified and enthralled by the suggestion of a local mystery.

"Child snatchers. Bad men. Her mother says the fairies took her. They never found her, either way." I shivered and drew my knees up to my chest. I sensed that Elsie wanted to say more but thought better of it. "Anyway, it's nowt, really. Just folk's imaginations running away with them. I shouldn't be gossiping about Mrs. Hogan, 'specially since she'll be your teacher."

I lay still, thinking about my schoolteacher and her missing child and listening, all the while, to the distant rumble of the waterfall. "Can we go to the beck tomorrow?"

"Suppose so. If you can think of nowt better to do."

"What does *nowt* mean?"

"*Nothing. Nowt* means *nothing*. You've a lot to learn before we make a proper Yorkshire lass of you, Frances Griffiths. Now, get to sleep before my father comes up and tans your backside!"

"He wouldn't!"

"He might."

For all that my body longed to rest after our long journey, my mind was wide awake. I tossed and turned, willing myself to sleep. The mattress was too soft and then too lumpy, the room so dark I couldn't see my hand in front of my face. I thought of Daddy and wondered if he was lying awake, thinking of me. I wondered if gunners on the front lines ever went to sleep at all.

Eventually I forgot about my toes touching Elsie's and snuggled up beside her for warmth, glad of the companionship. With the rumble of the waterfall in the distance, I slipped into sleep and dreamed of a red-haired girl holding a posy of white flowers. The words of Mr. Noyes's poem crept from the pages of my picture book and tiptoed into my mind. "Then you blow your magic vial, / Shape it like a crescent moon, / Set it up and make your trial, / Singing, 'Fairies, ah, come soon!'"

NOTES ON A FAIRY TALE
Cottingley, Yorkshire. April 1917.

After a restless night filled with curious dreams of a little girl and a pretty woodland cottage, I woke to a bright peaceful morning. Elsie was already up and the sheets were cold beside me. I clambered to the end of the bedstead to peer out of the narrow window. A bitter chill still laced the air, but a generous sun gilded everything that had been so colorless and gray yesterday. The constant sound of the waterfall reminded me of Mummy's words of caution and Elsie's talk of the missing girl. Nevertheless, the trees beyond the little garden looked inviting and I couldn't wait to get out there.

I shivered as I washed at the basin. The water in the ewer was stone cold and the cracked tablet of Sunlight soap refused to produce anything much in the way of suds. Dressing quickly in a hand-me-down pinafore from Elsie that was still a good three inches too long for me (the portmanteau with my own clothes had not yet arrived from Plymouth), I tied my hair into bunches with white ribbons and rushed downstairs. Everyone was up and about, and all was chatter and clatter as porridge was spooned into bowls, bread was sliced, and fresh pots of tea were drawn. Aunt Polly read our tea leaves, predicting a happy marriage for Elsie and an interesting encounter with a stranger for me.

After breakfast and chores, I nagged at Elsie to show me the waterfall until she relented, despite insisting that our faces would be *frozzed* in no time. I didn't mind. I wanted to be outside in the fresh air, frozzed or not. Mummy and

Aunt Polly were delighted to see me and Elsie getting along so well, and although Mummy wasn't keen on the idea and suggested we stay indoors and play draughts, Aunt Polly encouraged our little expedition outside, as long as we wrapped up well and were back for dinner at twelve. I followed Elsie through the musty cellar and out into the garden that sloped steeply down toward the tree line at the bottom, my tummy tumbling with the excitement of Christmas mornings and birthdays.

The sky was a perfect blue and the sun cast a pleasant warmth over the garden, making glistening dewdrop necklaces of the spider webs draped between the slats of the fence between Elsie's garden and next door. While Elsie strode ahead, I stopped to inspect every new leaf and plant, and to listen to the unfamiliar songs of unfamiliar birds that perched on the rooftops. It would have been perfect if it weren't for the awful stench of grease and wool from the mill at the bottom of the village. I covered my nose and mouth with my hand.

Elsie laughed at me. "Manky, isn't it? I hardly notice it anymore. You'll soon get used to it."

I wasn't sure I ever wanted to get used to a smell like that.

"The beck's only small," Elsie explained as she opened the latch on the gate. "So don't say I didn't warn you when you're bored in five minutes."

I wasn't really listening. I was too busy picking my way around great clumps of stinging nettles and wild blackberry bushes that snagged on my coat and scratched the backs of my hands. As I walked, the rumble of the waterfall grew louder with every footstep, matching the heightened beating of my heart. Elsie told me to watch my footing as we clambered down a steep bank, grasping onto gnarled roots and embedded rocks until the trees opened up in front of us to reveal a narrow ravine.

I stopped walking and stood in silence.

At the bottom of the ravine was a glittering stream, about two feet in depth and six feet wide. A waterfall plunged from a shelf of shale rock to the right, tumbling in three broad steps toward the stream, where the water bubbled and boiled. Dappled shade from the trees cast intriguing shadows onto the water, while the flickering sunlight painted the early spring foliage in shades of gold and emerald and soft buttery yellow.

"Oh, Elsie!" I whispered. "It's lovely."

It was more than lovely. It was magical. It was wild and alive, and yet peaceful and serene. I could never have imagined somewhere so pretty could exist among the drab gray of the village I'd seen last night.

Elsie rubbed her hands together and pulled her scarf closer around her neck. "It's nicer in the summer, and nice enough at backend. Autumn," she added, seeing the confusion on my face. "You can spend a whole day here then. I don't fancy more than ten minutes on a day like this."

But I didn't feel the cold so much. Last night's disappointment of dirty snow and lightless streets fell away as I watched the water tumble and swirl. I already knew I could happily spend hours here, day and night, summer or winter. And there was something else. A sense of being watched, a continual urge to look over my shoulder. I didn't say anything to Elsie, afraid that she would tease me for being silly, but I felt it all the same.

Elsie picked up a stick, idly pushing a leaf around in the eddies that formed behind the larger rocks. I found a stick of my own and did the same, giving Elsie an idea. "Let's have races. Come on. We might find baby frogs if we're lucky."

The morning slipped away beneath the strengthening sun as we became engrossed in our game, searching for the broadest leaves to make boats for the baby frogs we found hiding behind rocks and among the long grass. I winced at the cool touch of their skin, shrieking when they sprang from my hands. On Elsie's count of three, we released our boats, running along the riverbank after them, eager to see which would reach the finish line first. Elsie won most of the races, and the baby frogs abandoned ship far too soon, but I didn't mind. I loved it there at the beck and couldn't resist taking off my shoes and stockings to dip my toes into the water.

Elsie laughed as I squealed at the icy cold. "You'll catch your death, Frances Griffiths, not to mention a slipper on your backside if your mother catches you! And mind you don't slip on those stones. The water's running fast. It'll knock your feet from under you easily enough."

I walked at the edge of the water for as long as I could bear it before following a path of slippery stepping-stones to the far bank, where I jumped up onto a bough of a willow tree. It made a perfect seat. I swung my legs beneath me, letting my bare toes skim the surface of the water. From my perch, I noticed a cottage, hidden almost entirely by trees. It looked familiar somehow, and as I narrowed my eyes against the glint of the sun, peering through the shifting branches to get a better look, I saw a woman standing at an upstairs window. She was looking directly at me.

I jumped down from the branch and ducked behind the bank. "Elsie," I hissed. "Who's that?"

"Who's what?"

"Through the trees. In the window at the cottage. Someone's watching us."

Elsie didn't seem at all concerned. "That'll be Mrs. Hogan. Your teacher. Remember, I told you about her last night."

"Why is she watching us?"

"Probably wondering who you are. She often stands at the window. Folk say she's looking for her little girl."

I stayed low as I walked back across the stepping-stones toward Elsie. As I turned to look over my shoulder, I caught a movement of the lace curtain as Mrs. Hogan disappeared into the dark interior of the cottage. "How sad for her. Is she nice?"

Elsie shrugged. "Keeps herself to herself, mostly. She speaks with a funny accent too—Irish—so the pair of you will get along fine."

"Was she *your* teacher?"

Elsie shook her head. "I went to the village school, but you're a clever clogs so you're going to Bingley Grammar, where Mrs. Hogan teaches." My stomach lurched at the thought. Today was Saturday. Monday would be my first day in the new school. I felt sick with nerves. "Mummy says she's also sad about Mr. Hogan being off at war," Elsie explained as we wandered back upstream. "He joined up last year when conscription came in. It wasn't long after the child went missing."

I knew all about being sad when people went off to war. "Why didn't Uncle Arthur go to war?"

"Too old. He tried to enlist anyway, but he failed the medical examination. He was assigned to stay at home and help at the mill and with other mechanical jobs for the farmers. He doesn't like to talk about it. He feels guilty not to be doing his bit at the Front."

As I followed Elsie back along the riverbank, I brushed my fingertips against the silky catkins on the willow trees and wished Daddy had failed the medical examination too. I stopped now and then to collect interesting-looking pebbles that clacked together satisfyingly in my pockets, and to pick the pretty wildflowers: stitchwort and ragwort, silverweed and harebell, lady's purse and cinquefoil. Elsie told me their names. As we walked, I repeated them over and over so I wouldn't forget them, storing them away like precious gems to admire again later, in private.

But it wasn't just the pebbles and flowers that enchanted me at the beck that morning, or the rush of water against my toes, or even the little ducklings that squeaked at us from their nest among the rushes. Perhaps it was just the excitement of being somewhere new, but I couldn't shake the feeling that something—or someone—was waiting for me there. And although I'd seen her for only a brief moment, I couldn't stop thinking about Mrs. Hogan's face at the window, or Elsie's tale of the missing child.

Lost in my thoughts, I whispered to myself as I strolled along. "'Out of that sand you melt your glass, / While the veils of night are drawn, / Whispering, till the shadows pass, / Nixie—Pixie—leprechaun.'"

Elsie poked playfully at me with her stick. "Do you believe in fairies then, Frances?"

I worried that Elsie would tease me if I said I did. "Do *you*?" I asked cautiously.

She smiled and walked on. "It's more fun to believe, isn't it? And one thing's for certain. You'll never see them if you don't."

And in that moment, as the breeze played among the bulrushes and the birds sang in the branches above us, I knew Elsie and I would become the greatest of friends. Although she'd been in my life less than a day, I knew with great certainty that Elsie Wright would be in my life, always.

That night, in the dark hush of the bedroom, I let my thoughts wander back down the cellar steps and out along the garden path, through the gate and down to the little stream where I walked over dew-wet grass, my eyes tipped toward the violet sky, somewhere between the end of night and the start of morning. I heard the sound of birdsong and laughter, bells ringing in the distance, the steady rush and tumble of the waterfall. I saw flashes of green, then blue as I felt myself being lifted, my feet dancing on air. And there, on the bough of the willow tree, sat a young child, hair like flames, her hand reaching out to offer me a single white flower. "For Mammy," she said. "For my Mammy."

Three

Ireland. Present day.

Lost in the words of Frances's story, Olivia jumped at the jangle of the shop bell, the pages in her hands fluttering in the breeze that rushed through the open door.

She looked up to see a child standing on the doormat. She appeared to be entirely alone, as if blown there on the wind like a miniature Mary Poppins.

"Hello. Can I help you?" Olivia stood up and walked over to her. The child was clearly distressed. Tears fell like fat summer raindrops from pale eyelashes that glistened, heavy with more.

"I'm lost."

Her words limped away through the dim light of the shop, the acknowledgment of her predicament triggering a fresh downpour of tears. She was a striking child, all rosy-cheeked innocence and tumbling red hair, a Pre-Raphaelite painting come to life. Her navy school uniform was at odds with the silver fairy wings sprouting from her back.

Instinctively Olivia hunkered down so that she was on a level with her. "Have you lost your mammy?"

The girl gulped in a breath of air. "I don't have a mammy."

Olivia's heart crumbled at the words. She knew them too well. She wanted to say that she *did* have a mammy, that we all have a mammy, even if she isn't with us anymore, but all she could do was offer the same insincere reply she'd heard so often herself.

"I'm very sorry to hear that."

"Daddy went into a shop and I can't find him and now I'm lost and I don't know where he is . . ." More tears prevented her from saying anything else.

The child's distress was unsettling and made Olivia fidgety. She took a tissue from her skirt pocket and offered it to the girl with an encouraging smile.

"It's all right. You're safe here. I'll help you find your daddy. I promise." For good measure, she said she liked her fairy wings, which produced a half smile in response as the girl took the tissue, sucking in great mouthfuls of air through her sobs as she wiped her nose.

"It was dress-up day at school. I was Titania, but I lost my wand."

"Titania? Queen of the Fairies?"

An emphatic nod. "Daddy read me a story about her. It's called *A Midnight Dream*. Or something like that."

Olivia's heart melted a little. As a rule, she found children noisy, unpredictable things. Whenever she was with Jack's many nieces and nephews she felt inadequate: not funny enough, or cool enough, or interesting enough to hold their attention. She tired of their company easily, and they of hers. Perhaps that was why part of her had always suspected she would never be anyone's mammy, and yet when she'd seen it confirmed in black and white it was all she wanted to be. She thought of the letter in the drawer of her nightstand in London, the letter she hadn't told Jack about. *Dear Miss Kavanagh, Following your recent appointment with Dr. Kent . . .*

Shaking off the thought of it, she focused on the child again. Something about this little girl was different from other children she knew. Something in her eyes suggested an old soul.

"What's your real name, then, Queen Titania?"

"Iris."

"That's a pretty name."

"They were Mammy's favorite flowers."

Were. Was. The awful vocabulary of loss. Olivia said they were her favorite flowers too. "I fell in love with them when I saw Van Gogh's painting on a school trip."

Unimpressed, Iris passed the sodden tissue back to Olivia. "What's *your* name?"

"Olivia. I'm named after the heroine in *Twelfth Night* because I was born on Twelfth Night. My mammy loved Shakespeare too. She was a teacher."

"What's Twelfth Night? Are you a teacher? Will my daddy be here soon?"

This was something else Olivia found difficult about children: their endless questions.

She grabbed her coat and the shop key. "Come on. Let's go and find him." She held out her hand, then hesitated. Was hand-holding appropriate? What were the rules when you found a lost child? Thankfully, Iris showed no such hesitation, linking her fingers trustingly around Olivia's. It was such a simple gesture, and made Olivia pause. She'd forgotten how reassuring that connection could be; how something as simple as a hand to hold could make you feel useful, or safe, or loved, or any number of things you weren't feeling a moment before.

Jack wasn't a hand-holder. He preferred to link arms, as if they were a promenading couple from an Austen novel.

She smiled at Iris, who looked back at her with such innocence Olivia couldn't bear it. "He can't be far away. I bet he's outside wondering where on earth you are."

As she spoke, the door opened and a tall, bearded man rushed in, his panic-stricken face collapsing into folds of relief as he saw Iris.

"Iris! Thank God!"

"Daddy!" Iris wrenched her hand free from Olivia's and ran to him, throwing her arms around him as he sank to his knees. He wrapped his arms tightly around his daughter as they released their worry and relief in a jumble of hugs and tears.

As she observed their little reunion, Olivia thought of her own childhood. Had she ever been lost? Had her mammy ever held her like this man held Iris now? She shut her eyes, willing a memory to surface, but nothing came. This was Olivia's reality: imagined moments, always wondering. The truth was that her mother had become more like a dream to her than a real person, a story she'd once read but couldn't fully recall. Sometimes, Olivia could hardly remember her mother at all.

Iris unpeeled herself from her father and dragged him toward Olivia, telling him all about the kind lady who had saved her life.

"It wasn't quite that dramatic!" Olivia explained. "She just wandered in. We were coming to look for you."

"Thank you *so* much." He offered his hand. "Ross Bailey. This little monkey's dad." The relief poured off him like water.

They shook hands as if they were sealing a business deal, and Olivia wondered how it was that one moment you were dealing with the impact of your grandfather's last will and testament and wondering how to call off your wedding, and the next you'd inadvertently come to the rescue of a little girl and were being thanked by her father, who carried an intriguing scent of sea spray and turf smoke and whose eyes were the color of good whiskey.

Ross Bailey had the appearance of someone who didn't especially care what he looked like, or didn't have time to worry about it, but looked good anyway. In jeans, a crumpled gig T-shirt, and a floppy beanie worn casually over shoulder-length hair he was a negative image of Jack—perfectly groomed, perfectly fragrant, perfectly ironed Jack. Intrigued by his crumples and stubble and eau de mer, Olivia held Ross's hand a moment too long. Long enough to feel the hard edge of his wedding band against her palm. Long enough to feel a momentary pang of guilt at having taken off her engagement ring.

"Iris was very polite and brave," she said, dropping Ross's hand like a hot coal, and shoving hers firmly into her skirt pocket.

Iris beamed at the compliment, the color returning to her cheeks in perfect pink circles as she grasped her father's hand. She was the image of him. The same lived-in eyes. The same quizzical eyebrows.

Ross ruffled Iris's hair affectionately. "She's always wandering off, this one. Daydreaming. Chasing cats and clouds. I guessed she might have come here. I'm a writer, so I often drop in looking for inspiration or a cup of tea. Mac makes a great brew!"

"You know Grandpa Cormac?"

"Mac's your *grandpa*?"

Olivia nodded. *Is? Was?* How did you refer to the recently departed?

"Ah, he's a great man. Always finding interesting books for me, and *always* has a few stories of his own to tell. Is he around?"

This was what Olivia dreaded the most. Having to tell people. Having to explain it all, over and over, as if somehow her grandfather's death was her fault and she had to constantly apologize for it.

She turned to Iris. "There's a shelf full of lovely children's books over there. Do you want to have a look? I need to have a quick chat with your dad."

Iris skipped off to the far corner of the shop as Ross looked at Olivia, confused.

"I'm sorry." She dragged the words—*those* words—from the depths of her heart. "Grandpa Cormac died. A week ago."

The color drained from Ross's face. "No way. I'm so sorry. I had no idea."

"It's okay. He'd lived a good life."

It was a terrible cliché, and Olivia hated herself for saying it. Pappy had lived a quiet, gentle life, the life of a humble, hardworking man who'd given everything to make sure his family was happy—to make sure *she* was happy. In the days since his death, she'd thought a lot about who he'd been as a boy, as a young man in love, as a father at war. She'd never talked to him and Nana about those parts of their lives. Somehow she'd always sensed the past wasn't a place they especially cared to revisit. Eventually she'd stopped asking. Now she would never know those parts of their story, and like an old book with missing pages, it troubled her.

Ross said again how sorry he was. "I can't believe it. Mac was one of those people you imagine will go on forever. He was a good man. A really good man."

"It was all very sudden . . . his heart . . ." Olivia couldn't say the word *stopped*, unable to believe that a heart so big and strong *could* stop. "I just found out he left me the shop in his will." She spread her arms in a sweeping arc. "This is all mine now."

Ross whistled through his teeth. "Wow. That's quite an inheritance. Are you a bookseller, then?"

She laughed. "No! I don't know the first thing about selling books. I'm a bookbinder by trade."

"Cool. So you, like, stick old books back together?"

Ross reminded Olivia of an eager puppy. She couldn't help smiling at his enthusiasm. "Yeah. Something like that. I restore rare books. I'm contracting at the National Art Library at the V&A in London."

"Sounds impressive. So, how does owning a bookshop in Ireland fit in with that?"

Olivia rubbed her fingers around the edges of the engagement ring in her pocket. "I'm not sure yet."

Ross cast his gaze around the shop. "I've always thought this place was amazing. It's like something from another time. You know? Hidden gem."

"A bit too hidden. Typical Pappy, opening a shop where nobody can find it. He doesn't even have a website."

"Pappy?"

She blushed. "Nickname. It's what I called him when I was younger."

"Cute. I called mine Gumpa. Although I secretly called him Grumpa. He was a miserable old sod, God rest him."

Olivia laughed. It was such a spontaneous, bright sound that it took her by surprise. As did Ross. A total stranger to Olivia, and yet not to Pappy, who had always been a good judge of character. Olivia wanted to keep talking to Ross—about Pappy and other things—because something told her he would listen and understand, not judge or condemn.

"So, what's the plan, then?" he asked, peering over Olivia's shoulder to check on Iris.

"I don't have one." It was the truth. She didn't. Her plans were shifting by the minute, it seemed. "I haven't a clue where to start, to be honest. It's all a bit of a shock."

"Well, these things usually happen for a reason. I'm sure you'll work it out. Actually, now that I think of it, Mac was always talking about you—his Olivia. And Martha. How is she?"

Nana Martha. Olivia winced with guilt at the thought of her. "She's doing okay. Some days are better than others. It's not easy."

Olivia hated it: Alzheimer's. She hated to watch the agonizing demise of the vibrant woman she'd once known. She hated visiting the nursing home, not just because of the smell of the place or the quiet sense of defeat that hung in the air— she hated not knowing how Nana would be when she got there, hated not knowing whether Nana would recognize her. Olivia felt physically sick every time she walked through the nursing home doors, and that was where she was heading this afternoon.

Her thoughts were interrupted as Iris appeared at her side. "Who's this, Olivia?"

Iris had one of the Conan Doyle magazine articles in her hand. The one with the picture of Alice and the fairies. After not seeing the image for so many years, Olivia found it upsetting and for a moment she couldn't respond.

Ross took the page from his daughter. "Iris! You shouldn't be nosing around in other people's things." He handed it to Olivia. "Sorry. Iris, say you're sorry to Olivia."

Iris blushed and stared hard at her feet. "Sorry, Olivia. I liked the picture."

Olivia heard herself saying that it was all right. Not a problem. That it was just an old newspaper cutting. But it wasn't. It was so much more than that.

Ross apologized again. "Too curious for her own good, this one."

"Aren't all children?"

Iris tugged at Olivia's skirt, beckoning her to bend down and cupping her hand over Olivia's ear. "Are the fairies real?" she whispered.

Olivia looked into Iris's eyes, so full of hope and wonder. And there it was. The memory of a time when she'd felt the same hope and wonder, when she'd believed in fairies and happy endings. It was like looking in a mirror and she was a little girl again, asking her mammy the same question.

She held out the page so they could look at the photograph together. "That's a good question, Iris. This photograph was taken a long time ago. As far as I know, some people thought the fairies were real, and some didn't."

"Who's that? Is that you? Is it your mammy?"

"She's called Alice." The enigmatic smile. The knowing look in her eyes. "See? It says her name underneath."

"Who is she?"

"That I don't know." Olivia thought about Frances's manuscript, of the photograph signed to Ellen, of the file full of newspaper clippings, a trail of bread crumbs tempting her to follow them. "But I'd like to find out."

Ross bundled Iris away before she could interrogate Olivia any more. "That's enough of your questions, madam. Come on. We've things to be doing."

"Like what?"

"Homework and hot chocolate, for starters."

Ross thanked Olivia again for looking after Iris. He pulled a business card from his jeans pocket as he stepped outside into the lane. "Listen, I only live down the hill, so if you need a hand with anything, give me a shout. Mac helped me out plenty of times. I'd like to return the favor."

Taking the card, Olivia mumbled a "Thanks, but I'll be grand" and closed the door behind them.

She turned the business card over—"Ross Bailey, Writer"—and stood for a moment, forehead pressed against the cool glass in the door, as the wind blew Ross Bailey, Writer, and his daughter back to wherever they'd come from. She watched until they faded into the distance, and then she turned to walk back to the desk. As she did, she noticed a white flower on the doormat: a slender green stem, one leaf, five perfect bell-shaped blooms. Assuming Iris had dropped it, she picked it up, rinsed out her coffee cup, filled it with water, and placed the flower inside. The inscription *Live* seemed more appropriate than ever.

Settling herself back at the desk, she picked up her phone to check for any missed calls or messages. There were five e-mails from the wedding planner, two missed calls from the bridal shop, and three text messages from her two bridesmaids. She didn't have the energy to respond to any of them. She thought about calling Jack to check her reaction to hearing his voice, but he was in China on a business trip and she had no idea what time it was there. She tossed the phone into the bottom of her bag and picked up the Conan Doyle article again.

The photograph of Alice and the fairies stirred so many memories of that awful day of the accident. Olivia remembered how Pappy had gathered her into his arms in the pale light of early morning and wept quietly against her shoulder. She didn't remember how he told her, didn't recall his exact words. She remembered only the photograph in the silver frame lying on the bed beside her and how, as she'd looked into that little girl's eyes, she'd seen a lifetime of questions her mammy would never be able to answer.

The wind rattled the glass in the window frame. A reminder that there were things to do.

As a violin concerto danced among the bookshelves, Olivia made herself focus, working steadily through the official-looking correspondence. She was shocked to see how much it was costing to keep Nana in the nursing home every month, but at least all the bills were paid and everything appeared to be in order. It wasn't until she opened a letter from a solicitor that she realized everything was far from in order.

30th April 2017

Dear Mr. Kavanagh,

> *We refer to previous correspondence in this matter, and regret to inform you that our Client can no longer support the sizeable debt owing and our Client's patience is at an end.*
>
> *Please regard this letter as our final warning.*
>
> *All outstanding debts and arrears must be settled by three calendar months from the date hereof. Failure to do so will result in the issue of proceedings, without further notice, to recover the sums due . . .*

She couldn't bear to read on, guessing what must have happened. Pappy had poured all his money into keeping Nana in the nursing home and, as a result, the bookshop was in debt. It was now the middle of May. She'd already lost two weeks.

Olivia buried the letter in the bottom of her bag and switched off the shop lights. As an afterthought, she grabbed Frances's manuscript and the Conan Doyle magazine article. Maybe Nana Martha would remember something about Frances, or the fairy photographs, although Olivia doubted it.

Poor Nana didn't remember much about anything anymore.

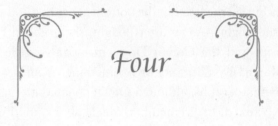

Four

Ireland. Present day.

St. Bridget's nursing home smelled of old chrysanthemums and loss. The cloying scent settled on Olivia's skin, working its way into her pores until she felt she would suffocate if she didn't go back outside for some fresh air. But she couldn't. She had to endure it. Like everyone else there, she had little choice in the matter of staying or going.

The nurses at reception directed her to the dayroom before returning to their endless form-filling and chipped mugs of milky tea. Carrying a packet of jelly babies, and with the bulky manuscript in her bag weighing heavy on her shoulder, Olivia walked along the corridor, passing the framed prints, of floral paintings that she found so hopelessly depressing. Her footsteps were muted by the soft linoleum flooring. Even her breathing quieted. Everything was done with a hush at St. Bridget's, as if the people there had a mute button permanently switched on. The silence provoked a nervous energy in Olivia, making her want to laugh when there was absolutely nothing amusing about the place at all.

At the dayroom door, she hesitated. Nana was in her favorite chair by the window, her eyes closed as one of the nurses read to her. Olivia leaned around the door frame to listen.

"'Up the airy mountain, / Down the rushy glen, / We daren't go a-hunting / For fear of little men.'"

Olivia whispered along with the words, recognizing the William Allingham poem "The Faeries," which Nana used to recite to her as a child. Nana had loved to tell her the tales of the Little People, reading from a favorite collection of Irish fairy stories. Olivia had vague memories of her mother scolding Nana, saying, *"You'll have the child ruined with a head full of fairies."* But Olivia had loved the old tales as much as Nana did, *The Stolen Child* and *The Fairy Hill* becoming firm favorites. She asked for them night after night, enchanted by Nana's storytelling, by the old-fashioned language and forgotten names and places. Nana brought the stories alive, until the *púca* and the *sídhe* became real to Olivia and she insisted on leaving out a saucer of milk and other little treats so they would keep her in their favor.

The nurse read on. "'Wee folk, good folk, / Trooping all together; / Green jacket, red cap, / And white owl's feather!'"

A slight smile played at the edge of Nana's lips. When Olivia saw her like this, so peaceful, it was hard to believe there was anything wrong with her at all. She looked for all the world like a happy, healthy ninety-seven-year-old. Her hair was neatly styled, her clothes smart and freshly laundered. Today's ensemble was a pair of black trousers and a bright yellow cardigan that brought out the color in her cheeks. Her penciled-in eyebrows were as much an accessory as the string of pearls that skirted the collar of her cardigan.

When the poem ended, the nurse made sure Nana was comfortable and smiled at Olivia, indicating that she should come over. Olivia stepped into the room.

"Hi, Nana. How are you?" She kept her voice bright and breezy, bending down to kiss Nana's cheek and squeezing her frail hands as tight as she dared. Nana seemed to shrink a little every time Olivia saw her. It was like watching melting ice—soon there would be nothing left of her, only memories frozen in time. She so desperately wanted the old Nana back. The Nana she knew and loved. The Nana who knew and loved her. "I remember that poem, Nana. It was one of my favorites." She pulled over a chair and straightened the blanket on Nana's knees.

Rheumy gray eyes studied Olivia in reply, not looking at her but past her, as if searching for something far away.

Nana pushed the blanket to one side, muttering to herself. "What is it this time? Temperature check?" She often thought Olivia was the nurse. Sometimes she was the minibus driver. Once she was a famous actress from the Gaiety. Rarely was she Olivia.

"No temperature checks today," Olivia said. "Just visiting." She passed Nana the jelly babies. "I brought you these."

Nana eyed them suspiciously, crinkling the plastic wrapper as she turned the bag over in her hands before placing it on the table beside her. "Do I like them?"

"They're your favorites. Especially the red ones. We used to bite the heads off them and laugh."

Olivia told Nana about the walk she'd enjoyed up Howth Head that morning and showed her some pictures of the rhododendrons on her phone. Nana remarked on them, trying to remember if it was rhododendrons or hydrangeas she grew in her garden.

"Hydrangeas, Nana. White and pink. They're always admired by people who pass the cottage."

"Which cottage?"

"Your cottage. Bluebell Cottage? At the top of the hill?" Everything was a question now. Everything punctuated with doubt and uncertainty.

Nana closed her eyes, exhausted by the effort of conversation, of remembering.

The room was stuffy and airless. It made Olivia claustrophobic.

They sat quietly for a while, the occasional rattle of the approaching tea trolley and the distant tinny voices from the television doing their best to cover up the gaps in their conversation. It was these silent minutes Olivia especially hated. She filled them with inconsequential fussing: straightening piles of months-old magazines, picking browned petals from wilted carnations in a vase at the window, organizing a deck of cards into suits. None of it mattered, but anything was better than the gaping silence.

She was relieved when the tea trolley arrived and Nana perked up a little. There was something reassuring about watching Barbara pour hot tea from the large stainless steel pot while she chattered on about the wind blowing the wheelie bins over in the night and how you wouldn't believe the mess she'd woken up to on her street that morning. Nana dunked a digestive biscuit and said what did people expect if they were silly enough to put bins on wheels? Olivia smiled. In brief lucid moments like this, she could hardly believe that life had brought them to St. Bridget's at all.

Pappy had never admitted it, but Olivia knew he found words like *dementia* and *Alzheimer's* frightening. "Away with the fairies. That's all. She'll be grand." He'd said he didn't want Nana to be labeled, insisting she was still the same Martha, deep down. He'd looked after her at home as long as he could, patiently making small adjustments to their routine, constantly trying to find a way to make the new Martha fit with the old Cormac as things became awkward, then difficult, and eventually impossible. He said it was like doing a jigsaw puzzle where the pieces kept changing shape. "You have to keep trying every piece until you find one that fits." It was the closest he'd ever come to complaining.

The fire finally brought things to a head. Nana was making chips, double fried, the way Pappy liked them, but she forgot about them during the second fry and popped out to the shops to get him a bottle of stout while he was at a friend's garden picking broad beans. He didn't even like stout. The kitchen was a charred shell by the time a neighbor raised the alarm.

Pappy found Nana at the bookshop. She couldn't remember how she got there or why she had a bottle of stout in her bag. Something Old was the place she'd instinctively gone to, knowing she would be safe there. Olivia thought it rather lovely that when real life was deserting Nana, it was the bookshop and the fictional lives she'd loved and lived through that stuck by her, like loyal friends. Arrangements to move her into the nursing home began the next day, and St. Bridget's became part of their lives—a comma separating everything life was before, and everything it had become since.

Olivia sipped her tea and took a deep breath before telling Nana she would be looking after the bookshop now.

"Which bookshop?"

"Something Old?" Olivia waited, hoping for the fog to lift, for Nana to remember.

"Has he straightened that sign yet? It's all off to one side. I suppose he'll be wanting his tea soon. Never stops eating, that man. Hollow legs. Or worms." Nana's eyes fluttered as she chased a memory back over the years. She leaned forward, studying Olivia's face. "You remind me of someone." Olivia's heart thumped. *Please remember. Please say my name.* "Hepburn. Is that it? Audrey Hepburn?" Nana looked pleased with herself and then frowned, confusion clouding her face. "What's your name?"

"Olivia."

"Pretty name." She took Olivia's left hand in hers. "Not married?"

Olivia winced at the thought of her engagement ring still in her skirt pocket. She should really put it somewhere safe. She wondered if she would give it back. What did you do with an engagement ring if you called the engagement off? "No, Nana. I'm not married." Again she felt a rush of childlike rebellion, a truth not fully told.

"Don't worry, dear. You'll meet someone. When the time's right. Or maybe when it's not."

Nana's gaze drifted off into the distance, lost somewhere Olivia couldn't reach her. It was a look Olivia had seen often, even before the onset of Alzheimer's, a look she sensed she wasn't meant to notice.

She picked up her bag from beside her chair and took out the magazine article and Frances's manuscript. "I found some interesting things at the shop today, Nana." She explained about the briefcase and the things she'd found and handed Nana the Conan Doyle article. "I thought you might like to see them."

Nana took the page from Olivia. It shook in her hands as she brought it closer to her face, studying it carefully before resting it on her lap. She ran her fingers across the photograph of Alice and the fairies as if she were reading braille, searching for a memory among the words and the picture. She chuckled lightly, a curious, faraway sound.

"Do you recognize it?" Olivia leaned forward, willing her to remember. There was a softness to Nana's face that Olivia hadn't seen for a long time. For the briefest moment, she looked like the old Nana Martha. Alive. Full of questions and stories.

Nana tapped the photograph with her fingernail. "That's Frances."

Olivia's heart sank. She tried to keep her voice calm and patient as she explained. "It's Alice, Nana. Look. It says underneath."

Nana fixed her with a determined stare. "I don't care what it says. That's Frances."

Olivia knew when to back down. "Did you know her? Mammy had the same photograph in a silver frame in her jewelry box." She paused, waiting for any sign of recognition from Nana, anxious not to upset her by stirring distressing memories. "I haven't seen it for years, but I've never forgotten it."

Nana looked back at the image. "Such a lot of fuss about a few photographs. It was all those men from London. Interfering. They never meant it to go as far as it did."

She remembered.

There were so many questions Olivia wanted to ask, but she didn't want to overwhelm Nana. She thought of the hope and wonder in Iris's eyes that morning when she'd asked if the fairies were real. She thought of the hope and wonder she'd felt in her own heart when she'd asked her mammy the same question. She hardly dared ask it again now.

"Are they real, Nana? The fairies?"

Nana turned her eyes to Olivia, her gaze settling firmly on her as she took hold of her hands. "Which ones, dear? The ones in the photograph, or the ones we can't see?"

Olivia looked at the photograph again. The girl—Alice or Frances or whoever it was—looked straight ahead into the camera. Why wasn't she looking at the fairies in front of her? Surely she would have been so captivated by them she wouldn't have been able to look at anything else. Perhaps there was another story to be told; another story behind the camera.

"There were some other things, too, Nana. Another photograph in an old children's picture book, and this." She lifted the heavy manuscript from her bag. "It was written by someone called Frances Griffiths."

Nana nodded. "The girl with the fairies in the photograph." She took the thick pile of paper and rested it on her lap, running her fingers over the violet ribbon.

"It's a sort of memoir," Olivia explained. "Do you know why Pappy might have had it at the shop?"

Nana shook her head and closed her eyes. Her memories couldn't keep up.

"I thought I could read the story to you when I visit. It's set in Cottingley in Yorkshire. Isn't that where you grew up?"

Olivia hesitated, wondering if she shouldn't have mentioned any of this at all. Perhaps it was something Nana didn't want to remember, even if she could.

"That's right," Nana said. "Cottingley. Pretty little place. There was a stream." A slight smile played at her lips as she spoke. She opened one eye and looked at Olivia. "Go on, then. Start reading."

After the first four chapters, Nana grew tired and asked Olivia to take her back to her room. Olivia sat with her until she slept and the evening nurses came around. Then Olivia kissed Nana's cheek and told her she loved her, as she always did, although she was never sure if Nana heard. Even if she did, she never said it back.

OLIVIA SLEPT FITFULLY that night, back in the bedroom of her childhood at Bluebell Cottage, Nana and Pappy's home in Howth. Despite the soothing hush of the sea that tiptoed through the open window, the emotional turmoil of the day cartwheeled through her mind, and her thoughts refused to settle. They jumped from Pappy and Nana to Frances and Elsie. They even settled—fleetingly—on Ross and Iris. But no matter who else resided there for a moment or two, it was to Jack and the wedding that her thoughts ultimately returned. Jack, and the future they'd planned over Michelin-starred dinners and expensive wine. A future that felt increasingly distant with each day that she moved hesitantly closer toward it.

It wasn't until the thick blackness of night made way for the navy hue of dawn that she eventually fell asleep, but even then she couldn't properly rest. Her dreams were occupied by visions of a little girl, hair streaming like flames as she placed a posy of white flowers on the doorstep of a woodland cottage before settling on the bough of a willow tree above a narrow stream. There she sang of fairies at the bottom of the garden and watched the flowers slowly unfurl their petals beneath the warmth of a gentle morning sun. Even from behind the veil of sleep, Olivia sensed that something about this dream was different, that although she inhabited it, it wasn't her dream at all.

Like the prospect of married life with Jack waiting for her in London, somehow she sensed it belonged to someone else.

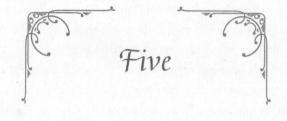

Five

Ireland. Present day.

She woke to the sound of the sea, the sound of home. A cool breeze floated through the open window, carrying a dande-lion seed inside with it. *Jinny-Joes* as she called them, although Nana Martha insisted they were called fairies in Yorkshire, and if you caught one you had to make a wish. Olivia watched it dance in a shaft of sunlight before it settled onto the pillow beside her. She picked it up and twirled it around between her thumb and finger. Something about its fragility spoke to her of letting go, of being blown on the wind to some unknown place. She closed her eyes and made a wish.

Propping herself up against her pillow, she watched the hyp-notic ribbons of sunlight that streamed through the window and cast a sheen against the peach silk curtains. Her mind flipped from London to Ireland and back again, her thoughts racing over the lists she had made and remade in recent months: flow-ers, wine, favors, gifts for the bridesmaids, band, DJ . . . She'd only wanted a small wedding. Close family and friends. How had it become so big and time-consuming? The Wedding and

The Dress were all anyone ever talked about so that she—
Olivia—was a mere afterthought, an accessory. As she stared
up at the purple lampshade that had accompanied so many of
her dilemmas over the years, she felt nauseated at the thought
of returning to that life, and exhilarated by the prospect of not.

There was nothing especially wrong with Jack, other than
the fact that there was nothing especially right about him.
An unlikely partner whom she'd met after being stood up on
a date, he had completely surprised her with a proposal the
following Christmas Eve. Most surprising of all was the yes
Olivia had heard herself saying. A yes formed from shock and
other people's expectations and the unavoidable sound of her
biological clock ticking. Marriage, family, a mortgage—it was
time she settled down, wasn't it? Yet that was the part troubling her the most. The settling down. Making the best of it.
Being content. *Content?* The word alone filled her with a deep
malaise. Contentment was a poor substitute for the fulfilling,
enriching life she'd imagined, but how could she get back to
that? Pappy used to say that an explorer without a map must
become a mapmaker. It sounded so romantic: plotting a different course, charting new waters. That was the life she wanted.
Not the paint-by-numbers predictability she found herself in
the middle of now.

Stepping out of bed, she opened the curtains, blinking against
the glare of the sun as it bounced off the sea. She grabbed her
sunglasses and pushed up the casement window, savoring the
purity of the air, the briny tang, the sense of well-being that
flooded her body with every breath. In the harbor the boats
bobbed gently in the swell, while above, wispy clouds raced
the seagulls and chased shadows across the water. The clang of
mast bells and the snap of rigging drifted back on the breeze.

Olivia's senses were attuned to the environment here, where they always felt numbed in London, smothered by the unrelenting pressure to live the perfect life.

She washed and dressed and made her way downstairs.

The house was hesitant and cold. It, too, was grieving.

She pulled up the kitchen blind, glad of the sunlight that streamed through the slats and pooled on the table like melted butter. She filled the kettle, switched on the heater, flicked on the radio. A lively piano concerto filled the silence with purpose and energy. She walked through to the sitting room, where an army of condolence and mass cards marched across the mantelpiece. "We are sorry for your loss." "In deepest sympathy." Several had toppled from their perch, forming a puddle of grief on the hearth rug below. Olivia gathered them up until the mantelpiece was cleared and the cherished family photographs that had sat there for decades were revealed once again. Among them was her favorite photograph of herself as a baby with her mother, the tips of their noses just touching, a look of absolute adoration in her mother's eyes. So much love, captured by the click of a button.

A knock at the back door disturbed her thoughts.

Dropping the collection of sympathy cards into the kitchen bin, she opened the door, delighted to see Mrs. Joyce, the neighbor who never seemed to age and had always reminded Olivia of a Russian doll with her headscarf and rouged cheeks.

Olivia threw her arms around her. "Mrs. Joyce! It's so lovely to see you."

"I'm not disturbing you, am I? I won't stop. I saw the curtains open and said to Joe I'd look in on you. 'I hate to think of that young girl all alone in there,' I says." She handed Olivia a Tupperware container. "Brownies. Fresh out of the oven."

"You're very good. Come in. The kettle's just boiled."

"Grand so, but I'll not stop. Just one cup." Mrs. Joyce stepped inside, rubbing her hands briskly together against the morning chill. "I like your hair, love. It suits you. Brings out your eyes." She hesitated a moment before adding, "You look just like your mam. The spit of her."

They sat together at the kitchen table, drinking sweet tea and eating brownies as the notes from a violin solo mingled with the steam that drifted in spirals from their mugs. Olivia was in no hurry—happy to find an excuse to put off the things she had to face up to—and neither, it seemed, was Mrs. Joyce. Her "just one cup" became a second pot as Olivia told her about Pappy's letter and the fact that he had left her the shop.

Mrs. Joyce wasn't surprised. "You always loved that shop. Martha used to say you would live there if you could! You'll do a grand job, love. I know you will."

Olivia didn't mention Jack or the threatening letter from the solicitor. She didn't admit that apart from her passion for books and her skill in restoring them, she felt totally unqualified for the task.

"Have you started clearing things out yet?" Mrs. Joyce asked. "Never a nice job, sure it isn't, but best to get it done rather than letting it hang over you."

"I promised myself I'd start today. I'm dreading it, to be honest."

She couldn't bear the thought of rummaging through drawers and cupboards, disturbing the private places where Nana and Pappy kept their secrets. She'd done it before when she'd helped Pappy sort through Nana's things, sifting through her life like museum curators, choosing the best pieces to display in her new room at St. Bridget's. Pappy had insisted on at least one of her china dogs going with her. The doctors said familiar things would create a sense of home for Nana and make the transition easier. Olivia wasn't convinced it had done either.

Mrs. Joyce's eyes glistened with tears. "No wonder you're dreading it. God love you. He was a good man, Cormac. I always said it to Martha. 'He's a good man, that Cormac Kavanagh.'"

They sat in thoughtful silence, just as they had after her mother's accident. Olivia remembered how she'd pushed a spoon around a bowl of lime jelly that she couldn't eat and how, as she'd watched Mrs. Joyce sob into her handkerchief, she'd realized that the sadness wasn't all hers to bear alone. She felt it again now, as Mrs. Joyce patted her arm.

"Will you let me help? I've nothing much on this morning and we'd get through it much faster with two."

Olivia was so grateful. "Would you mind?"

Mrs. Joyce smiled. "What are neighbors for, eh?"

While Mrs. Joyce tackled the back room, Olivia made a start on the front. Old magazines and TV guides were thrown into a bag for recycling. Half-empty bottles of Christmas sherry and rum were dragged from the back of the drinks cabinet and poured down the sink. Photograph albums were put in a box to look through later. Shelves and sideboards were cleared of china dogs and the lace doilies they'd sat on for decades, all of them going into the box for the charity shop with surprising emotional detachment. It was the smaller, unexpected things that broke Olivia's heart: an incomplete game of solitaire, Pappy's pipe resting on the edge of the ashtray, a half-finished jigsaw of the *Titanic*. A quiet, simple life on pause. In Pappy's honor, she cleaned the pipe and ashtray and completed the game of solitaire before finishing the jigsaw and returning it to its box. She stood back then, acknowledging how empty the room had become without its little trinkets and mementos, just the sofa and chairs left with nobody to sit on them. How quickly a lifetime could be cleared away. Too quickly. She wished she could put everything back as Mrs. Joyce appeared at her shoulder.

"All done, love?"

"It's as if they were never here, Mrs. Joyce. As if they never existed."

"I know, love. But you've your memories, and they're more important than ornaments of china dogs." She linked her arm through Olivia's. "God forgive me, but I never liked them dogs. Awful ugly things."

They both laughed until their laughter turned to tears, and Olivia felt much better for letting it all out.

"Here. You might want to look at this." Mrs. Joyce held a book and a folded piece of paper. "I always give books a good shake before I send them to charity. I used to work in the donation center at the St. Vincent de Paul. You'd be amazed what we found in coat pockets and books. The letter was inside this book."

Olivia took them from her. The book was a slim volume called *The Coming of the Fairies* by Arthur Conan Doyle. On the title page were two inscriptions. One "To Frances," signed by Conan Doyle, dated 1921. The other "To Martha," signed by Frances, dated 1978. It was in exceptionally good condition. It hardly looked as though the pages had been turned at all, and with the signatures, Olivia knew it could sell for a decent amount to the right collector. She turned the first page and read the opening paragraph:

Chapter one. How The Matter Arose. The series of incidents set forth in this little volume represent either the most elaborate and ingenious hoax ever played upon the public, or else they constitute an event in human history which may, in the future, appear to have been epoch-making in its character.

Intrigued, but anxious to read the letter, she closed the book for now, perched on the arm of Pappy's favorite chair, and unfolded the sheet of writing paper.

16th October 1978

Dear Martha,

Thank you for the very kind words in your recent letter, which I was delighted to receive after all these years. It is always a pleasure to hear from someone who believes my story. The recent BBC television play has stirred up a lot of memories and fuss. I'm still not sure it was a good idea to rake over the past—it usually isn't—but what's done is done. Elsie, at least, seems to be enjoying the attention. She was always more comfortable with the reporters.

Cottingley seems like a distant dream now, like something that happened to somebody else, yet whenever the press get involved (as they do from time to time), it all becomes very real again. Real, and not altogether pleasant. They forget that I was a child when it happened—a naive young girl, not the woman they see when they ask me their questions and raise their eyebrows at my replies. I know what they are thinking, but I also know what I saw all those years ago, and what I have seen time and again in the years since.

I'm often asked why I think our photographs caused such a sensation when they first became public all those years ago. Conan Doyle's articles appeared during a time of great despair in England. When you've lived through such a terrible war as we all had, lost friends and loved ones, you cling to anything that offers a sense of hope and comfort. People wanted so desperately to believe in fairies and the spirit world because if fairies could visit us from another realm, then perhaps our loved ones could too. I'm not surprised our fairies charmed so many people. Nothing much surprises me anymore.

I've enclosed a copy of Conan Doyle's book about the events of those summers, which I hope will be of interest to you (I somehow ended up with two copies). His account makes for interesting reading—if a little too scientific at times for my liking. I've recently started writing about the Cottingley events, to tell the story in my own words, as it were. I will send you a copy—if I ever finish it.

I wonder—do you still have the Princess Mary picture book? You admired it so much when you were a little girl. I was pleased to give it to you.

Do pass on my regards to Cormac and Kitty. It would be lovely to see you again, although I don't travel too far these days. Old age makes snails of us all. If only we had wings!

Yours sincerely,
Frances Way (née Griffiths)

Olivia read the letter a second time before folding it carefully, slipping it back inside the book, and walking through to the kitchen where Mrs. Joyce was scrubbing the sink with an ancient-looking bottle of Vim and wire wool.

Olivia sat at the table and took another brownie. "Can I ask you something, Mrs. Joyce?"

"Of course, dear."

"Did Nana ever talk to you about her life before she met Pappy?"

Mrs. Joyce stopped scrubbing, took off her rubber gloves, and sat down beside Olivia at the table. "Is everything all right, love?"

"It's just with Pappy gone and Nana not able to remember things, I regret not talking to them about the past. I hardly know anything about their life before Mammy was born. I know that Nana was brought up in Yorkshire, and that Pappy's parents both died during the Second World War. That's about it."

Mrs. Joyce sighed. "Martha wasn't one for dwelling in the past. After her parents died, she only went back to Yorkshire once—legal business or something, not long after Kitty was born. Martha was an only child, and any aunts or uncles had passed away. I think there were a few cousins, but she lost touch with them, as far as I know."

"Did she ever talk to you about someone called Frances Griffiths, or about photographs of fairies taken during the First World War? It seems that Frances and Nana were friends."

Mrs. Joyce played with the wedding band on her finger. "Well, there's a question. I do remember Martha showing me an old photograph once. A young girl watching some fairies. There was something on the television about it, except the girl was an old woman by then. I remember your mam being especially interested in the photograph."

"She was. She kept it in her jewelry box, in a silver frame. I'd love to know how Nana knew Frances, and why she never spoke about her life in Yorkshire."

"Why don't you ask her?"

"I tried yesterday, but she gets so confused. I hate to think I'm upsetting her by stirring up the past."

"Don't give up on her, dear. Keep asking. Keep encouraging her to remember. There are some things we can't forget. Even if we want to." Mrs. Joyce stood up and tied her headscarf under her chin. "I'd best be getting back. Joe'll be looking for his dinner and God love him but he's a grumpy auld bugger when he's hungry."

She kissed Olivia good-bye and shuffled off down the garden path.

The grandmother clock ticked away the minutes in the hall. Olivia closed the door and turned the radio up.

She spent the rest of the morning clearing out drawers and wardrobes and bookshelves, always hoping to find the photo in the silver frame, but it was nowhere to be found. Apparently, it was as lost as Nana's memories.

LATER THAT AFTERNOON, when Olivia arrived at the bookshop, she was surprised to find an envelope pushed through the letterbox, her name written on the front in child's handwriting. Beside it, on the doormat, was a single white flower. Inside the envelope was a sheet of pink writing paper. *"Dear Olivia, Thank you for looking after me. I hope you like this picture. Did you find out about the fairies? From Iris Bailey."* At the bottom of the note, Iris had drawn a picture of Alice and the fairies.

Tearing a blank page from a notebook, Olivia wrote a quick reply. *"Dear Iris, Thank you for your letter. Your drawing is lovely. I've put it in the window so people can see it. I hope you found your wand.*

Olivia." She placed Iris's letter and picture, and her own reply, in the window, where she hoped Iris would see them. The white flower she placed in the coffee cup with fresh water. She smiled again at the inscription in black marker. *Live.*

Switching on the radio for company, she settled herself at the desk, took a deep breath, and read the solicitor's letter again, Nora Plunkett's sniping words nagging at her as she did. *"Should have given it up when Martha went doolally. Bit off more than he could chew if you ask me."* Olivia's skin bristled. More than ever, she was determined to prove Nora bloody Plunkett wrong.

A phone call confirmed Olivia's worst fears. The letter she'd opened was the last in a long line of correspondence that, for some reason, Pappy had ignored. She arranged a meeting for the following afternoon, even though she would rather have stuck her head in a bucket of bees.

Her second phone call was to the V&A to explain that she needed to stay in Ireland a little longer than expected to sort things out. Her manager was very understanding and since Olivia was on a rolling weekly contract, agreed that they would talk again when she was ready to return to London. The temporary nature of her job was, for once, a blessing, even if the financial nature of it wasn't.

Her final call wasn't so easy.

Her final call was to Jack.

Before ringing him, she walked to the harbor, drawing strength from the breeze and the view and the certainty she'd felt at the top of Howth Head the previous day. She walked for hours, searching for clarity of thought as she watched the waves lap at the harbor wall. She ran her married name over and over in her mind—Olivia Oliver, Olivia Oliver, Olivia Oliver—the words tripping her up, like a tongue twister. No matter how often she said it, or practiced her signature, it didn't sound, or look, right. But Jack was a traditionalist. He wanted her to take his name. Less complicated for the children, he said.

And there it was again. The unavoidable facts of the letter hidden in the drawer of her nightstand.

Olivia could still remember the smell of the paper it was typed on: expensive perfume and antibacterial hand wash—the smell of the endocrinologist's office. It had turned her stomach at every appointment.

She'd first heard the words in the consultant's soft Derry accent. "Premature ovarian failure." She'd made it sound almost glamorous; something all the cool kids would want. Then Olivia had read it in stark Times New Roman font, confirming, in confusing medical terminology, that her biological clock had stopped. What had started out as a routine trip to the local GP about anxiety and unusual fatigue had led her to this.

It wasn't that she didn't know how to tell Jack, or that she worried about his reaction. She knew exactly how he would react: he would treat it like a business transaction, throw money at it and call in the experts. He would do what Jack always did. He would make her feel inadequate, as if it was her fault that she was lacking in the most fundamental part of being a woman. And that was why, when she should have needed him the most, her future husband was the last person she wanted to confide in. Her "future" husband, she'd realized, was not the husband she wanted in her future.

As the sun began to set, Olivia pressed the speed dial on her phone and took a deep breath. Her heart raced as the phone rang at the other end. Her cheeks flushed with adrenaline as the dial tone clicked into voice mail. His sure, steady voice. The same Jack. The same message she'd heard so often. Nothing had changed as far as he was concerned. And yet everything was different as she explained, as calmly and casually as she could, that she needed to stay in Ireland another week to sort things out with Nana and the bookshop. She could hear the crack in her voice: the pretense, the fake, breezy nonchalance.

After she hung up, she flicked through her e-mails and listened to her voice mails. Could she come back with a decision on the buttonholes? Would she mind if a friend brought a plus one? Was there another option on the bridesmaids' dresses because the ink blue might not suit everyone? The tightness in her chest intensified. Her breathing came fast and shallow. She took deep breaths and closed her eyes, telling herself to relax, to calm down. The last e-mail was from the wedding planner, sending on the information she'd promised about preserving the wedding flowers. There was no information about how Olivia might preserve herself.

She looked once at the engagement photo she'd set as her phone's wallpaper, and without planning to or thinking about it for more than a second, threw the phone into the harbor. It hardly made a splash. A feeble half protest at best before it was swallowed by the amber sea.

Olivia felt as if she'd thrown herself one of the orange life rings positioned along the harbor wall. For the first time in months, she could breathe properly, long deep breaths, in and out in time with the waves.

She stood for five minutes, maybe ten, watching the sunset and the seabirds and the planes coming in to land. Life carrying on, as life did. As she made her way back to the bookshop, she felt as light as the gull feather that swirled along the path in front of her.

Too full of adrenaline to eat or sleep, she poured a glass of wine and curled up in Pappy's favorite chair with a blanket and Frances's story. If Nana couldn't tell Olivia about her family's connection to Cottingley and the fairy photographs, maybe Frances could tell her herself . . .

NOTES ON A FAIRY TALE
Cottingley, Yorkshire. June 1917.

The weeks passed quickly, blown away by the stiff spring breezes that whistled down the chimney breast and blew the blossoms from the trees and tugged at my hat as I walked up the hill from Cottingley Bar tram. The only thing the wind couldn't blow away was the dark shadow of war that hung over us all like a thundercloud. But I was happy at Bingley Grammar, and as the days lengthened and the last of the snow thawed on the distant hilltops, so too did my indifference to Yorkshire. Best of all, the warmer weather meant more time to play at the beck at the bottom of the garden, where Elsie often joined me.

Aunt Polly called the pair of us as thick as thieves and Mummy teased me for admiring my cousin so much, dressing the same and styling my hair the same way Elsie styled hers. Or trying to. I didn't mind Mummy's teasing. Elsie was the sister I'd never had, and although she was sixteen, she still liked to make up games and tell tall tales and funny stories. She made up wild adventures as we whispered to each other in the darkness of the bedroom, setting me off into great fits of the giggles for which I earned a sharp "shush" and "get to sleep" from Mummy or Aunt Polly, which only made me giggle more. It was Elsie who told me to ignore the village bully, Mavis Clarke, when she called me a "funny foreigner" and kicked at my shins with her heavy wooden clogs. It was Elsie who explained that the village kids were jealous of my shiny leather shoes and smart school hat with its blue ribbons. It was always Elsie and Frances, or Frances and Elsie. I didn't mind which, as long as we were together. I could hardly remember a time when I hadn't known Elsie Wright. It was as if she had always been there.

But for all that I enjoyed Elsie's company, what I loved most was to be alone at the beck with the quiet chatter of the stream. In my wonderment, I often forgot to look where I was stepping and slipped on the stones, returning home sheepishly with wet shoes and skirts. Mummy said I would be the ruination of her, honestly I would, and that she didn't want me playing there if I couldn't stay on my feet. I'd heard her and Aunt Polly talking in low voices about the Hogan girl's disappearance and the rumors surrounding it. Mummy didn't trust the beck, but I couldn't resist going back, pulled there like the ball bearing Mrs. Hogan had shown us being pulled toward a magnet. I felt nothing but tranquility at the beck, tranquility and the suggestion of something else that lay beyond the flash of the dragonflies' wings and the ever-shifting shadows on the water. I couldn't explain the feeling I had when I was there, but as Daddy said in his letter when I asked him why so many men had to die in the battles, some things can't be rationally explained, but you still can't stop them happening.

It was an especially warm day when I first took the longer route home from school, mainly to avoid Mavis Clarke with her spiteful words and painful clogs, but also to walk beside the golden barley fields. I climbed onto the gate and dangled my legs on either side, closing my eyes as I listened to the ripple and rustle of the tall ears of barley, imagining they were whispering their secrets to the wind. It was hard to believe the world was at war when everything here was so peaceful and calm. I thought of all the poor dead men in France and pressed the palms of my hands together, saying a prayer for the war to be over and for Daddy to come home safe.

As my eyes grew heavy beneath the warm sun and the gentle lullaby of the barley, I leaned back against the gate-post and let myself drift into a gentle slumber, suspended in that magical place between sleep and waking where my thoughts were of birdsong and laughter, and a little girl, hair like flames, offering me a white flower. "For Mammy. For my Mammy."

"Frances?"

I sat up, squinting through the glare of the sun. "Mrs. Hogan?" I jumped down from the gate, sending my satchel tumbling to the ground, spilling everything across the dusty lane. "Sorry, Miss. I must have fallen asleep."

Mrs. Hogan bent down to help me gather my things. "There's no need to apologize. It's a grand day. Does wonders for the soul, sure it does."

I liked the way Mrs. Hogan ended her sentences with "sure it does." When I mimicked her Irish accent it made Elsie laugh.

"Is it very late, Miss? I should be getting home." I was annoyed with myself for falling asleep. I'd planned to go to the beck and now there wouldn't be time.

"It's not that late. Your cousin won't be back from work yet." I was pleased to hear this. Elsie made too much noise at the beck. She wasn't as patient as me and could only sit for a few minutes before she was up and striding about again, saying we should make dams and have races with the frogs. "Do you mind if I walk with you?" Mrs. Hogan continued. "I always think a walk is far nicer with two, don't you?"

I said of course Mrs. Hogan could walk with me, although I wasn't sure what you said to your teacher when you weren't in the classroom.

From my first day at Bingley Grammar, I'd taken a liking to Mrs. Hogan. The pale face I'd seen at the cottage window was barely recognizable as the enthusiastic teacher at the front of the classroom. Mrs. Hogan had lively eyes and brisk footsteps and a lovely Irish lilt to her voice that made me feel as if I were listening to music. I liked the way the heels of her shoes clacked against the boards as she moved around the classroom. I liked the rustle of her skirt and the lavender-scented trail she left behind her as she swished past the rows of desks. I liked the *tap tap tap* of the chalk as her neat handwriting danced across the blackboard. Even when I was having trouble with my algebra or thinking about Daddy, Mrs. Hogan always had a gentle smile and the right words. I felt as though nothing bad could ever happen as long as people like Mrs. Hogan were in the world. Still, I couldn't forget the haunted look I'd seen on her face through the window, and I couldn't stop thinking about her poor daughter who'd disappeared.

"I was sorry to hear about your little girl, Miss."

The words were out before I could stop them. I clapped my hand over my mouth, but it was too late. My thoughts had become a real living thing, striding along the laneway between us and spoiling what had been a perfectly nice walk.

Mrs. Hogan stood for a moment, breathing in and out, her hand at her chest. I stared hard at a new scuff on my shoe, thinking how Mummy would be vexed when she saw it. I stared at that scuff for what felt like an age until I had to say something to fill the silence.

"My cousin told me. Elsie Wright. She wasn't gossiping, Miss. She just . . ."

Mrs. Hogan placed a hand on my arm. "It's all right, Frances. There's no need to apologize. Sometimes it's better to talk about the difficult things. Ignoring them doesn't make them go away, sure it doesn't?"

I thought of the many nights I'd lain awake, worrying about Daddy, wishing he would get himself a Blighty wound so he could come home. "No, Miss. It doesn't."

Mrs. Hogan must have read my thoughts as we walked on because she said I must miss my father very much. "Do you know where he's stationed?" she asked.

"He was somewhere called Arras the last we heard, but Mummy isn't sure now. We haven't had a letter for a while."

"'Tis a truly terrible thing altogether, not to know where someone is. If only we knew they were safe . . . It's the not knowing. Never knowing . . ."

I heard the crack in Mrs. Hogan's voice and wished I could think of something helpful to say. I scolded myself for having a loose tongue and spoiling our walk.

We followed the rutted laneway where the mud had been baked into hard rough ridges by the sun and sent up puffs of dust as my boots crunched satisfyingly over them.

"How's your mammy keeping, Frances?"

I said Mummy was keeping well, although it wasn't really the truth. The truth was that her hair was falling out. She did her best to conceal it with hats and headscarves, but I'd seen her at her dressing table, the back of her head as smooth and pale as a tailor's dummy. I'd found a wig on her bed, mistaking it for the cat and getting an awful fright when I went to pick it up. Elsie reckoned it was all to do with worrying about Daddy.

"She'll be happier when Daddy comes home," I added. At least that was the truth. "We'll all be happy when the war is over, won't we, Miss?"

Mrs. Hogan pulled her head up high and turned her eyes skyward. "Yes, Frances. We will. And until then, we have to keep praying that our loved ones are safe." She crossed herself as she said this, in the Roman Catholic way—touching her forehead and chest and each shoulder. "Do you say your prayers every night?"

"I do, Miss. Me and our Elsie. We pray for Daddy. And for all the brave soldiers."

"You're a grand girl, Frances. 'Tis a pleasure to have you in my classroom. You're fitting in well now you've made some friends. Tell me, do you play with the village children at all?"

"Not really, Miss. I'm not sure they like me much."

"Oh?"

"They call me a funny foreigner because of the way I talk. Elsie says they're jealous of my grammar school uniform." I couldn't explain that I still felt like a stranger in Cottingley; that I stood out no matter how much I tried to blend in. I couldn't explain how I felt different at the beck; that I felt accepted there, as if I was among friends. Mrs. Hogan wouldn't understand. Nobody would.

"Don't be minding the village children. They can be wary of newcomers. I *still* talk like a funny foreigner as far as they're concerned! You'll fit in with them soon enough, Frances. Give it time."

We would be going back to Cape Town as soon as the war was over and Daddy was home, so it didn't matter anyway about fitting in with the local children, but I knew Mrs. Hogan was only trying to be kind and decided it was probably best not to say anything.

Mrs. Hogan noticed the book I was carrying. "*Black Beauty.* One of my favorites. I'm glad to see you're a keen reader. You can never have too many books or too much laughter in a house. Isn't that right?"

I looked up at her. "Mummy thinks I read too much. She says I live in a world of make-believe and it's not good to always be filling my head with stories. She gets cross with our Elsie when she catches her whispering to me at night about goblins and unicorns and fairies. Mummy says Elsie Wright will have my head so full of nonsense there'll be no room left for anything sensible."

Mrs. Hogan chuckled. I was glad to have lightened the mood. "Well, I'm afraid I have to disagree with your mammy," she said. "Make-believe keeps us going at times like this. We have to believe in the possibility of happy endings, sure we do, otherwise what's it all for?"

I didn't know how to answer that, and wasn't sure it was the sort of question that needed an answer anyway.

Reaching the crest of the hill, we stood to one side of the path to make way for a passing horse and cart. I gaped at the great Shire horse as it lumbered past, its brasses jangling on the thick halter around its sweat-foamed neck. One of the lucky ones not to have been shipped out as a war horse. Mrs. Hogan bid the farmer good afternoon. I recognized him as Mr. Snowden, who owned the beck and the land at the back of Number 31.

He tipped his hat to us as he passed. "'Ow do, Ellen. Miss Frances."

Ellen. Mrs. Hogan's name was Ellen. It was a gentle name. It suited her perfectly.

"How does Mr. Snowden know me, Miss?" I asked as we walked on, the familiar spire of Cottingley church appearing above the tree line ahead.

Mrs. Hogan smiled. "Everyone knows everybody's business in Cottingley, Frances. There are things people will know about you that you don't even know about yourself yet!"

She winked playfully, but her words made me uneasy. Still, I was glad of her company and enjoyed the rest of our walk into the village. Sometimes we talked. Sometimes we walked in comfortable silence as I tumbled the newly discovered name of my teacher around in my mind—Ellen Hogan—and all the while the gentle hush of the barley whispered its secrets in the fields beside us.

For Mammy . . . it whispered. *For my Mammy* . . .

NOTES ON A FAIRY TALE
Cottingley, Yorkshire. July 1917.

Summer bloomed over Yorkshire and Mummy was right—everything was brighter and better. I woke each morning to the sound of birdsong and the glow of sunlight through the window. School would soon be over for the summer, and the prospect of long, lazy days at the beck stretched out before me like a spool of thread. And what days they would be, because a week before the school holidays, everything changed.

It started out as any ordinary Monday, but it was a day I would never forget, even when—years later—people told me it couldn't possibly have happened at all.

Mummy went off to work at Uncle Enoch's tailor shop in Bradford. Elsie went to her job at Gunston's photographers. Uncle Arthur went to the Briggs', and Aunt Polly bragged about being the first on the street to get her washing on the line, remarking at least a dozen times on the whiteness of her sheets as they flapped in the breeze and how Edna Morris—our busybody neighbor—could stick that in her pipe and smoke it. It was a warm, oppressive day, the air heavy with expectation that stuck to my skin as I walked to Cottingley Bar to catch the tram to school.

The sense of anticipation followed me around all day like a playful puppy, nipping at my heels until I could give it my full attention. I was distracted and forgetful at school, making a muddle of the simplest of comprehensions. Mrs. Hogan sighed with frustration when she corrected my work, saying she didn't know what on earth had got into me, and did I have a fever coming on?

I was glad when the school bell rang, and I was glad to find the house empty when I returned home, a scribbled note on the table telling me Aunt Polly had popped in to Bingley and would be back at teatime. It was a perfect afternoon for dipping too-hot toes in cool water and for watching the painted lady butterflies fan their wings on the purple buddleia that grew by the riverbank. I didn't hesitate for a moment.

Dropping my satchel in the scullery, I ran straight out to the garden, skipping across the grass, scrambling down the bank and down to the beck, where I pulled off my stockings and shoes, hitched up my skirt, and walked along the edge of the shallow stream. My skin savored the cool of the water, drawing the clammy heat down through my legs and out through my toes. I dipped my hands beneath the surface, the water slipping like silver ribbons over my fingertips before I pressed my palms to my cheeks, absorbing the refreshing coolness. I repeated this several times before sitting on the bough seat of the willow tree.

Leaning back against the smooth bark, I closed my eyes and listened to the gentle gurgle of the stream, the splash of a fish snatching a fly from the surface of the water, the soft rustle of fern and leaf, disturbed by unseen riverbank creatures. I imagined Daddy sitting beside me, my head on his shoulder, the tickle of his five o'clock shadow on my forehead. He would love it here. I imagined the flowers and plants coming to life, uprooting themselves, joining leaf and petal, like hands, to form a circle, entwining themselves around and around the trunk of an oak tree, like eager children in a Maypole dance.

It wasn't a sound that disturbed me, more a sensation—

the feeling I'd experienced so often at the beck, the suggestion of others around me, the sense of being watched.

I sat up and let my eyes adjust to the light, watching the shadows and shifting shapes among the trees. The beck was alive. The air around me hummed as my attention was caught by a willow leaf spinning around in an eddy at the side of the beck. I followed it as it drifted free of the bank and floated out into the center of the stream, where it continued to twirl and spin before carrying on, not downstream to follow the natural course of the flowing water, but straight across to the other bank, as if guided by something, or someone.

That was when I saw the first flash of emerald, then another of blue, then yellow, glimpsed out of the corner of my eye. Not dragonflies. Not butterflies. Something else. Something moving among a cluster of harebells, the delicate white flowers nodding as their petals and leaves were disturbed by the slightest of movements, like a gentle breeze blowing against them and yet there wasn't the slightest breath of wind at the beck that day. All was perfectly still except for my heart thumping like a piston engine in my chest, my breathing fast and shallow. I pressed my hands against the solid bark of the tree trunk, anchoring myself as I leaned forward, wide-eyed in wonder, afraid to blink in case I lost them in the fraction of a second my eyes were closed.

Fairies.

They appeared to me like a thin veil of mist, translucent, almost—not quite there. But for all their misty peculiarity, they were as clear to me as the minnows in the shallows and the foxgloves on the riverbank and the but-

terflies fanning their wings. They flitted from flower to
flower, as swift as dragonflies, sometimes glowing brightly
like a candle flame suddenly catching, sometimes fading
like a breath of warm air on glass, so that you would never
know they had been there at all. Yet there they were. And
there I was, watching them.

I had never observed anything so intently, conscious
even amid my amazement and wonder that I had to remember this, had to take in every detail so I would be sure
of it later. As I looked, a beautiful ringing filled my ears, a
sound unlike anything I'd heard before, a sound I wished I
could hear always, because it filled my heart with joy.

Half of me was desperate for Elsie to appear so that she
could see them too. Half of me was anxious that nobody—
nothing—would come along to disturb them.

I watched for two or three minutes, maybe more. Time
was suspended in those magical moments. The stream
stilled at my feet. The birds paused mid-song. It was as if
all of nature watched with me in respectful silence. And
then, as suddenly as they had arrived, they disappeared.
The birds resumed their singing, a soft breeze ruffled the
foliage of the ferns, the stream trickled along its endless
course, taking my astonishment with it.

Giddy with excitement, I hopped down from the branch
and made my way slowly, quietly, along the center of the
stream, searching among the foliage for any last sign of
them. I sat on the riverbank for a while, tucking my knees
up to my chest, waiting, watching until the afternoon
sun grew too hot and I grew terribly thirsty. Reluctantly,
my heart bursting with the greatest secret imaginable, I

clambered up the bank and ran through the garden, back to the cool shade of the house where Aunt Polly's note was still on the table, my school satchel was still on the scullery floor, and everything was exactly the same.

Yet nothing would ever be quite the same again.

NOTES ON A FAIRY TALE
Cottingley, Yorkshire. July 1917.

A wonderful array of color burst from the hedgerows and marched jubilantly across the hilltops that summer, defiantly smothering the lingering shadows of war. When I arrived home from school, I often found Aunt Polly napping in the garden, a bowl of half-shelled peas on her lap, her head tipped back, her mouth wide open in a deep, heat-soaked slumber.

She complained about the heat, saying it made folk weary as she fanned her flushed cheeks with a tea towel. "We need a good dose of rain. I don't care for this weather at all. Can't get anything done." The previous month of "flaming-June" sunshine had scorched the front gardens so that, according to Aunt Polly, the whole street looked like it was suffering from a bad case of jaundice. But I loved the sultry warmth. I liked the tickle of pollen in my nose and the way everyone slowed down, languishing like cats at garden gates to talk to neighbors and friends whom they would have ignored in bad weather in their hurry to get indoors. Like the bees and the rambling roses that bloomed around the garden fence, I thrived in the summer heat. If only Daddy could have been here and the war were over, it would have been the perfect summer Mummy had promised.

Best of all, the summer brought school holidays and more time to play at the beck. Day after day I returned, eager to see the fairies again. Most days I saw nothing other than the usual birds and insects, but on the brightest, warmest days, my patience was rewarded with sightings of my little friends. They saw me, I was sure of it, and yet they never flew away or disappeared into the undergrowth. As I pottered about beside the stream, building dams and writing notes in my diary, they continued with their work among the flowers. I watched in peaceful wonderment, never disturbing them, never disturbed by them, until seeing these curious beings became almost as natural to me as seeing the plants and the birds. Distracted and delighted by what I saw, I often lost my footing on the mossy stones, and Mummy grew ever more annoyed when I continually returned home with wet shoes and sodden skirts.

"Oh, Frances. You've been at the beck *again*. I don't know what's so fascinating about it. Go up to your room and put some dry clothes on before you catch pneumonia."

Everyone dreaded the pneumonia. In the privacy of the bedroom, I said a silent prayer that I would be spared.

Time and again, I was forbidden from playing at the beck. Time and again, I disregarded Mummy's warnings, unable to resist the remarkable things I saw there. I took my secret to bed with me every night, where, disturbed by the oppressive heat and Elsie's snoring, I lay awake, playing the images of what I had seen over and over in my mind, determined to remember everything so that I would never forget, not even when I was an old lady back in South Africa.

I was restless at mealtimes, fidgeting in my chair and kicking my toes against the table legs. Mummy said I was giving her a headache with all my writhing around. I overheard her and Aunt Polly talking about me, wondering whether I might have worms and should be taken to the doctor. Aunt Polly suspected me of being lovesick for one of the boys at school. Uncle Arthur declared me "a bit of a rum'n" and delivered a verdict of sunstroke. I was sent to bed with a cold compress and a dose of Epsom salts and forbidden from playing outside for a week.

Elsie noticed the change in me too. She did her best to prize the truth from me as I changed into my night-dress.

"Come on, then. What's got into you? Summat's up and don't deny it, Frances Griffiths. It's written all over your face."

I wanted to tell Elsie. With all my heart I wanted to grab her hands and tell her everything, but I said I was weary from the heat. "Sunstroke. That's all."

With Rosebud in my arms, I lay on top of the bedsheet, too hot to snuggle down beneath it. I fell into a restless sleep in which my dreams carried me away over misty valleys and moonlit woodlands toward a fairy glen, where I watched their beautiful midnight revels in silent awe as I whispered the words of my favorite poem. "'You shall hear a sound like thunder, / And a veil shall be withdrawn, / When her eyes grow wide with wonder, / On that hill-top, in that dawn.'"

As the summer heat intensified, so did my dreams. I dreamed of Daddy walking up the hill in his uniform, smiling as I ran into his arms. I dreamed of wild winds blowing down from the distant hilltops, tossing dandelion seeds around the garden like summer snowflakes, but mostly, I dreamed of the fairies.

They came to me night after night, bright shimmering lights at the window, twinkling like moonlight on frost. They beckoned to me, the ringing in my ears becoming voices, urging me on. *Come, Frances. Come and play.* And then something changed, and my dreams became real, in a way I could neither understand, nor explain.

I knew I shouldn't follow the fairies and that I'd be in trouble if Mummy found out, but that particular night they were so beautiful I simply couldn't resist and slipped quietly from the bed, tiptoeing downstairs to the scullery where I pulled my coat over my nightdress and stepped into my boots, clean and shiny from my diligent polishing earlier that evening. I moved silently across the garden, silvered with moonlight, my feet barely touching the ground. I brushed past fern and tree, following the lights across the stream, toward the cottage in the clearing where I watched a little girl surrounded by light and laughter as the fairies threaded flowers through her hair. I stood out of sight, peering through the tangled blackberry bushes, but the girl saw me, rushing forward, her hand outstretched, a white flower clasped between her fingers. "For Mammy," she said. "For my Mammy." As I reached for the flower, I slipped and lost my balance, tumbling down the bank and into the water, and all I could think was that Mummy would be ever so cross . . .

Waking with a start, I opened my eyes. Sunlight streamed through the open window, drenching the room in a soft golden light as a dandelion seed drifted inside.

Elsie called them fairies, which I thought rather lovely. Birdsong pierced the silence.

When I stepped out of bed, I noticed a white flower on the floor beside my slippers. I picked it up, turning it over in my hands: a slender green stem, a single leaf, and five bell-shaped white blooms. I placed it between the pages of my picture book and, half in a dream, made my way downstairs.

Mummy was waiting for me in the scullery, holding my boots speckled with mud. "And what is the meaning of this?" Her voice was clipped. Stern.

I stared at my dirty boots. "But . . ."

"But what? I asked you to clean these yesterday, Frances, and what's worse, you told me you had."

"But, Mummy, I did. I had."

She slammed the boots down onto the back step. "You're to get a bucket of water and start scrubbing. Why on earth you can't do things when you're asked is beyond me, really it is. I've enough to be worrying about without you making things difficult."

I felt the tears coming. I didn't understand. I'd left the boots on the doorstep, perfectly clean, before I went to bed.

As Mummy clattered about in the pantry behind me, taking out her anger on jars of pickled onions and black currant jam, I filled a bucket from the pump, picked up my boots, and began to scrub at them with the brush.

"And put a bit of elbow grease into it," Mummy called. "There'll be no more playing at the beck. I don't know how many times I have to tell you, Frances. You're not to be playing there and coming back with muddy boots. D'you hear?"

I called back that yes, I heard, and rubbed my frustration harder and harder into my boots, until the water in the tin bucket turned a murky brown and I couldn't shake the feeling that I was scrubbing away more than the dirt. I was scrubbing away a memory or a message, but I couldn't remember what it was, or whom it was for.

NOTES ON A FAIRY TALE
Cottingley, Yorkshire. July 1917.

I soon came to understand that Aunt Polly and Uncle
Arthur were highly regarded in Cottingley. With Uncle Arthur working for Mr. Briggs, the Wrights were considered
close to the local gentry and regarded with a certain de-
gree of respect. I noticed it after Sunday service when
people stopped outside the church to shake Uncle Arthur's
extraordinarily large hands, and on Friday evenings when
friends gathered in the front room for a musical evening
around the piano. I loved to listen to Aunt Polly singing
"Four Indian Love Lyrics" and Uncle Arthur's deep baritone rendition of "Roses of Picardy." Sometimes Elsie and
I were allowed a slice of jam tart while we listened, and
although I never tasted it, I liked the musty smell of Ma-
son's nonalcoholic beer that Aunt Polly brewed especially
for the occasion. She said it was a chance for everyone to
forget about the war for an hour or two, to sing and laugh
"rather than worrit and cry," although I knew that everyone's thoughts were never far away from their loved ones.

But even with these social gatherings at the house, I
found it hard to join in. I was the girl who stood back, the
girl who remained quiet and reserved, happy to let Elsie do
the talking on behalf of us *young uns*, as we were called.
I wasn't necessarily shy, but I still felt like a stranger in
Cottingley, despite my efforts to adopt the local dialect and
throw in the odd *thee* and *thou* for good measure. Mummy
mithered at me to try harder to make friends with the
village children. "No wonder they talk about you behind
your back, Frances. They don't know what to make of you,

walking around with your head in the clouds. They think you sullen and unfriendly."

"But I'm not."

"Well, *I* know that, and *you* know that, but they don't, do they?"

I tried to explain that I had friends at school, although most of them lived in Bradford so I didn't see them in the holidays. I said there wasn't much point making new friends when we would be going back to Cape Town when the war was over and Daddy was home, and that, besides, I was perfectly happy playing with Elsie at the beck, or on my own. Mummy threw her hands in the air and said she gave up, really and truly she did.

It was on a thankfully cooler day when Elsie was off work with a head cold that I decided to explore a little further afield, clambering over the stile at the top of the lane and following the beck upstream, where it opened up into the glen and Cottingley Woods. From there, I walked along the far bank, following a little trail where the grass had been flattened, perhaps by other inquisitive young girls, or perhaps by a badger or fox. As I stopped to pick a handful of wild raspberries, I saw Mrs. Hogan's cottage among the trees ahead. It was almost completely concealed by the lush summer foliage, more woodland than house, as if made of flowers and trees, not of stone and mortar.

I picked my way through the tangled briars underfoot, drawn toward the cottage as if in a dream as something nagged at me, a distant memory of something I'd forgotten to do. As I walked, I thought about fairy stories of stolen children locked up by wicked old witches and I skirted the edge of the cottage wall with a mixture of excitement and trepidation as I peered into the garden. I knew I shouldn't have been there, and yet I sensed that I was welcome, that I had been there before and knew everything I saw in front of me: the rambling roses around the low white door, the patterned curtains at the windows and the posy of wildflowers in a willow pattern jug on the sill, the elder tree—heavy with white blooms—that grew in the center of the garden, the pair of man-sized black boots on the doorstep and the much smaller pair of child's boots beside them.

Everything was so peaceful, the only sounds the birds singing in the branches high above and the constant gurgle of the beck behind me, the waterfall just visible through a gap in the trees. I imagined Mrs. Hogan standing at her window, watching Elsie and me play that April morning. I wondered if she'd once watched her daughter play there too.

A click of the latch on the cottage door snatched me back from my thoughts.

"Frances? It *is* you. I thought it was." Mrs. Hogan stood in the doorway, her hands covered in paint, a bemused look on her face.

My cheeks blushed furiously. "I was taking a walk, Miss, and . . ."

"Exploring?"

I nodded.

Mrs. Hogan smiled warmly. "I'm almost completely hidden by the trees in the summertime. But you'll see the cottage easily enough in the winter when everything dies back. Come on in for a glass of water. 'Tis fierce thirsty work, exploring."

I followed her inside the cottage, as pretty on the inside

as it was on the outside. Tapestries and samplers hung on the walls with carefully stitched Irish proverbs and sayings. One in particular caught my attention.

Come away, O human child!
To the waters and the wild,
With a faery hand in hand,
For the world's more full of weeping than you can
    understand.

The words reminded me of Elsie's nighttime stories of changelings and fairies who stole human children and left monstrous things in their place.

Mrs. Hogan noticed me looking at it as she emerged from the pantry with a glass of water. "William Butler Yeats. 'The Stolen Child.' One of his most famous poems. Perhaps we should read it in class after the holidays."

She said this more to herself than to me as I turned my attention to the watercolor paintings of landscapes and flowers that filled the spaces between a hotchpotch collection of crockery on the dresser. I told Mrs. Hogan I liked her painting of the beck.

"I expect you like to play there," she said. "Hard to resist such an enchanting place."

"Me and Elsie make dams and race the baby frogs on leaf boats. You can hear the waterfall from our bedroom. It used to keep me awake at night, but I don't notice it now."

"Everything strange becomes familiar in time. I loved the beck when I was a young girl, although I was older than you when I played there—closer to your cousin Elsie in age. My parents moved to Yorkshire from Leitrim so my

father could get work in the mills." I sipped my water and
wished Elsie was with me and not at home in bed coughing
and sneezing. Elsie was much better at conversation than
me. "You'll have heard the stories, I expect, about the beck
and the woods and Gilstone Crags." I shook my head, even
though Elsie had told me some of the local folklore. Mrs.
Hogan lowered her voice. "Some claim to have seen the
Little People there. Pixies and fairies and such." Her eyes
sparkled like the water in the beck when the sunlight hit
it. "What do you make of that then?"

My heart thumped beneath my pinafore as I thought
about what I'd seen at the beck. I desperately wanted to
tell someone, and Mrs. Hogan was as good a person as any.

She mistook my silence for doubt. "Sure, you don't believe me." She smiled. "Most people don't. Most of the locals say it's a 'load of old codswallop.' And they say *I* talk
funny!"

"I do believe you, Miss. I really do. I . . ." My heart raced.
I felt as if I would burst if I didn't tell her, but I couldn't
find the right words.

"What is it, Frances?"

"Nothing, Miss." I fished around wildly for something
to say, remembering the leaflets I'd seen at home for the
Theosophist Society meetings in Bradford. "Is that what
the Theosophists are interested in? Fairies?"

"How do you know about the Theosophists?"

"I've heard Aunt Polly talking to Mummy about them."

"Theosophists believe in the existence of other beings,
and other realms," Mrs. Hogan explained. "Ghosts and
spirits, and fairy life."

"Uncle Arthur says it's all a load of old codswallop."

I was pleased to make Mrs. Hogan laugh. "But what if he could see fairies? He'd have to believe in them then, wouldn't he?" I sipped my water to stop myself talking. I'd already said more than I should, talking about Uncle Arthur out of turn.

"I suppose he would. There are stories going back years about fairies in Upper Airedale and Wharfedale. Some of them must be true, sure they must, but most people only believe what they see with their own eyes."

As I sat in Mrs. Hogan's cottage I felt I could tell her anything, and it would be all right.

"Do you think it's wrong to keep secrets, Miss?"

She thought for a moment. "I suppose it depends on what the secret is, and where it's being kept." .

"What do you mean?"

"Cottingley's a small village, and small villages can't keep secrets. They've a funny way of setting them free, and who knows where they'll end up?" She leaned forward. A gentle smile danced in her eyes. "If I had a secret, I'd hang on to it."

The sound of the rag-and-bone man's bell signaled that it was time for me to go home. "I should be going. Aunt Polly will be looking for me."

"You're welcome anytime, Frances. The woodland belongs to everyone, and my door is always open in case . . . well, never mind. It's open. That's all that matters."

I said good-bye and Mrs. Hogan disappeared into the dark interior of the cottage, closing the door behind her and humming a ditty that drifted through the open window. "'Up the airy mountain, / Down the rushy glen, / We daren't go a-hunting / For fear of little men; / Wee folk, good folk, / Trooping all together; / Green jacket, red cap, / And white owl's feather!'"

I hurried back along the mossy path, unable to shake the feeling that I had forgotten to tell her something very important.

It was now three weeks since my first sighting at the beck. More than once, I'd almost told Elsie. Like water coming to the boil in the copper, I could feel the bubbles of excitement rise to the surface, certain they would burst out of me if I didn't tell someone. But somehow, I bit my tongue. Only when I was alone in the bedroom did I even breathe a word about it.

"They're *real*, Rosebud!" I whispered, grasping my doll's hands. "*Very* real and so beautiful . . ."

"Who is beautiful?"

I turned to see Elsie standing in the doorway, a slight smile at her lips.

"Nobody. Nothing." My cheeks flared scarlet. "I was just making up stories for Rosebud."

Elsie stepped into the room and pulled the door to behind her, her eyes burning with excitement. "What happened, Frances? I promise I won't tell."

She looked so grown-up and pretty that I couldn't resist. I *had* to tell her. Jumping up onto the bed, I grabbed Elsie's hands, pulling her down to sit beside me. "You have to *promise* you won't laugh, or tease me, or tell anyone." She promised, twice, three times before I took a deep breath. "I've seen things at the beck."

Elsie squeezed my hand in encouragement and nodded for me to go on. "What sort of things?"

The word caught in my throat, emerging as a faint whisper. "Fairies."

Elsie said nothing. My heart sank. I'd known she wouldn't believe me.

"It doesn't make any sense," I continued, imploring my cousin to believe, "and you'll only think I'm making it up or imagining things, but I *see* them, Elsie. I promise I do. I see them just as I can see you now."

Elsie studied me carefully, her lively blue eyes searching deep into mine. "It's all right, Frances. I believe you."

"Do you, really?" Elsie nodded, her eyes sparkling with intrigue as I threw my arms around her. "Oh, Elsie. Can you believe it? Fairies at the bottom of the garden!"

My words came out in a rush then as I told her everything. How I'd first seen them and how they always appeared toward the end of the afternoon in fine weather, never in bad. I tried to describe them exactly as I'd seen them while Elsie listened and asked questions until we were both whispering about fairies as if we were gossiping about the neighbors. And it was as easy and as difficult as that. In a moment, the secret I'd kept so carefully in my heart wasn't mine anymore. It was Elsie's secret too.

That night, we lay in the dark and whispered for a long time about my remarkable discovery. Elsie assured me again and again that she wouldn't say a word to anyone, and although I trusted her and felt a delicious fizz of excitement in my tummy when we talked about it, I also felt a nagging sense of doubt. Of something not quite right.

I felt my words seep into the walls of the bedroom and under the door. I felt them slip through the gaps in the window frame and wished I could take them back, because when Elsie went to work the next morning, she would take the secret with her. It would leave 31 Main Street and travel to Bradford, where it would spread like a fever down the long line of girls who did the spotting work with her. It would be there at every mealtime, passing between us like salt and gravy. It was part of the house now, captured in the wind that whistled down the chimney and in the floorboards that creaked on the stairs.

As I squeezed my eyes shut and fell into a restless sleep, Mrs. Hogan's words raged through my mind like the whispers I'd heard among the barley. *"Cottingley's a small village, and small villages can't keep secrets. They've a funny way of setting them free, and who knows where they'll end up?"*

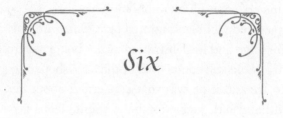

Six

Ireland. Present day.

After another restless night, disturbed by the same curious dream of a little girl and a woodland stream, Olivia woke to dazzling sunlight and the glaring realization of what she'd done. She lay still, her hands on her stomach, feeling her breath as it rose and fell in synch with the distant pull and push of the tide. The tightness in her chest had eased. Her body—her heart—felt lighter. Extending her stay in Ireland was just the start, the loose end of a messy tangle she would have to unravel if she was serious about making these seismic changes to her life, but as Nana had always said when she was winding a skein of wool, finding the end was the hard part. After that, all it took was patience, determination, and plenty of fresh tea in the pot.

Reaching instinctively for her phone, she winced at the thought of it lying at the bottom of the sea. A childish act of rebellion, perhaps, but the relief at not having to listen to notification alerts and read through missed messages was immense. For the first time in months, her head felt empty of noise and clutter. She had bought herself time to think—precious, vital time to be herself and not someone's fiancée, or a bride-to-be, or a name on a consultant's appointments list.

She pictured Jack's golf-tanned face, imagining his reaction to her message and his frustration at not being able to get hold of her. He could still contact her at the bookshop, or could even travel to Ireland if he was that concerned about her, but she doubted he would. Jack wasn't the spontaneous type. Theirs was a relationship of schedules and carefully coordinated diaries. Squash on Tuesdays (him). Pilates on Wednesdays (her). Date nights on Thursdays (Jack's business meetings permitting). How do you schedule spontaneity?

Determined to put Jack out of her mind, Olivia spent her morning in a series of unpleasant meetings.

The accountant—a Ms. Gilbert, who looked far too young to know anything about such things—talked about the bookshop's unique selling points and asked Olivia if she'd considered modernizing. Olivia tried to explain, as calmly as possible, that the whole point of Something Old was to be quaint and full of old-world charm, the antithesis of modernized, but her words fell on deaf ears as Ms. Gilbert pressed on about margins and bottom lines and Olivia retreated further and further into her chair until she was almost fetal.

The solicitor was equally bewildering, impressing upon Olivia how fortunate she was that her grandfather had been astute enough to grant her power of attorney over his and Nana's assets. Olivia wanted to say that she didn't feel fortunate, that she mostly felt sad and worried, but she pushed her feelings aside, diligently signed various forms and left Messrs. Comerford & Keogh to put things in motion. It came down to a simple, gut-wrenching decision: sell Bluebell Cottage and use the funds to pay off the bookshop's debts, or lose the book-shop and keep the cottage. Either way, she would be letting Nana and Pappy down; letting go of something they had trea-sured and had made them part of who they were.

She was grateful for the quiet, unassuming calm of the book-shop when she returned that afternoon, and although she hated to admit that Nora Plunkett was right, she had a point: the shop front *was* in desperate need of a spring clean. After a few hours of hard work, and with the addition of four new window boxes from the florist (whose ladder and head for heights Olivia was especially grateful for), Something Old looked much neater and brighter. Nora Plunkett might have had a point, but Olivia re-fused to give her the satisfaction of making it twice.

Inside the shop, Olivia found another note from Iris pushed through the letterbox. She wrote a reply and placed it in the window for Iris to see, trying desperately to ignore the urge to think about Ross Bailey, Writer, as she did.

Before making a start on the shop interior, Olivia took a few minutes to look through more of the newspaper clippings she'd discovered in the old briefcase.

In contrast with the articles written in the 1920s, more recent reports from the 1970s were skeptical of the fairy photographs, asserting they were fake. Some of the articles went as far as to accuse the two girls of being the perpetrators of England's greatest hoax. Olivia thought about the innocent photograph she'd discovered in her mammy's jewelry box all those years ago. She'd had no idea it had been the source of international media interest and speculation. It made her more determined to find it, and to understand the connection between Frances and Cottingley, and her own family.

The jangle of the shop bell disturbed Olivia from her

reading. An inquiring baritone voice followed as the bell fell silent.

"Anyone at home?"

Olivia peered around a column of books to see a smartly dressed elderly gentleman peering back at her through the door. "I'm not actually open," she said. "I'm closed for . . . re-furbishments."

"According to the sign, you're open."

The sign said OPEN on one side and NOT CLOSED on the other. Pappy's little joke.

Olivia stood up. "Ah, yes. The infamous sign."

The man stepped inside and removed a trilby hat. A tor-toiseshell cat was cradled in his arms. His face was kind and inquisitive and he looked at Olivia a little longer than might be considered acceptable. She felt herself blush beneath his scrutiny.

"You must be Olivia?"

"Yes. Olivia Kavanagh. The owner." It felt good to say it out loud.

The man's eyes flickered from Olivia to the bookshelves and back again, a broad smile curving across his mouth as he handed her the cat. "In that case, I believe this scoundrel be-longs to you."

"Hemingway?"

"The very same."

"I wondered where he'd got to." The cat wriggled from Oli-via's arms, stretched, and strode purposefully upstairs as if he owned the place, his tail waving in the air in pompous disregard.

"I'm terribly sorry to intrude, Olivia, and please do ask me

to leave if you're busy, but I promised Cormac I would look in on you from time to time."

Olivia smiled, partly at his voice and mannerisms, which wouldn't be out of place among the pages of a Wilde novel, and partly in relief as she realized who he was. "Actually, I'm not that busy. Nothing that can't wait, anyway. Please, come in."

Closing the door behind him, the man offered his hand. "Henry Blake. I thought I should look in sooner rather than later." His eyes scanned the undisturbed shelves, the shop without customers, the expectant hush in the air. "I'm rather glad I did."

Henry Blake was exactly as Olivia had imagined. Pigeon-gray hair. A generous mustache. Deep brown eyes that flickered with curiosity behind small circular spectacles. A yellow-and-blue spotted handkerchief sprouting from the breast pocket of a smart three-piece tweed suit. He reminded her of a younger version of Pappy, carrying that same joie de vivre like an extra item of clothing. She wasn't a bit surprised to see that he carried a walking cane. He was perfectly put together from top to toe.

Shaking his hand, she introduced herself properly. "Olivia Kavanagh. I'm very pleased to meet you, Mr. Blake."

"Henry, please."

"Sorry. Henry. My grandfather mentioned you in a letter. I was planning to get in touch." She pulled the scrap of paper from her cardigan pocket, waving it in the air as evidence. "I had your name written down to remind me to call you."

"Then I'm glad I looked in. I don't wish to interfere, but a promise is a promise, and here I am."

Here he was. Her knight in light tweed armor. "Can I get you a cup of tea?"

He shook his head. "Never touch the stuff, which is peculiar and inconvenient of me, I know. You cannot imagine the consternation it causes when I decline. I only drink peppermint tea, you see, and most people have never encountered such a curious thing."

"I have. I like it. I think I have some in the back."

"Is that so? Then we shall get along marvelously, you and I, but do you mind if we skip the tea altogether? I fancy a stroll since it's such a pleasant day."

Olivia hesitated.

"Ten minutes?" Henry prompted. "I'm sure *all* your customers will come back tomorrow." He winked.

Olivia relented. Much as she needed paying customers, she also needed Henry's help.

As they stepped outside, Mr. Blake remarked on the empty cottage beside the bookshop. "Wasn't Cormac trying to get his hands on that?"

Olivia sighed. "Yes, but his inquiries never came to anything. Nora Plunkett won't lease it. She says she'd prefer to leave it empty."

"Who?"

"Nora Plunkett. She's the secretary of the local shopkeeping society, or something. Likes to shove her nose into other people's business. Her husband used to run a furniture business. The empty cottage was his shop. Some of the shop owners think she does wonders, but Pappy never liked her—and he was always a good judge of character—so neither do I."

They walked together along Little Lane, passing the shops and the bakery with its delicious aromas of vanilla and buttery brioche that made Olivia's stomach grumble.

"What was Cormac planning to do with the empty shop?" Henry asked.

"I presume he wanted to expand. He didn't talk about it much. He knew Nora wouldn't budge. It's probably for the best anyway. I don't think adding any more debts to the business would have been a good idea."

"Indeed. Your grandfather had a great talent for discovering rare books, but in recent years he wasn't so good at selling them. All that dreadful business with Martha distracted him." Henry paused, the *click click* of his cane filling the silence as they walked slowly on. "How is she, by the way?"

"She's doing okay. I saw her yesterday. The strange thing is that she remembers the distant past quite well. It's the present she struggles with: what she did a few minutes ago, or an hour ago, or yesterday. She gets terribly confused—forgetting people and places. Even the words she wants to use. She gets very upset."

"I believe that can often be the case with her condition. Desperately sad. She was always such a vivacious woman."

Olivia glanced at Henry. "Did you know her well?"

Henry smiled warmly. "I did, yes. Although I knew a much younger version of her. People change so much over time, don't they? I couldn't claim to know her now."

"Nana might have changed, Henry, but I believe that same vivacious woman is still in there. Somewhere."

Henry said it would be nice to think so.

They sat on a bench beneath the harbor wall, glad to be sheltered from the breeze as they watched the passenger ferries setting out toward England.

"How did you know Pappy, Henry?"

"We met when I was a young man, starting out in lecturing at Trinity. Cormac was a few years older than me and I looked up to him. We became friendly through a mutual love of books, I suppose," he explained. "Cormac started collecting rare books as a hobby. It was always his dream to open a shop when he retired. I planned to do the same."

"And did you?"

"Sadly not. Life didn't quite turn out the way I'd hoped it would." He ran his fingers across his mustache and took his handkerchief from his pocket to wipe his glasses. "I fell in love, as all young fools do, but the woman I loved couldn't love me in return, so I took a teaching post in New Zealand. As far away from Ireland as it is possible to go before you start to come back. I lived there for nearly thirty years. Had a marvelous time. Beautiful country." He perched his glasses on the end of his nose. "I never forgot her."

Henry's words were a pinprick to Olivia's conscience. She acknowledged to herself how easily she'd pushed Jack toward the edge of her heart. Too easily. "What brought you back?" she asked.

"Oh, various things. A longing for home, mostly. I was happy over there. I had a grand life, but I never met anyone quite like her. I suppose you would call her my soul mate. Life always felt terribly off balance without her. I'm afraid this stick of mine makes a very poor substitute for the warmth of her beside me."

Olivia was touched by Mr. Blake's gentle humility. "That's such a sad story, Henry."

"In one way, yes, but in another, not at all." He tapped a finger to his head. "I have my memories, you see, and those I can always cherish. Memory is a wonderful gift, which is why it is so cruel to watch someone try to live without it." He returned his handkerchief to his pocket. "Anyway, I eventually tracked Cormac down here. I couldn't believe how much his small collection in our shared office had grown into an actual bookshop."

"And now it's all mine."

"So I believe. Cormac told me he planned to leave the shop to you. You know, when the time came."

"I'm not sure how long it will be mine, Mr. Blake . . . Henry. I love books and I adore the shop, but I don't know the first thing about the business side."

"Then I suppose it's fortunate that I do."

His words were like a balm to Olivia. "Really? You can help me with all that?"

"Yes, dear. I can help you with all that—with a little help from my nephew. I'm afraid I couldn't claim to be quite as sharp as I once was! It won't be easy and there will be difficult decisions to make along the way, but you don't strike me as the sort of person to shy away from a difficult decision."

She thought about her phone at the bottom of the sea and all the decisions it had taken down with it. Decisions that would still be waiting for her when—if—she chose to resurface from this self-imposed exile in Ireland, but decisions she would be better able to make because of it.

"Difficult decisions are easy enough, Mr. Blake. The tricky part is deciding to make them in the first place."

Henry peered knowingly at Olivia through his spectacles. "Quite so, my dear." He checked his watch and mumbled something to himself. "And I'm afraid I must be going."

"So soon? I can't tempt you to that peppermint tea?"

He saw the worry in Olivia's eyes. "You will do superbly well, Olivia. Cormac thought of you as a very special woman.

He wouldn't have entrusted his shop to you if he didn't believe you were up to the challenge."

"I don't want to let him down, Henry. I feel such a huge responsibility to get the bookshop back on its feet. It just . . . well . . . it's come at a strange time for me."

Henry studied Olivia with understanding in his eyes. "Life getting in the way of life?"

She smiled. "Something like that."

"Then perhaps by saving the bookshop, you might save an awful lot more. You've been given a beautiful gift. What could be more delightful than a shop full of treasured old books?"

"But nobody wants to buy them, Henry. People don't value old books anymore."

"Then your job is to remind them. Remind them what it's like to hold a real book in their hands. Remind them of all the stories they loved as children. There's magic in every book-shop, Olivia. You just have to bring people to it. The books will take care of the rest."

Olivia laughed. "If only it were that easy."

"But if it were easy it wouldn't mean anything, would it? Our greatest struggles give us the greatest rewards." He took hold of her hands, squeezing them tightly. "It was a delight to meet you, Olivia. You are very like Martha when she was younger." He adjusted his hat and pulled himself up with the support of his cane. "I'll pop by again in a few days, but do call if you need anything in the meantime."

Olivia almost told him about London, almost said she didn't know how long she would be in Ireland, but the words stuck to the roof of her mouth and she swallowed them down in a great guilty gulp and hoped she would never have to tell him.

As she watched Henry walk away, Olivia silently thanked

Pappy for his good foresight and his good choice in friends. It was only with a distance between them that she noticed how pronounced Henry's limp was, the extent to which he leaned to one side.

Whoever she was, he must have loved her very much.

RELUCTANT TO RETURN to the empty rooms of Bluebell Cottage, Olivia ate fish and chips on the harbor wall, dangling her legs over the side just like she used to as a little girl, even though it made her mam anxious.

The breeze nipped at the back of her neck and whipped up a fine sea spray that settled on her hands, leaving sparkling salt crystals as it dried. Fairy dust, she used to call it. She breathed in the fresh air and absorbed the view: tangerine sky and dove-gray sea, ripples on the surface of both, like dragon scales. She savored the sharp tang of vinegar on her tongue, letting her thoughts wander as the sun slowly melted into the sea, turning it to liquid gold. As a child chased the gulls behind her, she closed her eyes to listen to the rush of the waves, and there, among the crash of surf, she heard her mother's voice, gently urging her to come away from the edge, to come and sit beside her on the seat where she could keep her safe and warm.

It was so easy sometimes to drift back over the years, back to the golden light of a summer's evening and the comfort of her mother's arms around her. As she let herself go there now, she heard—so clearly—the voice of a little girl who had once believed in fairies, and in that moment she knew that it was time to start believing in something far more important.

It was time to start believing in herself.

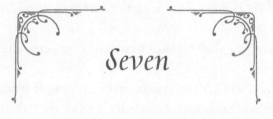

Seven

Ireland. Present day.

The decision to sell Bluebell Cottage didn't come easily, but despite the sense of abandonment that nagged at her heart, Olivia knew it was the right thing—the only thing—to do.

She hated to say good-bye to the little house on the hill, picture-perfect with its white walls and hyacinth-blue door and the pink and white hydrangeas that bloomed like fat marshmallows in the front garden. It was Nana and Pappy's fortress, and the thought of letting it go weighed heavily on her mind.

After the accident, Nana and Pappy had done everything they could to make her feel loved and safe at Bluebell Cottage, but it wasn't a home in the way her friends had homes, with parents and siblings and arguments, and she'd always felt a little like a visitor on an extended holiday. In many ways, Something Old had always felt more like a home to Olivia. It was neutral ground. Hers for the taking. The bookshop was always where her real affections lay.

Once the decision was made, a steady stream of surveyors and estate agents arrived with cameras and measuring tapes and the FOR SALE sign went up by the end of the week. Olivia observed it all with quiet detachment as she bubble-wrapped the breakable contents of her grandparents' lives and wished it were possible to bubble-wrap people. With each drawer she emptied and each black bin liner she filled with smart suits and pretty dresses that had once waltzed around the local dance hall, she felt both a little lighter and a little more heartsick.

When she wasn't packing away her grandparents' lives at the cottage, she began to transform the cluttered old flat above the bookshop, turning it into an acceptable living space, however temporary or permanent. It wasn't much, with only a sofa bed, a desk, a wardrobe, a kitchenette, and a tiny bathroom—a far cry from the impressive penthouse apartment in London—but there was a lovely rustic charm about the lofty space. With a few scented candles and a jug of fresh flowers on the window-sill, it charmed Olivia, whispering to her through the cracks in the window frame, daring her to be happy there.

THE WARMER WEATHER and the burst of color from the new window boxes brought several customers to the shop. Casual browsers and tourists, rather than serious collectors who might single-handedly save the shop from repossession, but Olivia was grateful for their patronage all the same. Each time the door opened and closed, she felt the shop inhale and exhale, each customer breathing a little life back into the place as the books were opened, remembered, enjoyed. She loved nothing more than to see the neat rows of perfectly ordered spines messed up at the end of the day, loved the gaps left by the books that had gone to new homes.

In the long, silent hours between customers, she started to transfer Pappy's catalog from his old ledgers onto a new website. She rearranged displays, and wrote up new information labels to replace the more dilapidated ones. Small changes, but big steps in the right direction. It still surprised her when someone brought a book to the desk and gave her money for it. Every time, she had to stop herself from hugging the customer in gratitude.

Most mornings, when Olivia arrived at the shop to open up, she found a note from Iris waiting on the doormat. The notes were often accompanied by a little white flower so that she now had quite a collection in her coffee cup vase, all of them obeying the instruction to *Live*. On his second visit to the shop, Henry Blake had told her they were rare white harebells that didn't usually flower until later in the year. He couldn't understand how they were in bloom this early, or where they could be coming from, suspecting Hemingway. Olivia preferred to believe that there was a more interesting explanation for the appearance of these little flowers than haughty cats.

Inspired by Frances's memoir and the books and articles she'd found relating to the Cottingley fairies, Olivia decided to create a fairy-themed window display. She added *Princess Mary's Gift Book* and Conan Doyle's *The Coming of the Fairies* along with the *Strand* articles and several rare editions of *Peter Pan* and *The Water Babies* and other collections of fairy stories. She hung Iris's letters and drawings on a line of string suspended from each end of the window—a laundry of correspondence—and started drawing a sign to add to the display, sketching out the words "Do You Believe In Fairies?" surrounding the letters with vibrant wildflowers and lush greenery, just like the visions from her dreams. It had been so long since she'd drawn for pleasure that she became completely immersed in her work and didn't notice the time passing. Only the sound of the shop bell disturbed her.

She smiled as she looked up and saw who it was. "Well, hello, Miss Iris! You're not lost again, are you?"

Iris giggled. "You wrote back! My letters are in the window!" She turned to call through the open door. "Daddy, come on."

Ross stepped into the shop, his hands held out in helpless apology. "Sorry to bother you—again. She insisted we come back and say hello."

"That's okay. It's lovely to see you." She directed this comment at Iris, hoping the flush in her cheeks wouldn't betray her. "I've been enjoying your letters, Iris."

"We wanted to bring you a present to say thank you for helping me when I was lost." Iris handed Olivia a purple gift bag covered in glitter. "I added the glitter myself."

"Wow. Thank you." Olivia glanced at Ross. "But you didn't need to get me anything."

Iris stood on her tiptoes, peering into the bag as Olivia took everything out: a miniature blue door, a tiny chair, and three tiny wooden stepping-stones. "It's a fairy door," Iris explained. "You put it somewhere and the fairies will come and visit. If you leave them a gift, they might bring you something in return."

Olivia glanced at Ross, who winked. She knew it must be tough for him being Mammy and Daddy and all the fairies too. Even as a child, Olivia had understood that it was hard for her mammy, raising her on her own. She'd asked only once about her father. The question was met with a pause and her mother had said he couldn't be with them and that she would do everything she possibly could to be the best Mammy *and* Daddy.

She had done more than that. She had also been Olivia's best friend.

"It's lovely, Iris. Thank you." She was genuinely touched by the gift. The fairy door was very sweet and the kindest thing anyone had done for her in an age.

She turned to Ross. "Thanks so much, but you shouldn't have."

He shrugged. "Nothing to do with me. Except the paying part."

Olivia smiled. "Well, I love it. Where do you think I should put it, Iris?"

"In the window?"

"Great idea. Why don't you go and choose a good spot."

Ross lowered his voice as Iris wandered over to the window. "Listen. Thanks a million for writing the notes. She's been through a tough time lately." Olivia felt the pause as he steeled himself to say it. "I lost my wife last year. Iris's letters to you and that photograph of the girl and the fairies are the first thing she's shown any real enthusiasm for since."

Olivia went through the routine of saying she was sorry and explained that she'd lost her mother when she was around Iris's age. "It's a tough time. If a few letters help, then I'm only too happy to write them."

"Thanks. But honestly, don't feel obliged. She's a bright kid but she gets these funny notions sometimes, especially when it comes to fairies."

"Don't all little girls?"

"I wouldn't know. I've never been one." His smile was infectious. A little *too* infectious. "Actually," he continued, "there was another reason I wanted to call in. The fairy door was a convenient excuse."

"Oh?" Olivia really hoped he wasn't going to ask her out for a drink. Infectious smile or not, a drink with another man would be all kinds of awkward right now. Maybe she should have kept her engagement ring on after all.

Ross cleared his throat and straightened his shoulders. "Okay. Here goes. I'm having some work done in the house, and Cormac had said I could use the flat to write for a couple of weeks, to keep out of the builders' way until I finish my book. I know we only just met and I hate to ask, but deadlines make me desperate." He stuck his hands in his pockets. "I guess what I'm asking is whether the offer might still be there?" He grimaced, as if the embarrassment of asking was causing him physical pain.

A drink would have been a far simpler proposition. Olivia offered an awkward apology, tripping over her words as she said she was sorry, but she would be staying in the flat for a while until she sorted things out.

Ross raised his hands in surrender. "Ah, listen. No problem. I totally understand. I wouldn't dream of dumping myself on you."

"I'm sorry I can't help."

"Honestly. Don't be. I was pushing my luck anyway."

"What will you do instead?"

Ross shrugged. "Kitchen table as usual. It's grand. I'm sure I can put up with a bit of noise and dust."

"It doesn't sound very romantic. I always imagined writers had panoramic ocean views or a chaise to lounge around on."

Iris called over to say she'd found the perfect spot for the fairy door. Olivia told her she could climb into the window to set it up.

"What do you write then, Ross Bailey, Writer?" she asked, turning her attention back to him.

"Kids' books. Fantasy stuff. Dragons and mythical beasts. I'm an illustrator too."

"Wow. Sounds impressive."

"Yeah. It's not, though, but I suppose there are worse ways to make a living. I sometimes think I have the best job in the world—except when I have a deadline. Then it's the worst."

Olivia thought about the flat upstairs. It was practically empty apart from a few boxes of trinkets from the cottage and the small case she'd brought over from London. It was only a temporary base for her, and there was something appealing about having a resident writer in the bookshop. Ross might be a stranger to her, but Pappy had trusted and helped him, and something told her that she should trust and help him too. Her mind was made up.

"Listen, use the flat. It's fine. It's really not a problem and . . . well . . . if you can make a decent cup of tea, it might be nice to have some company."

Ross looked genuinely surprised. "Are you sure? I don't want to impose."

"Honestly. You won't be. You'd be helping, if I'm honest. I can brag about having a Writer in Residence and maybe you can throw a few friends my way and I might sell a few books."

"That sounds fair enough."

"Deal, then?" Olivia held out her hand. "Start Monday?"

Ross laughed and smiled again in a way that Olivia didn't want to think about too much because she wasn't sure where her thoughts might lead. "Deal."

As they shook on it, Olivia wondered why it was that some hands felt right together, like pieces of a jigsaw slotting into place, and she remembered how Pappy always said that we didn't always have to look for an explanation. That sometimes it was far nicer to just let things be.

THE BRISK MORNING breeze became a reckless wind as Olivia made her way to St. Bridget's that afternoon. It propelled her forward, blowing her doubts and disappointments away, out of reach. She felt wild and free, like the scudding clouds above.

Still slightly breathless and with her cheeks flaring scarlet, she stood for a moment at the dayroom door, watching Nana as she straightened the magazines and newspapers into neat piles before plumping the cushions. She worked methodically, from one chair to the next, picking up a cushion, giving it a shake followed by three sharp bangs on one side, and settling it back onto the seat of the chair. She went around the seats three times, having forgotten which ones she'd already done. When her little task was complete, Olivia walked into the room and gave her the bunch of sunflowers she'd brought with her, disheveled and windswept now. Nana thanked her and said it wasn't every day you got flowers from the bus driver, and would she mind helping her back to her room before it was time to go.

Olivia took Nana's arm, leading her along the corridor while Nana talked about the visitors she'd had in the week. Nana often had imaginary visitors. The President had even been last month. Olivia was used to these muddled memories, although it didn't make them any easier to hear.

"You'd like him," Nana said.

"Who?"

"You know." Nana waved her hands in front her, conducting her memories into some sort of harmonious order. "What's his name? The one with the smart tie." She forgot who she was talking about then and turned to say hello to a gray-faced man in a tartan dressing gown who shuffled past with the aid of a walker. "Poor bugger," Nana remarked, a little too loudly. "He was in those Olympic Games, you know. Won a silver medal."

Olivia smiled at him as he passed them and pulled Nana a little closer to her. She sometimes thought it must be quite nice to exist in a world of your own imagination, where everybody used to be somebody, and nobody went home without a medal.

Nana's room was neat and functional. She'd hated it at first but had gradually accepted it as her own. The doctors had told Olivia and Pappy about *self-reflecting rooms*—medical speak for ways in which little reminders of home would help Nana settle in. In a painstaking process in which Olivia became something of an archaeologist of Nana's life, mementos and trinkets— including one lucky china dog—were carefully excavated from the cottage and brought to the nursing home. Most days, Nana looked at these things with the emotional response of a fish. But occasionally—increasingly less so in recent months—she would pick up a photograph or an ornament, scrutinizing it until she was able to drag the associated memory from wherever it was hiding, or until she gave up searching and put it down again.

Olivia settled Nana in her favorite chair beside the window, positioned so she could see the oak and rowan trees in the gardens. She liked to watch the world beyond the window, complaining of feeling "strangled" if she couldn't see the sky. It was one of the few parts of Nana's condition that Olivia understood. She often felt the same way in London. Suffocated by the soaring buildings and high achievers and the nagging sense that her property developer fiancé was constructing not only a new apartment building they would live in as Mr. and Mrs. Oliver, but was also constructing her life. It was ironic that she often heard Jack talking about solid foundations while it appeared that their impending marriage was built on nothing more than the flimsy premise of mutual contentment.

With Nana settled, Olivia perched on the windowsill beside her and continued to read from Frances's memoir. Nana, as usual, listened in silence. Olivia was never sure whether she was asleep or listening, or a little of both. Either way, it gave Olivia something to do, and the story was so interesting, it was a pleasure to read on . . .

NOTES ON A FAIRY TALE
Cottingley, Yorkshire. July 1917.

I said my story had many beginnings, and the day the
camera arrived was one of them. After all, without the camera, there wouldn't have been any photographs. Without the
camera, I wouldn't have a story to tell.

I first saw it when I came back from a morning playing
at the beck. It was sitting on the table in the scullery like
a magician's prop, unfathomable to me with its dials for
aperture, focus, shutter speed, and other things I didn't
understand. I walked around the table to look at it from all
sides, inquisitive fingers reaching out to touch the smooth
black box. Whenever I'd visited the photography studio in
Cape Town, I'd wondered about the mysterious machine
concealed beneath the dark cloth. It was all so strange:
the pop of the flashbulb, the backgrounds I had to pose
in front of, the props I had to hold, the same emotionless
expression, frozen on my face for endless minutes. I was
wary of cameras and the men who operated them, not least
because when my image was captured on the glass plate,
it would be there forever, whether I liked it or not, and I
didn't like most of the photographs I'd had taken of me.
They didn't look like the girl I saw when I looked in the
mirror. Daddy laughed at me when I complained, and said
the camera couldn't lie. I wasn't so sure.

"Quite something, eh?"

I jumped as Uncle Arthur appeared in the doorway. "I
didn't touch it," I said. "I promise." It wasn't a complete lie.
I'd only brushed the tips of my fingers against it.

"I should think not. Expensive equipment, that. You

and our Elsie are not to touch it or go anywhere near the darkroom beneath the cellar steps. The chemicals would strip your skin off." I winced at the thought. "It isn't a toy. Not to be messed with. Do you hear?" I said I did. "Right so. Now, be off with you."

I scampered upstairs, leaving Uncle Arthur to twiddle dials and press buttons and curse under his breath as he tried to figure out how to work the blessed thing.

When Elsie came home from work, she explained that the camera had arrived with Uncle Harry the previous night. He was a local timber merchant who often traveled to the port in Hull and came back with a collection of tall tales and new inventions. Everyone agreed that the Midg camera was the most interesting thing he'd brought since the leather tobacco pouch with a zip fastening, which Uncle Arthur liked to impress visitors with whenever he had the chance.

"I bet you're itching for a go with the camera," I said as we settled down to sleep that night.

Elsie turned onto her back. She was used to my nighttime ponderings now and knew she wouldn't be left alone until we'd had our little chat. "Why do you say that?"

"Well, with you working at Gunston's, you must know all about cameras and whatnot."

Elsie laughed. "I don't see the cameras, Frances. All I see are the gaps on the plates. I know about as much about the workings of a camera as you do." She yawned and turned onto her side. "I suppose it would be fun to try it out, though. I could take a picture of you to send to your father."

I quite liked that idea. "Do you think Uncle Arthur would let you use it?"

Elsie giggled into her pillow. "No. I do not. You'd think it was made of gold the way he fusses over it. Now, get to sleep, Frances. You might not have school tomorrow, but some of us have to go to work."

I settled down beneath the top sheet, dangling my leg and arm over the edge of the bed to let the cool air brush over my skin. I felt sorry for Elsie. Sometimes she had to be so grown-up, and yet when we played our games and made up stories together, she became a child again, like me. As I lay in the dark, listening to the distant rush of the waterfall, I hoped that part of me would always be nine and a half, and that even when I was an adult and had to face the world with all its grown-up responsibilities, part of me would always know the excitement of the fascinating things I'd seen at the beck. I couldn't imagine anything worse than a life without such wonders. How dull and sad life would be if it was all work and chores and war.

For the best part of a fortnight, I was intrigued by Uncle Arthur's camera and the images that emerged from the mysterious darkroom he'd set up beneath the cellar steps (much to Aunt Polly's consternation). After several failed attempts, he was delighted when he took the first success-ful photographs of Elsie and me. He followed these with several portraits of Mummy and me, and then of the two sisters, and eventually all of us together. I sent Daddy a portrait of myself and Mummy, telling him all about Uncle Arthur's new hobby. "It was great fun at first," I wrote, "but me and Elsie are fed up of having our games inter-rupted so that he can take another photograph of us. He even asks the tourists to stop to have their picture taken.

Aunt Polly says she wished he'd never set eyes on 'that ruddy camera!' You know how he likes to tinker. I think it takes his mind off things, stops him thinking about not being at war with the rest of you."

But as with most things that were once strange and then become ordinary, the novelty of the camera soon began to wear thin, and the summer started to drag. Without school to occupy me and with everyone at work, I found the days interminably long. I played skipping games and hoops and hopscotch with some of the village children in the street, but our games always ended in petty squabbles as the heat intensified and tempers frayed. If the heat didn't spoil things, Mavis Clarke and her spiteful tongue did. I tried my best to fit in, to talk like the locals, dropping my *h*'s and saying "me Mam" instead of "my Mummy," but square pegs won't go into round holes, no matter how hard you try. I was different. That was that.

I was secretly glad of the days when I woke to the rain pouring down outside. On those days, I stayed inside to work on my flower diary and wrote long letters to Daddy and my friend Johanna in South Africa, but still the days dragged.

There was only one place that kept me enchanted that summer: the beck. The place that held such magical secrets and crept into my dreams at night so that sometimes I wasn't sure where the dreams ended and the new day began. Mummy still worried about me playing there, and fussed at the slightest hint of damp on my skirts, but I couldn't resist.

It was on the warmest days when I saw them most clearly, days when the sun dawdled high in the sky, tinting everything with rich gold and amber as long shadows played lazy games of hide-and-seek among the trees and ferns. Like the wildflowers that decorated the riverbank, my fairy friends grew more abundant as the summer went on, multiplying in numbers and strengthening in color, the pale yellows and greens evolving into mauves and pinks. I loved nothing more than to be among them, to dip my feet in the cooling water and watch them work. To be able to spend my days in such a place was a gift I would be ever grateful for. I needed nothing and nobody while I was there, although Elsie was always keen to come with me when she stayed off work, which was often, her being of a rather delicate constitution. Aunt Polly encouraged our games. I was good for Elsie, she said, and so was the fresh air, although there was nothing fresh about the manky stench from the woolen mill, which only worsened beneath the summer heat.

On days when my patient waterside vigil was unrewarded and nothing emerged from the foliage, I returned to the house sullen and disappointed. "What's got into you?" Mummy would chide. "Your face will stay like that if the wind changes." Aunt Polly still teased me about being in love with one of the village boys. "Look at you, mooning around, lost in your daydreams. A lovesick schoolgirl if I ever I saw one." I didn't really mind the teasing. It was worth it to see the fairies when I did.

It was an especially muggy July afternoon when I returned from my latest excursion to the beck. By then, I had almost become used to the presence of my little friends while I played. I suppose a sort of understanding existed between us—a delightful harmony of the magical and the ordinary, a coming together of the world I understood and the world that fascinated me. I grew hot and bothered by the persistent tickle of thunder bugs on my arms and the back of my neck and started to make my way home, slipping and tumbling into the shallow water as I did. My heart sank into my sodden skirts. I knew I would be in trouble.

Mummy and Aunt Polly were in the scullery, making tea. Aunt Polly was making a pie at the table, pressing the rolling pin into a thick slab of pastry with brisk, firm movements before spinning the slowly emerging circle around and rolling the other end. I loved to help her bake but wished she wasn't doing it right now. There was no way for me to sneak upstairs to my bedroom and change. I peered through a crack in the door frame, chewing anxiously on my fingernails. I would get into trouble for that too.

"I see our Frances was up the beck again yesterday," Aunt Polly remarked, tutting for good measure. "Is she usually this disobedient, Annie?"

"That's the strange thing, Polly. She's usually such a good girl. I honestly don't know what's got into her. It's like she's walking around in a dream."

Mummy was distracted and distant, as she often was lately. The novelty of being back in Yorkshire had worn off, and she found it difficult to be in her sister's home, all five of us tripping over each other, having to wait for the lavvy and for the copper to boil to use the tin bath. She missed Daddy terribly and worried about him. I'd heard her talking to Aunt Polly about it as they scoured the newspapers for the lists of Missing, Wounded, and Dead. She dreaded the knock at the door from the telegram boy. Everyone dreaded the knock at the door.

"Can't for the life of me understand what the fascination is," Aunt Polly continued. "There's nowt down there in the summer but a great swarm of midges."

Uncle Arthur walked in then, his hands black with motor oil as usual. "Where's a great swarm of midges?" he asked, scrubbing at his hands with the bar of soap I would wash my face with later.

"Down the beck. Our Frances can't keep away from the place."

Frustration bubbled up inside me. If only they knew that there was far more than midges to be found at the beck, that there were wonderful things that drew me back there again and again. If only they could see the fairies for themselves, then they would understand. Then I would be able to play at the beck as often as I liked.

Tired of listening to them talk about me and things they didn't understand, I resigned myself to another scolding and stepped into the scullery.

Mummy was onto me like a cat onto a mouse. "Oh, Frances. Look at the state of you! I'll be scrubbing at those skirts for days to get them clean. I've a mind to set you to the task yourself. Honestly." I said nothing, holding my tongue, although my cheeks burned with a sullen temper. "I don't know how many times I have to tell you. You are *not* to play at the beck."

It was then that I saw Elsie listening at the door on the other side of the scullery. Aunt Polly and Uncle Arthur sat at the table in stony silence as Mummy grabbed the rolling pin from Aunt Polly, taking her anger out on the pastry.

"I don't understand you, Frances," she continued. "Fancy, playing all those hours up the beck by yourself when you could be out on the street with the other children, making friends. Well, there'll be no more of it. You are forbidden from playing at the beck for the rest of the summer. Do you hear me? No more." She thumped the rolling pin back and forth across the table before banging it down, making everyone jump. "Why do you insist on playing there anyway? It isn't good to spend so much time alone. No wonder the other children call you names."

The room fell into a shocked silence. I had never seen my mother so cross. It frightened and upset me. I stood in silence, pressing my fingernails into the palms of my hands. My nose prickled with the urge to cry as I blinked back hot tears. I could feel it coming, rushing through me like the water on the mill wheel, unstoppable. I couldn't hold it in any longer. The words I had promised never to say came tumbling out.

"I *don't* play on my own," I cried. "I play with *them*! I go to see the fairies!"

I had never answered back to my mother. I had barely ever raised my voice in temper at her. I trembled in shock and swallowed hard, and for the second time in as many weeks I wished I could take back my words, wished I could gather them up like wool and wind them carefully back into a ball.

For what felt like an age nobody spoke. A blackbird sang at a branch near the window. Uncle Arthur coughed. Someone whistled "It's a Long Way to Tipperary" in the street outside. Time stopped, and in those silent moments I knew things would never be the same. There would always be the time before I said I saw fairies at the beck, and the time after.

I watched helplessly as my words slipped out through the open window, drifting away with the dandelion seeds.

Mummy placed her hands on her hips and glared at me. "And now we are to have fibs as well as sodden stockings, are we?"

"I'm not telling fibs. I see them. I really do." My words came out in gasps, choked by my heartbroken sobs. I felt like a silly little girl telling tales. All I wanted was for Mummy to believe me.

Seeing Elsie lurking at the door, Aunt Polly turned on her in a flash. "Well, Elsie Wright. What do you have to say about all this? I suppose you've seen fairies at the beck too?"

Elsie stepped into the room. Her eyes flickered toward mine, wide and searching. I stared back at her, tears streaming down my cheeks. I stood, frozen to the spot, as she picked up a scrap of pastry that had been trimmed from the pan. I had no idea what she was going to say.

"Yes, Mummy," she said, without a care in the world as she popped the scrap of pastry into her mouth. "I *have* seen them." I stared at the floor, my heart pounding, my knees trembling like a jelly pudding. "Our Frances isn't telling fibs. There *are* fairies at the bottom of the garden."

Uncle Arthur spat his tea with laughing. "Never heard such a load of old codswallop. Fairies in the beck! What next? Pixies in the lavvy?"

I looked at Mummy. Her arms were folded defiantly

across her chest, her face a picture of incredulity and anger as she stood in broody silence beside the range.

Aunt Polly raised an eyebrow. "Well now, girls. Supposing, just for a moment, that you *have* seen fairies. What would they look like?"

Elsie stared at me. "Well, Frances. Go on. Tell them."

I stared at the floor, wishing I could disappear into it. How could I possibly describe them? How could I explain their misty, barely-there peculiarity, the ringing in my ears, the fact that I sensed their presence and beauty as much as saw it? "I don't remember."

Uncle Arthur burst out laughing again. "No wonder you don't remember. You never saw them in the first place."

"I really did," I whispered. "I really do."

Mummy harrumphed. "Well, if you say there are fairies at the bottom of the garden, then I suppose there must be, because I can't for the life of me think why you would say such a thing otherwise." She turned her back to everyone as she put the pie in the oven. "You can show us after tea."

I felt hot and prickly and for all that I nipped at the skin on my legs to distract myself, I couldn't stop the tears falling. I was relieved when Mummy told me to go and get out of my wet clothes and somehow I walked from the kitchen, my legs shaking, my head down, my cheeks burning hot in anger and shame.

I heard them talking about me as I made my way upstairs. Aunt Polly defending me, saying Uncle Arthur shouldn't tease me because I wasn't used to it like our Elsie; Uncle Arthur saying I'd want to get used to being teased if I was going around telling folk I saw fairies at the bottom of the garden.

"Fairies in Cottingley!" he laughed. "Never 'eard the like of it!"

"And wash your hands," Mummy called after me.

I knew Elsie would follow. Without turning around, I knew she was right behind me. She would know what to do next. I was sure of it.

In the bedroom I fell onto the bed, unable to stop my tears. Elsie closed the door behind her.

"I shouldn't have said it, Elsie. It was a secret. *My* secret."

"*Our* secret."

"I should never have told *you*, even."

"Well you did, and I'm glad. At least this way there's two of us saying it."

"They don't believe us anyway," I sobbed. "Did you hear Uncle Arthur? He thinks it's a load of nonsense."

"But they were interested all the same." Elsie hesitated for a moment. I knew what she was going to say. "Have you *really* seen them, Frances? Cross your heart and hope to die."

I sat up and made the most solemn face I could. "I have, Elsie. I really and truly have. Cross my heart and hope to die."

"Then you can show us all. After tea. Like Auntie Annie said."

"But they don't always come, Elsie. What if they're not there?"

Elsie thought for a moment. "Don't worry. I'll think of something."

And she did. The next day, after more teasing by our parents and several unsuccessful "fairy-spotting" excursions to the beck, Elsie came bounding upstairs where I was writing to Daddy. Full of excitement, she grabbed my hands and pulled me to my feet.

"I've got it, Frances! It's perfect!"

"Got what?"

"An idea. For how to prove to them about the fairies. We can borrow Daddy's camera and take a photograph of them. Then they'll *have* to believe us, won't they?"

It was a perfectly clever idea. "But what if the fairies don't come, Elsie? They don't come every day. Only sometimes."

But she wasn't listening. She was rummaging about in the trunk at the foot of the bed. "Where is it, Frances? Your book? Princess Mary's book."

I pulled it out from under the bed and handed it to Elsie, who flicked quickly to the page she was looking for, the Alfred Noyes poem "A Spell for a Fairy" with Claude Shepperson's lovely illustrations of fairies dancing.

"There," Elsie said. "If they want fairies, we'll give them fairies. We don't have to wait for *actual* fairies. We'll make our own!" She grabbed her box of pencils and paper and began to copy the illustrations from the book, and although her drawings weren't like the real fairies I'd seen, I said they were, because I didn't want to hurt her feelings.

I would often look back on that moment in the bedroom at 31 Main Street and wish things had been different. Had I known then how much trouble Elsie's idea would cause, I would have dismissed the whole thing as nonsense and continued to enjoy the fairies in private, hoping Uncle Arthur's teasing would eventually subside. But I didn't know what the future held, and the more I thought about it, the more I liked Elsie's plan. It was only a bit of harmless fun after all, a little joke to make Mummy and Aunt Polly and Uncle Arthur believe me about the beck fairies so that Mummy would stop fussing and let me play there as much as I liked.

It was agreed. Elsie would draw likenesses of the fairies, copying from the pictures in *Princess Mary's Gift Book*, and we would take a photograph of them at the beck with Uncle Arthur's camera.

As Daddy had said, the camera cannot lie.

If we could photograph fairies, everyone would have to believe me.

Wouldn't they?

NOTES ON A FAIRY TALE
Cottingley, Yorkshire. July 1917.

We made our plan in the bedroom as slivers of moonlight fell onto the counterpane. When we weren't whispering about fairies, I dreamed of them, and always of the little girl handing me a white flower.

We decided to take the photograph the following Saturday when Mummy and Aunt Polly were due to spend the day with Aunt Clara in Bradford. Elsie had everything worked out and explained what we were going to do. She just had to persuade Uncle Arthur to lend us his precious camera. I had my doubts he would, but I didn't say so. As Elsie said, it was worth a try.

Brimming with confidence, Elsie talked of nothing else in the days leading up to Saturday. She thought it a terrific joke. "Imagine their faces when they see the picture, Frances! It'll be as good as a Harry Houdini trick. You wait and see."

I perched on the edge of the bed while Elsie scrambled underneath and lifted a loose board. "Here. Grab this." A hand emerged from beneath the iron bedstead, pushing a biscuit tin toward me.

I lifted it onto the bed as Elsie wriggled out backward and stood up to brush the dust from her dress and stockings. Her smile was infectious. "Well, go on, then," she said. "Open it."

My tummy fizzed with excitement as I opened the lid. One by one, I lifted out four beautiful fairies, each about three inches in height. They had been drawn onto stiff card and cut out carefully. Even the tiny gaps between their fingers were perfectly defined. Their wings and dresses were shaded in soft pastel tones of lavender, lemon, and green, giving them an almost lifelike effect: real folds in their skirts, real sunlight in their hair. One was playing an instrument, and they all looked like they were mid-movement.

Elsie sat down on the bed beside me, a proud smile on her face. "What do you think?"

"They're beautiful, Elsie. You're so clever."

She couldn't hide her pride. "Took me longer than I thought, but I wanted to get the shading right to make sure they looked real. Not too flat."

I turned them over in my hands, picking them up in turn and placing them carefully back onto the counterpane. "They *do* look real, Elsie. *Very* real. I wish I could draw like you."

"If you keep practicing, you will. Anyway, what matters is that *they* think they're real when they see them on the plate."

Her eyes glittered with anticipation, and all my doubts were brushed away in an instant. It was impossible not to fall under Elsie's spell. There was something so alluring about her. If I was quiet and reserved at times, Elsie was an abundance of confidence. Like the pollen from the ragwort that left dusty marks on my hands, a little bit of Elsie had brushed off on me too.

I picked up the fairy cutouts again. "How will we stand them up? They won't look real lying flat."

Elsie winked and took a small box from her pocket. She tipped several of her mother's largest hat pins onto the bed. "We'll tape a pin onto the back of each cutout. Then we stick the end of the pin into the ground. Look, like this." She demonstrated by holding a pin against the back of one of the drawings and standing it upright.

I giggled. "Oh, Elsie. It looks like she's standing up on the bed!" I took the cutout and the pin from Elsie and held it up for her to see.

Elsie laughed too. "It's perfect. Better than I thought. Now all we have to do is convince Daddy to let us borrow his camera and we'll prove to them, once and for all, that there are fairies in the beck and you weren't telling fibs. Then they'll be happy to let you play there, and this can all be forgotten about."

Hearing movement downstairs, Elsie quickly put the pins and the drawings into the biscuit tin and slid back under the bed to return it to its hiding place.

"And not a word, Frances," she said when she emerged. "Not to anyone. Promise?"

I nodded with my most serious face. "I promise, Elsie. I promise I won't tell anyone."

"Not even Rosebud."

My rag doll was propped up on the pillow. My confidante. The one person I told my biggest secrets to. She'd been there all the time, and heard everything about our plans. But Elsie—although not too grown-up to believe in fairies—*was* too grown-up to believe in dolls being able to understand humans.

"I won't even tell Rosebud. I promise."

Saturday arrived with bright sunshine and a warm breeze that blew through the open windows and doors of 31 Main Street. The house was heavy with anticipation, the air laced with secrets shared and secrets hidden.

I had a spoonful of porridge halfway to my mouth when Elsie asked Uncle Arthur if we could borrow his camera, explaining that she wanted to take a picture of me with it. I couldn't move. I hadn't expected her to come out with it just like that, as casually as if she was asking someone to pass the milk jug. I glanced sideways at Uncle Arthur, who was equally surprised.

He put his cup down. "Well . . . no. You can't borrow the camera. Expensive stuff, that. *I'll* take a photograph of our Frances if that's what you really want it for."

I glanced at Elsie, throwing her an *oh, well* look as my heart sank into my boots beneath the table. I'd suspected as much all along. Uncle Arthur would never agree to us having his precious camera. The plan was ruined, and I would still be forbidden from playing at the beck.

Elsie wasn't as easily defeated. "*Please*, Daddy. I'll be very careful with it. I promise. I've watched you work it, and I've handled lots of the glass plates at work. We'll bring it straight back as soon as we've taken a picture, and you can develop the plate so we won't be near your chemicals and things." She looked at him with pretty pleading eyes, drawing every ounce of her infectious charm toward him.

Aunt Polly stood up to clear the breakfast dishes. "Oh, go on, Arthur. Let them use it. It'll get them out from under your feet if nowt else."

Elsie sensed her opportunity, pouncing as quickly as the cat catching a mouse. "*Please*, Daddy. Mummy's right. It'll get us out of the house for a while, and it's such a lovely day."

Everyone stared at Uncle Arthur. Eight eyes that he couldn't resist. I watched him melt beneath his daughter's gaze, and for a moment I forgot all about fairies and cameras. All I could think about was Daddy far away in France, and with all my heart, I wished he was here in the scullery so he could look at me that same way. Sometimes I forgot what he looked like. Sometimes, I struggled to remember him at all.

Uncle Arthur stood up, his chair legs scraping against the floor. "You're to bring it straight back, mind. And if there's so much as a scratch on it . . ."

Elsie was up and out of her chair before he could say another word, throwing her arms around his neck. "Thank you, Daddy. Thank you!" She turned to me. "Well, come on, then."

There was an urgency to her voice. I stood up without even realizing I had.

"Erm. Where do you think you're going, Frances Griffiths?" Mummy looked at me, arms folded, a quizzical look on her face.

"Can I leave the table?" I asked, itching to follow Elsie, who was already halfway up the stairs.

"*May* I?"

"*May* I leave the table?"

"Yes. You may."

With that, we were gone, thudding upstairs on eager feet, giggling and whispering as we left the adults to finish their breakfast and shake their heads and wonder about the peculiar ways of children.

I waited as patiently as I could in the narrow hallway while Uncle Arthur explained everything to Elsie: how to load the glass plates, how to set the aperture and shutter speed, and how to frame the picture through the small viewfinder. It sounded complicated, and I hoped Elsie was paying attention. She wasn't known for her ability to concentrate. I twirled my fingers around and around the curls in my hair, formed from the rags I'd slept in the previous night. I knew Elsie had the fairy cutouts in her coat pocket, and worried they would fall out and our plan would be spoiled before we'd even left the house.

As I waited, the grandfather clock ticked methodically beside me, sweeping the restless minutes away like dust being brushed out of the scullery door. Rather than taking time away, I imagined the passing minutes stretching out further and further, like bread dough rising and proving, filling the months and years ahead when I might not live in Cottingley and might never speak of fairies again. And for the first time, I understood why Peter Pan didn't want to grow up, because neither did I. I wanted to be nine years old forever. I wanted to stay in this summer of fairies. I wanted time to pause.

Eventually Elsie emerged from the front room, carrying the heavy camera by the handle, her eyes wild with impatience. We didn't speak a word to each other as we clattered down the cellar steps and followed the slope of the garden down toward the beck. Only when we'd negotiated the slippery stones and picked our way toward a mossy bank in front of the waterfall did we dare to look at each other and burst out laughing.

"Oh, Elsie. I thought he'd never agree. It's a good job Aunt Polly stepped in."

"He'd have given in eventually. I can nag for hours."

The waterfall was especially beautiful that morning,

falling in a veil of silver silk, the water perfectly smooth as it tumbled in arcs over the stepped rocks. The continual rumble had become so familiar to me since that first fretful night when I'd heard it from the bedroom. I dipped my fingertips into the water, savoring the icy tickle as it ran across my skin.

Taking one last look around to check that nobody had followed us, Elsie began to arrange the fairy cutouts. She'd already taped a hat pin onto the back of each and stuck the ends of the pins into the earth. I stood to one side, watching my cousin work as I picked idly at the wildflowers around me, threading them together through their stems to make a garland that I placed on my head like a May queen's crown.

Elsie laughed when she glanced up and saw me. "Look at you! The fairy queen. What was she called?"

"Which one?"

"The Shakespeare one? We learnt it at school."

"Titania? From *A Midsummer Night's Dream*?"

"That's it. You look like Titania!"

I admired Elsie's drawings again as she arranged them to make them look like they were dancing across the bank. I thought them very clever and beautiful, even though they weren't much like the real fairies I saw, but I supposed it didn't matter. Mummy and Aunt Polly and Uncle Arthur didn't know what the real fairies looked like anyway, so Elsie's attempts were good enough. While she fussed with the camera, I wandered along the stream, watching, listening, hoping to catch a glimpse of them.

"I'm ready, Frances."

Splashing back along the edge of the water, I stood behind the dancing figures so that only my head and shoulders were visible above the grassy bank. "What shall I do?" I asked. I couldn't suppress my dislike for being photographed. Not even now.

"Try and look like you're watching them dancing in front of you."

I tried a few expressions of surprise and wonder, which made Elsie laugh. "You look like you've seen a ghost!" she said. "Try to look a bit more . . . I don't know . . . dreamy."

I did, but Elsie still wasn't happy. "You look too stiff. Lean forward or something. Rest your elbow on the bank."

I followed Elsie's instructions, leaning forward onto my elbow and putting my hand under my chin. "Like this?"

Elsie bent down to peer through the viewfinder. "That's it!" she squealed. "It's perfect. Don't move."

As the waterfall tumbled behind me and the lightest of breezes ruffled the leaves on the trees above, I stayed as still as possible, and I couldn't be absolutely certain, but in the second before I heard the click of the shutter, I thought I saw something stir among the wild blackberries behind Elsie's shoulder. My eyes flickered away from the cutouts to follow the slightest glimpse of a lavender light disappearing into the foliage.

"Perfect!" Elsie was pleased with the setup. She couldn't wait to get back to the house and ask Uncle Arthur to develop the plate.

"Is that it?" I'd expected it to take longer.

"That's it."

"Did it work?" I dared not move until Elsie was certain we'd got the photo.

"Hope so. Come on, help me get rid of all this, and we'll take the plate back to Daddy."

To hide the evidence of our joke, we pushed the hat pins down into the soft ground and tore the paper fairies into pieces. I thought it a shame to destroy all Elsie's hard work, but she insisted. We scattered the torn paper into the beck, where it drifted downstream like fallen petals.

"There," Elsie said. "Now nobody will ever know."

We scrambled back up the bank and through the gate at the bottom of the garden, laughing as we ran to the house. I turned around once to check that we hadn't been seen. There was nobody about, but I couldn't shake the feeling that somewhere, between the ever-shifting shadows of the trees, watchful eyes had seen everything.

NOTES ON A FAIRY TALE
Cottingley, Yorkshire. July 1917.

Time limped painfully along as we waited for Uncle
Arthur to come home, the seconds and minutes ticking
idly by with no sense of urgency as the camera sat on the
scullery table, taunting us with the promise of secrets captured inside. I sat down, resting my chin on my hands as
I stared at the camera, wondering if our plan had worked.
From the outside, the camera looked the same as it had
that morning, and yet the longer I stared at it, the more
it felt alive; as if part of me was trapped inside, trying to
get out.

I was fidgety and distracted, my thoughts returning
continually to the cutouts we'd torn up and thrown into
the beck. What if someone saw them? I suggested to Elsie
that we go back to check they'd been carried off downstream, but she laughed and told me to stop worrying. I
distracted myself with a book of British butterflies while
Elsie worked on a new painting. She said it was a surprise
and that I wasn't to be looking over her shoulder.

It wasn't until much later, after a painfully slow teatime
punctuated with unsettling conversations about rationing
and the latest battles on the Western front, that Uncle
Arthur finally took the camera into his darkroom. There
wasn't room for all of us inside, so while Elsie squeezed in
with her father, I waited outside, pressing my ear to the
door to listen to what was being said. All I could hear was
the heavy hush of expectation.

With each passing minute I grew more restless and eager to know if our plan had worked, picking nervously at

the quick of my nail until I drew blood. I had just stuck my finger in my mouth when I heard Elsie's delighted exclamations through the door.

"They're on the plate, Frances! The fairies are on the plate!"

My heart thumped beneath my pinafore. It had worked. I jumped up and down on the flagstone floor, squealing with excitement.

The noise brought Mummy rushing to the top of the steps to see what the fuss was about. "What's all the commotion down there? Sounds like someone's being murdered."

Uncle Arthur emerged from the darkroom, peering at me through narrowed eyes. "Been up to summat, these two have, Annie. Seems they weren't alone today when they took their picture."

Hitching up her skirt, Mummy made her way carefully down the narrow steps. "What do you mean?"

"Seems their *fairies* showed up an' all." He said the word *fairies* as if it were a foreign word none of us would understand and flapped his hands like wings to help the translation.

Elsie stepped out of the darkroom, her eyes bright with secrets and mischief. "Go and look," she whispered, gripping my arm. "They're all there. It's ever so good!"

I stepped into the dimly lit room, my breath catching in my throat as I walked toward the bench where Uncle Arthur had laid out the glass plate. I don't know how long I looked at it—a minute or two—but it felt like forever as I stared back at myself: a perfect negative image of my face, of the flowers in my hair, of my hand resting on my chin, of four dancing fairies in front of me. I leaned forward to take a closer look. The cutouts had come out perfectly, far better than I'd imagined. I shivered, touched by the invisible thrill of mischief. I covered my mouth with my hand to stop my secrets escaping.

I heard Elsie telling Uncle Arthur he would have to believe us now. "You see, Daddy? There really *are* fairies at the beck, and now we have a photograph to prove it, so you're to stop teasing poor Frances." She must have turned to Mummy then. "Now you know why she loves to play at the beck, Aunt Annie. I know I'd much sooner play with fairies than horrible Mavis Clarke."

Mummy bustled into the room, her skirts brushing against the stone floor with a *swish* of starched fabric. She looked me straight in the eye. "Well? Where are these so-called fairies?"

I moved to one side to make room for her at the bench and held my breath as she scrutinized the image on the plate. Would she believe us? Would she notice the guilt that flared crimson on my cheeks? She looked at me only once in the two or three minutes she studied the plate. Then, without saying a word, she motioned for me to follow her out of the darkroom. She asked Uncle Arthur what *he* made of it.

He shook his head. "Must be sandwich wrappings. Whatever it is, I know it's not fairies. Nowt but a prank. That's all." He closed the darkroom door, locking it behind him before he made his way up the narrow stairs, telling Elsie to go and fetch her mother from the neighbor's. "A clever prank, granted, but a prank nonetheless."

I watched Elsie's boots disappear up the stairs and

wished she would come back. I stiffened my knees and arms, determined to hold on to my promise not to tell as the inevitable question came from Mummy, now we were alone.

"Well, Frances? Did you see fairies? And I expect the truth now."

I hardly dared look at her as my thoughts returned to that gray April evening when we'd first arrived in Yorkshire and she'd promised everything would be better in the summertime. She was right. Everything *was* better, mostly because of Elsie and my special friends at the beck. All I wanted was for Mummy to believe me and allow me to play there for the rest of the summer. Although my guilty conscience urged me to confess to the joke we had played, I remembered the solemn promise I'd made to Elsie and crossed my fingers behind my back.

"Yes, Mummy. I really do see fairies at the beck." It was, after all, the truth.

She raised a skeptical eyebrow in reply. "Hmm. Well, I can't for the life of me work out how you would make them appear on the plate if they weren't actually there, so I suppose I'll have to take your word for it."

I'd expected her to be cross. I'd expected her to doubt Elsie, if not me. She was always scolding Elsie for filling my head with stories and nonsense. But she did neither. If anything, her face softened as she looked at me and put her hand over mine.

"Fairies, eh?"

I nodded. "They're so lovely, Mummy. I wish you could see them." I wanted to tell her everything: about their misty peculiarity and their changing colors.

She let out a long sigh that could have stretched all the way back to Cape Town. "So do I, love. So do I."

"You do believe me, Mummy. Don't you?"

"I want to, Frances. If we can believe in fairies, perhaps we can believe in anything, even in an end to this damned war. And wouldn't that be something."

The crack in her voice was as wide as the crack in the flagstones beneath my feet. Almost as wide as the crack I'd felt in my heart since Daddy had left us.

In our room that night, with Elsie snoring beside me, I couldn't stop thinking about the photograph. My conscience nagged at me like an itch I couldn't scratch, more noticeable somehow in the quiet darkness of nighttime. Were we wrong to play the trick, even if it was done with the best of intentions, and only to stop me getting into trouble? Should I have told Mummy the truth? I tumbled her words around in my mind—*"If we can believe in fairies, perhaps we can believe in anything"*—and the more I repeated them, the more I felt that perhaps *believing* in fairies was more important than seeing them. In belief, there is hope and wonder. In seeing, there is often question and doubt.

With the steady rumble of the waterfall keeping its nighttime vigil, and the stars blooming in the sky, I knew with a sudden clarity that I would never tell Mummy the truth about the photograph. I wouldn't tell her not only because I had made a promise to Elsie, but because with the world still at war, we needed to believe in something better. In that moment, and perhaps for much longer, it seemed to me that the possibility of believing in fairies was more important than one little girl telling the truth.

Eight

Ireland. Present day.

*W*hen she reached the end of the chapter, Olivia followed Nana's gaze outside, where the wind tossed the branches of the cherry trees around, sending their blossoms skittering across the lawns.

"The bluebells are out, Nana. Did you see them?"

Nana nodded, a small smile on her lips. "A carpet of bluebells," she whispered. "It comes right up to the garden wall in the spring. We mustn't trample on them in case the fairies are sleeping inside."

Olivia moved closer. "Where is this, Nana? In Yorkshire? Cottingley?"

"Lovely place. Hidden among the trees. The beck runs along the bottom of the garden." She remembered these distant places and events so clearly, Olivia found it hard sometimes to understand how Nana couldn't remember what she'd had for breakfast that morning. "I can hear the waterfall from my bedroom," she continued, tilting her head to one side, leaning forward slightly. "Listen. Do you hear it?"

Olivia listened. The rush of the wind around the eaves did sound a little like a distant waterfall. "I do, Nana. Very faintly, in the distance."

"Must be a thaw. Did it snow?"

Olivia took her hand. "Not today, Nana, although the blossoms look like snowflakes dancing around on the lawns. Look."

They watched the pink snow for a moment as the clock on the wall swept the minutes carelessly away. Minutes they would never get back.

"Do you have a photograph of the cottage, Nana? I'd love to see it."

Nana pointed her walking stick toward the wardrobe. "In there. Get the book out, will you?"

Olivia took Nana's memory book from the bottom of the wardrobe, turning the pages until Nana told her to stop at a photograph of a woman and a child, side by side in the doorway of a pretty cottage, a small pair of black boots on the step beside them. The image was in black and white, but Olivia could imagine the vibrant colors of the flowers and plants around them.

"Who is this, Nana?"

Nana took the album from Olivia, resting it on her lap. "That's me. Chubby little thing, wasn't I." She tapped her fingernail on the woman in the photograph. "That's Mammy."

"What was her name?"

"Ellen," she said without missing a beat. "Ellen Hogan."

Olivia's mind whirled. Of course! That was why the name was familiar. Ellen Hogan—the schoolteacher Frances had written about so fondly—was *her* great-grandmother. Everything was starting to make sense.

Nana gazed at the photograph, as if puzzled. "I wonder

where Aisling was." She pronounced the name *Ash-ling*. "Probably playing at the beck with Frances. Frances often came to visit in the summer." She chuckled to herself; a childish sound. "She used to tell me all about the fairies."

"Frances Griffiths?"

"That's right. Or was it Elsie? I get confused."

There was so much Olivia wanted to know about her great-grandmother, and Frances, but Aisling was a new name to her. "Who's Aisling, Nana?"

A distant look clouded Nana's face. She pushed the album away and shut her eyes. Olivia knew the signs. Like a book being closed, the story was suspended. There was nothing more to know. Not today, at least.

Olivia sat with Nana for the rest of the afternoon, occupying herself by tidying up, changing the water in the vase of flowers on the table, and refreshing the jug of water by Nana's bed. She polished the photo of Pappy with her cardigan sleeve, so handsome in his uniform, off to war. But no matter how much she tried to distract herself, her thoughts kept returning to Frances, and Cottingley, and her great-grandmother, and the connection between them all.

At teatime, Olivia took her cue to leave, kissing Nana's cheek and telling her she would visit again in a few days. She left Nana with a bowl of soup and a quiz show on TV, the volume turned up so high she wasn't sure if Nana heard her say she loved her.

On the bus home, Olivia thought about the story unraveling in Frances's memoirs, and in the Arthur Conan Doyle book Mrs. Joyce had found at the cottage and which Olivia had been reading in quiet moments at the shop. One paragraph in particular had resonated with her:

There are certain facts which stand out clearly and which none of the evidence I was able to obtain could shake. No other people have seen the fairies, though everyone in the little village knew of their alleged existence.

Everyone in the village included her great-grandmother, Ellen Hogan. Had she seen fairies too?

The more Olivia thought about Frances and Elsie's photographs and the cottage in the woods and Ellen's missing child, the more she felt an urge to visit Cottingley. Something was pulling her back there, a sense of family connection. Like a skein of wool being wound, she was being drawn in.

Back in Howth, she followed the slope of colorful houses that decorated the street, so pretty in the evening sunlight, and there was Bluebell Cottage at the crest of the hill. Tonight was Olivia's last night there. Tomorrow she would say good-bye.

SHE SPENT THE evening poring over mountains of paperwork to make some sense of it all. Business transactions. Orders. Invoices. Rent. She checked her e-mail, a wall of black unread messages. She scrolled through as quickly as she could, and there it was, a message from Jack asking if her phone was broken because the wedding planner had been on to him to say she couldn't get hold of Olivia. He added that everything was going well in China and that he might have a trip to Germany the following week but would make it up to her with dinner somewhere fancy when he got back. She felt more like his mistress than his soul mate. She didn't have the desire, or the energy, to reply.

Too restless to sleep, she took Pappy's old radio upstairs and listened to classical music into the small hours: concertos and symphonies, Mendelssohn's "Fairies' March," Tchaikovsky's "Waltz of the Flowers." It soothed her soul. When she did drift into sleep, she dreamed of forests and glistening streams and the voices of children, laughing and whispering, their faces and secrets concealed behind the leafy trees. Sometimes she felt the sensation of cool, wet grass under her feet, and always there was a little girl, hair like flames, handing her a white flower. "For Mammy. For my Mammy."

The dreaming had started after the accident, her darkest fears and insecurities manifesting in curious images and strange people and faraway places, so vivid that when she woke up, she wasn't sure if they were dreams or reality. She didn't tell anybody at first. It was when the sleepwalking started that her grandparents became aware of it. Anxiety, the doctors said; the result of trauma and shock. They said she would grow out of it, but she hadn't, and she was glad.

Her dreams brought alive happy memories of a time when she had laughed and loved, when she'd fought for what she believed in. They reminded her of what she'd once wanted and who she once was. It was her dreams that now urged her to wake up from a reality she no longer believed in.

ON HER LAST morning at the cottage, Olivia woke early. Everything felt visceral as she dressed and made her way downstairs: the brittle cold of the kitchen tiles, the rattle of bubbles as the kettle came to the boil, the bitter aroma of coffee as the water hit the freeze-dried granules.

She cupped her hands around her favorite mug and stood at the window. She'd always been an early riser, her otherwise lazy body instinctively aware that it was a privilege to be awake at dawn to watch as the sky turned from navy to gray, lavender to violet and rose. Pappy would often join her, just the two of them and the winding thread of tobacco smoke from Pappy's pipe as they watched the world wake up. Those were some of Olivia's favorite moments. Catching the start of a new day when nothing was yet done, and everything was possible.

After dressing, she worked her way methodically through each room of the house, taking one last look, pulling the curtains, closing the door on all that once was. She paused at Nana's dressing table, gazing into the mirror, searching for the younger Olivia in the glass. What would she say to that lost and frightened child who'd once stood here, more alone in the world than she had ever imagined it was possible to be? Would she tell her to believe in fairies, or would she say there was no such thing? Or would she simply tell her that whether you choose to believe in something or not, the joy is more often in the wondering than in the knowing?

In the back of a drawer at the bottom of the dressing table, so hidden she almost missed it, she found an old Instamatic camera. She checked the exposure reader. It still had film in it. Her mam always carried an Instamatic camera in her handbag, forever snapping away as Olivia played, catching her off guard. As she slipped it into her pocket, Olivia wondered what secrets this camera might reveal.

Turning to leave, her leg banged on the edge of the dressing table. She heard a rattle, and only then did she notice a narrow secret drawer beneath the mirror. Her heart thumped as she pressed against it and it sprang open.

She knew what was inside even before she saw it.

The silver photo frame.

She lifted it out, remembering that night when she'd grasped it so tightly beneath the bedcovers, smooth and cool to the touch. Beneath the dusty glass, the familiar photograph of the little girl and the fairies looked back at her, the little girl she now knew was Frances. That playful smile at her lips. So many questions, still unanswered.

She put the photo frame into her bag, pushed the drawer shut, and left the room, closing the door softly behind her before she walked downstairs and out the front door. The cottage released a long sigh as it fell into a peaceful slumber behind her, the wrought-iron gate squeaking a reluctant good-bye as she closed it for the last time. Her heart broke at the finality of it all, but she knew it was the right thing to do—the only thing to do to save the bookshop.

The morning light was clear and melodic, lending everything a bright-edged quality as she made her way down the hill, the breeze at her back, pushing her on to find the next chapter of her story. As she walked, she thought about the photograph in her bag. Whatever secrets it held, she was certain that Frances would tell her, in her own words, in her own good time . . .

NOTES ON A FAIRY TALE
Cottingley, Yorkshire. September 1917.

Our fairy photograph became something of a party trick over the summer, displayed with excessive theatrical flourish by Aunt Polly at her musical evenings and whenever the Bradford relatives came for Sunday tea. It was a source of great amusement and intrigue, the print Uncle Arthur had taken from the plate passing around eager hands so that everyone had their turn to study the image and decide if the fairies were real, or if not, how on earth we'd done it. Elsie and I played along, spinning ever more elaborate tales about how we'd found the fairies and what they looked like and how Elsie had taken the photograph. The trick had done its job, and although Mummy still fussed when I got my petticoats wet, she didn't worry quite as much about me playing at the beck.

But as the weeks passed, Elsie and I grew tired of the teasing and speculation, and I began to wish the photograph would disappear and be forgotten about. Aunt Polly, especially, kept talking about it, pulling at it like an errant thread in her needlework to be unpicked. I heard her discussing it with Mummy while I was outside, their voices drifting through the open window.

"What do you make of the girls' photograph, then, Annie?" Aunt Polly asked. I recognized the tone of her voice. Slightly too curious. Slightly meddlesome.

"I don't know, Polly. Honestly, I don't. Frances says it's real, and she isn't one for telling lies."

"Arthur still thinks it's a trick of some sort, but I'm not

sure. You know as well as I do that folk have been talking about fairies in Cottingley since we were young girls."

"That's just folklore, Polly. Old tales told around the fire on winter nights."

"What about the Hogan child? That's not folklore, is it?"

Aunt Polly pulled the thread further, teasing and tugging to see what might be revealed. My skin prickled at the mention of the Hogan girl. I thought of the look in Mrs. Hogan's eyes, the hushed silence of the cottage in the woods, the absence of the chatter of children.

"Poor little mite. She must have fallen down an old mineshaft, as they said. I don't for one minute believe she was taken by the fairies. That's the ramblings of a mother grieving for her child, and I can't say I blame her for that." I could hear the *click clack* of knitting needles as they worked furiously on more comforts to send to the troops. "Still," Aunt Polly continued, "I'm sure there are stranger things than fairies in the world. Things you and I will never understand, at any rate." A chair scraped against the floor as she stood up. "There's a meeting of the Theosophist Society in Bradford next week. Will you come with me?"

I heard Mummy sigh. "Oh, I don't know, Polly. Are you sure it's wise to be getting involved with the likes of all that? Arthur says it's black magic and conjuring the dead."

Aunt Polly snorted with laughter. "Arthur Wright wouldn't know how to conjure the dead if he was surrounded by corpses. Don't mind him. Come with me. You might learn something. We both might. Don't pretend you're not as intrigued by that photograph as I am. It must be real. What other explanation can there be? If fairies can exist in another world, maybe our loved ones can too. If I'd lost my son in France, I know I'd rather believe in the possibility of seeing him as a spirit than never seeing him again. Wouldn't you?"

"I suppose so." After another moment of quiet knitting, I heard Mummy agree. "I'll come to your meeting, then, but only on the condition that you put that silly fairy photograph away and forget all about it. You're worse than the girls. And they're bad enough."

Elsie stayed home from work again the following week, suffering from hay fever or a summer cold or "lazy-itis," as I heard Uncle Arthur muttering one day. When she was well enough, she loved to come up the beck with me, where we spent hours building dams or sketching the wild poppies and bee orchids or just talking and making up new adventures for a story we were writing. We didn't discuss the photograph much, or the fairies. If the photograph of pretend fairies was *our* secret, the real fairies were mine.

I saw them when Elsie wasn't with me, most often on the warmest days when they appeared to be busiest, tending to the flowers on the riverbank and in the hedgerows. Like the right notes played to make a chord on Aunt Polly's piano, we resonated in peaceful harmony, the fairies and I. I played my games. They got on with their work. It was the most ordinary extraordinary thing. The sort of thing you never forget, no matter how many years weave themselves between the present and the past.

As the weeks slipped by and the golden days of summer turned toward the amber days of autumn, the fairy photograph was brought out less often, until I thought it forgotten about altogether. Only once did I see Aunt Polly take it from the drawer when she thought nobody was looking. Only once did I do the same, studying my face, that distant look in my eyes, captured by the camera as I'd glanced over Elsie's shoulder to follow the glimmer of something far more interesting than a paper cutout. As I stared at myself, it was like looking into my past, because I knew that even when I was old and gray like my grandmother, or fretting about the laundry being mangled like Aunt Polly, part of me would always be that nine-and-a-half-year-old girl, playing with the fairies at the bottom of the garden. The photograph had captured that moment forever. It was a thought I carried with me as I fell asleep at night, drifting away beyond the bedroom window to chase my dreams of fairy glens and a little girl with red hair who entwined white flowers among the curls in my hair, and sang songs to me of the Little People.

Yorkshire's autumn was as great a gift as Yorkshire's summer. I loved watching the rusting of the leaves while the dales mellowed to shades of ochre, and rose hips and blackberries grew deliciously fat on their branches. The morning mists were mystical and magical to me, and the rose-glow of the evening sun lent the sky a hypnotic light that matched any Cape Town sunset.

It was harvest time: a time for thanks and prayer and reflection, but a time also tinted with sadness for the mothers and fathers who had lost loved ones in the latest offensives in Ypres and Passchendaele. The war was unceasing and cruel. I saw the telegram boy visit the same house three times in as many days, each chilling knock at the door bringing news of another son lost, until there were no more telegrams to deliver. No more sons to mourn.

In those honey-dipped days, I felt Daddy slip further away from us. I couldn't even seek solace in the fairies since they had gone from the beck with the passing of the summer. Worst of all, Mummy said we had outstayed our welcome at 31 Main Street, that we were starting to get under everyone's feet and it was time for us to look for a house of our own. With no end to the war in sight, she felt it best for us to start making alternative arrangements sooner rather than later.

Aunt Polly wouldn't hear of such a thing and said whatever would the neighbors think if she couldn't give her own sister and niece a roof over their heads? Uncle Arthur was more sympathetic to Mummy's point of view, saying, "If our Annie feels she'd be happier in a place of her own, then who are we to stop her?" Aunt Polly told him to shush and mind his own, that this was a matter between sisters and nothing for him to be concerning himself with. In any event, I was relieved when it was agreed that we would stay at Number 31 until the war was over and Daddy was back. I'd grown very fond of Aunt Polly and Uncle Arthur, and couldn't imagine not seeing Elsie every day. She'd become everything to me: sister, friend, confidante, coconspirator. Elsie was a spark to my guttering flame. With her, I was a brighter, better me. With Elsie, anything was possible. With Elsie, you never quite knew what was coming next.

"We need another photograph, Frances." Her words fell on me like lumps of rock as I lay in the bed beside her. "This time you can take one of me."

I didn't like the idea. The more I'd studied the first pho-tograph, the more fake the fairies looked. I could hardly believe anyone thought they were real. "What if we get caught, Elsie? Isn't it best to forget about the photographs now?"

"You've heard Mummy and Daddy talking. They still doubt the photograph, even though they don't know how we could have faked it. If we took another, we would really convince them." She sat up in bed, her hair silvered by the light of the full moon streaming through the window. "Don't be a stick-in-the-mud. It'll be fun."

I had reservations but I supposed it was only fair for Elsie to be in a photograph since she'd taken the first one of me. And so it was agreed. Elsie would start work on a new cutout the next morning. I asked her if she needed *Princess Mary's Gift Book*, but she said no.

"This one will be different. It'll be a surprise."

It was more than a surprise. When Elsie showed me the new cutout, I didn't know what to say. It wasn't a fairy but an odd little man.

"What is it?" I asked, peering at the strange-looking creature.

"It's a gnome, silly. They'll be expecting us to take an-other photograph of fairies, so we'll surprise them with this. They'll be more likely to believe us if we photograph something different. Come on. We'll take the photo in top field. They won't be expecting that, neither."

It was a misty Saturday morning, far from ideal condi-tions for photography. I winced when Elsie asked Uncle Arthur if she could borrow the camera again. His "no" was quickly brushed aside by Aunt Polly, who came to our rescue again, telling him not to be a spoilsport and to let us have the camera for half an hour.

"Up to summat, you mark my words," he said as we put on our boots at the back door.

Aunt Polly said that we might very well be up to summat, but at least we were up to summat outside and not under her feet and that he shouldn't be complaining.

"Up to summat, you mark my words," Elsie mimicked as we ran through the garden. I laughed so hard I thought my sides would burst.

It was an unusually still day. No breeze. No clouds. Not the faintest swaying of grass or fern. I picked campion for my flower press while Elsie sat down in the field and arranged herself and the cutout, using a hat pin as before to position the "gnome," as she called it. She looked pretty in the bridesmaid dress she'd worn for our cousin Judith's wedding the week before. It was one of Mummy's designs, beautifully stitched as always. I had one to match but hadn't wanted to wear it to play outside, knowing how prone I was to slipping and falling. Elsie also wore her favorite hat and had left her long hair to fall in loose tumbles around her shoulders. I peered nervously at her through the camera lens, terrified that I would get it wrong and spoil the one plate Uncle Arthur had given us.

Elsie patiently explained how everything worked until I felt better about it. "Is the camera ready?" she asked.

I checked everything again. "Yes. I think so."

Elsie reached out her hand so it looked as if the gnome was going to hop onto it. "Go on, then. Press the lever." I hesitated. "Today, preferably."

I checked one last time that the pointer for the exposure time was set at the correct number for the distance between Elsie and the camera. On the count of three, I pressed the lever.

Elsie gathered up her skirts and the "gnome" and rushed over. "Come on. Let's ask Daddy to develop it right away."

She was all excitement and enthusiasm, but I was uninspired by the whole event. The cutouts had been harmless fun the first time. This I wasn't so sure about. "I'll stay by the beck for a while," I said. "You take the camera back. I'll follow you in a bit."

Elsie didn't question or try to persuade. She wasn't that sort of girl. "Promise not to tell?"

"Promise not to tell."

"Ever?"

"Ever."

Elsie pushed the hat pin into the ground and ran off through the field, leaving me to dispose of the cutout. I did the same as last time, tearing the paper into pieces and tossing them into the stream, before settling myself on the willow bough seat, hoping for my real little friends to appear.

I wasn't sure how long I'd been there when a voice made me jump.

"What you up to, then, Frances Griffiths?" Mavis Clarke stood on the opposite bank, arms folded, face screwed up in smug satisfaction.

"Sitting," I replied, trying my best to sound bored. "Why? What's it to you?"

"What were you and Elsie doing up in top field?"

My heart thumped in my chest. Had she seen us? "None of your business, nosy parker."

"Up to no good, you two. That's what. And when I find out, I'll tell on you both."

I swung my legs beneath the willow branch and tried to sound nonchalant. "Tell. See if I care."

But I did care. Very much. If Mavis Clarke had seen what we'd done, she would tell everyone. And then we would be in awful trouble. She stuck her tongue out, laughed, and stomped off upstream, beneath the stone bridge, toward the quarry, where I hoped she would fall in and never be seen again, like the poor Hogan girl.

As soon as Mavis was out of sight, I jumped down from the branch and ran back to the house as quickly as I could. I had to tell Elsie not to develop the plate.

But I was too late.

She was already waiting for me on the back step, a great smile on her face. "It worked!" The excitement made her voice all shrill, like Aunt Polly's. "The photograph came up!"

She showed me a funny-looking image. It wasn't half as nice as the one of me with the fairies.

"Why does your hand look all big?" I asked.

"Daddy thinks it must have been overexposed."

"What did he say?"

"He still thinks it's a trick, but Mummy thinks it's real."

I grabbed Elsie by the elbow and walked with her back down the garden. "I think Mavis Clarke saw us. She was down by the beck, all sneering and know-it-all."

Elsie laughed. "Well, Mavis Clarke can get knotted. Everyone knows she's a troublemaker. Nobody would believe her even if she said something, which she won't. I'll make sure of it. Come on. You can show Aunt Annie the new photograph."

The photograph of Elsie and the gnome was discussed at length over tea. The same speculation and questions from the adults, the same assertions from Elsie and me that it wasn't a trick, that we *had* seen a gnome in the top field. The words scratched in my throat like a bad dose of the mumps, choking me with my lies. I watched Mummy from beneath my fringe, which was badly in need of a cut. She didn't say much about the photograph. She was often quiet these days, her words squashed away by all the worry brimming inside her.

The rest of the month was given over to haymaking, an event I enjoyed immensely. I loved the musty smell of the freshly cut hay and the scent of the honeysuckle that threaded through the hedgerows beside the fields. I loved to hear the song of the mistle thrush that trilled until dusk as we worked, and I loved the jokes and laughter that took my mind off the knowing looks and snide comments from Mavis Clarke.

It pleased me to see Mummy and Aunt Polly with their sleeves rolled up to the elbow, a flush of red to their cheeks as they pitched forkfuls of the dry hay onto the cart. Mr. Snowden almost disappeared under the great flurries of straw tumbling down on him as the women encouraged each other to pitch faster, giddy in their exertions. I loved the *swish* and *rustle* as they worked, and laughed when the prongs of Aunt Polly's pitchfork reached the seat of Mr. Snowden's trousers, sending him hopping about like a madman. These were the days I loved the most. Being outside, working hard, doing our bit while the men were away. And after the day's work, we sang songs of thanks for a bountiful harvest and the generous weather, and I fell into bed at night, too exhausted to dream or to worry about Daddy in France, far away from haymaking and the simple pleasures of country life.

By the time the last field was ploughed and the swallows had flown south, the two "fairy" photographs had been put away in a drawer, brought out only occasionally, when a relative came to visit. I was glad. I'd grown tired of talking about fairies and gnomes, tired of Uncle Arthur's teasing, tired of pretending. With the changing seasons, my fairy friends had moved on, and although I sometimes overheard Mummy and Aunt Polly talking about the Theosophists and whether it might be possible that fairies did exist, for the most part, their interest faded and their talk returned to the more somber matters of war and the prospect of another Christmas without any sign of an end to it.

Life moved on, and my summer of fairies had come to an end.

Or so I thought.

Part Two
The Beginning of Fairies

Dear Miss Elsie Wright, I have seen the wonderful pictures of the fairies which you and your cousin Frances have taken, and I have not been so interested for a long time.
—LETTER FROM SIR ARTHUR CONAN DOYLE TO ELSIE, JUNE 1920

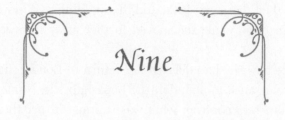

Nine

Ireland. Present day.

The wild winds of May dissolved into the peaceful balm of June as Howth village exhaled beneath a bright sun that brought pale-faced office workers for weekend strolls and lured café tables and parasols outside to decorate the pavements. While the rhododendrons flourished beneath the better weather and longer days, Olivia felt herself wilt. Better weather and longer days meant that time was slipping by, and still she was no closer to solving the bookshop's financial struggles. Bluebell Cottage had yet to sell and provide the much-needed injection of cash to settle the bookshop's debts, and despite launching a new website and adding Pappy's handwritten catalog to the site, the shop remained empty of customers and the books lingered on their shelves, stuck there, like the barnacles that clung to the hulls of the boats in the harbor.

As the fortunes of the bookshop hung in the balance, Olivia's dreams intensified, taking her on curious nighttime meanderings toward woodland streams where a little girl offered her a white flower, and always, when she woke, she felt a strange sense of disquiet, a sense that something was unsettled. It left her restless and impatient.

And then there was Jack, and the wedding that moved ever closer in time, while she moved further away from it in her heart.

Twice now she had delayed her return to London. It wasn't just a reluctance to abandon the bookshop and Nana. It was a reluctance to confront what was waiting for her there. Her thoughts swung daily from strident conviction that she couldn't marry Jack to a reluctant acceptance that she had to. The plans had surely gone too far to back out now, and yet when she climbed to the top of Howth Head and looked out across the view, something told her that her plans hadn't gone nearly far enough.

They'd had a couple of difficult conversations. Jack was exasperated by Olivia's loyalty to the bookshop. He couldn't understand why she wouldn't just leave it to Henry Blake, or the solicitors, to sort out. He didn't understand her emotional attachment to it at all. As far as he was concerned, she was re-acting to her grandfather's death and having perfectly normal pre-wedding jitters. He urged her to come home so they could talk about it like adults, but she flinched at the word *home*. London had never really felt like home. The poky little flat above the bookshop felt more like a home than any of the sleek west London apartments she'd lived in. She tried to explain herself in lengthy e-mails and frustrating conversations on the old rotary-dial phone in the shop but could never adequately express what she wanted to say. She deleted the latest attempt on her laptop and retreated to a rare edition of Dickens's *A Tale of Two Cities*. The words pricked at her conscience. "It was the best of times, it was the worst of times . . ."

AFTER AN AWKWARD first week, Ross Bailey, Writer, was firmly established "In Residence" at Something Old. He'd arrived on a rainy Monday with his laptop, a bottle of wine, a guitar, and a smile that could flip even the most troubled of hearts upside down and made Olivia wonder things she shouldn't have been wondering.

"Okay," she said. "I get the laptop and the wine, but . . . the guitar?"

"Never write without it. Helps me think when I'm stuck. If it gets annoying, just say."

It wasn't annoying at all. It turned out to be rather lovely.

Their first day together was clumsy, peppered with overly polite apologies for disturbing each other and tentative questions about how they took their tea and where the sugar was and whether the guitar was too loud. The second day was a little more relaxed, the third even more so. Friday was actually pleasant.

By the start of the second week, Ross had learned that Olivia only took a splash of milk, that she liked silent movies and Fleetwood Mac, and that she stuck her tongue out when she was concentrating. What he hadn't discovered was that she had a fiancé in London and a wedding dress fitting to reschedule. It hadn't come up in conversation, and wasn't something Olivia especially wanted to talk about. The more she and Ross conversed, the greater the omission of her marital situation became. The elephant made itself firmly at home between Children's Books and Irish Folklore, waiting for Olivia to acknowledge it, while she hoped it would eventually get bored and go away.

For her part, Olivia discovered that Ross took his tea builder-strong with two sugars, that he liked fig rolls and Pink Floyd and was allergic to gooseberries. This Olivia found hilarious. "Who the hell is allergic to *gooseberries*? Who even *eats* gooseberries?" Ross conceded it was a fairly useless and bizarre thing to have an allergy to as far as allergies went, but still, he would appreciate it if she didn't leave them lying around the place, just in case.

As the days passed, an easy friendship began to develop between them, and Olivia looked forward to the jangle of the shop bell at nine and the occasional strumming of the guitar upstairs. She even found that five o'clock on Friday came around too soon. Only once, in a cheap-white-wine-fueled moment of self-pity, did she entertain any romantic notions about Ross. To her enormous relief, the notions left after breakfast the next morning. Romantic notions confused and complicated things. Olivia had quite enough confusion and complication in her life already.

As much as she hadn't been expecting to share the flat with anyone other than Hemingway, she grew fond of Ross being around. She liked that she could hear the scrape of chair legs and floorboards creaking, and the *tap tap tap* of his fingers against the laptop. She liked the sound of his guitar. She liked the serendipity of it all, that while he was writing a new book upstairs, she was selling old ones downstairs. However unexpectedly the arrangement had come about, there was something perfectly cyclical about it. It felt as natural as breathing in and out, and the coming and going of the tide.

As the hours slipped harmoniously by each day, Olivia occasionally glanced at the photograph of Frances and the fairies in the silver photo frame that now sat on the shop desk, and she smiled to herself. It was a reminder to her that impossible things could happen, that the narrative of our lives was constantly be-

ing rewritten, and none of us knew how our story would end
until we turned the last page.

ON TUESDAY AND Friday afternoons, Olivia took time away
from the bookshop to visit Nana. One of the benefits of having
Ross around was that he could mind the shop while she was out.
Annoyingly, he always sold more books when she wasn't there
than she ever sold on her own. Ross had a natural ease with
the customers that Olivia couldn't match. It had become something of a competition between them, but as long as money was
going in the till, Olivia was happy to let her pride take a fall.

Tuesdays and Fridays were quieter days at St. Bridget's,
which meant Olivia could slip in and out without having to
endure painful conversations with well-meaning relatives of
other residents. She couldn't bear the doleful expressions in
their eyes, the endless discussion about treatments, and the
sense of death and despair that clung to everyone like the support stockings that clung to the residents' legs. There was still
life left in Nana, and Olivia refused to become *that* relative, nib-
bling on custard creams, awaiting the inevitable.

On days when Nana was in a more restful mood, Olivia
read to her from Frances's book. Sometimes she would nod off.
Sometimes she would listen intently, stopping Olivia midsen-
tence to ask her to repeat something, or to explain something
she couldn't understand or a word she couldn't remember the
meaning of.

Today Nana was in her room, listening to the radio. She
was dressed like a tiger in an orange-and-black-striped top and
black trousers, so elegant and strong, and yet so fragile. Nana
had difficulty swallowing and only ate very little as a result.
She didn't wear her clothes anymore. They wore her, the fabric

folding in on itself in crumples and creases, trying to find a way to fit her better.

They spent a difficult hour together, talking about a job Olivia didn't do and the time when Nana won the lottery and the newspapers came to take her photo and the visitors who came and went when Olivia wasn't there: old friends and neighbors and "that terribly nice man." Nonsense conversations and half-remembered fragments of memories about things that had never happened. It frustrated Olivia so much that she wanted to scream by the time Barbara came around with the tea.

A doctor had once explained Alzheimer's to Olivia by telling her to think of the brain as an orange, the skin and pith peeled away first, and then the segments slowly being eaten, piece by piece, until there was nothing left. That, he told her, was when a patient would die, when the last segment of orange had gone. It was an inevitability now, a matter of time that neither Olivia nor Nana had any control over.

Olivia nodded along to Nana's stories, her thoughts drifting further away from the suffocating room, her conscience ever more guilty with each retelling as she wished precious minutes away. Minutes that brought Nana that bit closer to the last segment of the orange.

In a brief moment of lucidity, Nana asked Olivia to fetch her memory book from the wardrobe, and they spent a pleasant half hour together looking at the photographs. Some of the faces Nana remembered immediately. Others were lost to her now. It was only when she saw her wedding photograph that she stopped turning the pages and started to cry.

"I'm so sorry, Nana. Let me put that away. We'll go for a walk. Or a trip out, maybe. It's a lovely day. We can look at the bluebells."

Olivia started to take the book, but Nana shook her head and pushed Olivia's hand gently away. She ran her fingertips across the photograph.

"It's all right, dear. I'm crying because I remember. I remember the church bells the most. They'd been silent during the war, you see." Her eyes flickered shut and her head tilted to one side: listening, remembering. She looked wistfully out of the window then. "You never forget a feeling like I had that day. It becomes part of you. Like these bloody wrinkles and liver spots. Happiness like that leaves its mark forever."

As Nana spoke, it struck Olivia more than ever how little she knew about her family's past. Like a sea mist warmed beneath the sun, she'd watched Nana Martha slowly fade away in recent years, but only now, as she looked at the frail old lady beside her, did she realize that she didn't know her at all. Yes, she knew a gentle-hearted woman called Nana, but she didn't know Martha Kavanagh, the wife and mother, or the Martha Hogan she'd been before she met Pappy. When she looked into Nana's eyes, Olivia didn't know what made her laugh or what frightened her. She didn't know her favorite color or her favorite song. She didn't know what she and Pappy had danced to on their wedding day. She didn't even know where they were married, or who'd made Nana's dress. She felt that part of her own story would always be missing without these precious fragments of the past.

"What year were you married, Nana?"

Nana told Olivia to take the photo from the page. Olivia removed it from the plastic slot and passed it to her. She turned it over and asked Olivia to read what it said on the back.

"'Cormac and Martha. St. Michael and All Angels Church, Cottingley. 16 March 1946.' That wasn't long after the war, was it?"

"He'd been in France. Asked me to marry him before he'd even dropped his kit bag on the cottage floor."

"The cottage in Yorkshire?"

"Yes. We met in a hospital in Leeds. I was nursing there. He was sent back to recover from a shell wound. I thought him funny with his Irish accent. When he got better he went back to fight, but we wrote as often as we could. When the war ended, he came to find me."

Olivia rested her head on Nana's shoulder as they continued to look through the photographs together. Only briefly did her thoughts jump to her own wedding day. She'd always imagined an autumn wedding: russet leaves and black velvets and dancing to Fred Astaire. The wedding she would be part of in a matter of weeks had none of that. She could hardly remember how all those simple ideas had become so lost.

"How did you know Pappy was the one, Nana?"

Nana laughed and coughed. Olivia passed her a glass of water and rubbed her back until she recovered. "I didn't! We fell in love through our letters, through our words. We've had our problems over the years, but we made it work."

"What sort of problems?" Olivia was aware she was being insensitive in asking, but something about her own relationship problems compelled her to hear about other people's too.

Nana shifted in her chair and asked Olivia to fetch her a blanket. She didn't answer the question.

They carried on turning the pages of the album until they came across a photograph of Pappy outside Something Old, his smile as broad as the flourish on the sign above his head.

"He loved that shop, loved those books like his own children."

Olivia closed the book and took it back to the wardrobe. "He doted on Mammy, didn't he? She loved him very much." Nana looked at Olivia through narrowed, expressionless eyes. Olivia knew that look. Nana didn't know whom she was talking about. "Katherine. Kitty. Your daughter? My mam?"

Questions without answers. She didn't remember.

Reaching for her walking stick, Nana pulled herself up out of the chair. "I want to go to the bookshop."

Olivia was taken aback. Nana usually complained whenever Olivia suggested they go out somewhere for the day. She always said it was too far. Everywhere was too far these days. Too much of an ordeal.

"We'll go one day soon, Nana. When you're feeling up to it."

Nana pushed Olivia's hand away with a determined shove as she rummaged in the wardrobe for her coat. "I want to go today. Where's my coat? Have you seen my blue coat?"

She hadn't worn her blue coat for decades. Olivia remembered seeing it in the wardrobe, musty with damp. She'd put it in a bag for the charity shop.

Like a pan of water coming to the boil, Olivia could feel her grandmother's frustration rising as she rifled through the wardrobe.

"Where the bloody hell is it?" Nana's arms physically shook against her sides.

"Let's have a cup of tea, Nana, and I'll find it for you. Listen. I can hear Barbara coming with the trolley."

It was too much. Nana's frustration boiled over. She turned to Olivia. "I don't want tea. I want to go to the bookshop, *now*, silly girl."

Olivia hated it when Nana got angry. It frightened and upset her. She wanted to say it wasn't her fault. She wanted to shout back and say she *wasn't* a silly girl. She wanted to say, "I'm your granddaughter, and I love you and I'm doing my best." But she said nothing. With tears smarting in her eyes, she fetched the nurse, who spoke calmly to Nana and assured her she would go to the bookshop soon and why didn't she sit down and have a rest for a minute.

Like a child after a bad dream, Nana was exhausted and confused by her outburst. With the nurse comforting her, she fell asleep in minutes.

The nurse assured Olivia she would be okay. "She won't remember anything about it when she wakes up. If you want to take her out anytime, though, love, let us know and we'll have her ready."

Olivia said thank you, she would. She kissed Nana's cheek and told her she loved her before reluctantly picking up her bag and leaving the nurses to it. She loathed herself for being afraid; loathed this awful disease for stealing Nana away from her so cruelly.

That night in the flat, Olivia dreamed that she was walking in a woodland glade lit by a bright moon that hung low in the sky. Her footsteps were soft upon the velvet moss beneath her feet as angelic voices whispered like a hundred distant bells, "Fairies, fairies, ah, come soon." Flashes of green, blue, and purple whirled around her, leading her to a cottage with a white door, where a child with hair of flame red held a bunch of wildflowers in her hands. She offered them to Olivia, smiling. "For Mammy," she said. "For my Mammy. Cinquefoil and harebell, for love."

OLIVIA WOKE THE next morning, groggy, as if she'd hardly slept at all. Stepping out of bed, she paused. On the floor beside the spare pillow that had tumbled from the bed in her sleep was a single yellow flower. Five heart-shaped petals. As fresh and as pure as if it were in full bloom in a summer meadow.

Drowsy and mind-fogged, she crept downstairs to look for a book on Irish wildflowers. It took her a while to find anything that resembled the yellow flower, but eventually she found an image and description that matched: "Cinquefoil, a flower renowned for its healing properties and a flower also said to be favored by fairy folk. Meanings associated with it include money, protection, sleep, prophetic dreams, and beloved daughter." She placed the yellow bloom in the coffee cup vase with the others. Henry Blake must have been right. The cat must be bringing them in. There wasn't any other rational explanation.

Unsettled by her dreams and the unusual flower, Olivia couldn't get back to sleep. She made coffee and sat in the window seat, watching the sunrise and wishing more than ever that Pappy was beside her, reminding her that nothing had happened yet today, and that everything was possible.

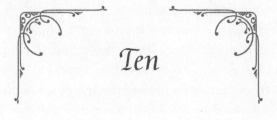

Ten

Ireland. Present day.

$\mathcal{I}$t was five weeks since Pappy's funeral, four since Olivia had watched his words fly away across the sea and had taken off her engagement ring in a moment of reckless defiance. Still her future, and that of the bookshop, hung in the balance, and still the weeks slipped away too quickly beneath unpredictable skies. Days of moody granite clouds made way for days with skies the perfect blue of every child's imagination. The weather had always affected Olivia's mood, and she found it hard not to let her emotions sway from sunny highs to colorless rain-lashed lows.

As time marched on, Olivia's life in London, and the future she'd been planning there, felt increasingly distant. She was surprised at how easily she had detached herself emotionally from it all, like a page come free of its bindings—part of the story that didn't belong there in the first place.

Jack insisted, with increasing irritation, that she come home now. He said it was becoming difficult to explain her continued absence. "People are starting to ask questions, Olivia. It doesn't look good." She wasn't especially surprised that he was more concerned about the clients he had to impress and the reputation he had to uphold than he was about their relationship. An absent wife-to-be didn't fit within Jack's carefully orchestrated life. It was awkward. Not how things were supposed to be. "My secretary is finalizing dinner arrangements for the Willoughby contract next week, and she needs to know if you'll be there. It will be rather embarrassing for me if you're not."

With every conversation she tried to tell him about the letter, about her "condition," but the tone of the exchange was always wrong, and the words escaped her. Her secret remained in only two places: her heart, and the drawer of her nightstand.

Through the ever-shifting weather and emotional turbulence, Olivia stuck resolutely to her task, working hard to learn the business of selling rare books. She visited house clearances, where substantial private libraries often yielded rare ex libris treasures. She contacted auction houses and specialist librarians. She studied websites and catalogs of other booksellers and, all the while, she continued to work on uploading Pappy's catalog to the new website. Something Old held such treasures. She just had to find a way of connecting the right book lover or collector with the right book.

Even in sleep, there was no escape from the overwhelming responsibility to save the shop. In her dreams the books came to life, flying up from their shelves like a flock of seagulls startled from the sand, their pages flapping wildly beneath cracked spines, carrying them up and out of the open door where they swooped across the dazzling lights of the city, intending to settle on deserving nightstands, gifts for sleepy book lovers when they woke in the morning. Except the books never made it. Something interrupted them and they forgot how to fly, falling from the sky like shot game as Olivia watched, helpless. They landed in graffiti-covered skate parks and litter-strewn rivers and empty housing estates, until they were lost and ruined, and it was all her fault.

The sense of guilt and helplessness nagged at her as she opened the shop each morning and saw Pappy's carefully collected books. Unread. Unloved. Beautiful narratives and prose trapped among their closed pages. She ran her fingertips along their spines, like a child running a stick along a fence. There was something pleasing about the rhythmic undulation of the smooth leather against her skin. Silently she promised Pappy she would bring customers to them, promised she *would* breathe life back into the shop's hollow lungs, even if she didn't know how.

THANKS TO A continual stream of correspondence between Olivia and Iris, the fairy-themed shop window bloomed like a summer garden. Olivia added greeting cards she found in the gift shop with Arthur Rackham's classic fairy illustrations. She added several editions of Cicely Mary Barker's Victorian flower fairy books she'd found in a bag of donations, and inscribed favorite quotes from fairy tales onto chalkboards. She watched people stop to admire the display, willing them to come inside, but it was Ross who first noticed the most curious addition to the window.

Olivia was cataloging a shelf of Irish Poets when she saw him outside, arms folded, face scrunched up in confusion. Ross was one of life's quiet observers, so it was no great surprise to see him standing still, pondering. Olivia liked the way he made time to think. She liked the way he listened to her properly when they had their chats over coffee. She liked that she could tease him about trying to be one of the cool kids with his gig T-shirts and man-bun and the beanie he wore even on the warmest days. She liked *him* . . .

Lost in her thoughts, Olivia didn't realize he'd seen her until he started to wave his arms around, beckoning frantically for her to come outside. Embarrassed at being caught staring at him and at how much she'd been thinking about him lately, she ducked behind the shelf and pretended she hadn't noticed.

The bell jangled as he pushed the door open. "I know you're in there, Kavanagh. Stop checking me out and come here for a minute. I want to show you something."

Olivia grabbed a pile of books and stepped outside. "I was *not* checking you out. As if! I'm busy. What is it?"

"There." He pointed at the bottom corner of the window. "Look at the fairy door."

Olivia leaned forward to take a better look. A slender green shoot was entwined around the lintel of the little blue door. "That's so weird. How did it get in there?"

Ross moved close beside her, their breaths misting up the window as they both stared at the fairy door. "Dunno. It's pretty cool, though." He tugged at Olivia's sleeve. "There. Look at the window box."

The plants in the window boxes had flourished beneath the mix of sunshine and rain in recent days. The one closest to them had sent out a shoot that had found its way through a tiny crack in the frame.

Olivia walked back inside and leaned into the window to take a closer look.

Ross followed. "Must be all your fairy juju working its magic. Here, take this before it goes cold."

He passed Olivia the latte he habitually picked up for her

now on his way to the shop, always with a different instruction written in black marker on the side: "Laugh." "Dance." "Fart." Anything other than her name.

"And what do we have today?" she asked, smiling as she turned the cup 'round.

"Today, Ms. Kavanagh, I bring you a cup of 'Hope' with a capital *H*. Enjoy!"

As Ross went upstairs to the flat, Olivia sipped her coffee and listened to the scraping of chair legs and windows being opened and the cat being shooed out of the way. She smiled to herself as she glanced back at the shop's front window. However it had gotten there, something about that little green shoot spoke to her of new beginnings, of hope.

Fairy juju or not, five new customers arrived that morning, and every one of them left with a book in their hands and a promise to come back soon.

OLIVIA WAS STILL thinking about the shop window when Henry Blake arrived later that morning, peering around the door to ask if it was a good time.

Olivia put down the pile of books she was rearranging. "It's always a good time to see you, Henry. Come in. I'll put the kettle on."

They drank peppermint tea while Henry asked how she was and how business was going and whether there had been any offers on Bluebell Cottage.

"We've had a few viewings, but no offers yet. To be honest, part of me hopes it doesn't sell."

Henry looked surprised. "But surely you're keen to release some cash?"

Olivia sighed, a big heart-heavy sigh of resignation. "I am, I suppose. It's just that Nana and Pappy loved that little cottage so much. It's been in the family for years. I hate the thought of someone else living there." She rummaged in her pocket and pulled out a piece of paper. "I even bought a lottery ticket today. My first ever. Maybe if I win the lottery, I can keep the cottage *and* the bookshop." Henry eyed Olivia studiously. She felt as if she had been scolded without him having said a word. "It's a big *if*," she conceded, returning the ticket to her pocket. "A very big *if*."

Henry looked at her with compassion then. She sensed that he understood her reluctance to let go.

"Everything must move on, dear. Houses. Shops. Books. People." He stood up and took his teacup for a walk as he paced up and down the shop. "Let someone else love the cottage as much as your nana and grandfather did. Let a new family make it *their* home. Sometimes we have to let go of the things we cherish the most. Sometimes it's the only way we can move on."

Henry talked such sense. Olivia often wished she had a notebook to write everything down. She imagined his wisdoms on fridge magnets and notecards. "Henryisms," as she called them.

He put his cup down, took a book from the shelf beside him, and opened it to the front page. "Take all these books with their sentimental inscriptions. Here. Listen to this. 'Christmas, 1915. To my darling Beatrice. Think of me as you read these glorious words. Yours always. Patrick.' Young lovers separated by war, no doubt." He opened another book. "And this. 'August, 1933. Follow your dreams, wherever they may take you. Bertie.' These words, these books, meant the world to someone not so long ago, and now here they are, giving joy to us as we romanticize about who these people were. When someone buys these books, those sentiments will become theirs to cherish." He sat down again. "There's a provenance to everything, Olivia. The only reason anything has a story is precisely *because* it moves on. Books, paintings, houses—they all hold a trace, an echo, of the people who once cherished them." He took a sip of tea and added as an afterthought, "Not so dissimilar to people, I suppose. We are the sum of those who have touched our lives in one way or another."

Olivia remembered how Pappy used to talk about the provenance of books. He found great romance in the notion of books acquiring new owners and a new history. Henry was right. She was being overly sentimental. She desperately needed the money and Bluebell Cottage was, after all, just bricks and mortar.

"Did you ever look into that old picture book you found in the drawer?" Henry asked. "Or the Conan Doyle book you found about the girls and the fairies?"

Olivia said she had and that they were both cataloged and on the website. "It's all really interesting. I found an old manuscript in the desk drawer, as well. It was written by Frances, the younger of the two girls who took the fairy photographs, and what's fascinating for me is that her schoolteacher, Ellen Hogan, was my great-grandmother."

"That *is* fascinating."

"Isn't it? I'd love to take a trip over to Yorkshire. Nana Martha grew up in Cottingley, where the girls took their photographs, but she never talked about her life there, so I hadn't made the connection. We didn't talk about the past much. My mam died when I was young. I suppose it was too upsetting for everyone to look back. So we didn't."

Henry put down his cup and touched Olivia's hand. "I'm so sorry, dear."

His words carried such meaning that they moved Olivia to tears. She'd heard "I'm sorry" so many times but had rarely believed anyone truly meant it. Henry's compassion was so honest and heartfelt. It wrapped around her like the little green shoots entwined around the fairy door.

Sniveling into a tissue, Olivia thanked him for his kindness. "With Pappy gone and with Nana as she is, I feel like I'm losing touch with my family's past. I'd like to go back to the start of their story. See the village where Nana grew up. Maybe the cottage is still there. I don't know. I've done a bit of research online and found out there's a collection of materials relating to the Cottingley fairy photographs in the library at Leeds University. I know it doesn't make much sense, but I feel that I need to go."

"Then do. I'd be very happy to look after the shop for you. I find the days interminably long. It would be nice to fill them here."

"Would you really?"

"It would be my pleasure. I made a solemn promise to your grandfather, and I will do whatever I can to help you, Olivia, for as long as I can. If that includes sending you off on a fairy trail to Yorkshire, then so be it."

He winked, and Olivia felt a crack heal in her heart. She hadn't seriously thought she *would* go to Yorkshire, but now that Henry had made it possible, why not?

"But what about Nana? I can't just abandon her."

"Then don't. I'll visit her while you're away."

They *had* known each other, after all, although Olivia doubted Nana would remember Henry after so many years.

Henry placed his hand on Olivia's. "It would be my pleasure."

SINCE ROSS HAD started working in the flat, Olivia found a quiet solace in the shop after he'd gone home. She loved the click of the lock on the shop door, loved to kick off her shoes, pour a glass of wine, and take half an hour to read or just to think. She knew that wedding tasks were piling up and people were waiting for her to get back to them, but in those quiet moments alone, she could pretend nobody was waiting for an answer from her and nothing mattered, other than the sound of the sea beyond the window, echoing the sound of her breathing: in and out, in and out.

Such was her reluctance to acknowledge the life she'd left on pause in London that it was with a mixture of joy and regret that she opened a parcel from her manager at the National Art Library, sent with a note to say she hoped Olivia would be back soon and that she might find a use for these in the meantime.

She was delighted to see her bookbinding tools: her bone folder and awl, her French pointe knife and brushes, even her cutting mat. Her manager had thrown in a "few extras," as she put it, which included book cloth, Somerset text pages with deckle edges, and a selection of flyleaves and silk headbands.

Olivia inhaled the lush vanilla scent of the paper, her hands itching to get to work. She'd always found great comfort in bookbinding, finding something calming about the diligence and care required. As she scanned the shop for inspiration, her eyes settled on the photograph in the silver frame, and then on the manuscript on the desk beside her. Frances's story. She knew exactly what she would do. While the pages of her own story were unraveling, she would stitch Frances's story together the only way she knew how: with thread and glue and beautiful gilded leather.

After opening the windows to enjoy the balmy evening, she switched on the radio. Her heart quickened as she heard what was playing—an old Beatrice Lillie recording, and she was singing Mammy's song. "There are fairies at the bottom of our garden! / It's not so very, very far away; / You pass the gardener's shed and you just keep straight ahead— / I do so hope they've really come to stay. / There's a little wood, with moss in it and beetles, / And a little stream that quietly runs through; / You wouldn't think they'd dare to come merrymaking there— / Well, they do." Olivia sang along to the end. It was a sign, she was sure of it. A new pebble for her bucket.

Before she switched off the lights downstairs, she checked the fairy door in the window, remembering how Iris had said if you leave a gift for the fairies they might leave something in return. Olivia looked around the shop but couldn't see anything small enough for fairies other than paper clips and staples, and she doubted whether fairies would have much use for either. Then her gaze fell on the coffee cup. She took out two of the flowers and set them in front of the little door. "There you are, fairies. A thank-you. From me."

Feeling more positive than she had for a long while, she settled into bed with Frances's words, happy to let a young girl's memories transport her back over the years, to a place where fairies really did exist at the bottom of the garden and anything was possible, if you believed . . .

NOTES ON A FAIRY TALE
Cottingley, Yorkshire. Winter 1917.

Time passed quickly among the familiar routine of school, piano lessons, Monday wash day, Thursday baking day, church on Sunday, and all the things that now formed my life at 31 Main Street. I watched the last months of the year race away over the distant hills along with the swallows and the starlings, taking autumn's russets and golds with them and leaving the muted tones of winter behind: bare branches, gray skies, barren moorland, empty hedgerows. Winter was coming. It was time for nature, and little girls and fairies, to hide away.

Although my heart was still drawn to the beck, I mostly found it too cold to play there. Even on rare days when the winter sun hung low in the sky, tempting me outside and lighting the way toward the bottom of the garden, it wasn't the same. Like the leaves and petals that had fallen from the trees and flowers along the riverbank, the magic I'd felt at the beck that summer had drifted away downstream, taking the long journey west along the River Aire.

Uncle Arthur joked about there being "nowt so miserable as a hard Yorkshire winter," and all too soon I experienced for myself how bitter and unforgiving it was. I dreaded every trip to the lavvy and every bath night, my bones aching with the cold until I thought my blood would freeze like the water pump in the garden. Elsie and I spent long evenings huddled beside the fire, knitting comforts for the soldiers, darning holes in our stockings, reading or drawing by candlelight whenever we could. I felt like a prisoner in the house with everyone's bad tempers and rotten colds getting on top of each other. Elsie grew ever taller, leaving hardly any room in the bed for Rosebud and me. No wonder our occasional trips to the Picture House in Shipley became such a treat. We spent many happy afternoons there, captivated by the Gish sisters and Mary Pickford, whom I found as enchanting and magical as my fairy friends at the beck.

The winter nights were the worst. In those endless hours, waiting for morning, I longed more than ever for the warm breezes that had ruffled my hair in Cape Town as I walked on the beach with Daddy. I missed him more and more with each week that passed and worried about him being too cold in the trenches, even with all the hats and scarves we'd sent him. I took his portrait from between the pages of *The Water Babies* every night, shivering as I knelt on the cold floor and prayed with all my might for his safety. When I opened my eyes and looked at his face, I could hardly remember what he sounded like when he spoke or laughed. The picture was worn from being held so often, the image not as clear and sharp as it once was. Like the year, and like my hopes of ever seeing him again, my Daddy was fading away.

It was a rare frost-free day, two weeks before Christmas, when Aunt Polly asked me to take some wool to Mrs. Hogan. "She's knitting a balaclava to send off to Mr. Hogan in his Christmas parcel, but she's run out of wool, and the haberdashery is closed until Monday. Be a pet and take this 'round to her, would you, Frances?"

Glad to get out of the house for a while, I put on my wellingtons and coat and set off around the fields, following the woodland path toward Mrs. Hogan's cottage. It was easier to see without the summer foliage concealing it, but it looked terribly lonely there in the woods, with only a few evergreens for company.

Lifting the latch on the gate, I followed the narrow path to the front door. The two pairs of black boots still stood on the step: one big, one small. The perfect circle of toadstools still grew beneath the elder tree, and just as I had when I'd first come here in the summer, I felt, again, a nagging sense that I'd forgotten to do something.

I knocked tentatively at the door and listened for the sound of footsteps approaching inside.

Mrs. Hogan was delighted to see me when she opened the door. "Frances! What a lovely surprise!"

"Hello, Miss. Aunt Polly asked me to bring you this." I handed her the two balls of wool.

"Ah, well now. Isn't that terrible kind of her? Come on in for a minute. You must be frozen stiff."

A fire crackled in the grate, and I was glad of its warmth as I took off my hat and coat and gloves, which Mrs. Hogan took to hang on the stand. The cottage was as inviting as I remembered from my visit in the summer, but Mrs. Hogan looked as thin and pale as the bare branches on the elder tree outside.

I sat at the small table as she set the kettle on the stove and cut a thick slice of something—cake or bread, I wasn't sure.

"Tea brack," she said, putting it on a plate and handing it to me with a smile. "My mammy's recipe. Best brack in Ireland. Tuck in."

I hadn't tasted tea brack before so I couldn't say if it was the best in Ireland or not, but it was certainly delicious. As I ate, I noticed several new paintings had been added to the collection on the dresser.

"Started as a hobby to keep me busy while Robert . . . Mr. Hogan . . . was away," Mrs. Hogan remarked as she saw me admiring them. She sighed and placed a hand to her heart. "There have been a lot of days to fill."

I wished there was something I could do to take away her sadness about her husband being at war and her little girl gone missing, but as I knew only too well, no matter how much you wished someone was with you, it wouldn't bring them back. "My cousin Elsie likes to paint," I said, trying not to drop crumbs. "She's very good."

"Is that so?" Mrs. Hogan sat in a chair opposite me and poured tea from the pot. "What does she like to draw?"

"Landscapes. Nature. And lots of fairies." I froze as I realized what I'd said. "But mostly landscapes."

Mrs. Hogan looked at me for a moment as if she wanted to say something, but changed her mind. "Well, every-body likes fairies, don't they?" she said with a knowing smile. "And it's a great skill to draw something purely from imagination." I nodded in agreement and stuffed my mouth full of tea brack so I couldn't speak. "My granny used to tell me stories about the *daoine maithe*—the Good People," she continued. "She lived all her life among the ancient thorn trees and faerie forts in Ireland. What she couldn't tell you about the faeries wasn't worth knowing."

There was a rare brightness in Mrs. Hogan's eyes as she spoke, a dreamlike quality to her voice. I put down my brack and listened. It was like hearing my own heartbeat.

"She taught me the ballads and tales she'd been told around the turf fires when she was a *coleen*. I was enchanted by the stories of the *sídhe* and the *púca*, of changelings and leprechauns, the *Far Darrig* and the *banshee*. My favorite poem was one she used to recite by William Allingham: 'Up the airy mountain, / Down the rushy glen, / We daren't go a-hunting / For fear of little men; Wee folk, good folk, / Trooping all together; Green jacket, red cap, / And white owl's feather!' Do you know it, Frances?"

I shook my head, almost in a trance. I wanted her to keep talking.

"Perhaps we'll read it in class. Some people dismiss it all as nonsense, but I believe in the Little People. Some tend the flowers and plants. Some tend the rivers and streams. Others are more mischievous." She took a sip of her tea. "Not unlike humans, I suppose."

My secret burned on the tip of my tongue. The desire to tell the truth raged inside me, the need to tell *someone* about the muddle Elsie and I had got ourselves into with the photographs. But the words wouldn't come. I sat in silence and gazed at the tea leaves in the bottom of my cup, wondering what secrets they would tell if I could read them.

"If you ever want to talk about anything, Frances, I'm a good listener. It must be difficult for you and your mammy with your father away. Sometimes it's easier to talk to someone who isn't as close to you as your own family. Isn't as involved?"

The question in her voice was an invitation. Did she know? Had she seen us taking the photographs? In our excitement, we'd forgotten that Mrs. Hogan could see the beck from the cottage, even if we couldn't see the cottage from the beck. I stared harder into my teacup.

"You know, Frances, I sometimes think there's too much truth in the world. Too much certainty and scientific fact. We don't always need an explanation, do we? Sometimes all we need is something to believe in, something to give us hope and to remind us how remarkable the world can be, even in the middle of a war." She stood up and walked to the window. "Perhaps that's why we've always made up stories—created our own truths—because sometimes they're easier to believe. That's not so terrible, is it?"

Before I said something I would regret, I told Mrs. Hogan I'd best be getting home.

"Come and see me again before Christmas, Frances. And bring your mammy. There's plenty more brack where that came from!"

I said thank you and that Mummy would like that. As I buttoned my coat, my eyes were drawn to a small oval painting on the windowsill. It was of a child with red hair. Her face was familiar, but I didn't know why.

I thought about Mrs. Hogan's stories of the Little People all the way home and all through tea and all that evening over card games in the front room. I was still thinking about them as I fell asleep that night, where my dreams were filled with waterfalls and woodland glades and a girl with flame-red hair, handing me a white flower. "For Mammy," she said. "Please. For my Mammy."

Christmas came and went in a disappointing manner. Wartime rations meant meager pickings for Christmas dinner, although Aunt Polly's figgy pudding was declared a triumph, and we all had second helpings to fill the gaps in our bellies. I was disappointed not to find the silver sixpence I'd planned to send to Daddy for good luck. He needed it now more than ever. Mummy tried to protect me from the worst of the news, but Elsie told me about the headlines she saw on the newspaper stands in Bradford and about the things the older women at Gunston's talked about over tea break. The battles were fierce and the casualties many.

With the arrival of a new year, everyone made an effort to be full of good cheer and to talk of victory coming soon, but I couldn't allow myself to believe it. The world had been at war for nearly a third of my life. War was as much a part of me now as three of my fingers and toes. All I could do was pray for Daddy's safety and an early spring and an end to it all.

Mrs. Hogan had said that we didn't always need an explanation for things. Fairies, I understood entirely. War, I couldn't fathom at all.

NOTES ON A FAIRY TALE
Cottingley, Yorkshire. Spring 1918.

According to Aunt Polly, Uncle Arthur had ears like an African elephant. "He can hear the dead turn in their grave, that man," was her favorite turn of phrase. His ears were almost as big as his hands, so I suppose it was no surprise that it was Uncle Arthur, and nobody else gathered in the front room that Whitsuntide evening, who heard the latch on the gate. He wasn't in the best of moods and certainly not in the mood to entertain uninvited guests.

He flicked down the top of his newspaper. "Who the 'eck's that coming 'round at this time?"

Aunt Polly tutted. "It'll be Edna Morris. Wanting to borrow something again, no doubt. Any excuse to stick her great snout in where it isn't wanted."

I burst out laughing, and both Aunt Polly and I earned ourselves a scolding from Mummy for being rude about the neighbors. Elsie winked at me and pushed her finger against the end of her nose to make it resemble a snout. I stuffed my mouth into the crook of my arm to smother my giggles.

But it wasn't Edna Morris wanting to borrow something.

I heard the front door open and gently close with a quiet click. I heard soft footsteps.

And I knew.

I held my breath as the front room door swung open, and everything became nothing and there was only him.

"Daddy!"

One minute he was a distant fading memory, the next

he was standing right there, in the front room, laughing and smiling and telling us he'd been through the delousing center and it was safe for us to hug him. As if all the months and weeks and days and hours without him had never happened, Daddy was home, tin hat in one hand, kit bag in the other, and all my heart was held in the smile that lit up his eyes.

I remember crying out his name, remember my petticoats wrapping themselves around my legs as I tried to stand up, remember his arms squeezing me tight, remember the peculiar smell of him: earth and salt, cigarettes and some other bitter tang I imagined was the smell of war.

My prayers had been answered. Daddy was home. Everything was going to be all right.

Mummy couldn't stop sobbing. Even with her scrunched-up face and snotty red nose, she looked ten years younger and ten inches taller. She looked like Mummy again.

When Daddy finally had a chance to get a word in edgeways between all the fussing and hugging and back slapping, he explained that the war wasn't over, but he had a week's leave after which he would have to go back. Mummy said we would deal with that when the time came. For now, all that mattered was that he was home.

I sat on Daddy's knee, the finest seat in all of England, as Aunt Polly went to put the kettle on and Uncle Arthur groused about the price of coal. Life at Number 31 Main Street felt wonderfully normal.

I had never been prouder than when Daddy sat beside me at church the next day, so smart and brave and important-looking in his uniform. My friends admired him and made a great fuss of me. Fathers were a rare sight in those days, and the boys wanted to ask him about the whizzbangs and the tanks and the trench rats. When one of the girls asked if the horses would be coming back, Daddy shook his head and said the horses had been very brave, which made us all cry.

I didn't mind sharing Daddy for a few minutes, but what I loved most were the quiet, ordinary moments we spent together as a family at the house, Mummy sewing in the window seat, Daddy lying on the bed beside me as he read from *The Pickwick Papers*, making up terrific voices for the characters and causing me to laugh so much my sides ached.

I couldn't wait to show him the beck, and on the first rain-free day, I insisted he come with me. We sat together on the willow bough seat, just as I'd often imagined.

"So, tell me what you and our Elsie have been up to. Your mother says you two have become the best of friends—and what about these other friends you've made, eh?"

I'd told Daddy about the photographs in my letters because I knew Mummy would mention them. "Did Mummy show you the photographs?" I asked. Nobody had seen them for months.

"She did. Quite something, eh? Our Frances playing with fairies. Captured forever in a photograph."

I'd been waiting for the right moment to tell him about *my* fairies. More than anyone else, I knew Daddy would believe me. But when it came to it, I was terrified to say anything in case he didn't.

"Do you believe in fairies, Daddy?"

"I've no reason not to I suppose, but I've never seen one myself." He swung his legs beneath the bough and threw sycamore seeds into the water. "Do you know the story of the Angels of Mons, Frances?" I said I didn't. "There was a big battle at the start of the war, in a place called Mons in Belgium. The British soldiers suffered heavy losses but said they'd seen phantom bowmen, troops of angel warriors storming the skies above them, firing flaming arrows down on the Germans to help the British forces. They became known as the Angels of Mons."

"Were there *really* angel warriors in the sky, Daddy?"

"That's the question, isn't it? The soldiers say there were, but how can *we* be sure if we didn't see it for ourselves? That's why I can't say I don't believe in fairies—but I can't say I do, either, because I haven't seen one."

I couldn't keep it in any longer. I had to tell him. "Daddy, if I tell you something, do you promise not to make fun of me?" Daddy was as bad for teasing as Uncle Arthur. Worse, in fact.

He promised. And he was true to his word. He didn't comment or question as I spoke. He sat beside me as I told him about the glimmers of light and the misty visions I'd seen day after day through the summer. He listened quietly as the stream carried my secret away beneath our feet.

"Mrs. Hogan, my teacher, says there are lots of different types of fairies," I explained, feeling clever to know so much about them. "She's from Ireland and calls them the Little People. Some are nature fairies. Some are water fairies. They change with the seasons and the weather. Some fairies are mischievous, but most are kind. The ones I see are kind."

"And what about the ones in your photographs? What type are they?"

I stiffened. I had never been able to tell Daddy a lie. He had a way of looking at me as if he could see straight into my mind, could hear what I was thinking. He looked at me that way now.

Should I tell the truth? Should I show him the mound of earth where the hat pins were pushed into the ground? But then he would have to tell Mummy and Aunt Polly and Uncle Arthur and they would be ever so cross, and what would Elsie think of me if I broke my promise? The photographs were mostly forgotten about, hidden away in a drawer. I thought about the Angels of Mons and Mrs. Hogan's words—that we don't always need an explanation. That sometimes all we need is something to believe in, something to give us hope. No, I wouldn't tell him. Not now.

"The fairies in the photograph are different from those I see when I'm alone. The ones in the photograph only appear when me and Elsie are together."

Without actually telling a lie, I had managed not to betray my secret.

Daddy didn't mention the fairy photographs again.

We packed every minute of that week with laughter and fun. Daddy filled a hole we'd all felt but hadn't been able to explain. He was the missing piece of Uncle Arthur's jigsaw puzzle and Elsie's lost button. He was Aunt Polly's stray earring and Mummy's misplaced glove. He was the lines I'd forgotten in the recital at school. Everything was right with him here. Everything was complete.

Which is why it was always going to be unbearable to say good-bye again.

We spent his final morning together at the beck, pulling faces at our reflections in the water and making each other laugh. The stream laughed with us, capturing our giggles in its gentle chatter as it meandered along. I buried my face in the warmth of his neck, breathing in the scent and feeling the shape of him, so that I wouldn't forget.

"I'm very proud of you, Frances. Very proud of the way you've settled in here." My heart swelled with pride as he spoke. "And as for fairies at the bottom of the garden," he added, lowering his voice to a whisper, "I believe you. Don't ever let anyone tell you they're not real. Don't let anyone take that away from you."

I stored his words away in my heart, to treasure like precious jewels.

"The war will be over soon, and I'll be back for good. I promise." He made me look into his eyes. "You believe me, don't you?"

"Yes, Daddy. I do."

As the sun sank low behind the horizon that night, I thought of all the poor children whose daddies had never come home, not even for a week, and I was so grateful to have had this time with him, even if it broke my heart to lose him again so soon.

I cried myself to sleep that night as Elsie held my hand.

"It's all right to be sad, Frances," she whispered. "You have to let all the sadness out to make room for the happiness again. Remember your daddy's promise and try to get some sleep." She squeezed my hand. "I'm here if you need me."

Seven months later, Daddy's promise came true and the war came to an end at last.

The fog of fear and worry lifted from Cottingley, leaving everything brighter and clearer. Finally we could live and breathe and hope again.

I wrote to my old school friend Johanna in Cape Town, telling her how we were preparing the Union Jack flags for a victory party. *"I am sending two photos, both of me, one of me in a bathing costume in our backyard. Uncle Arthur took that, while the other is me with some fairies up the beck. Elsie took that one. Rosebud is as fat as ever, and I have made her some new clothes. How are Teddy and Dolly?"* On the back of the photograph of myself with the fairies, I wrote, *"Elsie and I are very friendly with the beck fairies. It is funny I never used to see them in Africa. It must be too hot for them there."*

Over the following months, arrangements were made for me and Mummy to leave Cottingley and start a new life in Scarborough on the East Yorkshire coast, where Daddy would join us as soon as he was demobbed. In Scarborough we would be a proper family again. I couldn't wait, and yet I was sad to leave Cottingley and the family I'd become part of there.

Mr. and Mrs. Hogan invited Mummy and me to tea to say a proper good-bye. Like everyone else, something about Mrs. Hogan had changed since Mr. Hogan came home. The haunted, distant look I'd seen cloud her face during lessons had all but gone. I overheard her telling Mummy that she still felt a shadow beside her where her daughter should be, but that things were much easier now that Robert was home, and perhaps the Lord would bless them with other children. She crossed herself as she said this, and Mummy closed her eyes and prayed for the Lord to be generous.

As a farewell gift, Mrs. Hogan gave me a book of poetry by someone called W. B. Yeats and a play of his called *The Land of Heart's Desire*. She had underlined the words "Faeries, come, take me out of this dull world, / For I would ride with you upon the wind, / Run on the top of the dishevelled tide, / And dance upon the mountains like a flame." She said, "You can never have too much Yeats, or too many fairies in your life," and her eyes spoke to me of secrets known and secrets kept.

My last view of the cottage in the woods was of Mr. and Mrs. Hogan standing together in the doorway, a small pair of black boots beside them on the step, and although I promised to visit in the school holidays, I couldn't shake the feeling that I'd forgotten to tell Mrs. Hogan something very important.

Elsie was the hardest good-bye of all.

"I'll miss you terribly, Elsie," I sobbed as I clung to her. "And so will Rosebud."

In typical Elsie manner, she laughed affectionately at my tears. "You're a daft beggar, Frances Griffiths. True friends never grow apart. We'll always be friends, no matter where we call home. Here. I drew this for you."

She gave me a parting gift of a sketch she'd drawn of us dancing together in the front room on Armistice Day. She said it was one of the happiest days of her life. I said it was one of the nicest things I'd ever been given.

As for the fairies, I knew I would always have my memories, but I hated to say good-bye to them all the same. As I sat on the willow bough for the last time, I wished I could stay young forever so that I could always play with the fairies at the beck. But I wasn't Peter Pan, nor was I a page in a fairy story.

As all little girls must do, I grew up.

And although I thought them forgotten about, the story of our fairy photographs grew with me.

NOTES ON A FAIRY TALE
Scarborough, Yorkshire. 1920.

There was much about the seaside town of Scarborough that reminded me of Cape Town. With its long golden beaches and sweeping ocean views, I soon felt at home.

Scarborough had an event for every season and occasion: brass bands in the market square on Christmas Eve, Shrove Tuesday skipping on the pier, and Michaelmas Day market, where the farmers hired dairymaids and laborers. Most of all, I loved to watch the spectacle of the returning herring fleet when crowds of women lined the harbor wall with their stalls, working quickly to behead and tail the fish, scales scattering like jewels against the cobbles as the fillets were deboned and placed in salt barrels. They worked for hours among the stench of fish oil and brine until the catch was processed. I loved to hear the screeching of the gulls that wheeled overhead before swooping down to snatch a fish head. Mummy didn't like the fish women's cursing and bawdy jokes and bustled me past as quickly as she could.

Away from the seasonal events that marked the passing of the months, I loved to walk along the promenade past the magnificent pastel-colored hotels that stood shoulder to shoulder like refined old ladies: the Majestic, the Imperial, the Britannia, and the mighty Grand, which still bore the scars from the German naval bombing during the war. Sometimes I hung upside down on the promenade railings, imagining the sky was the sea and the water the rushing cloudscape, until it made me dizzy and reminded me of how impossibly large the world was, and how little I knew of it.

At weekends and after school, I loved to play in the sheltered sandy coves, loved to run among the sand dunes and pick the wildflowers and collect shells from the shoreline: periwinkles, scallops, and mussels. And above it all stood the ancient castle on the cliff top, where I imagined the battles that had played out along the castle walls and turrets in centuries past. In the evenings, Mummy and Daddy often attended the concerts at the Floral Hall. Nellie Melba and Clara Butt were their favorites. Mummy sang the songs for me the next day, as she always had, but with greater joy and energy.

Life returned to something like normality. I was a happy, carefree twelve-year-old girl. I missed the beck fairies and thought about them often at first, but as the months passed I thought about them less and less, my days occupied with picnics at Cayton Bay, crabbing in the rock pools, Punch and Judy shows on the promenade, and all the other new experiences. It was only at night, with the sound of the seagulls and the wind and the crash of the waves rushing through my open bedroom window, that my dreams pulled me back to Cottingley; back to the pretty cottage on the far side of the stream and the girl with hair like flames holding out a flower for her Mammy.

Some things will always follow you, no matter where, or how far, you travel.

The sky was a sultry gray the day the letter from Aunt Polly arrived. Heavy brooding clouds threatened rain as I arrived home from school to find Mummy hovering anxiously at the kitchen window, ready to fetch the washing in off the line at the sign of the first drops. She made idle chitchat about my day, as she often did when there was something difficult she didn't especially want to talk about.

The letter was sitting on the table, bearing a Bradford postmark.

"What's this?" I asked, pulling it toward me. "Is it from Elsie?"

Mummy turned the tap too far, spraying water everywhere as it bounced off the scrubbed potatoes in the pan. "It's from Polly."

"Did Elsie write?" Elsie was dreadful at replying to my letters. I missed her terribly and loved nothing more than to hear a few lines from her, but Elsie wasn't one for writing and, as Mummy reminded me, Elsie was a young woman now and probably courting and had other things to think about than writing letters to her cousin.

"She didn't, love. Not this time. Read it if you like, but I wouldn't take too much notice of it if I were you."

I read Aunt Polly's neat handwriting. And then I read it again, to make sure.

Cottingley. 5 March '20

Dear Annie,

I hope you are all keeping well in Scarborough. We are all well here. I am writing with a bit of news.

You'll remember the meeting of the Theosophist So-

ciety we attended together at Unity Hall in Bradford, not long before you and Frances moved to Scarborough. They spoke about fairy life, and at the end of the meeting, I showed the photograph of our Frances and the fairies to a Mrs. Powell. You might recall she found the photograph interesting and asked if she could borrow the negative plate and the sepia print our Arthur had made.

A letter arrived last week from an Edward Gardner at the Headquarters of the Theosophical Society in London. He has seen the photograph and is very interested in it. The best example of its kind—anywhere—he says. He has many questions: where it was taken, what time of year, what model of camera, etc. I asked Edie Wright to help me write a reply (you'll remember her from our musical evenings) and I sent the negative plate as requested.

Well, another letter arrived a few days ago, in which Mr. Gardner offers to send our Elsie her own Kodak camera and negative plates so that she can take more pictures of the "Yorkshire fairies," as he calls them. He asks if her "friend" can join her (her friend being our Frances). He has asked to borrow the negative slide of the goblin photograph (I corrected him and explained that it is a gnome)—which I will send on.

A peculiar turn of events, isn't it.

I'll let you know if anything comes of it, although I expect it will all blow over, as these things usually do.

Do you see the Bainses often? They've always been good friends to us. I imagine it must be nice to have a few familiar faces around.

Our Elsie gets taller every day. Maybe you could visit in the school holidays? We would love to see you all.

Much love,
Polly
xxxxx

I sat quietly for a moment as Mummy scrubbed at a saucepan with iron wool. The scraping and scratching set my teeth on edge. It was a long time since I'd thought about the fairy photographs. None of my friends in Scarborough knew anything about the beck fairies, and it wasn't spoken about between my parents and me. It felt like the whole episode had happened to somebody else, a story I'd read and left behind on the shelf in Cottingley.

"What do you make of that, then?" Mummy's voice was matter-of-fact, but I could tell she was putting it on.

I didn't know what to say. As far as Mummy and Aunt Polly were concerned, the fairies and the gnome in the photographs were real, so why would Elsie and I mind if important men in London took an interest in them? But we knew the truth, and it was alarming, to say the least, to discover that the photographs were being scrutinized by "experts."

I decided the best thing to do was act matter-of-fact, like Mummy. "It would be nice to see Elsie again," I said, taking an apple from the fruit bowl. "And I promised to visit Mrs. Hogan whenever I went back to Cottingley. Do you think this Mr. Gardner will *really* send Elsie a camera and plates?"

Mummy wiped her hands on a tea towel. "I don't know, love. He sounds serious enough." She leaned against the stone sink. "I didn't know your Aunt Polly had taken the photographs to the meeting. I was as surprised to see them as Mrs. Powell was. I thought that was all forgotten about."

"Me too." A sick feeling stirred in my tummy. I didn't want to talk about it anymore. "I'm going out to play. Betty has a new skipping rope. She promised me a go with it."

As I made my way out of the kitchen, Mummy called after me. "Frances? Just a minute."

I stopped and turned around. For a moment, I thought she was going to ask me, and part of me wanted her to. Part of me desperately wanted to sit down at the table and tell her and Daddy everything—about the cutouts and about it only being a bit of fun to get me out of trouble for always falling in the beck. But as she looked at me, Mummy seemed to change her mind about whatever it was she'd been planning to say.

"Nothing, love. You go on out and play. Don't be going far, though. Tea's at five o'clock."

My chance to confess blew away down the street as I opened the front door.

As the day wore on, my thoughts wandered back to Aunt Polly's letter. Why had she shown the Theosophist people our photographs? I didn't like the idea of important men in London studying them with their clever contraptions and intellect. I was sure they would make out the hat pins, or the corners on the card where Elsie's cutting out wasn't as smooth. I thought about Mrs. Hogan's words: *"Cottingley's a small village, and small villages can't keep secrets. They've a funny way of setting them free, and who knows where they'll end up?"* I hoped Aunt Polly was right and that it would all blow over.

Aunt Polly was wrong.

It was over tea a few months later that I sensed tension in the air between my parents. Mummy huffed and sighed her way through her lamb chops while Daddy buried his face in the evening paper.

Eventually he cracked. "Tell her, Annie, will you? She's involved now, whether we like it or not."

"Tell me what?" I asked.

Mummy took an envelope from her apron pocket. "Your Aunt Polly wrote again. You'd best read what she has to say."

I took the letter tentatively. As I read Aunt Polly's words, the paper felt like lead in my hands.

2 July '20

Dear Annie,

> *More news about the fairies.*
>
> *Edward Gardner has written several times now. He is most excited about our "Yorkshire fairies." He is clearly a well-educated man and believes, firmly, in the existence of fairy life, having heard many accounts of them through meetings of the society. He believes in the authenticity of the girls' photographs and sent our Elsie a box of chocolates, along with his latest request for her to take more photographs, and another offer to send a camera. I replied to say that Frances doesn't*

live here and that Elsie can use Arthur's camera and we'll send on any more photographs if she manages some. He also asked for permission to make copies of the photographs. Elsie says he can do what he likes with them. He forgets Elsie is a young woman of nineteen now, and not especially interested in fairies.

The two negative plates have also been analyzed by a Mr. Snelling—a top photography expert in London. He has declared them extraordinary and entirely genuine. He even pointed out the evidence of movement of the wings during exposure. So it would seem the girls were not making up stories as Arthur suspected.

And that's not all. Gardner showed lantern slides of the photographs to a meeting of the Theosophical Society at Mortimer Hall in London, where they caused a great fuss. A lady called Mrs. Blomfield saw them, and has brought them to the attention of Sir Arthur Conan Doyle!

In the latest letter from Gardner, Conan Doyle enclosed a note to Arthur. He wrote very politely to say how interesting the photographs are and that he would like to know more about them. He happens to be writing an article about fairy life for The Strand Magazine *Christmas number and has asked for permission to use the girls' photographs. He assures us he won't mention them by name and has offered to pay £5, or supply a free copy of the magazine for three years. He has since written directly to Elsie, saying how wonderful the fairy pictures are (he mentions Frances too), and says that if he wasn't traveling to Australia he would like to visit Cottingley and talk to her about the fairies.*

It is a lot to take in—I know.

I have invited Mr. Gardner to visit at the end of the month. Hopefully a visit to Cottingley will satisfy his curiosity and he will leave us alone. Elsie isn't especially keen to meet him. I think she would prefer it if Frances were here. Would she be able to come?

> *Love to everyone.*
> *Polly*
> *xx*

The color rushed to my cheeks, staining them scarlet with each astonishing line. *"The two negative plates have also been analyzed by a Mr. Snelling—a top photography expert in London. He has declared them extraordinary and entirely genuine."*

How could they believe it?

Folding the letter, I returned it to the envelope and passed it back to Mummy, hoping she didn't notice the tremble in my hands.

"Lucky Elsie," I said, "getting chocolates."

Daddy laughed. "Is that all you have to say about it?"

"Do you think Mr. Conan Doyle *will* write about our photographs?" I placed my elbows on the table and pressed my palms against my cheeks to conceal the deceit evident in the hot flush that had erupted there.

Daddy peered over his newspaper. "Quite probably, yes, so if there's anything you want to say about it, you should probably say it now."

An awful silence hung in the air. It was already too late to tell the truth. With prints of the photographs in circulation and magazine articles being planned and money and gifts being offered, how could we ever admit our "Yorkshire fairies" were nothing but silly cutouts of Elsie's drawings? We would be in dreadful trouble if we told the truth. If Elsie wasn't confessing—which she obviously wasn't—then neither would I. We had sworn each other to secrecy, and a promise was a promise after all. The best we could hope was that we managed to stage one or two more photographs that would satisfy everyone's curiosity.

"At least our real names won't be used," I said. "Nobody will ever know it was us. Will they?"

Mummy patted my hand reassuringly. "That's right, love. Nobody will know, so you're not to be worrying about it. You've miles of beaches to play on. Castles to explore. Fresh herring straight off the boat. What on earth could any of us possibly have to worry about?"

But I did worry, and so did Mummy. I saw her reading Aunt Polly's letter over and over, taking it from her apron pocket, sighing and putting it back again. As the days passed, I couldn't stop thinking about it, either. The fairy photographs were far away in Cottingley, but they were part of me now, part of my story, and there were more pages to be written yet, I felt sure of it.

Letters were exchanged like gunfire between Mummy and Aunt Polly over the following weeks. After a successful visit with Elsie, it was agreed that Mr. Gardner would visit me in Scarborough. I would then spend two weeks of my school holidays in Cottingley with Elsie, where we would try to take more photographs of the fairies with new cameras sent by Sir Arthur Conan Doyle, or "ACD," as we called him for short.

As the day of Mr. Gardner's visit drew nearer, I wished more than ever that Aunt Polly hadn't taken our photographs to the Theosophist Society meeting. I wished they had stayed in the drawer, forgotten about. Most of all, I wished I hadn't lost my temper that sultry afternoon in the scullery of 31 Main Street. I wished I'd kept my secret locked away, safe in my heart.

But I hadn't, and now I would have to face the consequences. Whatever they might be.

NOTES ON A FAIRY TALE
Scarborough, Yorkshire. 1920.

Mr. Gardner arrived on a muggy Saturday afternoon, the heat sticking to me like my bad mood. I hadn't slept well the night before. Neither had Mummy. She was anxious about what this man "all the way from London" would think of our humble home and northern ways. I was worried about the questions he might ask, and what he might already know. I didn't think it fair that I had to wait around the house to talk to him. I didn't want to talk about the fairies—especially not to a stranger—and I certainly didn't want to talk about the photographs. I'd made a solemn promise to Elsie, and that meant I would have to tell Mr. Gardner a lie. It made my stomach tangle up in tight knots so that I couldn't eat my breakfast.

I sulked all morning until Daddy insisted on taking me for a walk along the seafront, where he hoped the breeze would blow my temper away.

We sat on the harbor wall, waiting for the herring boats to come in. I dangled my legs over the edge, letting my bare calves rub against the cool stone.

Daddy threw stale bread for the gulls. "Come on, then. Spit it out."

I sighed and leaned my head into his shoulder, cherishing the fact that I could, that *my* daddy had come home when so many others hadn't.

"Why does Mr. Gardner want to talk to me, Daddy?" I kicked the heels of my shoes against the wall, enjoying the feeling as they bounced off again.

"Well, it isn't every day you see photographs of fairies, is it? I suppose he wants to ask you about them to understand them better."

The summer sun had reddened Daddy's cheeks, like it used to in Cape Town. He looked more like the man I remembered. For a long time after being demobbed, he'd looked like a ghost, as if part of him was still at war.

"We never meant for the photographs to be seen by anyone else though," I said. "They were only meant for us."

I felt his grip tighten around my shoulder as tears pricked my eyes. If only I could tell him. He would know how to make it all better.

"I know, pet. But other people *have* seen them now. Best to talk to this Mr. Gardner. Answer his questions. Tell him what you can." He ruffled my hair with the palm of his hand. "That doesn't sound too bad, does it?"

I closed my eyes, enjoying the warmth of the sun on my face. "No. I suppose not."

Mummy twitched at the lace curtain in the front room until the motorcar pulled up outside.

"Frances! He's here, love!"

I stiffened as I heard the car door opening and closing. I was in my bedroom, reading through the letters Johanna had sent from Cape Town. I wished Johanna or Elsie were with me. I wished I could go cycling along the leafy back lanes with my friend Mary. I'd rather do anything than talk to this Mr. Gardner. Elsie usually did the talking. Without her, I was sure I would trip myself up and say things I shouldn't say.

Mummy called up to me again, and I made my way

downstairs on heavy feet, my heart thumping in my chest, the knots still tangled in my tummy.

Mr. Gardner stood in the hallway, sun streaming through the stained-glass panels in the door behind him. He wore an expensive-looking brown wool suit with a brown bow tie and smart brown trilby hat. His brown eyes were intense, but he had a pleasant smile that stretched his slim mustache above his top lip.

Mummy did the introductions, her voice all up-and-downy again.

Mr. Gardner held out his hand. "I am delighted to meet you, Frances." He spoke softly, with a crisp London accent.

I shook his hand and thanked him for coming, as I had been told to, and while Mummy fussed over him, taking his hat and coat, I stood quietly at the bottom of the stairs, wishing I could sink into the floorboards.

Mummy showed him through to the front room, which had never been tidier or more vigorously polished. "Thank you for coming all this way, Mr. Gardner," she said. "It isn't often we get visitors from London, is it, Frances?"

I said, no, it wasn't, and sat at the opposite end of the table from Mr. Gardner—whom I kept wanting to call Mr. Brown—while Mummy excused herself to make the tea.

The carriage clock ticked away the seconds on the mantelpiece as Mr. Gardner settled himself into the chair, pulling at the fabric of his trousers in brisk movements before crossing one leg over the other and remarking on how pleasant it was to breathe the fresh sea air. "You wouldn't believe the fogs we get in London. Have you ever been?"

"No," I said. "But I've read about the pea-soupers in Mr. Dickens's novels."

He smiled. "Indeed. And his descriptions are astonishingly accurate." He tugged at his trousers again, and I wondered if he was a little nervous too. "I'm very grateful for your time, Frances. I hope I'm not intruding on your weekend too much."

His smile put me at ease. He wasn't as stiff and intimidating as I'd imagined. "Not really. But I hope to get out bicycling if the weather holds."

He rubbed his hands together like Aunt Polly did when she was cold or vexed. "Of course. And I won't keep you long. As you know, we were intrigued by your photographs. Most intrigued." I glanced at my feet and wished Mummy would hurry up with the tea. "Your cousin, Elsie, told me all about the fairies you saw together. I visited her recently and took a walk to the beck. It certainly is an enchanting place. Exactly the sort of place one might expect to find elementals."

To my relief, Mummy reappeared with a clattering tea tray, and for a while the room was filled with the noise of best china cups and teaspoons and sugar tongs rather than the sound of my guilty conscience. I ate two slices of parkin while Mummy and Mr. Gardner spoke politely about the weather and the coal strike and other dull things.

After the customs of tea had been dispensed with, Mr. Gardner suggested we talk in the garden, it being such a warm day. "I like to hear the gulls whenever I'm by the sea," he said. "And the fresh air does wonders for the soul."

Mummy said that was a nice idea but insisted I put my coat on since the wind was blowing from the east.

I sat beside Mr. Gardner on the bench Daddy had made last summer. My feet touched the ground now, where they hadn't six months ago. I was pleased to be growing into a tall girl, like Elsie.

"I know this must all be rather unusual for you, Frances," Mr. Gardner explained, "and I can assure you we only wish to understand the circumstances in which the images were captured. It isn't every day one sees fairies at the bottom of the garden, is it?"

I said no, it wasn't, and swung my legs nervously beneath the bench.

"Perhaps you could tell me how the photographs came about. Take me back to that summer's day. Try to re-create the scene for me, as if it were a painting."

I thought about those carefree days I'd spent by the beck, when I saw the fairies in abundance. It seemed silly to me now that we hadn't tried to take a photograph of real fairies. Elsie was so intent on her idea of the cutouts, we'd never discussed it, let alone tried. "It was all done in a hurry, Mr. Gardner. We were only allowed the camera for a short while and only had one plate. We didn't have time to think about what we'd seen. I stood behind the fairies and Elsie pressed the shutter. That was it."

Mr. Gardner asked questions about the weather that day and how we'd reacted when we saw the image on the plate.

"It was a warm day," I said. "Hot and sticky. We were very excited when we saw the plate. We wanted to prove to the grown-ups, you see. That there were fairies in the beck."

"And did they believe you?"

"Mummy and Aunt Polly did. Uncle Arthur teased us about it."

"How did that make you feel? When he teased you and said the fairies weren't real?"

Finally he was asking some interesting questions. "I didn't mind. It was only harmless fun, so I ignored it. Uncle Arthur was always teasing me and Elsie about something or other. But I knew what I'd seen."

Mr. Gardner jotted things in his notebook as we talked, and I began to relax in his company.

"Do you believe the fairies are real, Mr. Gardner?"

He paused for a moment as the sun lit up his face, making him look less brown and more interesting. "I do, Frances. I believe there are other realms, other places, where fairies and elemental spirits dwell. For those who doubt, I say only this: Does something not exist simply because you cannot see it? You cannot see Conan Doyle right now, but you know he is real, don't you?"

"Of course he's real. He wrote a letter to me. And he wrote all his books about Sherlock Holmes."

Mr. Gardner chuckled. "Ah, but how can you be *sure* he's real if you've never seen him yourself?"

I was starting to feel confused by Mr. Gardner's puzzles and was grateful for Mrs. Hogan's words, which popped into my head. "Sometimes, we just have to believe, don't we?"

He made some more notes in his book. "You are a wise young lady, Frances. I couldn't agree more."

Mummy appeared at the back door to say tea was ready. "It's only egg and chips, Mr. Gardner. Nothing fancy. I hope that's all right for you."

"Egg and chips is my favorite of teas, Mrs. Griffiths. Thank you. I shall enjoy it very much."

I let Mummy do the talking while I ate. I copied the way Mr. Gardner dipped his chips into his egg, because I knew Mummy wouldn't have let me if we were on our own.

By the time Mr. Gardner said good-bye, I was almost sorry to see him go. He hadn't mocked me or teased me or dismissed what I'd seen as some trick of the light—or sandwich wrappings. He believed me. And even if the photographs were staged, he believed in fairies, and for that alone, I liked him well enough. I was surprised he hadn't asked me to describe the fairies in detail, or to speculate on what I thought they were doing, or how they appeared and disappeared, and why, but I presumed he must know the answers already. He was a clever man from London, after all.

He left a smart new Cameo camera and six packets of plates for me to practice with. "So that you'll know what to do when you get to Cottingley," he said.

Over the following weeks, I had great fun photographing my friends and the views from the castle and the harbor. I enjoyed messing about with the camera, so much so that I almost forgot its real purpose. It was only when Mummy said the Bainses would be coming to collect me at ten o'clock the following morning, to accompany me on the train journey to Cottingley, that my stomach churned.

"And stop taking silly photographs, Frances. You're to save those plates for the fairies, remember?"

I remembered only too well.

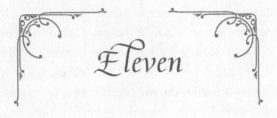

Eleven

Ireland. Present day.

The more Olivia read of Frances's story, the more she felt drawn back to Cottingley.

Reading Frances's memories of Ellen Hogan was like having a front-row view into her family's past. Olivia had never known or thought much about her great-grandmother. She vaguely remembered seeing her once or twice in old family photos, but the past is such a distant, colorless place to a child's eyes, and it was only now that Olivia saw Ellen as a young wife, worrying about her husband away at war; as a mother, grieving for her lost little girl.

As she read Frances's words, Olivia wept for Ellen's loss, wishing she could step back in time to help her, or comfort her, or find some answers for her. More than ever, Olivia wanted to stitch together the scraps and fragments she was discovering about her family. Just as Nana used to make patchwork quilts, Olivia was sure she could create something meaningful from all the disparate parts. She just wasn't sure how yet.

Taking Henry at his word, she made arrangements to travel

to England. First to London, because the longer she stayed away, the more certain she was that in order to walk away from her future, she had to confront it. She would travel from London to Cottingley and to the library at Leeds University, where the archives about the fairy photographs were kept.

Despite the soothing lullaby of the sea, Olivia slept fitfully, her mind a confusing tangle of questions and doubts. She sensed her mother beside her, and always she saw the red-haired child, surrounded by flashes of brilliant jeweled light, handing her a flower. "For Mammy." Each morning when Olivia woke, her body ached as if she hadn't slept at all, and often she found the flowers from her dreams dropped on a stair, or on the floor beside the bed, or tangled between the crumpled bedsheets. She collected them and placed them in the coffee cup, suspending her disbelief and choosing, instead, to trust in the things she couldn't easily explain or understand, but which charmed the childish wonder in her heart nevertheless.

As her dreams intensified, the red-haired girl became so real to Olivia that she found herself absentmindedly sketching her image during the day, bringing her to life on the page. She drew her surrounded by the flowers she held in her hands—white harebell, pink campion, and yellow cinquefoil—entwining them into the curls in her hair, until the flowers and plants were not around her, but part of her. A true child of the woodland.

AFTER SEARCHING ONLINE, Olivia found a photography studio in Dublin that could develop the film from the Instamatic camera she'd found in Nana's dressing table. She took the bus into town and left the camera with the owner of the studio, an expert in older film formats who was delighted to see the Instamatic. He told her the prints would be returned in the post.

There were only twelve exposures, but they were her mammy's, and the tantalizing prospect of the images that might be captured on the film meant everything to Olivia. It was like leaving a piece of her heart behind, and she couldn't help feeling a little anxious as she made her way back to Howth on the bus.

Back at the shop, Ross bounded downstairs as soon as he heard the jangle of the bell.

"Good. You're here."

"Why? What happened?" Olivia passed him the Americano she'd picked up for him on her way back and tried to ignore the touch of his fingers against hers as she did. "Did you sell *all* the books? Okay. You win."

He laughed. "A reporter from a local newspaper called in. He wants to interview you."

"Me?"

"Yes. You, Kavanagh! He's doing a feature on the Little Lane shops. Part of a commemorative history project or something. He left a card and asked you to give him a buzz or drop him an e-mail."

Olivia took the business card. "Cool. I hope you told him you're the Writer in Residence."

"Obviously. He wants to interview me for their Arts page. He didn't know there was a bestselling author in town. Good, eh?"

Sometimes Ross was so unintentionally charming and so humble about his work and his success that it took all Olivia's resolve not to throw her arms around him and tell him she was so pleased Iris had wandered into the shop that day and that he'd wandered in after her.

"Liv? Are you listening?"

"Sorry. What?"

He rolled his eyes. "You're worse than Iris with your day-dreaming. The reporter. He liked the window. He's sending a gardening expert over to have a look."

"A *gardening* expert?"

"Yep." He laughed and went back upstairs. "Olivia Kavanagh. Local celebrity and the darling of gardeners everywhere."

Olivia threw a packet of mints at his head and switched on the radio as she walked over to the window. Everyone who came to the shop was fascinated by it. One customer had left a coin for the fairies, for good luck. Others followed until the collection of copper coins in the window began to grow as quickly as the foliage.

The single green shoot that had first wrapped itself around the fairy door had grown into several green shoots, some of which had formed buds and flowers. Even when Olivia had moved the window box so that the original shoot was no longer attached, the flowers and plants inside the window still thrived. There was no logical explanation for how it continued to grow, but remembering the words from Frances's story, Olivia stopped trying to find a rational scientific explanation for it, allowing herself the far greater pleasure of simply being enchanted by it. A wild garden growing in the bookshop window was too magical to spoil with rationality. Olivia embraced it without question, because something told her that as long as the window bloomed, so would the bookshop—and so would she. She often left little gifts at the fairy door—flowers, leaves, feathers, shells, pebbles—things she found during her walks along the harbor and the cliff tops.

The fairies would bring a gift to her in return. She was sure of it.

THE COMMEMORATIVE ARTICLE on *Lána Beaga* was published a few days later, along with a piece in the Gardening pages about the bookshop window, which Ross teased Olivia about relentlessly. Word of mouth about this "magical" bookshop began to spread among the local community, rushing along the narrow streets like the white-tipped waves that rushed toward the shore. At the same time, the new Something Old website was officially launched. Slowly, new customers began to ring and e-mail to order books or to check if Olivia had something particular in stock. By the end of the week, a dozen new customers had visited the shop after seeing the feature in the newspaper. Collectors and curators of specialist libraries and museums sent inquiries. The wind had changed direction. Finally, good fortune was blowing Olivia's way.

The reporter had been especially interested in Pappy's antique book press and Olivia's bookbinding tools. At his suggestion, and despite being nervous, Olivia organized a bookbinding and restoration demonstration evening. The level of interest was far higher than she'd expected, and the shop buzzed with the sounds of conversation and questions and clinking teacups on saucers. Olivia was glad she'd kept Nana's china tea set. It seemed fitting that a small part of Nana and Pappy was there that night. It was such a success, Olivia decided to hold an Evening of Fairy Stories the following week.

And the good news kept coming. A call from the estate agent confirmed that an offer had been made on Bluebell Cottage, at the full asking price. The buyers were a couple with a young family who loved everything about it.

Henry and his nephew sat with Olivia to go over the details and the finances, assuring her the sale would cover Nana's nursing home bills for at least another year, and would also allow Olivia to clear the outstanding debts on the bookshop and leave sufficient in reserve to cover the rent for a couple of years. When the sale went through, she would effectively be back in the black. Her heart exhaled with a wave of relief. The shop had been given a temporary reprieve, and while her personal problems still loomed beneath the surface, the good news was enough to buoy her for the rest of the day.

Partly to distract herself from thinking about Jack and weddings, and partly to celebrate the sale of the cottage, Olivia insisted on taking Ross for a drink. A couple of phone calls settled arrangements for Iris to have a sleepover with her best friend, and when the shop closed for the day, Olivia and Ross made their way to the Abbey Tavern.

"Thank God for the school mums," Ross said as they walked down the hill. "They're forever offering to take Iris for the day or the weekend. She's a great kid, but it's hard. You know?"

Olivia didn't know, but she could imagine, having been a child of a single parent. "This is all most unlike me, by the way," she said as they strolled.

"What do you mean?"

"I never invite people for a drink without having planned it for weeks."

"So why did you?"

"I'm not sure. Good mood. Offer on the cottage. Fairies in the window . . ."

"Who needs a reason, anyway? We deserve it." Ross held the door for her as they stepped inside. "So, what will it be? A glass of white wine for 'the lady'? Tequila shots?"

Olivia elbowed him in the ribs. "I'll have a pint, you eejit."

They stayed longer than either of them had planned to. It was one of those unexpectedly perfect evenings when the con-

versation flowed as easily as the drinks, and neither Ross nor
Olivia wanted to bring the night to an end. Ross made Olivia
laugh. She made him drink gin and tonic. He talked about Iris
a lot, and Olivia talked about books. After the fourth drink,
she told him about her mother's accident, and he told her about
his wife's short battle with cancer, after which they shared a
packet of crisps and a moment of quiet reflection. Only once
did Olivia consider telling Ross about Jack, but she didn't want
to spoil the evening, so she pushed him from her mind and said
nothing.

After the fifth drink and a disastrous game of darts, Ross
told Olivia about the book he was working on, and she confessed to her secret dream of buying the empty cottage next to
Something Old and opening a shop for new books. Ross said
she should call it Something New, which made them laugh hys-
terically for twenty minutes as Olivia tried to scribble it drunk-
enly onto the back of her hand so she wouldn't forget.

After the sixth drink and a shot of tequila for the road, they
stumbled back to the bookshop, where Olivia lit a dozen tea
lights and Ross opened a bottle of Sancerre she'd been saving
for a special occasion, even though it was described as having
undertones of gooseberry, which made them both hysterical
again as Ross checked the mirror after every glass to see if his
lips were swelling up.

They sat together on the threadbare Turkish rug and drank
the wine by candlelight while Ross played bad renditions of
Van Morrison and Jeff Buckley on his guitar. By the time the
bottle was empty, there wasn't much about each other they
hadn't shared, their secrets and inhibitions falling from them
like autumn leaves. There was just one secret that Olivia held
tightly in her heart.

The end of the bottle came too soon, and Olivia kicked herself for not having another in the fridge. Their glasses sat empty on the floor beside them.

"I guess that's my cue to leave," Ross said as he stood up and pulled on his jacket.

Olivia scrambled to her feet. "Sorry there isn't anything else. I told you I hadn't planned this."

"Probably just as well. That second bottle is never a good idea."

"Yeah. Probably just as well."

"Probably."

For the first time since they'd met, Olivia let her guard drop. There was no filter, no joking, no wondering. She was simply in the moment, her cheeks warmed by the glow of alcohol and candlelight and something else she couldn't explain. She saw it in Ross's eyes too. An acceptance. A letting go.

She leaned forward first.

The kiss was inevitable and unexpected and different from any kiss Olivia had ever known. It was a kiss of a thousand days of sadness lost in a single moment of tender, searching connection. It was a kiss full of question and doubt and fear. It was a kiss of life, each of them breathing hope back into the other, and despite the many reasons she shouldn't, Olivia grasped the moment and held on to it as if it were the only thing that mattered.

Whether it would matter only for that night or for a lifetime, she didn't know. What she *did* know was that she had floundered for far too long, and in that brief, perfect moment as Ross Bailey, Writer, cupped her face so gently in his hands, she felt wildly, wonderfully alive in a way she had never felt before.

It was only later, as she lay alone in the dark, staring at the stars spinning in the clear skies through the skylight, that her conscience taunted her. She hadn't told Ross a lie, exactly, but by saying nothing about Jack or her impending wedding, she hadn't exactly told him the truth, either.

She remembered her mother had once told her that a lie told often enough can become its own truth. Over the past few weeks, she had distanced herself so entirely from her life in London that *it* had now become the lie. A lie she had been living for too long. Now, as she lay in a blissful fog of illicit kisses and alcohol, watching the unfathomable enormity of the heavens spinning above her, she found the answer she'd been searching for.

She could not marry Jack.

Twelve

Ireland. Present day.

*N*ana was wearing her blue coat, red hair licking around her face like flames. Olivia held so tightly to her hands that her fingers ached. Nana was all she had now.

The church fizzed with silence. It pressed in on her like the moody heat before a thunderstorm. Everything was magnified. Her footsteps echoed off the flagstones. Someone coughed. Someone sobbed. Someone sneezed. She could smell lilies and the other flowers Mammy liked. She didn't know what they were called, but the colors reminded her of rainbow drops and candy bracelets. She kept walking, her hand gripping Nana's as they reached the front pew.

She sat on the hard bench and blinked back her tears.

The casket was made of glossy wood; a garland of flowers trembled on top as the pallbearers set it down on a table with too-thin legs. What if it buckled under the weight of everyone's sadness? It was all she could think about as the priest said Mass. At one point, she gasped and wondered if her Mammy could hear her.

The hymns and the prayers from the congregation went on and on, droning like bees. She wanted to scream.

As everyone filed back out of the church, Nana hugged her and whispered that it was over now. But Olivia knew this sadness, this dark ache in her bones, would follow her everywhere.

It would never be over. Her mother's absence would be with her, part of her. Always.

LEADEN GRAY RAIN arrived as Olivia woke on the Monday morning, bringing with it the anniversary of the accident. Another year without her mother. Another day to be a little more aware of her absence.

She picked up the photograph from the windowsill. The one of herself as a baby, gazing adoringly at her mother. It was one of only a handful of photographs of the two of them together. So much love, captured by the click of a button.

She settled back against the pillows, watching the raindrops slipping down the windowpanes, imitating the tears that fell down her cheeks as she sang their favorite song. "'There are fairies at the bottom of our garden! / It's not so very, very far away; You pass the gardener's shed and you just keep straight ahead— / I do so hope they've really come to stay.'"

She lay in bed for an hour, thinking, remembering, and cringing after Friday night's unexpected developments with Ross. At least they'd had the good sense to stop with the kiss. Ross had walked home and Olivia had fallen asleep fully clothed. They hadn't contacted each other over the weekend. Their kiss remained the lovely, spontaneous thing that it was, and Olivia was glad it hadn't been spoiled by either of them overthinking it.

But her conscience pestered her.

Loose ends remained.

Truths must be told, despite the inevitable consequences.

WHEN ROSS ARRIVED for work, Olivia was relieved to discover that she was neither love-struck nor mortified in his presence. She was just pleased to see him, and Iris, who breezed into the shop like a daisy in yellow and white, her red wellies squeaking against the floorboards. A hassled-looking Ross skulked in behind her, saying he had a huge favor to ask.

Olivia raised her eyebrows and wished he would stop looking so casually handsome.

"Is there any chance you could mind Iris for a few hours? I've a meeting with my editor, and school's closed for teacher training or something. I forgot, because I'm an idiot. It's only for a few hours. I wouldn't ask, Liv, but I'm really stuck."

He couldn't have known that today of all days wasn't the best for Olivia, but she couldn't say no when the child was already standing beside her and besides, Olivia liked Iris. Perhaps it was that she saw a lot of herself in her: head always in a book, endless questions, the knowing sense that she was different now, forever changed beneath the gaping absence of her mother.

"It's fine. Go on. But you owe me."

He went to hug her but changed his mind, and what might have been a lovely embrace became an awkward sort of chest bump. "You're a star, Liv. Thanks a million."

Olivia turned to Iris. "You don't mind hanging out with me for a while, do you?"

"Nope. Can I watch cartoons?"

Olivia looked at Ross, who nodded his consent. "Go on then. I'll come up in a minute."

Iris followed Hemingway upstairs to the flat, leaving Ross, Olivia, and Friday night's kiss alone in the shop.

They both started to speak at the same time.

"Listen, about Friday night . . ."

"I hope you're not . . ."

Olivia waved Ross's explanation away. "It's fine. A drunken mistake. Don't worry."

He smiled shyly and said that was a relief. "I've been thinking about it all weekend, worrying that you might be expecting a marriage proposal! Thanks for being cool about it. I told you gooseberries were bad for me."

Olivia wished him good luck for his meeting and closed the door behind him. As the bell fell silent, she felt utterly deflated.

Why hadn't she told him about Jack? Why had she let it all get so complicated?

IRIS WAS A pleasant child, but she was still a child, and after an hour spent trying to keep her occupied while she got on with some work, Olivia realized she couldn't indefinitely keep a seven-year-old entertained in a small bookshop. To her relief, Henry appeared—as he was apt to do whenever she needed him—and offered to mind the shop while Olivia took Iris out for some fresh air. Monday mornings were always quiet, so Olivia agreed, grabbed her coat and bag, and left Henry to it. It was Iris's idea to go to the Fairy Tree in Marlay Park. It was a long journey, but she promised Olivia it would be worth it.

By the time they arrived, the rain had stopped, leaving sunshine and puddles for Iris to splash in as they walked through the park.

Iris pulled Olivia along, eager to get there as quickly as possible, leading her along a shaded path that wound through the trees until she took a left turn down an even narrower path, and there it was: an ancient-looking tree trunk in a clearing, with castle turrets on top. Around the side of the tree, spiral steps led up to tiny windows, dainty washing lines suspended between them. At the foot of the tree was a miniature door. Iris stood on tiptoe to peer into the windows before crouching down to knock on the door, whispering secret messages. Olivia's attention was drawn to the things pinned to the trunk.

"What's all this, Iris?"

"Those are the wishes. For the fairies."

Olivia took a closer look at the strange collection of trinkets tied to the tree: baby soothers, pictures, flowers, and messages. "I wish for Mammy to be better soon." "Dear fairies, please look after my baby brother what's in heaven." "Thank you for bringing the money for my tooth." Such simple, beautiful sentiments.

Olivia asked Iris if she wanted to make a wish.

"I already did," she said. "I always wish the same thing." She came closer to Olivia and whispered, "I wish for Mammy to come home." Olivia's heart broke as Iris grasped her hand. "But I don't think the fairies can hear me, because it never comes true."

Olivia bent down and placed her hands on Iris's cheeks. "Oh, sweetheart. Some wishes are just too big, even for the fairies."

"That's what Daddy says. He says Mammy is with the fairies now and that they're all looking after me, even if I can't see them."

"And I think he's right." She hugged Iris and wished she could take away some of her heartache. "You know, my mammy went to play with the fairies, too, when I was only young."

"Does she still look after you?"

"She does. All the time."

"I wish Daddy had a fairy to look after him. I think he's sad."

"Well, we'd better do something about that, then." Olivia rummaged around in her bag until she found an old envelope and a pen. "Here. Make a wish for your Daddy. If you leave it at the tree, the fairies will read it."

When Iris had written her note, Olivia helped her push it into a knot in the tree. Iris stood back to admire it before rushing off into the trees beside them.

"Where are you going?"

"To find a flower. You have to leave them a gift."

She returned with a handful of bluebells, which she laid at the door.

Olivia hoped with her whole heart that the fairies were listening and watching, because of all the little girls she had ever met, she couldn't think of one who was more deserving of her wish to come true than little Iris Bailey in her red wellies.

IT WAS ONLY when Olivia was locking up the shop for the day that she noticed a package on the desk. It was addressed to Olivia Kavanagh, Something Old, Little Lane, Howth, County Dublin. It must have arrived while Henry was minding the shop and he'd forgotten to mention it to her.

She opened the padded envelope and removed an early edition of *Peter Pan in Kensington Gardens*. Inside the frontispiece was an inscription. "For Olivia. 'And that was the beginning of fairies.'"

There was no signature. No date. No note.

There never was.

A book had arrived on every anniversary of her mother's death, secretly, quietly, without fuss or flourish. Sometimes it was left on the bottom of the bed. Sometimes she would find it in her schoolbag. Sometimes it was sitting on the stairs, and always there was a simple inscription to her inside, but never a note saying whom it was from. She knew they were from Pappy, although he never admitted it. He admired the books when she showed them to him, joining in the charade of the mystery. And yet this couldn't possibly have come from him. So who was it from?

The rain returned during the evening, casting everything into an autumnal gloom. Glad to be alone after she'd locked up, Olivia kicked off her shoes and took the Peter Pan book upstairs to the flat, where Hemingway had made himself at home on the foot of the bed. She wriggled beneath the duvet and started to read.

It was nearly dawn when she reached the final pages: "Jane is now a common grown-up, with a daughter called Margaret. . . . When Margaret grows up she will have a daughter, who is to be Peter's mother in turn; and thus it will go on. . . ."

Olivia thought about the family photographs lined up on the mantelpiece in Bluebell Cottage, the memories safely stored away behind the glass frames: great-grandma Ellen on the doorstep of the cottage in the woods with a baby in her arms; Nana Martha with her baby daughter in her arms; the photograph of her own mother cradling her in her arms, their whole uncertain life stretching out before them like the sea in the background. Four generations of women, each of their stories continuing through each other. Four generations of women, of which Olivia was currently the last—and always would be.

The reality of it all hit her hard.

Finally, she let go of the anguish she'd carried since reading the letter from the consultant. She let go of all the hours spent in consulting rooms being prodded and poked, and all the hours spent lying awake at night, hoping for a different answer than the one she received. It seemed especially unfair that after losing her own mother in such traumatic circumstances, she was now unable to become a mother herself.

Silently, the tears came. One by one, they slipped onto the pillow, each taking away part of a future she'd always imagined—assumed—would be hers. She would have been a good mother, in honor of her own. She would have created special memories for her children to collect and keep in buckets of their own. She would have done the best she could.

As her tears subsided, she lay back against the pillows and read the final words of the book. "Of course in the end Wendy let them fly away together. Our last glimpse of her shows her at the window, watching them receding into the sky until they were as small as stars."

That night, in her dreams, she sat on the harbor wall, legs cool against the concrete, cheeks reddened by the sun, heart warmed by the shape of her mammy beside her.

And while she slept, a note from Henry sat unseen where it had fallen beneath the desk downstairs.

A note saying that someone had called in earlier, looking for her.

Someone called Jack.

Thirteen

Ireland. Present day.

Olivia was processing new orders from the website when the shop bell jangled the next morning. She glanced up, expecting to see Henry or a customer. What she saw took her breath away.

"Jack?" The inflection in her voice carried a dozen questions she couldn't articulate.

The tightness in her chest constricted her breath, her thoughts, her words, while her hands trembled against the desk as she tried to steady herself and process what was happening: Jack was here. In Ireland. In the bookshop.

"But . . . I thought you were overseas," she added. "What are you doing *here*?"

He closed the door behind him and stood in the middle of the shop, legs slightly apart, hands in his chinos pockets. His business stance.

"I'm *here* to take *you* back to London. It's been six weeks, Olivia. It's ridiculous. People are starting to talk." He tilted his head to one side and frowned. "What did you do to your hair?"

She touched her hand self-consciously to her neck. "I cut it."

"I can see that. You look weird."

She was used to his critical views on her appearance. His words fell off her now like raindrops. "So do you, Jack. You look . . . different."

He looked terrible. Dark shadows lurked in the hollows beneath his eyes, stubble peppered his chin, and his hair was unusually tousled. Everything about him was wrong, but what struck Olivia most was how wrong it was that he was standing in her shop, how wrong it was that he had invaded this happy little world she'd created from nothing, and how wrong it was that when she looked at the man she was supposed to love more than any other, it was like looking at a stranger, and her heart felt numb.

"So, this is the famous bookshop," he continued, his eyes scanning the shelves and the teetering piles of books leaning against the edge of the desk. "This is it? *This* is what's been keeping you here?"

There was an edge to his voice that Olivia didn't like, a look in his eye she'd seen when business deals didn't go his way. It wasn't anger. It was something deeper than that. A seething dissatisfaction at not getting his own way.

Olivia opened her mouth to speak, but didn't have the words or the energy to defend herself or the shop, or to explain—again—why she'd needed to stay. She'd repeated herself so often whenever they had spoken over the past few weeks, but Jack couldn't understand her emotional attachment to the shop. It was a business. There was no place for emotion as far as he was concerned.

"What are you trying to prove, Olivia? Because, really, a secondhand bookshop in a poky little Irish town isn't exactly going to change the world."

"Perhaps I'm not going to change the world, but I can change my small part of it."

Jack smiled in reply. Or was it a sneer? It was hard to tell the difference sometimes.

Olivia caught a whiff of alcohol as he swayed on the spot. "Have you been drinking?"

He laughed. A loud, false laugh. The one he used in business dinners when he was trying to weasel his way into the favor of someone he secretly loathed. He sauntered toward her, the smell of brandy unmistakable as he leaned forward, placing his hands on the desk. "When were you going to tell me, Olivia?"

"Tell you what?" Her mouth was paper-dry. Her hands clammy.

He slid an envelope across the desk.

She recognized the crest of the consultant's practice on the front. Her heart thumped double-time in her chest as Jack perched on the edge of the desk, a little too close. Instinctively, she leaned back. "Where did you find that?"

"I *found* it in your nightstand when I was looking for your birth certificate for the church." He stared at her. Cold, glassy eyes that she had once fallen for because they had glittered with confidence and she'd been too easily impressed. "You do remember we're supposed to be getting married in seven weeks?"

She reached for the letter, but he snatched it away. Tears pricked her eyes. She refused to let them fall.

"Jack, we can't talk about this now. Not here." She glanced over his shoulder, anxious about customers coming in and finding them in the middle of a domestic.

"Why not? When *can* we talk about it, then, Olivia?" The crack in his voice was unexpected. Was it emotion? Was Jack Oliver showing his feelings? "Where, then, if not here and now?

At the top of the aisle? On our honeymoon? When exactly *were* you planning to tell me I can never be a father? Where did you think it was going to be convenient for me to find out my wife is infertile?"

His words hit Olivia like a punch in the stomach. Yes, there was emotion in his voice, but it was all for himself. There was no compassion for her. No concern. No offer to help her cope with this devastating news. It was the reaction she'd been dreading, only worse, because it was happening here, in the one place she had always felt safe and sheltered and protected; the place he had belittled and insulted. She could almost feel the books shrink back on their shelves, unwilling spectators to the drama unfolding before them.

Olivia glanced at the photograph of Frances and the fairies on the desk, drawing strength from the memory it stirred of her mother, and her Nana and great-grandma Ellen. Strong, determined women.

She took a deep breath, stood up, and walked around the desk. "I don't know what you want me to say, Jack. I only found out a few weeks before Pappy died. I'm still trying to come to terms with it myself. I didn't know *how* to tell you."

"But it changes everything, Olivia." He waved the letter frantically in the space between them. "*Everything.*"

"Does it?"

"Of course! It changes *you*. It changes our future. You don't just put something like this in a drawer and forget about it."

The anger built inside her. "*Forget* about it? Are you serious? Do you really think I could ever forget something like that? I've thought about it every day. Every. Single. Day. This might affect *our* future, Jack, but it's *my* body. The truth of that letter will be with me forever. I'll *never* be able to forget it."

"I don't know what to say to you, Olivia. First you disappear to Ireland and ignore everything to do with the wedding, and now this? If you're prepared to keep this a secret, how can I trust you?" He threw his hands in the air in exasperation and walked toward the door. When he turned, Olivia saw resentment in his eyes. "Clearly you're not the person I thought you were."

Did he mean because she had kept the letter a secret, or because she couldn't have children? The fact that she wasn't sure what he meant told her everything she needed to know.

A breeze rattled the letterbox. A rush of air. A reminder. *"You don't need anybody's permission to live the life you desire, Olivia. You need only the permission of your heart."*

Her heart beat a steady, determined rhythm. "Or maybe I'm just not the perfect cutout wife you want me to be? How very inconvenient of me to end up infertile." Jack studied her for a moment, clearly surprised by her resolve. She felt nothing as she stared back at him.

"I'm going back on a flight at seven," he said. "I've booked you a seat, and I've made an appointment with a fertility expert next week."

Olivia's mind was reeling. "You've done what?"

"I know people, Olivia. We can get a second opinion and get you fixed."

It was so typical of Jack. So absolutely typical of him to believe he could fix things with his influence and contacts.

Olivia was furious. "I don't need *your* people, Jack. I have my own, and I've already had a second opinion. And a third. It is what it is. Nothing will change it. '*Get me fixed*'? This isn't a business deal you can throw more money at and salvage at the eleventh hour. This is real life, Jack, with real people and real feelings." She opened the door. "I'm not sure what you thought you would gain by coming here and arranging my life, but I think you should go."

Jack glanced at her hand on the door handle. Whether he noticed the absence of her engagement ring or not, he didn't say anything.

"The flight departs at seven." He placed a boarding pass on a shelf beside Olivia. "If you're not there, I'll assume you've decided there are better things for you here. It's your decision, Olivia."

Yes. Yes, it was.

She closed the door behind him, leaning back against it to take a moment to catch her breath and to steady the trembling in her hands. Whatever questions she'd had, Jack had just answered them all for her.

It was only when she heard the scrape of a chair upstairs that she remembered Ross. He must have heard everything. The look on his face as he walked downstairs made Olivia feel small and foolish.

"Ross, I'm so sorry. I . . ."

He waved her apology away. "I'm putting the kettle on. Do you want one?"

"Please."

"I think we might both need two sugars."

She smiled a weak smile. "Will you let me explain?"

He glanced over his shoulder. "You can if you want, but I think Jack-Ass there just did all the explaining for you."

SHE DID WHAT she always did when she needed to think. She climbed.

It was a warm afternoon, the breeze unusually calm even at

the top of Howth Head, just enough to ruffle the gorse slightly, and yet in Olivia's heart, a tempest raged.

If things were right between her and Jack, she would have told him about her appointments, let alone the letter. He would have been the first person to confide in, not the last. He'd accused her of hiding the truth from him, but there were far greater truths she'd hidden from herself: That this marriage could never work, that things would never get better, that she would never be happy simply being content.

She thought about something Ross had said when she'd told him everything over a pot of sweet tea. "You have to be passionate about the things you put in your life: the music you listen to, the food you eat, the friends you hang out with, even the bloody towels you hang in the guest bathroom. It's about choice, Olivia. It is always about choice."

And her choice came down to this: Did she want to follow convention and settle for the security of a marriage that might work if she made herself believe it could, or did she want to explore a new life in Ireland, with nothing but herself and an old bookshop for company?

Did she want to follow a well-worn trail, or did she want to become a mapmaker?

JACK'S FACE LIT up when he saw her walk into the check-in area.

"I knew you'd see sense." He hugged her and patted her on the back as if she was a client. "You've done the right thing, Olivia. We'll get you sorted out and everything will be fine."

As her cheek pressed against the lapel of his blazer, she closed her eyes. She had never felt more certain about anything as she pulled back from him and gave him her boarding pass.

"I'm not coming with you, Jack."

"What? Of course you are. Don't be silly."

She shook her head. "You can't *fix* me, Jack. And *I* can't fix *us*."

His face was as pale as milk. He wasn't used to losing, to not getting his own way. Olivia wasn't sure what she felt as she looked at him. Pity? Perhaps a slight tinge of regret that it had come to this. But love? No.

"I'll contact the wedding planner. I'll let people know . . ." She looked at him. She even reached for his hand, but he drew his back. "I'm sorry, Jack, but it's the right thing. For both of us."

Surrounded by people returning from journeys and setting out on new ones, Olivia turned away from a future she had never truly believed in and walked out into a balmy evening, one step at a time, toward a new future.

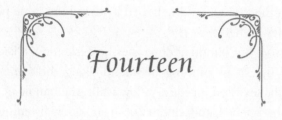

Fourteen

Ireland. Present day.

The Evening of Fairy Stories came around quickly. Olivia held Nana's hand as she sat beside her in the taxi on the way from the nursing home and hoped she'd done the right thing in bringing her. It was hard to know how she would react, but Olivia wanted Nana to see the bookshop full of happy readers and book enthusiasts, just as it had been in its heyday. Nana sat quietly, gazing out of the taxi window like a child caught up in the thrill of a day out. The late afternoon sun made ripe peaches of her cheeks and set life dancing in her eyes.

At the bottom of Little Lane, Olivia helped Nana out of the taxi and looped her arm through hers for support as they picked their way slowly over the cobbles toward Something Old.

Nana paused in front of the old black door, running her hand gently across the grain, as if feeling the contours of a familiar face. "Could do with a lick of paint," she said. "Tell him, will you? When you see him. To give the door a lick of paint."

Olivia said she would and pushed the door open.

She remembered how the smell of the shop had struck her

that May morning when she'd first learned it belonged to her: pipe tobacco and leather. She wondered if Nana recognized the smell in the same way. She hoped it stirred the same poignant memories for her if she did.

Nana set her handbag down on the desk and walked slowly around the shop, running her hand along the spines of the books, the textured mustard-yellow walls, the handle of Pappy's pipe. She opened and closed the front door, listening to the jingle-jangle of the bell as Hemingway wound around her legs. He remembered Nana, even if she didn't remember him. Olivia followed at a distance, giving Nana the space she needed as she walked to Pappy's chair, resting her palms against the worn faux-velvet fabric. She chuckled and nodded to herself. Olivia hoped she remembered. She hoped, with all her heart, that Nana could feel him here, as she did.

Walking back to the desk, Nana picked up the silver photo frame, running her fingers across the glass.

"There was another photograph," she said. "Frances took it when she and Elsie had those cameras."

"There were five photographs in total, Nana." She took Conan Doyle's *Strand Magazine* articles from the old briefcase. "The first article printed the first two photographs and two more photographs were printed in the second article a few months later." Olivia took the fifth photograph from the desk drawer. "And I found this in a children's book called *Princess Mary's Gift Book*. It is signed to Ellen from Frances. '*The fifth photograph*.'"

Nana peered at the photographs and the yellowing pages. Olivia recognized the look, as half-formed memories flickered across Nana's face, like butterflies she couldn't catch. "No. Not these," she said. "Another one. Fairies at a stream. A waterfall."

Not wanting to cause any upset, Olivia said she would look for it and settled Nana into Pappy's chair with a pot of tea and a plate of biscuits while she put the finishing touches to the window display.

When Henry arrived, he offered to sit with Nana to keep her company while Olivia finished setting up. Nana looked so at home in the bookshop, as if she had stopped fighting with herself and her memories and was happy just to be there. Olivia smiled as she noticed how Nana brightened around Henry, charmed by his attentiveness as he made sure she was warm enough and comfortable enough and whether she needed a hot drop of tea. He listened with such patience to Nana's muddled stories and when she grew tired they sat quietly together, observing what was going on around them.

By seven, the shop was full. By half past, people were still arriving. Chairs were borrowed from the other shops on the lane, and impromptu seats were found on windowsills and steps and other people's knees. Children sat cross-legged on the floor as Olivia, Ross, and Henry each read a short extract from different fairy stories and poems. Ross surprised them all by reading something he had written called *The Fairy's Tale*, which had everyone spellbound and earned him the longest and loudest applause of the evening.

At the end of the readings, Olivia encouraged everyone to stay and browse and buy as many books as they could carry home. Lots of people were interested in the Cottingley articles and the photographs Olivia had displayed around the shop. She was surprised to hear herself talking so knowledgeably about it, drawing on everything she'd read in Frances's memoir and the newspaper articles and Conan Doyle's book *The Coming of the Fairies*, which one customer took a particular interest in.

"His involvement in the Cottingley affair is fascinating," he said, turning the book over in his hands.

"Do you know much about it?" Olivia asked.

"A little. It's generally believed that his interest in spirituality and fairy life came about in the same way as many other people's did at that time, as a result of the war. People wanted—needed—to believe their loved ones lived on. Conan Doyle lost his son in the war and never got over it. He was involved in writing war propaganda, and held himself partly responsible for his son's death, and for the deaths of so many young men who volunteered. They didn't realize the extent of the horrors awaiting them at the Front because the papers withheld the worst details." He studied the book again. "What are you asking for it?"

Olivia was glad she'd looked up the value. "With the two inscriptions and in such excellent condition, it would be worth around five hundred euros to the right buyer."

"And are you selling?"

She hesitated. "I'm not sure. It's part of a private collection. It isn't currently listed in the catalog."

"I'd be very interested if it was."

Olivia took his details and said she would let him know.

AT THE END of the evening, Olivia took Nana back to St. Bridget's. Far from finding it upsetting, she had enjoyed the evening and Olivia was pleased she'd taken her. She only wished Pappy could have been there to see the shop so alive. He would have been so proud.

At St. Bridget's, the nurses made a great fuss over Nana, asking her all about her day out. Olivia waited until Nana was settled in bed before she kissed her good-bye. She hated to leave her, always wondering if it would be the last time. She hugged her as tightly as she dared and told her she loved her, but Nana had already dozed off and didn't hear.

When Olivia returned to the shop, she found a note on the desk from Ross to say well done on a fantastic night and that he'd sold loads more books after she'd left (ha ha). She loved that he'd written her a note. She loved that he'd signed it "Ross Bailey, Writer." She especially loved the illustration of a fairy he'd added at the bottom. It looked a lot like her and whether coincidence or intentional, she loved that something so simple could make her smile from her eyes to her toes.

She spent a little while reading the wishes the children had left for the fairies in the window, where the yellow cinquefoil and white harebells bloomed and green shoots were entwined around the window frame. Taking a piece of paper from her notebook, she wrote her own wish, adding it to the others beside the fairy door.

Upstairs, in the flat, she searched in the boxes from Bluebell Cottage and looked through the family albums, but couldn't find anything that resembled the additional fairy photograph Nana had described.

Despite being physically exhausted, Olivia couldn't sleep. She began packing for her trip to England, more eager than ever to get to Cottingley and more reluctant than ever to go back to the apartment in London to pick up a few things. Even though, in one of their few curt e-mail exchanges since his brief visit, Jack had told Olivia he would be away on a business trip, it would still be difficult to be back there. She'd already started the tricky business of canceling the wedding—endless apologies from her, endless tears from shocked family and friends. Their understanding and condolences were tough to take since she was the one causing all the upset, but she reminded herself constantly that an unhappy marriage would have been far tougher and would have lasted far longer. As Henry had told her when she'd confided in him about the wonderful mess she'd made of everything, this, too, would pass.

To take her mind off things, she lit a candle and set the radio playing quietly in the background. With Hemingway purring at her feet, she reached for Frances's manuscript, happy to escape from real life for a while and lose herself among the forgotten pages of someone else's story . . .

NOTES ON A FAIRY TALE
Cottingley, Yorkshire. August 1920.

I would travel to Cottingley with our family friends, the Bainses, who were returning to Bradford after holidaying in Scarborough.

Mummy said her good-byes to me amid the bustle and noise on the station platform. I promised to behave for Aunt Polly and Uncle Arthur and to try my best to take more photographs of the fairies so that the men in London would be pleased.

"Do try, Frances," she urged, dabbing at my cheek with a moist handkerchief to wipe away a smut of smoke. "I know how daft you and Elsie can get when you're together." She gripped my shoulders and lowered her voice as she looked me straight in the eye. "This isn't a holiday. You're to remember why you're going." I nodded. "And when you're done, we can put the whole business behind us."

I'd always trusted those dolphin-gray eyes. I hoped she was right.

The slamming of the carriage doors and a great hiss of steam signaled that it was time to go. I stepped into the carriage as the stationmaster blew his whistle, the shrill cry following me inside the compartment, prodding and poking at my conscience. *Tell her!* it shrieked. *Tell her!* I pressed my glove to the window as Mummy blew a kiss and the pistons began to turn, and I knew it was too late. With a jolt and a judder, the great locomotive groaned along the tracks until I couldn't see Mummy anymore and the soot-blackened walls of the station gave way to green countryside as the confession I had almost made faded into the

distance, smothered by the great clouds of smoke streaming from the funnel.

The locomotive ate up the miles between Scarborough
and Bingley, whistling intermittently to the village children who ran through the fields to wave at the passengers. I held the new camera on my lap and wondered why
it was that life kept pulling me in such strange directions;
why it was that only a few years ago I'd been happily
playing on Cape Town's beaches, all thoughts of fairies
confined to the pages of my books, and now fairies were
all I ever thought about. I closed my eyes and pretended
to sleep so that Mrs. Bains couldn't interrogate me about
my visit to Cottingley, or the new Cameo camera I was
taking with me.

Despite my apprehension, I couldn't deny the prickle of
excitement when I stepped onto the platform at Bingley
station, nor could I resist the smile that returned to my
lips as I watched the familiar view through the motorcar
window: the gorse and heather, the sweeping views, the
rolling hills and steep valleys, the soaring chimney stacks
from the distant mills and factories. It was like looking
at old friends, and when Uncle Arthur pulled up outside
Number 31, it was like coming home.

Elsie was waiting at the gate. She was nineteen now,
more woman than girl. I felt shy in her company, unsure of
her full bosom and the elegant limbs she draped across the
furniture like silk fabric. Elsie wasn't just older. She was a
different shape. A different person altogether.

Aunt Polly was all smiles and lavender water, exactly as
I remembered her. "Eee, Frances Griffiths. You get taller

every time I see you. Must be all that sea air, eh? Come into the front room, love. Kettle's on."

The subject of fairies was fiercely avoided as we stuck to more comfortable topics of conversation: How was Scarborough? How was Annie? How was my father settling into his new appointment as a regimental sergeant major in Catterick? How was school? All this from Aunt Polly, whose questions poured out of her without end, much like the cups of strong tea she poured from the cracked pot. It was almost a relief when she finally acknowledged the elephant in the room.

"Quite a turnup for the books, this business with the photographs, isn't it, Frances? Who'd have thought they would be considered so interesting? Gentlemen from London visiting the likes of us!"

I did my best to smile and agree that it was quite something, but in my heart I felt deflated about the whole episode. I couldn't relax until Aunt Polly left Elsie and me alone and we took a walk down to the beck where the waterfall tumbled gently over the shale rock, and the water— patterned with the dappled shade from the trees—gurgled at our feet as we sat on the bank beside the mossy mound where we'd taken the first photograph. I still loved it there, but something had changed. I was no longer a nine-year-old girl full of curiosity and mischief. I was a twelve-year-old girl full of guilt and worry.

"It all seems silly now, doesn't it?" I said as I pressed my fingers into the cool moss. "Don't you wish we'd admitted the photograph was a prank that first evening? I do."

"We did what we did, Frances," Elsie said. "There's no

use crying over spilled milk." She picked petals from a pink flower, muttering "He loves me, he loves me not" to herself. "I'm just fed up with all these men from London and experts from Kodak. Some experts!"

She threw pebbles into the stream, and we watched the ripples spread out in ever-increasing circles. Like the interest in our photographs, they were unstoppable, spreading wider and further, seemingly without end.

"What did you think of Mr. Gardner?" Elsie asked.

I shrugged. "He was nice enough, I suppose. A bit brown. Everything he wore was a shade of brown."

Elsie laughed. Her voice was a tone deeper than I remembered it. "I've two cutouts prepared," she said, reading my thoughts. "One each. A fairy handing me a harebell. Another one of a flying fairy for you. A fairy in midair! That'll get those *experts* in London talking!"

I dipped my toes into the water, relishing the cool memory of hot summer days when the real beck fairies had appeared in such abundance. It was a long time since I'd last seen them and I wasn't even sure I *could* see them anymore. Although I was older and should probably have grown out of such things, part of me missed them.

"What's got you so narky, then?" Elsie asked as she passed me a posy of bindweed she'd tied with a stalk of grass. "You've hardly said two words since you got here."

Elsie always knew when I was in a bad mood.

"I'm not sure it's right to keep telling lies, Elsie. Everyone's taking it too seriously now. And what about the article Conan Doyle's writing for the magazine? What if lots of people read it? Then *they'll* believe the photographs are real too."

Elsie had already resigned herself to the fact that we had to see it through. "I don't see what else we can do, Frances. Conan Doyle and Gardner already think the first photographs are real. We'll only get into more trouble if we tell the truth now, especially after all their meetings with experts and whatnot. Best to go along with it. Give them a few more photographs to study and write about, and that'll be the end of it."

I hoped she was right.

"I heard Daddy telling Mummy that it's too late for us to tell the truth now anyway, even if it *was* a joke," Elsie continued. "He says we can't be making the likes of Conan Doyle look like a fool. Not with him being so well respected. He says we'd be the laughingstock of England, never mind Cottingley, or the West Riding." She ran her fingers through her curls. "Let's do what they ask, and in a couple of months, it'll all be forgotten about. You wait and see."

"Do you really think so?"

Elsie threw another pebble into the stream before turning to look at me, her blue eyes full of intent. "I'm sure of it. People have more important things to be worrying about than a few photographs taken by some girls in Yorkshire. And Conan Doyle won't use our real names in his article. I'm to be called Iris Carpenter, on account of me being so tall, like the flowers, and you'll be Alice Carpenter, after Alice in Wonderland. We're to live in a made-up village called Dalesby. Nobody will ever know it was us."

Like a dandelion seed caught on the wind, our joke had already traveled much farther than we'd ever intended. I knew how dandelions liked to spread and grow, how they stubbornly grew back no matter how many times you pulled them up. Mrs. Hogan was right. *"Small villages can't keep secrets."* They would always escape in the end.

Elsie stood up and brushed grass from her skirt. "At least we were clever enough to hide the evidence. Those torn-up cutouts will be out in the Irish Sea by now. Or the English Channel. I don't know which direction the Aire flows."

I didn't know, either. Whichever direction it was, I hoped those scraps of paper were at the bottom of the sea. Lost forever.

As we walked back to the house, I wished more than ever that I'd held my tongue when Mummy was vexed with me that summer afternoon in the scullery. I wished I'd never told anyone about the beck fairies and I wished I was back in Scarborough, cycling along the laneways with Mary or swimming in the sea.

But wishes, like fairies, are fickle things. They rarely do what you want them to do.

NOTES ON A FAIRY TALE
Cottingley, Yorkshire. August 1920.

The weather was dreadful for the first week of my visit. Aunt Polly groused about the incessant rain and mithered at the pair of us for getting under her feet. She had insisted Elsie stay off work until some satisfactory photographs were taken.

"Maybe you should go out and try," she said, sighing at the rain-spattered window and polishing the brass for the second time that week.

"The fairies won't come in such awful weather," I explained. "And besides, we don't want to get water into the cameras and damage them." It was, after all, the truth.

Aunt Polly said fairies were fussy little beggars and we would have to hope for better weather, then, wouldn't we.

As the rain spilled down outside and the cameras and glass plates sat idle on the table in the front room, Elsie and I occupied ourselves by sketching and reading and taking trips to the pictures in Shipley, like we had before the end of the war. In the evenings, we wound our hair into rags to make curls when we woke the next morning. We fell easily back into our familiar routines, and I was happy to be with Elsie again. Even though she was distracted at times and talked a lot about the young men she knew, she still made me laugh with her stories and wicked sense of humor.

After the first week, I began to feel restless and homesick for Scarborough. Aunt Polly wasn't her usual cheery self, either. She was irritable and short-tempered, snapping at Uncle Arthur at the slightest provocation. He retreated to the safety of the Briggs's manor and his beloved motorcars, happy to leave us to it. Aunt Polly wrote to Mr. Gardner in London to explain that the rain was preventing us from going outside, but that we would try as soon as there was a break in the weather.

I missed Mummy and Daddy and Scarborough's sea breezes and mooched about the house, complaining of being bored. Aunt Polly said she wished *she* was bored and found endless chores for me to do, such as running errands into the village, where I bumped into Mavis Clarke. She had doubled in size and was even more unpleasant than I remembered. Now thirteen, her sharp tongue had grown sharper, her mocking taunts even crueler. She goaded me with vague remarks about what Elsie and I had been up to at the beck that summer before the end of the war. Elsie told me to ignore her, but I couldn't. Mavis Clarke unsettled me. As the days dragged on, everything about Cottingley began to unsettle me.

In another attempt to pass the time, I read some of Aunt Polly's books about the Theosophist Society, the afterlife, spiritualism, and the occult. The ideas they contained had intrigued me when I'd first found them during the years I'd lived at Number 31, but they troubled me now, disturbing my sleep as I tossed and turned, my thoughts lingering in the mysterious parlor room séances described between the pages. I was glad when my more familiar dreams returned, taking me back to the stream where the girl with red hair was waiting for me and led me to a woodland cottage, where she lay a posy of wildflowers on the doorstep—ragwort and bindweed and campion—singing a song of old Ireland and the Little People before she sat on the step and wept, tears spilling onto her hands with a gentle pitter-patter . . .

I woke to rain-speckled windows and a murky mist. Not a day for photographing fairies.

With nothing much else to do, I put on my wellingtons and mackintosh and took a walk around the fields toward Mrs. Hogan's cottage. I'd promised to visit whenever I was back and looked forward to seeing my old teacher again.

The cottage was concealed even more by bushes and trees that had grown lush and dense in the year I'd been away. Where the small black leather boots used to sit on the doorstep, a pair of stone boots now stood in their place, flowers growing out of the holes in the top, like plant pots. A perfect circle of toadstools still grew beneath the elder tree in the garden, the same sense of something I'd forgotten to do still whispered through the canopy of leaves above.

I knocked tentatively at the door, unsure whether Mrs. Hogan would remember me. I needn't have worried. She was delighted to see me.

"Frances Griffiths! Well, would you look at you! So tall and pretty. Come in! Come in!"

The cottage was exactly the same inside. I remembered the tapestries and samplers on the walls, the array of paintings on the dresser. A couple of new ones had been added. A posy of wildflowers sat in a milk jug on the table: ragwort and bindweed and campion. I couldn't stop staring at them. They were the same flowers from my dream.

A baby's cry interrupted my thoughts.

"And we have a new addition to the family, Frances!" Mrs. Hogan excused herself as she rushed from the kitchen, returning a moment later with a tiny bundle swaddled in her arms. "Meet our beautiful Martha."

The baby was as pink and as pretty as the rambling roses that grew around the cottage door, her hands tiny grasping fists. I peered into the blankets to admire her and let her grip my finger.

"She's our special gift," Mrs. Hogan said, beaming as she set baby Martha into her cradle. "I still can't believe she's ours to keep." The catch in her voice betrayed her anguish, and when she continued, she spoke as if to herself. "We'll never forget our beautiful little Aisling. I may only carry one child in my arms, but I will always carry two children in my heart." She looked up then and smiled, as if she had forgotten I was there.

For the want of anything else to say, I told Mrs. Hogan I liked the name Aisling. "It's very pretty."

"Thank you," she replied. "In Gaelic it means *vision*, or *dream*. And Martha was the name of a nurse who cared for my husband when he was badly injured during the war. He promised to call any future daughter after her if she made sure he recovered."

While baby Martha cooed beside me, Mrs. Hogan made tea and asked me about my new home and school in Scarborough. Her face had lost the deep lines of worry that had been there before. She looked younger, despite the time that had passed since I'd seen her.

We chatted for half an hour or so before the door opened and a handsome man walked in.

"What's this? Visitors?" He winked at me and washed his hands at the stone sink. "Frances, isn't it?" I nodded and thought it nice of him to remember me after only meeting me briefly once, not long after he'd been demobbed. "Ellen . . . Mrs. Hogan still talks about you," he continued. "Best pupil ever, she says."

I blushed.

Mrs. Hogan laughed and said it was the truth and that the classroom was quiet without my questions. "Some people don't wonder enough, Frances. Isn't that right?"

I agreed and said I'd best be getting home before the next downpour.

"I suppose you and Elsie will be busy with your cameras again," Mrs. Hogan said as I put my coat on. "I saw Elsie recently, taking pictures at the beck. It's a lovely hobby to have."

I couldn't think of anything to say and mumbled a good-bye as she opened the door. As I stepped outside, my attention was caught by a painting in an oval frame on the windowsill. A little girl with flame-red hair, a posy of wild-flowers in her hands.

I knew her.

She was the girl from my dreams. The girl who always gave me a flower. *"For Mammy."*

Mrs. Hogan noticed me staring at the painting and picked it up. "It's a favorite of mine. That's our daughter. Aisling." Her voice cracked with emotion.

"It's a lovely painting," I said. "She was very pretty."

Was.

The word hung heavy in the air. An acknowledgment that Aisling lived in the past now. I wanted to take it back. I wanted to shout out, "Is! *I meant* is *very pretty.*" My mistake was so awful I practically ran out of the door, muttering a thank-you for the tea and nearly tripping over the stone boots on the step that Mrs. Hogan explained had been carved by her husband, to replace the leather ones. "More permanent," she'd said.

"Come and see us again before you go back to Scarborough," Mrs. Hogan called after me.

I called back that I would.

I thought about the painting of the red-haired girl all the way home and all through tea and all that evening in the front room as the rain danced against the windows. I thought about her as I fell asleep. Finally, I understood who the flowers in my dreams were for. They were for Mrs. Hogan. The little girl's Mammy was Ellen Hogan, the kind, gentle woman whose heart had been silently breaking for the last four years, and in my dreams, my heart broke for them both.

By Thursday of the second week, the weather finally improved, and the early morning mists cleared to bright sunshine. Perfect weather for fairy hunting.

Elsie teased the curls in my hair before tying my favorite violet ribbons into them. "If half of England is going to see us, we might as well look our best."

She took the cutouts and hat pins from the biscuit tin beneath the bed. I didn't like to say much after the effort she'd gone to, but they looked rushed, not as detailed or delicate as the first ones. The sight of them made me sick to my stomach. Were we really going to do this again?

After dinner, Aunt Polly shooed us out of the house. "I'm off to Bradford to have tea with our Clara. I'll leave you to it." She stood at the cellar door, arms folded, as we trudged miserably off down the garden, our wellington boots squelching over the rain-soaked grass. "Mind those cameras and make sure you take some good photographs," she called after us.

Her words crept along my spine, like guilty fingers pushing me on.

We were careful with our new cameras, a gift from Conan Doyle. Uncle Arthur said they were much more sophisticated machines than his Midg and that the lenses alone cost £20 each and we should be very careful with them.

In the top field where we'd taken the photo of Elsie and the gnome, we set up a picture of Elsie with the fairy handing her a harebell. As I peered through the viewfinder, I could hardly believe that anyone with sense or intelligence could think these cutout fairies real. This one looked especially stiff and flat, its feet in a balletic second position.

After I'd clicked the shutter, we gathered everything up and returned to my favorite spot at the willow tree to set up the next photo. Elsie used a hat pin to stick the cutout of the "leaping fairy," as she called it, into the branch of the tree. After a short discussion, we agreed that a two-second exposure would be enough.

"Stand in front of it, with the side of your face turned to me, and look straight at the fairy," Elsie said. "It'll seem as though she's jumping toward you."

I followed Elsie's instructions but had no real enthusiasm for it. Elsie had to remind me to look enchanted more than once as she measured the distance and set the speed for the shutter, allowing a longer exposure time due to the dim lighting with the leaves and bushes around us. I moved my head slightly as Elsie pressed the shutter. I hoped it wouldn't spoil the plate. We stuck the hat pins into the ground and threw the torn-up cutouts into the stream, as before.

"That's it, then," Elsie said as we clambered up the bank. "We never have to take pictures of ruddy fairies again."

We burst out laughing because it was such a funny thing to say.

We idled for a while by the water, remembering lazy days of racing our leaves and baby frogs and watching Mr. Snowden's ducklings. The blackberries were hard green bullets on the bushes, and I was glad to know I would be back in Scarborough long before they ripened. I was still fond of Cottingley, but it didn't hold the same magic it once had. Perhaps there was only a limited time for anyone to feel what I'd felt at the beck during those wartime summers. Perhaps it was someone else's turn now. Time for another little girl to play here and continue the story.

While Uncle Arthur developed the plates that afternoon, I practiced my scales at the piano. I had no inclination to wait outside the darkroom, no inclination to see the photographs at all, not even when Elsie popped her head around the door to say they had come up nicely.

When Aunt Polly returned from Bradford, she was pleased enough with the photographs, but disappointed we'd only managed the two, and neither of them with the fairies flying as Elsie had promised. She muttered and grumbled as she set the kettle on the stove. "I'll write to Mr. Gardner to tell him. You can go out tomorrow and try again."

My heart sank into my boots. "How many more photographs do we need, Aunt Polly?"

"Well, I should think half a dozen wouldn't be too much to ask, not after all the trouble and expense Mr. Conan Doyle went to, sending you those new cameras and plates."

I kicked Elsie under the table. I knew she didn't have any more cutouts prepared.

"But the fairies only come in good weather, Aunt Polly," I said. "They won't come in the rain."

"Then let's hope for good weather tomorrow, Frances."

I prayed for bad weather as I knelt beside the bed that night, and I prayed for poor little Aisling too.

NOTES ON A FAIRY TALE
Cottingley, Yorkshire. August 1920.

On my last day in Cottingley I woke to the steady patter of rain against the window. Murky gray clouds covered the sky like ink spots. Mists rolled over the valleys, washing away the hilltops and distant views and any hope of seeing fairies.

But this was not a task to be given up lightly, especially now that the time and expense of important men from London were at stake. Also, there was Aunt Polly's Yorkshire stubbornness to take into account. Despite the drizzle and the mist, she insisted we try one last time to get another photograph. She sent us out straight after dinner with our cameras and two glass plates each.

We made a sorry pair in our mackintoshes and boots. I felt as gloomy as the weather as we trudged toward the beck, where we mooched about for a while, sulking about everything to do with fairies, and talking about Elsie's plans to emigrate to America.

It was only toward the middle of the afternoon, as the rain stopped and a weak sun poked through the clouds, that Elsie said we should take one picture each.

"You never know," she said. "We might catch a *real* fairy! I'll go down to the bridge. You take something here."

Elsie was only gone for ten minutes when I saw a flash of color beside the waterfall. My heart quickened. Another flash came. Then another.

They were here.

It wasn't only what I saw that thrilled me. As before, I heard a light ringing in my ears. As before, my skin tingled with the sensation of being watched. I tiptoed as quietly and as quickly as I could toward them. There they were, just as I remembered them, so magical in their misty barely-there beauty. I watched, spellbound, for a minute, before I remembered the camera. Quickly I set what I hoped would be the correct aperture and speed. I looked through the viewfinder and pressed the shutter. When I glanced up from behind the lens, they had gone.

Elsie was striding along the bank, calling to me. "Frances! I said, shall we try up near the reservoir?"

I stood up and brushed the damp from my skirts. As I walked away from the beck, I instinctively knew I'd seen the fairies for the last time. They had come to say good-bye.

In the field beside the reservoir, we spread our mackintoshes on the ground and sat down to discuss what we were going to do, and how we would explain the lack of photographs to Aunt Polly. I didn't tell Elsie what I'd seen. I didn't know if I'd captured the fairies, anyway, and didn't want to get her hopes up.

Elsie picked at the grass beside her, placing a blade between her finger and thumb and blowing through it to make a high-pitched whistle. It reminded me of the sound I heard when I saw the fairies. She suggested we use our last two plates to take a picture of a tree or the bushes. "We can say the fairies flew away just as we pressed the shutter. Or we can say we can't see them anymore. I read a book of Mummy's about psychic abilities. It said children can communicate with other realms, but that when they grow up, they lose the ability. They'll believe that."

It was a muggy afternoon. Bees and wasps buzzed around us as I let my thoughts wander back to the beck, grateful that I had seen them one last time. As Elsie blew her grass whistle, a movement in front of me caught my eye. Leaning forward to take a closer look, I saw something resembling a bird's nest, almost hidden in the grass. Without stopping to think, I unfolded the lens sleeve, pointed my camera, and took a five-second exposure.

Elsie looked up. "What are you doing? Don't waste the plates."

"I thought I saw something."

"What sort of something?"

"I'm not sure. Something in the grass. A nest of some kind."

"Probably a field mouse." Elsie stood up. "Come on then. It's better than nothing, I suppose. We'll say it was the best we could do."

We wandered back to the house, lost in our thoughts, all talk of fairies quite done with.

Aunt Polly was waiting for us in the garden. "Well? What did you manage?"

"We're not sure," Elsie said.

"What d'you mean, you're not sure? Did you see fairies or not?"

"We thought we saw something in the grass in the top field, but it moved too quickly to get a close look. Hopefully it'll come up clearer on the plate."

Aunt Polly sighed. "Let's hope so. Otherwise I'm afraid Mr. Gardner and Mr. Conan Doyle will think you a pair of silly girls only able to capture two fairies with all those plates and such good cameras. Two fairies. Honestly!"

Uncle Arthur developed the plates that evening, declaring them all duds, even the one I'd taken of the waterfall.

Only the photograph of the nest in the grass was considered half decent and even that Uncle Arthur didn't think looked like a nest at all. "More like a basket of jumbled up washing if you ask me. It's a dud. That's about all it is."

Aunt Polly rubbed her hands on her apron and peered at it again. "Dud or not, it'll have to do. I'll send the prints to Mr. Gardner in the morning."

That night before I went to bed, I asked Aunt Polly if she thought the men from London would be happy with our photographs.

She patted my arm reassuringly. "They'll have to be, won't they? I suppose you can't get fairies to order, like buttons and ribbon in the haberdashery. It would have been nice to have more, but we'll make do."

"You still believe the beck fairies are real, though, don't you, Aunt Polly?"

She thought about this for a moment as she smoothed the front of her skirt and let out a long sigh. "Yes, Frances. Happen I do. If we can't believe in fairies at the bottom of the garden, then I'm not sure there's much point believing in anything."

That was good enough for me.

By the end of the week, I was back in Scarborough, enjoying my cycles along the quiet country lanes with Mary. We watched the cricket festival and county matches at the Queen's ground, swam in the sea, picked flowers for our presses, and knit jumpers for our dolls. All thoughts of Cottingley and fairies slipped away, like the tide carried out to sea.

If I'd known what lay ahead, perhaps I would have made more of those quiet, simple days in Scarborough that summer. Perhaps I would have lingered longer in the water before rushing back for my towel. Perhaps I would have relished the quiet joy of being alone, with only my thoughts. Perhaps I would have appreciated the days that I had, rather than wishing for the days that were yet to come.

I had never liked reaching the end of a story, and mine wasn't finished yet.

While I enjoyed Scarborough's summer, the next chapters of my particular fairy tale were being written in a London townhouse as Sir Arthur Conan Doyle evoked the marvel of our so-called "Yorkshire fairies" in words, sentences, and eloquent paragraphs. Soon his pages would be in the hands of the typesetter. By the end of the year, my story would be clattering along the great machinery of the printing presses, our photographs displayed on newsstands across England as the much-anticipated Christmas issue of *The Strand Magazine* went on sale, bearing the dramatic headline:

FAIRIES PHOTOGRAPHED
AN EPOCH-MAKING EVENT DESCRIBED BY
A. CONAN DOYLE

My story was far from over.
In many ways, it was only just beginning.

NOTES ON A FAIRY TALE
Scarborough, Yorkshire. January 1921.

Within days of Conan Doyle's article hitting the news-stands, talk of the fairy photographs reached Scarborough. Speculation was rife. How could it not be when the article claimed to contain "the two most astounding photographs ever published"? I pulled my hat over my eyes when I heard people talking about it on the bus, afraid someone would recognize me, even though our names had been changed to Iris and Alice, and Cottingley was described as the "quaint old-world Yorkshire village of Dalesby." Conan Doyle had written, "We are compelled to use a pseudonym and to withhold the exact address, for it is clear that their lives would be much interrupted by correspondence and callers if their identity were too clearly indicated."

Our lives were "much interrupted" regardless.

Mr. Gardner wrote to me straightaway. My hands shook as I read his words, my mouth as dry as toast. "Dear Frances, I send just this line at once as the *Strand* is out today and I am already getting numerous inquiries about the fairies. . . . It is just possible you may be found out and an attempt made to interview you despite my endeavor to protect you and yours from discovery . . ."

Far from concealing our identity, Conan Doyle had left enough clues that even an amateur Sherlock Holmes could work out who we were. Yorkshire folk are not easily dis-suaded once they set their mind to something, and I knew it wouldn't take long for someone to recognize us. I thought about Mavis Clarke's sneering and Mrs. Hogan's knowing looks. I curled my toes inside my boots as I looked at the photographs. They had been labeled "Alice and the Fairy Ring" and "Iris and the Gnome." There was also a picture of Mr. Gardner looking serious beside the waterfall, and another of Elsie that made her look sulky and heavy in the face, which I knew she would hate.

What surprised me most was the paragraph relating to Mr. Snelling, the photography expert. "He laughs at the idea that any expert in England could deceive him with a faked photograph. 'These two negatives,' he says, 'are entirely genuine, unfaked photographs of single exposure . . .'" Much as the whole thing worried me, I couldn't help smiling when I read that Mr. Gardner had tested Elsie's artistic skills, suspecting that she might have drawn the fairy figures. The article stated that "while she could do landscapes cleverly, the fairy figures which she had attempted in imitation of those she had seen were entirely uninspired and bore no possible resemblance to those in the photograph."

Clever Elsie.

The only redeeming thing about the article was a paragraph in which Conan Doyle supported the existence of fairies. That was what interested me. Not the tedious analysis of our photographs to prove if they were genuine or fake, but the study of fairy life: where they live, what their purpose is, how some people see them and others can't. "These little folk, who appear to be our neighbors, with only some small difference of vibration to separate us, will become familiar. The thought of them, even when unseen, will add a charm to every brook and valley and give romantic interest to every country walk. The recognition of their existence will jolt the twentieth-century mind out of its heavy ruts in the mud, and will make it admit that there is a glamour and mystery to life."

These words, more than any others, I agreed with. Still, I hated to see the photograph of Elsie with that silly gnome.

Over Christmas, I tried to put the *Strand* article out of my mind, even when more plates arrived from Mr. Gardner, which I thanked him for in a letter, saying I hoped to take photographs of fairies in the snow. The New Year did bring snow flurries, but it also brought another letter from Aunt Polly, which added another twist to the tale.

15 January '21

Dear Annie,

> *Trouble at mill. The girls' identities are out.*
>
> *A reporter arrived from the* Westminster Gazette. *He'd been sniffing around, asking folk what they knew about the Yorkshire fairies and the girls in the* Strand *article photographs. His questions eventually led him to our Elsie.*
>
> *I answered his questions as best I could and assured him Elsie has always been a truthful girl but he tracked her down at work (she's at Sharpe's card factory now, in Bradford) and asked her lots more questions. She told me he was quite polite and that she answered his questions as best she could. Having read his report, I'm not sure she did. I've told her to give better answers next time, and not so much "I suppose" and "I can't say" and "you don't understand."*

*I've enclosed a copy for you to read. It's a pity he
gives your address. I'd hoped you might escape some
of the attention.*

Love to all,
Polly
x

I put Aunt Polly's letter down and read the enclosed article from the *Westminster Gazette*. It was very long and detailed. I hardly had the patience to read it all, but one particular paragraph drew the breath from my lungs. "The 'heroine' of Sir Arthur Conan Doyle's story is Miss Elsie Wright. . . . When Miss Wright made the acquaintance of the fairies she was accompanied by her cousin, Frances Griffiths, who resides at Dean Road, Scarborough."

It didn't take long for the more tenacious newspaper reporters to track me down. They waited for me after school, lurking in the shadows with their trilby hats and notebooks and awkward questions.

"Did you really see little men and fairies?"

"Are you and your cousin playing a prank on us all?"

"Are there fairies in Scarborough?"

I wanted to say it was none of their business what I had or hadn't seen, but Daddy told me not to be cheeking the reporters or they might write unpleasant things about me. I answered their questions curtly. "Yes, I did see fairies up the beck" and "No, I haven't seen any fairies in Scarborough." I found different routes home from school, cutting through back lanes and narrow side streets, avoiding the reporters as best I could. But no number of back lanes and side streets could help me avoid the girls at school. If I didn't answer the teacher's questions right away, they'd say, "Thinking about fairies, then?" and giggle behind their slates. The headmaster even asked to talk to me about the "Yorkshire fairies." I didn't want to talk to him about fairies. I wanted to be a normal teenage girl, like my friends.

I became sullen and withdrawn.

Daddy tried to cheer me up with walks along the prom. He told me not to take it so seriously. "Nobody's come to any harm," he said. "People are fascinated with fairies, that's all. It's not such a terrible thing, is it?"

"I wish we'd never taken those photographs, Daddy. We only wanted to show Mummy and Aunt Polly and Uncle Arthur. Not the whole world."

He wrapped his arms around me and said people would find something else to talk about soon enough.

In a way, he was right. The reporters eventually lost interest in me, finding me a difficult, uncooperative child. Elsie was much more amenable. She quite enjoyed the attention. To my relief, the focus of their questioning shifted from me to her. But alone in my bedroom at night, I worried, and when I worried, I dreamed, and still the images of a little girl with red hair nagged at my conscience.

Through the dreary winter months, the guilty secret of our photographs clung to me like my rain-sodden wool coat that pulled my arms to my sides and made my footsteps uneasy. The newspapers continued to report on our photographs. The *Times* of London said, "I would suggest to Miss Elsie that she has carried her little joke far enough, and that she should tell the public what the 'fairies' really are." Other reports suggested we had been pulling Sir Arthur Conan Doyle's leg. Mr. Gardner wrote to advise us to keep hidden any copies of the final three photographs we'd taken the previous summer. He said we were not to worry about the speculation in the newspaper, writing, "We will surprise them all with the new fairy photographs. We will win through and Elsie and Frances will be justified everywhere."

Our joke had already gone too far, and as Mr. Gardner took our photographs around the country on his lecture tour, interest in them and in us spread further and further until eventually Mr. Gardner and our photographs crossed the Atlantic Ocean and we were being talked about in Elsie's beloved America.

Like the ripples I'd watched on the surface of the beck, I was absolutely helpless to stop it.

Part Three
Fairies Revealed

One mystery remains. It concerns a photograph in which the girls, unusually, are absent, and transparent fairies are depicted apparently in a sunny grass bower. Mrs. Griffiths maintains that she took the photograph and it is the only genuine one. . . .
—THE TIMES, *1983*

Fifteen

Ireland. Present day.

The first weeks of summer arrived with a parade of warm days and balmy evenings. Windows were left open at night and bedsheets kicked off as hot limbs searched for cooler air. Olivia was buoyed by the bright days and the support of those around her, especially Henry and Ross, who cheered her on when business was good and cheered her up when things got on top of her. The heavy coils of doubt she'd hefted around for so long gently unfurled as she accepted that whatever happened now, it happened because of her. She was in charge. She made the decisions.

It was her decision to arrange more bookbinding demonstrations and themed evenings: Irish Poetry, Gothic Horror, and British Classics were all a huge hit. It was her decision to repaint the shop door hyacinth blue in honor of Bluebell Cottage. It was her decision to leave a Welcome to Your New Home bottle of wine on the doorstep of the cottage for the new owners. It was her decision to invite Ross to stay on as Writer in Residence when he'd finished his book. She said she'd gotten used to him being around. He said he'd hoped she would say that.

The arrangement suited them both, and neither was especially keen to change it, particularly Friday evenings when they wrapped up the week over a bottle of wine. Only occasionally did they stray into the realms of harmless flirtation: a look, a smile, a pause while words left unsaid circled around them, teasing and provoking. Olivia didn't need another boyfriend. She needed a friend, and in Ross she had found exactly that. They both agreed their one drunken kiss had been a mistake. Still, it was a lovely mistake and one Olivia thought about often, and sometimes when a certain look passed between them, she wondered if Ross thought about it too.

As Olivia and Something Old flourished, so did the garden in the window. Local interest became a national curiosity, and Olivia found herself on the evening news, talking about it. Nobody knew how the garden continued to thrive, even when the window boxes were moved and without ever being given a drop of water. When she was asked what she attributed the phenomenon to, Olivia said that explanations were the thief of wonder, and that she was happy to live without one. She didn't mention the wish she'd left at the fairy door. Those for whom it was intended had heard.

Soon the "Garden in the Window" became a story in itself. Customers arrived in the dozens to take a look, and when they ventured into the shop, the books flew off the shelves. Something Old was alive again. Each morning, when Olivia went downstairs to open up, she discovered new green shoots, newly unfurled blooms and perfect glossy leaves, gifts that had arrived during the silent hours while she dreamed. And her dreams bloomed too.

As she read more of Frances's story, Olivia realized that her dreams mirrored Frances's dreams; the present reflecting the past. Like the tendrils and shoots entwining themselves around the shop window, Frances's story had wrapped itself around Olivia's heart, capturing there Frances's memories of Ellen Hogan and the traumatic loss of her daughter.

Cottingley called to Olivia. She waited, impatiently, for the day of her trip to arrive.

ON SUNDAYS, THE shop closed. Pappy had never agreed with Sunday trading and Olivia honored his tradition, taking the opportunity to hike around the cliff tops. She enjoyed the fresh air and the views, and enjoyed it even more when Ross and Iris started to join her. It was good to have some company. Up on the breezy cliff tops, Olivia and Ross spoke about things in a way they couldn't in the shop. There was something safe about sharing their thoughts and feelings up there. It was liberating in the same way that London had been restricting, and once she let herself open up, Olivia found she had a lot to say.

Iris loved the view, pondering what might lie beyond the horizon, just as Olivia used to when she was a little girl. As they looked down at the miniature sailing boats in the harbor, Olivia pointed out the ruins of the abbey and Little Lane.

"If you look hard you can see the bookshop, Iris. See? Just there."

Iris screwed up her eyes, following the direction of Olivia's finger. "Why do you like the bookshop so much?"

"I spent a lot of time there when I was younger. I always felt there was something magical about it." They threw pebbles over the edge of the cliff and watched them race down, bumping off each other and landing in some distant place they couldn't see. "Shall I tell you a secret, Iris?"

"Yes! I love secrets."

"I think the books come alive at night. When the shop is closed and the lights are turned out, I think they open their covers and fan out their pages like wings and start to fly. Imagine it. Hundreds of books, flapping their pages, soaring and swooping because they're so alive with stories they can't possibly sit still on the shelf."

Iris giggled. "You're funny when you talk about books."

Olivia laughed. "I suppose I am! Do you remember the photograph of the little girl and the fairies?" Iris nodded. "I'm reading a story about her."

"Are the fairies in it?"

"Yes. I think you might like it. I can give it to your Daddy to read to you if you like."

Iris grabbed Olivia's hand. "Would you read it to me? Daddy tries hard, but he doesn't do the voices properly. Not like Mammy."

Olivia promised she would do the best voices she could, although she knew they would never be good enough.

They walked on, following the path around the headland.

"We used to walk a lot, before Hannah died," Ross said as Iris ran ahead, skipping between the gorse bushes and clambering over stones. "Iris loves it up here. Look at her. She's in her element."

"Jack and I never went for walks, unless it was to a wine bar or to *somewhere*. We never walked for the sake of walking. He didn't see the point."

Ross stopped to admire the view. "This might be a stupid question, but why did you agree to marry him?"

It was a question Olivia had asked herself many times. She stared out over the sea, too ashamed to look Ross in the eye. "Because he asked me. I was afraid of being alone. Afraid of being left on the shelf. It felt kind of inevitable that I would settle down one day, and when he asked, I said yes."

"Did you love him?"

"I did. For a while. Or at least, I thought I did. Now I'm not sure." She turned to face Ross. "How do you know? How does anyone know what proper love feels like?"

Ross glanced at the wedding band on his finger and let out a long, heartfelt sigh. "Oh, you know, Olivia. You definitely know."

They walked on, the sun at their backs, the sweet gorse scenting the air around them.

"You had a lucky escape, then," Ross said.

Olivia smiled. "Actually, I prefer to think of it as setting out on an adventure. Illusionists escape. Adventurers go exploring."

"And how's that working out for you?"

She wrapped her arms around herself. "Pretty good so far."

They looked out across the harbor, unspoken words and thoughts shifting between them like the waves that lapped at the hulls of the boats. In those quiet moments, Olivia realized how lovely it was to have someone to do nothing with, to just stand with, and watch and think with.

"Did you ever read *Ulysses*?" she asked.

"Did anyone?"

"You should give it a go. There's a lovely scene written here."

"On Howth Head?"

"Yep. Molly Bloom's soliloquy. 'The sun shines for you he said the day we were lying among the rhododendrons on

Howth head in the grey tweed suit and his straw hat . . .'" She stopped short of completing the passage.

"I never knew that."

"There you go, then. You should read it. You might learn all sorts of things."

He promised he would.

Ross was fidgety for the rest of the afternoon. He kept looking at Olivia as if he wanted to say something but kept changing his mind. She knew him well enough by now to pick up on his moods.

"Ross, is everything all right? You seem a bit distracted."

He took a deep breath. "Did I ever tell you my family are originally from Kerry?" he asked.

"No. You didn't." Olivia sensed he was going to tell her something she wasn't going to like.

"We're going back. Iris and me. We're moving back to Kerry."

Olivia's heart raced. "When?"

"Two weeks. At the end of the school year. I've been trying to find a place since Hannah died. Iris has no family here. She has cousins and aunts and uncles there. A Nana and a Grandad. I can't deprive her of that. I've been looking for so long, I thought it would never happen, but I just had an offer accepted on my house, and I've had an offer accepted on a house in Kerry. The owners moved out months ago so it's vacant possession. Everything's happened really quickly."

Olivia didn't know what to say. She kept walking, one foot in front of the other, as Iris skipped ahead in her red wellies, oblivious to the drama playing out behind her.

"And do you know what's mad?" Ross continued.

"What?"

"When I told Iris we were moving, she asked if you could come with us."

Olivia stopped walking. "Did she?"

"Yep. She's taken quite a shine to you. I told her she'll still be able to write to you. I hope that's okay?"

"Of course it is." It would have to be okay. It would all have to be okay.

"Anyway, I wanted you to know. At least you'll get your flat back. You can hang your knickers everywhere and run around naked!"

Olivia punched him playfully on the arm. "Bugger off to Kerry, then. See if I care."

"Will you miss me?"

"I'll miss your guitar."

Ross laughed. "Is that all?"

There was so much she would miss. His smile. His silly coffee cup names. His company. His kindness. His belief in her.

"Of course I'll miss you. Who am I going to moan to about everything now? Seriously though. You've been great. Especially the past few weeks."

Ross shrugged his shoulders. "What are friends for?"

He held out the crook of his elbow, and Olivia linked her arm through his as if it were the most natural thing in the world.

Perhaps it was the wildness of the scenery, or perhaps it was the way the sun wrapped itself around Olivia so that her entire body felt as if it were made of sunlight, but whatever it was, it felt right to be walking arm in arm with Ross Bailey, Writer.

When Iris and Ross started a game of hide-and-seek, Olivia let them run on ahead, but as she picked her way through the rhododendron tunnels, she could feel the weight of Ross's arm in hers.

Without it, everything felt a little off balance.

As THE SHOP became busier, Olivia struggled to find as much time as she'd like to visit Nana. Ross helped out by minding the shop as often as he could, and Henry was only too happy to visit Nana on the days when Olivia couldn't. Old friendships had been easily rekindled at the fairy evening; Olivia had secretly watched Nana and Henry stroll together in the gardens, arm in arm. It was the first time she'd seen Henry walk without his stick.

St. Bridget's no longer held the same sense of dread for Olivia that it once had. She'd stopped fighting her anger and frustration about Nana's illness and focused on what she could do to love and care for her for as long as she could, and to make her remaining days comfortable and pleasant. As Henry said in one of his Henryisms, "We can't always change the situations life puts us in, but we *can* change the way we respond."

Olivia continued to read to Nana from Frances's book, and listened with renewed patience to Nana's invented stories. Sometimes she took red lemonade and they sat beneath the shade of a rowan tree, sipping the lemonade through straws and giggling as the bubbles went up their noses.

Olivia told Nana she would be traveling to England for a few days and that Henry would look in on her while she was away.

"I'm going to Cottingley, Nana. To see where you used to live."

There was a flicker of recognition. "That's nice, dear. If you see Aisling, tell her it's time to come home now. Mammy is terribly worried."

Olivia couldn't hide her tears. Nana looked increasingly frail in recent days so that Olivia hardly dared hug her as she kissed her good-bye. "I'll be back in a few days. I love you, Nana."

She thought she saw the edge of a smile at Nana's lips but couldn't be sure.

That night, as she lay in bed thinking about her trip to England, Hemingway curled up on the pillow beside her, purring as Olivia rubbed behind his ears. Despite his initial haughty indifference, he'd realized she wasn't going anywhere and had finally accepted her as his flatmate and, possibly, his friend.

Olivia picked up the final pages of Frances's story, losing herself in the events that had happened in Cottingley so long ago, and in the people who had lived through them. Events and people that felt closer with every turn of the page . . .

NOTES ON A FAIRY TALE
Scarborough, Yorkshire. March 1921.

Mummy always said, "Beware the Ides of March." I'd never paid much heed until that March day in 1921 when the second *Strand Magazine* article came out, blazing the sensational headline:

THE EVIDENCE FOR FAIRIES

BY

A. CONAN DOYLE

WITH NEW FAIRY PHOTOGRAPHS

Trouble was coming. I could feel it in my bones.

The day the article was published, I climbed to my favorite spot on the cliff tops above the bend in Marine Drive and watched spring rush in across the North Sea. The winds were wild and sent the waves crashing against the rocks below. I loved this time of year, before the tourists arrived from the West. Summer brought the thrill of Catlin's Pierrot shows in the Arcadia, the Punch and Judy shows on the pier, and Cricket Week, but spring gave me dunes to play in and empty beaches and the castle all to myself. I loved the rush and boom of the water in the caves. I loved to walk along the prom as waves raced across the road, sloshing around the omnibus wheels and soaking anyone who got in the way. But no matter how long I lingered by the sea, no matter how much I dawdled on my way home, I couldn't avoid Conan Doyle's article. It was waiting on the kitchen table when I got home.

The new photographs that Elsie and I had taken the

previous summer were included, the names Iris and Alice still used in the descriptions. I could hardly bear to look, wincing at the photographs of Elsie (Iris) and the fairy with the harebells and of myself and the leaping fairy. And yet despite the guilty conscience that nagged as I read the article, I again found myself interested in Conan Doyle's thoughts on fairy life and especially in his detailed accounts of fairy sightings from all over England and Ireland, the descriptions matching that of my beck fairies. "Taking a large number of cases which lie before me, there are two points which are common to nearly all of them. One is that children claim to see these creatures far more frequently than adults. . . . The other is, that more cases are recorded in which they have been seen in the still, shimmering hours of a very hot day than at any other time." It gave me great confidence to know that others had seen what I had.

Again, the reporters were waiting. I did my best to avoid them and their intrusive questions, but they were more persistent this time, and the mocking from the girls at school was more sustained. Things became so difficult that my parents considered taking me out of school and sending me to relatives in Bradford. I was relieved when Mummy said they'd decided against it.

"You'll just have to put up with a bit of ragging until this all dies down," she said. "And it will. I promise."

I remembered that cold April evening in Cottingley when Mummy sang Nellie Melba and promised better times would come in the summer. I had to trust her again.

But all hopes of an end to the fairies were dashed when Mr. Gardner made an unexpected visit to Scarborough.

Over apple pie and a pot of tea, it was suggested that I return to Cottingley once again that summer during my school holidays, when Elsie and I would be joined by a Mr. Geoffrey Hodson, a renowned psychic friend of Conan Doyle's.

"Mr. Hodson is a gifted spiritualist," he explained. "He will try to create the right aural conditions for the nature spirits to appear and will be able to authenticate your fairy sightings. He will use a new cinema camera to film the events. If he can capture the elementals on film . . . well!"

I wasn't sure what "aural" conditions were, but didn't want to appear ignorant by asking.

"And ACD is working on a book about the events," he added. "Isn't that something?"

"A book about us?" I asked, my apple pie sticking to the roof of my mouth.

"Yes. I believe the title is to be *The Coming of the Fairies*. He hopes to publish next year. I imagine it will be of great interest."

I felt sick and asked to be excused, but curiosity got the better of me and I listened secretly at the door. Mr. Gardner told Mummy he believed I was "mediumistic"—that I had the power to see things other people couldn't. "Frances is surrounded by an etheric material, Mrs. Griffiths. I believe it is this material that draws the nature spirits to her."

Whatever it was that drew the nature spirits to me, I had no desire to be observed by strange men from London when it happened. And anyway, I doubted the beck fairies would make an appearance with so many people around. They were shy, quiet creatures, not performers on the stage at the Spa.

By the time Mr. Gardner left, it was agreed that I would travel to Cottingley during the final week of my summer holidays. A few days later, I found a letter Daddy was writing to confirm things. ". . . We will do whatever we can to meet your requirements next August and will wait for further word from you re the arrangements. Meanwhile, Mrs. Griffiths and her sister will fix up Frances's stay at Cottingley. . . . We were interested to read in Monday's issue of the *Scarborough News* a short account of your Manchester lecture. We must certainly keep our eyes open for fairies when next we have flowers in the house."

I was now nearing fourteen, and Elsie nearing twenty. If *I* found the thought of sitting by the beck for hours looking for fairies a tedious prospect, I dreaded to think what Elsie would make of it all. Worst of all, I would miss my beloved Cricket Week when all the stars came to Scarborough. It wasn't fair. I sulked in my bedroom and wrote to Johanna in Cape Town. I told her that even if I did see fairies in Cottingley that summer, I wouldn't tell Mr. Hodson. If he wanted to see fairies, he would have to do so himself.

I tried to forget about Cottingley over the following weeks and months as I enjoyed the sea air and long walks along the foreshore. Only occasionally did I find myself looking for signs of fairies among the long grasses and cliff top meadows, but I didn't see them. I presumed it was too cold for fairies in Scarborough's wild spring breezes. It was barely tolerable for a girl with a thick woolen coat.

NOTES ON A FAIRY TALE
Cottingley, Yorkshire. August 1921.

Summer arrived in a rush, and too soon I was back on
the train, hurtling toward the West with Mummy beside
me. I was sullen and quiet and kept my head in my book all
the way there. I had no interest in the passing landscape
that had once intrigued me. I just wanted to get this over
with and get back to Scarborough.

But despite my frustration at being dragged back to
Cottingley again, my mood lifted as soon as I saw Elsie
leaning against the door of Number 31, as tall as a lamp-
post and prettier than ever. She squeezed my hand as
we stepped inside and whispered, "Ruddy fairies," which
made me laugh and made me feel much better.

When I asked why the curtains in the front room were
drawn in the middle of the day, Aunt Polly said it was to
keep the sun off the good furniture and that I wasn't to
be worrying about curtains. When she stepped out of the
room, I asked Elsie if people had been snooping.

She nodded. "'Fraid so. Fairy hunters. Cottingley's
swarming with them, carrying nets and cameras. Daft
beggars. As if they're going to see fairies making that
much of a clatter."

"Fairy hunters." My stomach tightened into a painful
knot so that I didn't even fancy any of Aunt Polly's parkin.

Apart from the "fairy hunters" who trampled over everything and made far too much noise to ever see fairies,
the beck hadn't changed, other than perhaps appearing a
little smaller because of the inches I'd grown since the previous summer. Like a reliable old friend, it welcomed me

back without question or hesitation. The yarrow and dog roses bloomed brighter than ever, and the waterfall slipped smoothly over the shale rock, the familiar sound sending a shiver along my spine. Through the dense foliage, I caught a glimpse of Mrs. Hogan's cottage, and visions of a little girl tugged at my conscience. I had to tell her.

Elsie and I walked for a while, discussing what we were going to do about the fairies, and how boring we found it all. We linked fingers and renewed our solemn promise never to tell the truth. We understood that this was far bigger than the two of us now. Somehow, we knew it would be part of our lives forever. Like our shadows, the photographs of the fairies would always be there, following a few steps behind.

"We might as well have a bit of fun with this Mr. Hodson while he's here," Elsie said. "I bet he isn't really a psychic, and anyway, I've had it with chuffin' fairies." She said she would do the talking when Mr. Hodson arrived. "Your cheeks always go bright red when you tell a lie."

I was grateful for Elsie's sense of humor. Grateful that she was there, beside me.

As we mooched about by the beck that afternoon, I watched our reflections in the water, fragments of both of us, moving in the ripples stirred by a gentle breeze. But I didn't just see a tall teenager and a young woman. I saw the reflection of two younger girls, happily playing in the innocence of summer days when Mummy would stand on the back step and call us in for tea, just as she did now.

"Frances! Elsie! Elsie! Frances! Tea!"

I smiled. It was always Frances and Elsie, or Elsie and Frances. That was how it was, and I was glad to know that some things hadn't changed from those summers during the war, even when so many other things had.

I was admiring Aunt Polly's costume jewelry in the front bedroom when the hansom cab pulled up outside with a great crunching of brakes. Concealed behind the lace curtains, I watched as a round-faced man and a strangely angular woman stepped out of the car. The man fastened the buttons on his tweed jacket, which was too small for him, adjusted his hat, and pushed open the front gate. The squeak reminded me of that magical day when Daddy arrived home on leave. The house was so happy then. Such a contrast with the awkward tension that filled the rooms now.

Mummy was all of a fluster and got one of her headaches. She'd been polishing and sweeping all morning, silently cursing Aunt Polly under her breath and muttering about it being all very well for Aunt Polly and Uncle Arthur to take off to the Isle of Man whenever it suited them. I crept to the top of the stairs and peered through the banister as Mummy took off her apron and fussed with her hair in the mirror before opening the door.

The usual pleasantries were exchanged between Mr. and Mrs. Hodson and Mummy: "Pleased to meet you." "How was the journey?" "Delighted to be here." "Shame about the weather." Mummy spoke in her posh voice, rounding out her vowels and finishing every word with a crisp *t* or *d* or whatever letter was required. It made me uncomfortable when she used her posh voice. It made me feel stiff and prickly at the backs of my knees.

The pleasantries dispensed with, Elsie and I were summoned to the front room, dressed in our Sunday best. "We can't be having visitors from London looking down on us and thinking us common northerners," Mummy had said. I was tempted to ask if it wouldn't be better if I wore my "etheric material" instead, but somehow managed to bite my tongue.

I shook Mr. and Mrs. Hodson's hands, and Elsie did the same. Mrs. Hodson sat quietly by the fireplace while her husband did the talking. He had squinty currant eyes that I didn't trust, and sagging jowls like Mr. Briggs's dog. He spoke through his nose in a way that people do when they pretend to belong to a better social class than they actually do.

His hand was clammy in mine as he gushed about how thrilled he was to meet us. "It's quite marvelous to be in your presence at last. I've read a lot about you both. It is rare one gets to meet with such special girls."

My toes curled inside my boots. I hated to think of people reading about me. I'd learned a lot about newspaper reporters in recent months and knew they didn't always stick to the facts.

Mr. Hodson looked at me strangely as we drank tea and chatted politely—or rather, he looked around me, his eyes flicking from side to side as if he were following a fly. Elsie mimicked his mannerisms behind his back, and I had to bite my lip and put my hand to my mouth to stop myself laughing.

After an excruciating hour or so, the Hodsons returned to their hotel, and Elsie and I were dismissed.

I didn't go to the beck that afternoon. There were too many strangers there with nets and cameras.

That night, I fell into a deep, travel-weary sleep, lulled by the familiar sound of the waterfall beyond the window. I dreamed of the beck fairies, a blur of lavender and rose-pink and buttercup-yellow light, flitting across the glittering stream, beckoning me to follow them toward the woodland cottage. There, the little girl with flame-red hair picked daisies in the garden, threading them together to make a garland for her hair. She picked a posy of wildflowers—harebell, bindweed, campion, and bladderwort—and gave them to me. I carried them to the cottage door where I left them on the doorstep beside a pair of stone boots. The girl then sat on a willow bough seat and wept, her tears spilling into the stream, merging with the reflections of the stars until they faded, one by one, and the sun rose in the east, and when I looked at the willow tree again, she had gone.

The next day dawned with rain and cloudy skies, but as I knew from the previous summer, fairy hunting didn't stop for bad weather, and Mummy sent us outside between showers.

While the silly people with their butterfly nets crept about as subtly as elephants, some of them claiming to have spotted a fairy every now and again, Mr. Hodson took endless photographs of me by the beck or Elsie by the waterfall as he claimed to sense this, that, and the other. We couldn't summon the enthusiasm to smile, despite his encouragement. His effusive manner was irritating, and neither Elsie nor I cared for the way he spoke to us, as if we were children. Mrs. Hodson kept herself to herself, sitting a short distance from our sullen group. The relentless *click-clack* of her knitting needles set my teeth on edge. At regular intervals, Mr. Hodson would inquire in a sickly voice if she was happy, to which she would smile sweetly and say, "Very happy, darling," before resuming her knitting.

In our bedroom that night, Elsie mimicked the Hodsons until tears rolled down our cheeks with laughter.

That was how the week passed. Miserable weather. Miserable girls. Long, boring hours spent at the beck, waiting for something to happen, and all the time Mr. Hodson whispering in his strange voice, muttering about "auras" and "heavenly bodies" and his experiences in the world of the occult. It was like watching an act on stage at the Arcadia. We couldn't take him seriously at all.

Mr. Gardner stayed at the Midland hotel in Bradford for the duration of the Hodsons' stay. He came to Cottingley a few times to ask us how we were getting on with our "field trips," as he called them. I often saw him spying on us from behind a tree, scribbling notes in his book. Elsie laughed whenever I pointed him out to her, especially if he ducked down, suspecting he'd been caught out.

Elsie often grew bored and made her way back to the house early. I had more patience and sat by the stream for hours, always aware of Mr. Gardner observing me from a distance. When I made my way home he would ask if anything had occurred at the beck that day. I always said no, there was nothing doing, or that it was too wet for fairies. As I'd decided months earlier in my bedroom in Scarborough, I wouldn't tell, even if I had seen something.

As the days passed, our boredom spilled over into something like a hysteria and Elsie and I began to have a little fun with Mr. Hodson and his auras.

Elsie started it. "Over there! Look!" She winked at me and pointed to an oak tree, saying that she could clearly see a figure like a fairy godmother.

Mr. Hodson hopped to his feet, instantly declaring that yes, he could see it too. "Do you see it, girls? Look. It is materializing as we watch."

I giggled into my hair as Elsie added more and more detail and Mr. Hodson became more and more animated, agreeing that he could see exactly what Elsie described. I had always suspected he was as fake as our photographs. Now I knew for certain.

From that moment, our daily vigils with Mr. Hodson became far more enjoyable as we claimed to see fairies six feet tall and fairies flying around our heads. I said I saw water nymphs and wood elves, and Elsie saw a golden fairy and little men trooping along the path in front of us, giving us a soldier's salute. Mr. Hodson scribbled frantically in his notebook, embellishing our descriptions with his low-voiced mutterings about the spirit world and auric fields and elementals. I was still surprised at the lack of proper scientific investigation into why the fairies appeared when we said they did, or what we believed their purpose was, or how they appeared to us and to nobody else. The most interesting questions were never asked, and therefore never answered.

When the week was over, Mummy, Elsie, and I waved the Hodsons off and breathed a sigh of relief.

"That's that, then," Mummy remarked as she flopped into a chair, exhausted by the endless cooking and cleaning she'd been doing.

Elsie said, "There's nowt so queer as folk, eh? Nowt so queer as *them* folk, anyway!"

We all laughed, and although I was relieved it was over, part of me felt a tinge of regret that I hadn't seen the beck fairies once more.

As Mummy packed our cases for the trip back to Scarborough, I took one last walk around the village. Privately I knew I was saying good-bye. Even if the men from London asked Elsie and me to try again, we had already decided—in agreement with our parents—that enough was enough. We had done everything that had been asked of us. It was time to draw a line under it. I spent a while in quiet reflection at the beck before making my way to Mrs. Hogan's cottage.

As always, she was delighted to see me when she opened the door, baby Martha in her arms, a delightful chubby bundle of smiles and gurgles.

We sat at a bench in the garden, Mrs. Hogan beaming with maternal pride as she dandled Martha on her lap and blew raspberries on her tummy. I talked about Scarborough and school and how Daddy was getting on with his new job, but we couldn't avoid the issue of the fairy photographs entirely.

"You and Elsie have caused quite the sensation in Cottingley," Mrs. Hogan said. "Reporters swarming about like bees and folk rushing about with nets. I've never seen the like of it."

I said it was all a lot of fuss over a few photographs and explained how we'd only taken them to show the family, but they had fallen into other hands.

Mrs. Hogan said she understood. "Sure, don't I know what it is to be the cause of local gossip. It isn't a pleasant experience, but it doesn't last forever. They'll be talking about something else come Christmas."

As we stepped inside the cottage to take Martha out of the sun, I noticed a posy of wildflowers in a jug on the dresser—harebell, bindweed, campion, and bladderwort.

Mrs. Hogan noticed me staring at them. "Pretty, aren't they? The most curious thing. I found them on the doorstep this morning beside the stone boots. And it isn't the first time. I often find a single white flower or a posy of wildflowers there." I felt my skin prickle as she spoke. "I know it sounds silly, but I still see her, you know. Aisling. I see her everywhere. Hear her laugh. Hear her cry in the middle of the night."

For a moment, I couldn't speak, and then it all came out in a rush as my dreams flooded my mind, clamoring for my attention, like a persistent knock on the door that I couldn't ignore any longer.

"I see her too."

Mrs. Hogan's face furrowed into a frown. "You see who, Frances?"

"Your daughter."

"Martha?"

I swallowed hard, my breaths coming quickly, my cheeks flushing red as I spoke. "Aisling."

Mrs. Hogan's face paled as she gripped the edge of the table and nodded, encouraging me to go on.

"Ever since I came to Cottingley, I've dreamed of a little girl with red hair. She always gives me a flower. 'For Mammy,' she says. She looks just like the girl in your paintings." My hands trembled as I spoke. "It's *her*, Mrs. Hogan. I think she wants to let you know she's all right."

Mrs. Hogan's eyes filled with tears. She clutched the locket that hung from a chain around her neck, her voice small and fragile as she spoke. "Is she alone when you see her?"

"No, Miss. She's never alone." I took a deep breath and said it. "She's always with the fairies."

A peacefulness fell over the room, like a cloud lifting.

Mrs. Hogan reached forward and took my hands in hers as tears slipped down her cheeks. "Thank you, Frances. Thank you for telling me. It means more than you can ever know."

We spoke then as we had never spoken before. With the door open to let in a breeze, there were no more secrets to hide. I told her all about the fairies I'd seen at the beck that first summer, about how beautiful and charming they were, and how natural it had become for me to see them. She told me she'd seen them, too, when she was a young girl, and that Aisling had often talked about the special lights she saw at the beck. We talked for a long time, of things I had never been able to talk about with anyone else. Not even with Elsie. Mrs. Hogan didn't question or doubt. She listened and understood.

Before I left, I asked Mrs. Hogan if she believed our fairy photographs were real. It was the one secret I'd kept from her.

She paused for a moment before answering. "I believe

there is more to every photograph than what we see—
more to the story than the one the camera captures on the
plate. You have to look behind the picture to discover the
truth. That's where you find the real story."

She smiled, and I smiled in return, and that was all that
needed to be said about it.

I slept peacefully that final night in Cottingley; no dreams
came to me. Aisling had gone.

And so, it seemed, had my fairies. I thanked them silently and promised I would never forget them, or the
magic and hope they had given me when I'd needed it the
most. In my heart, I hoped I might see them again one day,
but as I always said to Elsie, fairies will not be rushed.
They would come back when they were ready.

On the train to Scarborough, as Mummy dozed beside
me, I read the final pages of *The Water Babies*. It was still
a favorite of mine, but I no longer cried when I reached the
end. "But remember always, as I told you at first, that this
is all a fairy tale, and only fun and pretence; and, therefore, you are not to believe a word of it, even if it is true."

As the sun streamed through the carriage window,
I closed my eyes and thought about the men from London and Mr. Hodson's "aural senses" and Mr. Snelling's
photography expertise. I couldn't help smiling to myself.
Without realizing it, Elsie and I had written our own fairy
tale. It was, after all, only fun and pretense. In the years
since we'd taken that first photograph, I'd come to understand that whatever we might say on the matter now,
people had made up their minds. They wouldn't believe
we had faked the photographs even if we said we had, be-

cause they didn't want the truth. They wanted something magical.

People wanted to believe in our fairies, whether we liked it or not.

And perhaps, after all, that was the best way for the story to end.

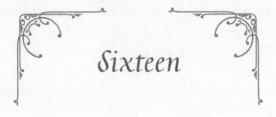

Sixteen

London and Leeds. Present day.

*L*ondon was even more chaotic than Olivia remembered. After spending melodic weeks surrounded by nothing but the gentle hush of the bookshop and the nighttime lullaby of the sea, everything was too loud and too frantic. As soon as she stepped into the arrivals hall at Heathrow, the sickening sense of dread that had started on the plane began to swell. It grew all the way through the airport, and on the train into the city center, and on the Underground across London to Waterloo.

Her breathing quickened with each station the train hurtled past: Vauxhall, Queenstown Road, Clapham Junction, Wandsworth; each stop ticked off in her mind, just as she used to mark the stops on her daily commute home: three more stops, two more stops, one more stop. She'd often been relieved to find the apartment empty when she got there.

At Putney, she left the train station, mechanically following High Street toward the river, passing wine bars where she used to drink and the tapas restaurant where she and Jack met and had their first date, all on the same night. She'd been stood up.

He was meeting a client whose flight was canceled. The champagne he'd put on ice to celebrate his business deal became Olivia's first drink with him. He had saved her from eternal mortification and swept her off her feet in the process. For a while, at least.

As she walked, she felt as if she was looking through an old photograph album, turning the pages on memories and moments, fast-forwarding through the life she'd known here.

There was no sense of regret. None at all. Yet, when she reached the apartment block, the tightness in her chest intensified.

When they'd agreed on a date for her to collect a few things, Jack had promised he wouldn't be there, but still Olivia's heart raced as the lift ascended. She counted the floors until the doors opened and she stepped into the penthouse apartment.

She could smell him. His aftershave. His hair gel. His leather brogues.

Putting her bag down, she walked to the floor-to-ceiling windows, telling herself to calm down. "Breathe, Olivia. Breathe." The Thames and all of London spread out before her like a Turner painting in the early evening haze. It was a view that had always held the promise of more, a view she'd often wished she could reverse, so that she was out there among it, not stuck in a flashy penthouse admiring it from a distance. Everything had felt inside out. Disjointed.

She noticed Jack had removed their canvas engagement photo, the pale rectangle against the sun-faded wall the only sign it had ever existed. The empty space reflected perfectly the hollow void their relationship had become, had perhaps always been.

Not wanting to stay too long, Olivia got on with the task. In the guest room wardrobe she found her boxes of books. Disorganized and mismatched and imperfect with their cracked spines and slightly torn dust jackets, brimming with personality and so out of keeping with the high-gloss apartment and its floating shelves. More show house than home, it left Olivia cold and she longed for the cramped coziness of the flat above the bookshop.

It didn't take long to do what she'd come for. After a couple of hours, she had everything she needed repacked and labeled for the courier who arrived just after seven. Once again, she was shocked to discover how quickly a life could be cleared away.

It was as if she had never been there.

In many ways, she never had.

Before she left, she placed an envelope on the kitchen island. Inside was her engagement ring and a single piece of paper on which she'd written, "I didn't need diamonds. I needed a best friend. Olivia."

She took a final moment to look around, a moment to leave behind the memories of the five years she'd spent there. This was where that part of her story ended, where the old Olivia would always be.

She closed the door behind her with a thud, and in that single sound, it was over.

From London she traveled to Leeds, dozing as the train sprinted northward. At her hotel, she sent a text to Henry to ask how Nana was. Having managed without a phone since throwing hers into the sea, it was with a sense of regret she'd bought a new one, but being away from Nana worried her, and she wanted the nursing home to be able to contact her should anything happen while she was away. Henry replied to say Nana was comfortable and Olivia wasn't to be worrying. She typed a text to Ross then, but deleted it. Too exhausted to read, she fell into bed, too exhausted even to dream.

THE FOLLOWING MORNING, she woke to rain thudding against the window, and a message from Ross wishing her good luck for her trip to Cottingley. The fact that he'd remembered, that he'd thought about her that morning, brought a smile to her face, and although it was very inconvenient given the circumstances, her heart grew a fraction fonder of him.

The Leeds University library was a stunning domed building of white brick that reminded Olivia of the White House as she made her way up the impressive steps outside. At the registration desk, she filled in various forms and was given directions to Special Collections, where the Cottingley materials were held.

The main library was a circular room, the domed ceiling arching above a polished parquet floor. Sunlight seeped in through lofty windows, sparkling against an impressive art deco chandelier and illuminating the long reading benches that spread out from the central desk like spokes on a bicycle wheel. A concentrated hush filled the air as Olivia walked around the edge of the room, past rows of deliciously old books. Her heels echoed off the floor, and she instinctively went on tiptoe to quiet them.

In Special Collections, the staff spoke in almost-whispers as she was asked to place her things in a locker and given the first box of materials, which she carried to the reading room. It was already a quiet hive of research. Half a dozen people studiously consulted the contents of gray archive boxes and pored over ancient books and photographs, their white gloves carefully turning the fragile pages. Olivia sat at an unoccupied table and opened her box. There was so much information on the Cottingley fairies, she hardly knew where to start. Miscellaneous Press Cuttings was as good a place as any.

She worked through half a dozen boxes filled with many letters, newspaper reports, and photographs, losing herself entirely in the story of Frances and Elsie and the childish prank that became a national sensation as two young girls from working-class backgrounds were consumed by the greater influence of men who moved in the right circles of polite society.

The newspaper correspondence interested Olivia especially. She read the sensational headlines from the 1920s when Conan Doyle had written his *Strand Magazine* articles. Many of these early reports were sympathetic to the notion of fairies at the bottom of the garden, their tone one of curiosity and amazement. Experts were quoted as confirming that the photographs could in no way have been faked. One report stated, "We must either believe in the almost incredible mystery of the fairy, or in the almost incredible wonder of faked photographs. Which is it to be?" Another article made Olivia smile. "For the true explanation of the fairy photographs what is wanted is not a knowledge of occult phenomena, but a knowledge of children." Through it all, she heard Frances's voice, telling her own version of events.

More recent articles suggested some sort of practical joke was at play, but always when they were asked by reporters, Frances and Elsie maintained their story. The most recent article from the *Times*, dated 1983, carried the headline: THE COTTINGLEY FAIRIES: SECRETS OF TWO FAMOUS HOAXERS. Below the headline was the familiar photograph of Frances and the fairies, her enigmatic smile gazing back at

Olivia through the years. The distance between them felt so narrow now that Olivia could almost hear the waterfall and the girls' laughter. In some ways, Frances felt like part of Olivia's family.

Family.

It had always been something of a strange notion to Olivia. Her family wasn't conventional. It was misshapen. Different from the families she observed around her. Pappy used to tell her that family is what you create, not what you're given. Olivia thought about Henry Blake and Nana. Ross and Iris. Mrs. Joyce. The bookshop. Hemingway, even. They were like a family to her now.

Box after box revealed more astonishing details of the Cottingley story and the level of scrutiny the photographs had come under, not just in Yorkshire or England but all over the world. It struck Olivia how overwhelming it must have been for Frances and Elsie. No wonder Frances had shied away from all the publicity.

As Olivia read on, it became apparent that, of all the Cottingley photographs, it was the curious fifth one that, in many ways, was considered the most interesting. Several copies of the photograph were included in the archive boxes, the same photograph Olivia had found between the pages of *Princess Mary's Gift Book* on the back of which Frances had written, "To Ellen. Real fairies!" The image was more defined in the enlarged archived prints than in the copy Olivia had. She studied the enlargements carefully and could just make out what appeared to be winged female forms among the nest-like object in the grass. Could Frances have unintentionally photographed her real fairies, after all?

An interesting piece of correspondence from Edward Gardner referred to this fifth photograph as "The Fairy Bower." He described the peculiar phenomenon of the fairy cocoon as "a magnetic bath woven by the fairies and used after dull weather and in the autumn especially." Olivia remembered Nana talking about a sixth photograph, but there was only mention of five in all the boxes of letters and articles.

She worked steadily all morning, taking a short break for lunch. Toward the end of the day, she opened the final box, which contained several envelopes labeled Miscellaneous Correspondence. In one she found a small cutting from the *Bradford Telegraph and Argus*, dated October 1948. It carried a report of a missing child from the area, and referred to a previous incident of a missing child from around the time of the First World War. "The child's mother, Ellen Hogan, a resident of Cottingley but originally from County Leitrim in Ireland, believed her daughter was taken by the fairies. The child was never found, nor was the stone fairy figurine her father had carved for her and which went missing at the same time. The mother and father are now deceased."

Olivia's heart ached for her poor great-grandmother, and for Nana Martha and for little Aisling, the sister Nana had never known, but as she picked up the next envelope, everything else faded into the distance. The other people in the room and the occasional scraping of chair legs melted away as she absorbed the words written on the archive note: "Ellen Hogan's personal letters, written to her husband during the Great War. Ellen Hogan was Frances Griffiths's schoolteacher."

With great care, Olivia removed the fragile papers from the envelope, her heart full of curiosity as she ran her fingers across her great-grandmother's neat script. Through her words, Olivia traveled with her, back over the years to Cottingley and the cottage in the woods . . .

Cottingley. May 1917

My darling Robert,

I am writing this as I sit by the cottage window, watching young Elsie Wright play at the beck with her cousin Frances, who has come to stay while her father is at war. Their laughter is such a joy to hear. It is a rare treat nowadays. I lap it up like a cat drinking cream and wish you were here to listen with me. We must try to laugh more when you come home.

I think often of the past during these long summer days, reflecting on distant places and times and the fairy stories Mammy used to tell me of Old Ireland. It was Mammy who taught me the William Allingham poem: "Up the airy mountain, / Down the rushy glen, / We daren't go a-hunting / For fear of little men; Wee folk, good folk, / Trooping all together; / Green jacket, red cap, / And white owl's feather!" Do you remember I used to sing it to Aisling when she was a baby?

Dear, sweet Aisling. The world is unrecognizable to me since she went away.

They say time is a great healer, but they are wrong. Time is a great illusionist, that's all. It tricks and it taunts. It sweeps away minutes and hours, months and years without any release from this endless wondering.

In brief moments, I can believe I am happy. I smile at the lambs capering in the fields. I appreciate the beauty of a summer's day. I'm thankful for the food on my plate. And yet, when I blow out the candle at night, it is there, waiting for me. My grief roars in like a winter storm, knocking me down to leave me broken and crumpled. It is during those dark hours when I feel the ache of her absence, when I cannot accept that I will never hold her hand again, or whisper to her of the sídhe and the púca.

And now you are gone from me too, Robert. Is there no end to this war? No end to my anguish?

I fill my days with insignificant things. I set the kettle on the stove, fill the ewer with water, peel potatoes, scrub the floors, and wash the windows until they gleam like jewels. I paint and knit and sew. I help on the farm—we are all needed to do something or other with the men away. But I can never escape this torment, no matter how many ways I try to occupy myself. If only they could tell me where she is. It is the thing that haunts me the most, the thought of our beautiful little girl alone and afraid in the dark and the cold. That cannot be how her story ends, so I create my own story for her, one where the fairies took her somewhere safe and where she will play in their world until we can meet her there.

I keep her boots beside yours on the doorstep, ready to welcome you both home. Wildflowers and moss already grow around Aisling's. Never around yours. I take comfort from it, to know that nature thrives around her, that her boots will become as much a part of this woodland cottage as she is a part of me. Of us.

Come home to me soon, dearest. The world is too dark without you both in it.

Your ever loving wife,
Ellen

x

Cottingley. July 1917

Darling Robert,

    In these balmy summer evenings, I sit at the window and pick over old tapestries that still hold the smell of the turf fires from Ireland. I pick and I stitch. I knit comforts to send to you and the boys. I knit and sew as if my life depended on it. You will think me silly, but I set myself little milestones: by the end of this spool of thread, he'll be home. By the end of this skein of wool, it'll be over.

    It never is.

    I watch the girls—Frances and Elsie—as they play at the beck, lost in the beauty and magic of the place. It pleases me to hear them. Elsie blossoms from a girl into a young woman, unfurling like the rambling roses around the cottage door. She comes alive in the company of her cousin, who encourages her to be a child again. They make a curious pair. One so tall. The other so slight. Watching them through the summer foliage is like watching a mother and child. I am reminded of how Aisling and I used to play there. How many inquisitive pairs of adventurers have sat at that old willow tree, I wonder?

    No news as such. Arthur Wright has a new camera—the whole village knows about it. Most of us have been photographed by him at some point or another! The girls brought it down to the beck yesterday. I didn't mean to pry, but their laughter drew me to the window and I watched Elsie take a photograph of Frances near the waterfall, flowers arranged on the bank in front of her. They scattered the petals into the beck before they clambered up the bank, giggling as girls do.

    I took my usual walk along the stream yesterday evening.

I like to listen to the soft cooing of the wood pigeons in the branches as the sun gilds the fields and the sheep. I stopped to pick some wildflowers and my eye was drawn to something caught in an eddy. At first I thought it was pieces of old cardboard, all sodden and bent out of shape, but I noticed drawings on them. I brought the sodden pieces back to the cottage and set them on the windowsill to dry. Only then could I piece them together, like a jigsaw puzzle, and would you believe it, they were drawings of fairies. Quite lovely too. I wonder if that was what I'd seen the girls scatter into the water, if Elsie's photograph wasn't of flowers in front of Frances—but paper fairies! I've placed the fragments of paper into my special box of Aisling's things.

I still keep the lock of her hair and yours in my locket. It is all I have to know that either of you were ever real: a single lock of hair. One as black as night, the other as red as a harvest moon. And here I am, trapped in a permanent twilight where nothing makes sense and I must dream my unquiet dreams of our beautiful little girl, playing with the fairies. Hair like flames in the setting sun. The beauty of all things around her.

Stay safe, my love.

You are always in my heart and in my prayers.

Your ever loving wife,
Ellen

x

Tears slipped silently down Olivia's cheeks as she read her great-grandmother's words, some of them almost erased with the passing of the years and the many hands that, like hers, had held these fragile memories. In reading Ellen's letters, Olivia felt incredibly close to her and to this distant part of her past. Her great-grandmother Ellen, like her Nana and her mother, was part of who *she* was, part of her story.

It didn't surprise Olivia that Ellen *had* seen Frances and Elsie take the photographs, and had found their torn-up cutouts, as Frances had worried somebody might, but she was glad Ellen had kept the girls' secret safe. She wondered what had happened to the fairy cutouts. Lost, she imagined, over the decades.

At the bottom of the box was a withered posy of dried wildflowers. Olivia knew them: harebell, bindweed, campion, and bladderwort. With the letters was a collection of paintings, some small enough to fit inside a locket. All of them were of the same red-haired girl, and always she was surrounded by fairies and flowers. Olivia knew the girl in the paintings. It was, unmistakably, the girl from her dreams.

"Aisling." The name fell from her lips in a whisper, as if someone else spoke for her.

"Excuse me, but we're closing now."

Olivia jumped at the voice beside her. The librarian smiled and apologized for giving her a fright.

Olivia began to gather her things. "Sorry. I lost track of time."

"Don't worry. Everyone does. Did you find what you were looking for?"

"Yes. More than I was looking for actually, but there's one other thing I'd like to find." She asked where she might find local newspaper reports from the early 1900s.

"Do you have a name you wish to search for?"

"Yes."

"Our microfiche might bring something up." He checked his

watch. "The main reading room is open for another half hour if you want to try."

It didn't take Olivia long to find several reports from local Bradford and Bingley newspapers regarding the disappearance of five-year-old Aisling Hogan. They stated that she was last seen by her mother when she'd checked on her before going to bed, and that the child was reported missing the following morning. She was known to sleepwalk, the reports said, and the conclusion reached by the local constabulary at the time was that she had fallen into a disused well or an old mine shaft. Only one report mentioned that the mother, local schoolteacher Ellen Hogan, of Irish descent but now living in Cottingley, believed her child had been taken by the fairies.

Olivia hadn't heard the name Aisling used in connection with her family until Nana had first mentioned it shortly after Olivia had started to read Frances's story. Having read about Frances's dreams of the little girl, and having read Ellen's heartbreaking letters to her husband, Olivia now understood why Aisling's name had never been mentioned. Her disappearance was so distressing that nobody in the family could bear to talk about it. Aisling's was an incomplete story that had tormented her mother until her dying day. No wonder she chose to believe her daughter had gone to play with the fairies.

As people began to return books to the desk and pack away their bags, Olivia scrolled through the last few reports. Her hand stilled as she read a short article from a local newspaper from the 1950s.

The remains of a young child were discovered yesterday when excavation began on a new housing

estate in Cottingley, West Riding. Although formal
identification is not usually possible in such cases,
investigating officers were able to confirm that the
remains are those of Aisling Hogan, a young child
who was reported missing in 1916, close to the area
of their discovery. The remains were found with
a small stone figurine, carved into the shape of a
fairy. It was described in detail to investigators at
the time of the disappearance by the child's mother,
the child's father having made it for her. A surviv-
ing relative, Martha Kavanagh (née Hogan), who
now lives in Ireland, attended a private ceremony
where the child's remains were interred at St. Michael's and All Angels Church cemetery, alongside
her parents.

Tears fell silently down Olivia's cheeks as she read the report. Nana had known. She'd been able to say good-bye to
the sister she'd never met, but whom she remembered when so
many other memories were now lost to her. It gave Olivia some
small comfort to know that Aisling had been found and given a
proper burial. Perhaps it was better that Ellen had died believing her own version of events, because believing in fairies was
far easier than knowing her little girl had died in such tragic
circumstances.

Olivia was the last to leave the library. Her footsteps echoed
as she walked out of the lofty room—reminding her of all the
women in her life who had come before her, and whom she
knew walked beside her still.

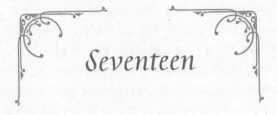

Seventeen

Cottingley, Yorkshire. Present day.

Cottingley was everything Olivia had imagined as she'd read Frances's story, her descriptions were so vivid and true: the heather-clad moors that dropped into wide, tumbling valleys, the narrow streets, the terraced houses like books on a shelf, Number 31 propping them all up like a bookend. She recognized it all, just as it had been seen through Frances's impressionable young eyes. But Olivia didn't just see the familiarity. She felt it, deep within her bones. Just like when she returned to Ireland, she had a sense of coming home, a sense that she had been here before, had once walked these streets and pulled her hat over her ears against the sharp prick of the cold east wind.

She stood opposite the humble stone-built house, where so many stories had been told and so many secrets were once held. She imagined Aunt Polly standing in the doorway, excited to see her sister and her niece, all the way from Cape Town. She could picture Uncle Arthur with his great big hands, and Elsie, as tall as the lampposts, a spark of mischief in her eyes. She saw

Frances, hesitant at the gate, because something had drawn her attention away toward the darkness beyond the end of the street.

And then she heard it. Faintly at first, and then louder as the wind changed direction: the unmistakable rush and tumble of water. Following the sound, Olivia walked through a small opening between two of the houses where the ground sloped sharply down toward a shallow stream. The beck.

Everything was exactly as Frances had described it and yet even lovelier. The little waterfall. The willow bough seat. The sunlight illuminating the leaves on the trees. It was perfect.

Glad to be alone, Olivia sat for a moment, absorbing the essence of this enchanted place where her family had once lived and played, laughed and cried, and where magical things had caught the attention of watchful young girls. She listened to the breeze as it whispered through the leaves, listened to the quiet chatter of the water as it gossiped about the things it had seen long ago. She took off her socks and boots, dipping her toes into the frigid water, smiling to herself as she heard the distant echo of laughter as Frances and Elsie had planned their joke.

After crossing the stream on the stepping-stones, Olivia dried her feet with her cardigan, put her socks and boots back on, and clambered up the other bank. She followed a narrow pathway through the trees where the grass had been flattened by other walkers and secretive nocturnal creatures. As if in a dream, she walked on, led by some instinct, by a distant memory.

Emerging into a clearing, she saw the remains of a small stone cottage, the roof having collapsed long ago, exposing rotting timber beams where crows now sat in silent respect. A low wall ran around the perimeter, enclosing what would once have been a garden but was now overgrown with a dense wilderness of long grass and weeds and wildflowers. Olivia picked her way through, resting her hands against the old walls, absorbing the soul of this place her dear Nana and great-grandmother had once called home: the cottage in the woods where bluebells came right up to the door in the spring and a fairy ring grew at the base of an old elder tree.

Birds sang in the trees around the cottage while the waterfall rushed ever onward behind the canopy of foliage. It was beautiful and serene. A private place that had known such grief and pain, and such unremitting hope and love. Olivia walked around the damaged walls, following a mossy path toward the ruined remains of the house. She peered through glassless windows, imagining the places where her family had once slept and eaten and where her great-grandmother had once sat as she'd watched two young girls play at the stream.

At the front of the cottage, she bent down and pushed aside the long grass. There they were, just as she'd known they would be. A pair of small stone boots on the step, wildflowers entwined between, around, and inside them, poking through weather-worn cracks. The sight of them, so small, gave Olivia pause as she thought about the little girl who had once lived here, once played here. She had been much loved. And she would be remembered.

Gathering a small posy from the wildflowers around her, Olivia took a moment for quiet reflection before leaving the cottage to its silent recollections, retracing her steps back through the woods, following the sound of the church bells that chimed the hour.

It didn't take her long to find the grave.

The headstone was small and weathered, the inscription partly erased by decades of rain and wind. And yet Olivia walked straight to it, crunching over the gravel pathways, past neatly tended plots, and around the church walls where pigeons roosted in the eaves and rooks cawed their rowdy welcome from the rafters.

It was the most colorful and vibrant of all the graves. Purple and pink, lavender and yellow, blue and green wildflowers bloomed all around it. Not one shop-bought bouquet. Not one pot plant. Something else had tended this grave.

Olivia bent down, running her fingertips across the lettering on the headstone.

"Here lies Aisling Hogan, who went to play with the fairies. 1911–1916."

Blinking through her tears, Olivia placed her posy of wildflowers at the foot of the headstone.

"For you, Aisling. You can rest now."

The breeze stilled around her.

All was silent.

All was as it should be.

She sat for a long time, thinking, remembering, paying her respects at the graves of her great-grandparents, Ellen and Robert, and paying her respects to little Aisling, on behalf of all those who hadn't been able to. Only when the sun dipped low on the horizon and a cool breeze nipped at Olivia's arms did she walk back into the village, to her room at the local pub.

She had just turned the key in the lock when her phone buzzed in her pocket. It was the nursing home. Could she come as soon as possible? Nana had taken a turn for the worse.

SHE WASN'T TOO late, but the nurse said it wouldn't be long. She must prepare herself, but how? How would it ever be possible to say good-bye to this woman who had become everything to her?

She took a coffee, although she didn't really want it, and crept quietly to Nana's bedside. The room was neat and tidy, everything in its place. It was as if the room knew Nana was leaving and was already packed and waiting with her suitcase, ready for wherever she was going next.

She looked unbearably frail and fragile in the bed, dressed like a summer meadow in her nightie speckled with pink and white flowers. Olivia brushed her fingers lightly over Nana's hands, remembering how Nana used to rub the backs of *her* hands when she couldn't sleep, troubled by dreams she couldn't understand.

The minutes passed slowly as the sun sank below the trees and the moon rose in an inky-blue sky, speckled with the first pinpricks of starlight. Olivia told Nana about her trip to Cottingley and how lovely the moors were beneath their heather blankets. "I found the cottage, Nana. It was exactly as you remembered it. A carpet of bluebells coming right up to the door." She took a breath before she carried on. "And I found Aisling. She's sleeping now, Nana. She's safe."

Perhaps there was the slightest flicker beneath paper-thin eyelids. The slightest movement of fingertips. A distant sigh.

Olivia could never be sure.

As darkness fell, she sat in silence, watching the rise and fall of the blue blanket. Up and down. Up and down. In these final moments, everything else fell away and life came down to nothing more than the desire for the heart to keep beating, for the bedsheets to keep up their continual ebb and flow.

"I love you, Nana," she whispered, squeezing her hand gently. "Very, very much."

Nana slept.

She didn't hear.

The hours slipped slowly away.

Olivia had nothing with her other than the few remaining pages from Frances's story. Pulling them out of her bag, she wrapped a blanket around her shoulders and began to read aloud. Whether Nana heard her or not, she wasn't sure, but she read on until the words began to swim about on the page and her eyelids became leaden, and she couldn't fight the urge to sleep any longer. As her eyes closed, the final pages of Frances's story fluttered to the floor like feathers, floating beneath the bed, where the final secrets would remain unseen, unread.

THE NURSE SHOOK Olivia gently awake at dawn. She opened her eyes and glanced toward the bed. The blanket was still. The room echoed with the sense of a life departed.

She was shown into a private room. While the nurse went to make tea and toast, Olivia stood at the window and watched the sunrise. It was peaceful and full of hope. A perfect day for a stroll along the harbor. Pappy would be waiting for Nana. She knew he would.

The nurse set the tea on a table. "She always spoke very fondly of you, Olivia, even when she wasn't entirely sure who you were." Olivia watched the clouds, rose-tinted by the sun. "But there were moments when she remembered and knew exactly who you were. And she always told me she loved you very much."

Olivia's hand stilled on her teacup as she turned around. "Did she? Really?"

The young nurse nodded. "She often told me, after your visits. 'She's a grand good girl, that one. Always says she loves me. Isn't that nice?'"

It was all she'd ever wanted to hear.

The nurse sat with her for a while, and they shared stories and memories of Nana. The tea had gone cold in the pot by the time a gray-faced man knocked lightly on the door. He was in a tartan dressing gown. Olivia recognized him as the man Nana had told her was an Olympic swimmer.

He touched Olivia gently on the arm. "Please excuse me for interrupting, but I wanted to say that I am very sorry for your loss. Martha was a special lady. It was an honor to know her." He crossed himself as he said this, and as he did, his dressing gown gaped slightly at the neck, revealing a thick ribbon and a flash of silver.

When he'd gone, Olivia asked the nurse who he was.

"That's Tom. Swam for Ireland in the Olympics once. Never goes anywhere without his medal."

Olivia smiled through her tears. Perhaps Nana had remembered more than she'd given her credit for.

The nurse placed her hand lightly on Olivia's arm. "Take your time, love. There's no hurry."

There really wasn't. On days like this, time simply wasn't relevant. This was a day to be slowly absorbed, not swept away. Today was a pause before the page was turned and the story continued.

Before Olivia left St. Bridget's, she stepped into the dayroom. The cushions were all messed up. Out of line. She plumped and straightened each one and imagined her dear Nana smiling from somewhere far away, telling her she was a grand good girl. A grand good girl, altogether.

Eighteen

Ireland. Present day.

The shop fell into a quiet mourning, and the window stopped blooming. The leaves began to brown and curl at the edges as petals tumbled from the flowers. Even the collection of white harebells in the coffee cup began to wither and die as the bright purpose Olivia had felt in recent weeks was clouded by fresh grief and the all-too-familiar ache of loss. Nana had gone, and Ross and Iris were leaving to start their new life in Kerry. The unexpectedly lovely world Olivia had discovered since returning to Ireland was disappearing too soon.

She tried to take her mind off things by throwing herself into her work. While Henry looked after the shop, she went to meetings and house clearances and auctions. With each bang of the gavel, she forced herself to stop thinking about "what if" and "what might have been" and focus instead on what she needed to do for herself and the bookshop. In the evenings, with just the radio and Hemingway for company, she took out her bookbinding tools and began to work on Frances's book. She'd forgotten how much she enjoyed the delicate intricacies of the task, how nothing else mattered while she worked. It seemed fitting that as she stitched and glued Frances's memories together, she felt herself begin to come back together a little too.

Over their final week together, Olivia read Frances's story to Iris as she'd promised she would, doing her very best voices, even though Iris giggled at her attempt to mimic the Yorkshire accents. As Olivia read, Ross worked on illustrations for *The Fairy's Tale*, which had sold to his publisher for a nice advance. He used the illustrations from *Princess Mary's Gift Book* as inspiration for his fairies.

They were pleasant, happy hours spent together, but hours in which Olivia's emotions often tripped her up, lurching from resignation to regret, acceptance to denial. Her rational mind knew it was for the best that Ross was leaving. She was, after all, still clawing her way out of one relationship. The last thing she needed was another. And yet her impetuous heart disagreed with such unromantic common sense, and as the day of Ross's departure crept closer, Olivia's heart grew closer to his.

THEY LEFT ON a peaceful sunlit morning.

Olivia promised to write as Iris sobbed onto her shoulder. "Here. This is for you." She gave Iris a package. "I made it especially for you."

Iris unwrapped the paper, beaming when she saw what it was. "You stuck Frances's book together!"

Olivia laughed. "I did. I made a copy of all the pages and bound it, just for you. It's a very rare and special book. I hope you'll take extra special care of it."

Iris was delighted, and promised she would.

As she settled into the car with her book, Ross and Olivia

stood side by side outside Something Old, gulls crying above them, clouds scudding by.

Olivia wrapped her arms around herself. "Well, here we are, then."

"Here we are, then."

Ross looked at Olivia. It was one of *those* looks. A look that made her heart turn somersaults.

"Ah, for crying out loud, Kavanagh. Come here, would you." He opened his arms, and she gave up all her grand plans to stay emotionally detached as she let herself sink into the crumples of his favorite ridiculous T-shirt. "Thank you for everything," he whispered, hugging her tightly. "You'll be okay, you know. You're back on your feet now."

She pressed her face to his chest. Yes, she was, and it was funny, because where Jack had once swept her off her feet, when she was with Ross she always felt she had them planted firmly on the ground. Far more stable. Much more secure.

Ross pulled back and brushed a tear from her cheek. "Promise you'll visit?"

"Promise."

"Often?"

"As often as I can." She almost forgot the gift she had for him. "Here. I got this for you." She pressed a book-shaped packet into his hands.

"*Ulysses*?"

She laughed. "How did you know?"

"Because you knew I would never get around to buying it myself. Thank you. I promise I'll read it." He jumped into the car and wound down the window. "I'll call you Friday. Maybe we can still have our end-of-the-week chats over a glass of wine."

"I've already put a bottle in the fridge."

Olivia waved as Ross's Mini trundled off over the cobbles, tooting a good-bye as he turned the corner and disappeared, Iris waving madly from the backseat. It was far from the fairy-tale ending Olivia might have briefly allowed herself to imagine, but as the wind swirled around her feet, blowing an unknown future away over the sea, she felt alert and alive and purposeful. She understood that whatever lay ahead for her and Ross, theirs was a quiet relationship, slowly unfurling like petals on a rose. She had to let nature take its time. Nana had always said the most beautiful blooms on her rosebushes were the last of the season. The most fragrant. The most colorful. "Those late blooms always flourish the most. They'll be around long after the others have been blown away. You wait and see."

A FEW HOURS after Ross and Iris had left, a package arrived from the photography studio in Dublin. With so much happening lately, Olivia had forgotten all about the Instamatic camera she'd found in the drawer at Bluebell Cottage. She sat down to open the package with hesitant hands.

Dear Miss Kavanagh,

I hope you are satisfied with the enclosed prints. I brought them out as clearly as possible. I think they are rather lovely.

She removed the wallet from inside the envelope and took out a dozen prints.

Everything stilled. Even the cry of the gulls receded into the background as she worked her way slowly through the prints, laying them out on the desk in front of her. In each image, her mammy smiled back at her: happy, playful, laughing. She was standing at the top of Howth Head, her belly swollen, her hands resting on her bump, the wind blowing her hair around her face. The gorse blazed vibrant yellow behind her in one photograph, the blush of red and pink rhododendrons lit up the background in another. Olivia wept tears of grief and joy, remembering her mother as clearly as if she were standing beside her. She remembered the bright peal of her laughter, the powder-soft scent of her perfume, the smooth touch of her hand against her cheek. She closed her eyes and let her mind burst with memories she had thought lost to her forever.

She wasn't alone. She never had been. All she had to do was close her eyes and remember, and her mammy would be with her.

Only briefly did Olivia wonder who had taken the photographs, recalling her great-grandmother Ellen's words from Frances's story: *"You have to look behind the picture to discover the truth. That's where you find the real story."* Whoever had taken them, they had captured her mother at her most beautiful, and for that she would always be grateful.

HENRY WAS A rock of support after Nana's passing, and Olivia grew terribly fond of him. She looked forward to their Sunday "putterings," as he called them, when she would close the shop and they took a thermos of peppermint tea to enjoy by the harbor.

Olivia was a little surprised at how much Nana's death had affected Henry. As they strolled along the harbor, she asked him to tell her what Nana had been like when she was younger.

"Oh, she was great fun. I was a good few years younger than her and Cormac, but they often invited me to join them for a drink, or a bite to eat. They were a very happy couple, and always willing to make space for one more. I was eternally single, you see. Martha used to tease me about being too choosy with the ladies. She said I would end up bitter and alone if I didn't get on with finding myself a wife. Said she didn't know what I was waiting for."

Olivia laughed. "That sounds like Nana, all right. Never one to mince her words!"

"She was a very confident woman, and very beautiful. I often thought of her like a bird, flitting about from one party to the next." He smiled to himself at the memory. "The three of us became good friends over the years." He coughed and cleared his throat as he stopped walking. "I'm afraid I fell in love with her."

"With Nana?"

He nodded. A sure, steady nod. "I was young and my heart was easily broken. It was the greatest agony of my life, to meet the woman I felt with all my heart I was meant to be with, but couldn't be."

Olivia's heart raced. "Did Pappy know?"

"Not at first. It was my secret. But it gradually became obvious, as these things tend to do. I couldn't bear to be in the same room as her and not tell her how I felt."

Olivia could hardly bear to ask the question, but she knew she had to. "Did Nana feel the same way?"

Henry hesitated before shaking his head. "She was very confused when I first told her. A little too much sherry at a Christmas party and . . . well . . . you know how it is. It was just a kiss. Nothing more. A misunderstanding."

Olivia thought about Ross and the kiss they'd admitted was a mistake, but which had felt so right.

"I felt absolutely terrible," Henry continued as they walked. "Cormac was such a devoted husband and a dear friend. It was all terribly upsetting for a while, but Martha's heart belonged to Cormac first and foremost. He was a very lucky man."

It was almost too much to take in. Another part of Olivia's family she'd known nothing about.

"What happened then?" she asked.

"I tried to forget about her," Henry said. "Tried to get on with my life, but I couldn't. That was when I knew I had to leave. I suppose you could say I ran away."

Olivia held Henry's hand. It trembled beneath her touch. Suddenly it all made sense. His easy friendship with Nana. His heartbreak over her death.

"She wrote to me," he added. "Just once. She sent a photograph of herself with her baby." He fumbled in his jacket pocket and pulled out his wallet. "I've kept it with me ever since."

Olivia took the photograph from him. Nana as a young woman, a tiny baby in her arms. "That's my mam."

"Yes. Katherine. Kitty, as she was affectionately known. I always thought it the most beautiful picture. Martha never looked happier. As soon as I saw that photograph, I knew I'd done the right thing by leaving, no matter how I felt." He wiped his eyes with his handkerchief. "I never met anyone else who came close to how I felt about Martha. Perhaps we would have been together if we'd met in different circumstances, a different time or place. You never forget a feeling like that, though. Not over a year. Or a decade. Or a lifetime. It will always be there."

Olivia thought of that breezy morning when Ross had rushed into the bookshop looking for Iris. She thought about how empty the shop had felt after he'd left at the end of each day. She thought about the kiss they had found at the bottom of the empty bottle of gooseberry-flavored wine and how full her heart was whenever she thought about him.

"I heard about your mother's accident," Henry continued. "I didn't know Kitty, not in the true sense of the word, but in another sense I did. She was Martha's daughter. Martha was part of her, the same way Kitty is part of you. I looked at the photograph every day and wished, with all my heart, I could help ease Martha's pain. That was why I came back in the end. I couldn't bear to be so far away, and although I knew I could never be with her, just to see her occasionally was enough. It was more than enough."

Olivia passed the photograph back to him. "It's all such a shock, Henry. I had no idea."

"I know this must be difficult to hear, but I want to be honest with you, Olivia. When Cormac told me he planned to leave you the shop and asked me to look out for you, he gave me a very special gift." His hands trembled in hers. "I could never have been the devoted husband and loving grandfather that Cormac was, and I owe him a great debt of gratitude for his friendship over the years. Whatever I can do to help you, I will. He especially asked me to be there for you on the anniversary of your mother's death."

Olivia thought about the book she'd found in the shop on her mother's anniversary. "Was it you who left the copy of *Peter Pan*?"

He nodded. "I hope I did it properly, the way Cormac would have done."

"You did, Henry. Thank you. It meant everything to me."

They sat together as the clouds raced each other overhead, and Olivia linked her arm through Henry's and knew it would be okay.

"We have each other now, Henry. You'll always have my support."

He patted Olivia's arm. "Thank you, dear. And I hope that if you ever find that special person, you manage to hold on to them."

THE LETTER ARRIVED from St. Bridget's the next day.

> *Dear Ms. Kavanagh,*
>
> *Please find enclosed a piece of writing that I believe belongs to you. It was found in the room occupied by your Nana, Martha Kavanagh. It had fallen beneath the bed.*
> *If it isn't yours, please return it.*

Olivia removed several folded sheets of paper. She recognized the typeface. The thin paper. The crackle of anticipation. There was one final chapter to Frances's story . . .

NOTES ON A FAIRY TALE

Epilogue

Like fairies, stories will not be rushed. Mine would take longer than most, unraveling slowly over the years like a winding stream, trickling ever onward, carrying us all along without end or pause.

I'd arrived in Cottingley as an uncertain young girl and left as a confident young lady, changed forever by the experience of the newspaper reporters and the extraordinary interest in our photographs.

Shortly after returning from the disastrous last trip to Cottingley with Mr. Hodson and his auras, my family left Scarborough. I was sorry to leave. I'd grown fond of the salty sea breezes and the crashing winter waves and the castle, standing like a sentry above us all on the cliff tops. But once again, my father's work took us elsewhere. We were on the move, blown to the market town of Shrewsbury, where life, finally, began to settle into something like normality for a teenage girl.

Sir Arthur Conan Doyle published his book *The Coming of the Fairies* in the spring of 1922. It created a bit of a stir for a while, but didn't sell as well as he might have hoped, or as well as I had dreaded. He sent me two copies, presuming, I suppose, that I would be keen to pass one to a friend as a gift. I put them both in a drawer in my bedroom, reluctant to read it, but curiosity eventually got the better of me, and I read the book over the course of several nights. It was peculiar to read about Elsie and me in ACD's words, but, as with the *Strand* articles, I was again interested in his thoughts on the subject of fairy life. When I reached the end I was surprised to have quite enjoyed the book, despite trying very hard not to.

Had I been a little older when it all happened, I'm sure I would have found ACD very interesting. It would have been nice to meet him in person. I've often wondered over the years if he might have asked me *why* I thought the fairies were there, and what they did—the questions everyone else ignored, and which I'd always found the most fascinating.

Mr. Gardner visited us once more. He was in Shrewsbury giving his Cottingley Fairies lecture to the Theosophist Society. Like Aunt Polly, my mother had developed quite an interest in the Theosophists' ideas, although my father, like Uncle Arthur, didn't particularly agree with any of it. Mummy and I went along to the lecture to hear Mr. Gardner speak, eager, I suppose, to hear his conclusions on the matter. I'd naively hoped to sit in obscurity at the back of the room and slip away unnoticed when it was over, but at the end, Mr. Gardner rushed to me, insisting on introducing me to a group of people he'd assembled in the foyer. They all fussed over me and wanted to shake my hand and said what an honor it was to meet me. I had never been so embarrassed. As we traveled home, I cried hot tears of frustration and swore that I would never have anything to do with the Theosophists or Mr. Gardner's lectures ever again.

Elsie emigrated to America, as she'd always said she would. Aunt Polly joined her there after Uncle Arthur's sudden death in 1924. It was a difficult time, but Mummy told me Aunt Polly took comfort from her Theosophical beliefs. She believed Uncle Arthur was with men he'd known all his life and that they were enjoying themselves together again, which made it easier for her to accept his death. I imagined him wringing his flat cap in those enormous hands of his, and accusing Elsie and me of being "up to summat." His funny Yorkshire ways and sayings always made me smile.

I visited Cottingley once more in the summer of 1929 while passing through on a holiday. It was midsummer and the wildflowers were in full bloom. I walked up the hill along Main Street and stopped for a moment outside Number 31. It looked exactly the same from the outside, although I could imagine Aunt Polly tutting and saying the windows needed a good clean. I followed the path around the back of the village and picked my way carefully along the riverbank, as I had done many times before. I stopped for a while at the willow bough seat—reflecting, remembering—before walking to the cottage in the woods, concealed, as always, behind the trees.

I'd kept in touch with Ellen over the years, as I'd promised I would.

Her daughter, Martha, had turned nine that spring. She was a bonny, lively girl. "Full of mischief," her father said, winking at her affectionately. We sang songs from Ireland, songs I remembered from my days in Mrs. Hogan's schoolroom. I gave Ellen a print of the first photograph Elsie had taken of me by the waterfall, and one of the curious fifth photograph, which had become known as "The Fairy Bower" and which had caused the most interest and consternation among the so-called experts. I also gave her the photograph I'd taken of the fairies at the waterfall— blurred misty images to the untrained eye, but something far more interesting to those who looked beyond the obvious. I signed a copy of *The Coming of the Fairies* for her, and gave Martha my copy of *Princess Mary's Gift Book*. It held difficult memories for me. Every time I saw those illustrations of the fairies, I thought of Elsie's cutouts, wondering if they ever did get washed out to sea. Martha was delighted with the book, and I was glad to know it had found a good home.

That was the last time I saw Ellen and Martha. We exchanged Christmas cards and occasional letters, but over the years the letters became fewer and eventually stopped altogether. The inevitable silence that descends when old friends pass away.

Interest in the Cottingley photographs also faded as the years went by and England became preoccupied with a new war. I never spoke about the events of those summers, not even to my own children, but in these, my latter years, I find quiet moments to look back through wistful eyes and think about the fairies in Cottingley beck. Occasionally, as I'm doing the washing up or weeding the garden, I catch a flash of something out of the corner of my eye, and I smile and whisper a silent thank-you.

I suppose a part of me always knew that there would be another chapter to our story, that the secret Elsie and I had kept for so many years would eventually be heard, so I wasn't entirely surprised when, forty years after that last summer at Cottingley, Elsie sent me a cutting from a newspaper interview she'd done with a reporter from the *Daily Express*, sparking interest in our photographs for a whole new generation. Neither was I surprised when, six years after that, I was contacted by a TV producer who was making a documentary about the Cottingley photographs for *Nationwide*, nor five years after that, when another TV producer contacted me about a documentary for Yorkshire Television.

The child within me had often wished for an opportunity to talk properly about the fairies. Sixty years is, after all, a long time to keep a secret, but on each occasion we were interviewed, Elsie and I remained faithful to the promise we'd made all those years ago. Our answers to the questions about the authenticity of the photographs were suitably evasive and never entirely conclusive. I wasn't sure the watching millions *wanted* our answers to be conclusive. I always remembered an American newspaper report that came out at the time the first photographs were revealed. "The soul of the fairy is its evanescence. Its charm is the eternal doubt, rose-tinted with the shadow of a hope. But the thrill is all in ourselves."

Doubt. Hope. Thrill. Words that encapsulated everything I felt about the whole event.

I suppose it was inevitable that one of us would break our silence in the end.

It was Elsie who first confessed to the trick we had played. Our secret was finally free.

I was cross with Elsie at first, but I couldn't stay cross

for long. In many ways I was glad to tell the truth. I felt a weight lift from my shoulders, despite the sensational headlines that raced across the printing presses as the story broke:

FAIRY LADY ADMITS PHOTOGRAPHS WERE FAKED! THE COTTINGLEY PHOTOGRAPHS: A HOAX!

I read the headlines while sitting in my garden, the birds singing in the hedgerows and bees buzzing around me, normal life going on as I turned the pages and read other people's accounts and awful misrepresentations of our story. It is those inaccuracies that spurred me on to tell my own version of events. As Elsie once said in an interview, "Frances and I don't care anymore. People can enjoy the fairies any way they like as far as we are concerned (so long as they get their facts right)."

As interest in the photographs revived, I started to write this book. A memoir of sorts. The record set straight. Sometimes my memories elude me: gaps I can't quite fill, names and places and dates I can't quite grasp. But all the important things are there, as clear as the day they happened. Clearest of all are my memories of the fairies, and my dreams of a little girl with flame-red hair, standing in a woodland glen. I've known many people in my life who refuse to believe in things they can't explain with scientific fact, but I'll never forget what I saw, or the comfort Ellen Hogan took from the posy of flowers I gave to her, a gift from another realm.

I met Elsie recently. Frances and Elsie, together again.

Apart from the wrinkles and the gray hair, we hadn't changed much over the years. Elsie still made me laugh with her deadpan Yorkshire humor, and I still made her wonder about things. We talked about our families mostly, swapped photographs of our children and grandchildren—so proud of them all. We didn't talk about the fairies. We'd done all our talking about that.

When we said good-bye, I wished Elsie the very best. I was so grateful to have known her, so grateful that when I stepped into the front room of 31 Main Street that cold April night, it was Elsie waiting by the fireplace with mischief in her eyes. I'm grateful that it was Elsie who first showed me the beck and that it was Elsie, and nobody else, who shared the whole experience with me. Two peas in a pod, Aunt Polly used to say. Elsie was the sister I'd never had. The friend and ally who took a photograph of me in a quiet sunlit moment in one of the most perfect places I have ever known, and captured forever a young girl with wonder in her eyes and the belief in magical things in her heart.

For many years, I could only look at that photograph with guilt and anguish. Now? Now I look at it and smile, because whatever conclusions the experts may reach about our photographs, I alone know what that little girl saw, and she will hold that treasure in her heart forever.

THE END

But it wasn't quite the end.
Olivia turned the page and read on.

Afterword

My first memory of Frances Griffiths is sitting beneath an elder tree, looking at a children's picture book with her. I admired it so much she said I could keep it.

I was a young girl of about nine and lived in a pretty cottage beside a stream—the beck—in the West Yorkshire village of Cottingley. Frances knew my mother well—she had been Frances's teacher in Bradford during the Great War. They became friends of sorts, drawn together by their shared worries of loved ones at war and what my mother described as "a particular sensitivity to nature."

I knew nothing about the Cottingley fairy photographs until that summer when Frances came to visit. She gave Mammy some photographs, which they talked about for a long time, and when she left, I begged Mammy to tell me about them. I especially liked the photograph of Frances leaning on a mossy bank, surrounded by fairies, and was thrilled when Mammy said I could keep it. She put it in a silver frame for me and I treasured it, believing—like everyone else—that the fairies were real. I spent the rest of that summer playing by the beck, sitting on the willow bough seat, watching, waiting, hoping.

Mammy died long before the truth behind the famous photographs was revealed, but shortly after her death I found some letters she'd written to my father during the war in which she told him how she'd watched the girls take their photographs and that she had found the drawings they'd used to create them. She never told anyone, of

course. That was her own part in the secret. Paper drawings or not, when Frances and Elsie finally admitted to
their trick, Frances firmly maintained that she really did
see fairies at the beck.

I was much older when my mother first told me about
Aisling and although I'd never known her, I felt as if I did.
I'd often dreamed of a little girl with red hair, playing in
the woods, and I often found flowers in our cottage, particularly white harebells and an unusual yellow flower called
cinquefoil, known to be symbolic of dreams and a mother's
love. Mammy said she believed they were little gifts from
Aisling and the fairies.

Poor Mammy took her grief to her grave. Aisling's remains were found several years later and I was glad to be
able to travel to Cottingley to see her laid to rest. She is the
sister I never knew, but she is never forgotten. I often feel
her—an echo, a shadow, a flash of light, the sense of someone walking beside me. I talk to her sometimes. People
think I'm going daft in the head, hearing voices, seeing
things. But I know what I see, what I hear.

Frances wrote to me a few years ago to say she was writing her account of the Cottingley events. She eventually
sent on the finished pages with a note saying she thought
I might like a copy, since so much of the story included
my mother and my dear sister. I am pleased to have it,
although not entirely sure what to do with it. My husband
says if he ever opens his bookshop he'll have it bound and
kept on display. Cormac doesn't believe in fairies, but he
does believe in the power of stories. We both believe that
Frances's story deserves to be told.

In many ways, I wish the story had ended that autumn

of 1917, that the girls' secret had remained theirs alone. But some secrets are too big to keep and even as I write these final comments, I have a feeling that Frances's story will go on. In interviews, Frances often spoke about the curious fifth photograph—but she never referred to it as the last.

I wonder.

People speculate about why Frances and Elsie didn't admit to the hoax sooner, but I can understand why. So many people made the story their own, twisting and turning the facts so that in the end it almost wasn't Frances and Elsie's truth to tell anymore. The story they had created— albeit unintentionally—filled people with excitement and wonder and hope. The truth would have destroyed the girls and their family, not to mention the hopes of a nation recovering from war.

In Frances's final years, people still asked her if she really *had* seen fairies at the bottom of the garden. Now that her story is written down, I suppose people will make up their own minds. I only hope that Frances and her fairies will be talked about for many years to come.

Perhaps I'll write my own story one day. It would be nice to capture my memories before I become too old and forgetful.

For now, dear reader, thank you for setting Frances's words free. May they fly ever onward.

Martha Kavanagh
July 1987

Beneath these last typed words of Nana Martha's was a handwritten note. Olivia's heart roared with emotion as she read it.

Dear reader,

My mother once told me that if a lie is told often enough it will eventually become the truth. Like any story well told, with each re-telling it grows and strengthens so that over many years we might forget it was ever anything but the truth. That is, after all, how legends and myths are born. She always believed that was what happened in Cottingley. A little white lie, told for good reason, became a story in itself. A story that has endured for decades.

The photograph of Frances and the fairies has passed down through several generations of my family, and now belongs to me. I keep it in my jewelry box in the same silver frame my Nana Ellen first placed it in. One day I'll show it to Olivia and tell her all about Frances and Elsie and the fairies in Cottingley, just as my mother told me, and as her mother told her. Like all good fairy stories, it should endure and grow.

Photographs have always fascinated me; the way they offer a portal into our past, the way they capture a fleeting moment and make it last forever. There is one particular photo of myself and Olivia that I especially love, the tips of our noses just touching as she gazes into my eyes. When I look at it, I'm instantly transported back to that moment: her adorable fat little hands scrunched into tiny balls, the delicious folds of her skin, the ripe-peach smell of her, the velvet touch of her hair, her searching eyes following something around the room as she gurgled into space. I wonder what she saw.

I found Frances's book when I was clearing out the back bedroom at my parents' cottage. I read it on quiet afternoons while the wind howled around the eaves and Olivia sent her teddies and dolls on great adventures.

I can hear her now as I write this, making up her innocent little stories.

I love her more than I can find the words to say.

It breaks my heart to know that she will grow up and have to try to understand the world, with all its complications and uncertainties. I hope she won't try to understand everything, and that some of the magic she knows now will stay with her.

Perhaps she'll ask about her father one day, and I will tell her what a kind and clever and wonderful man he was. Like every good story, I will make him the best sort of hero, because that is the father she deserves. I will invent a story for her, one we can believe in together, because she deserves more than the truth as far as he is concerned. We will learn to do this together, Olivia and I. She will teach me how to be a good parent, and I will teach her how to tie her shoelaces and how to tell the time on a dandelion clock. As in all good fairy tales, we will find our happy ending.

Our story is just beginning, but Olivia will write her own conclusion. And perhaps that is the greatest gift I can give her: the confidence to fill the blank page, the desire to live a life full of tomorrows in which everything is possible and all our best stories are waiting to be told.

Katherine (Kitty) Kavanagh
April 1988

The wind rattled the door frame.

Time seemed to stop, a respectful silence in which a lifetime shifted and found a new center. Olivia clutched these final pages to her chest as tears slipped down her cheeks in silent silver ribbons.

Frances had not only written a fascinating account of her incredible fairy photographs, but in doing so, she had brought together all the disparate parts of Olivia's story too.

Olivia worked late, stitching and gluing until these final loose pages became part of Frances's account, and everything was encased in a new leather cover. With painstaking care, she added the title in gold lettering on the front:

"Notes on a Fairy Tale, by Frances Griffiths."

The story, complete.

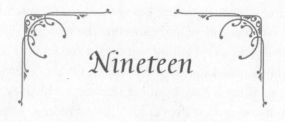

Nineteen

Ireland. Three months later.

*I*reland was at its loveliest in the autumn: sun-gilded and rosy-cheeked. It was a season of growth and abundance, the season when Olivia felt most alive. This was her spring. Her renewal.

Since Nana's death, life had taken on a different shape. Losing the last link to her past, the last remaining member of her immediate family, had left Olivia feeling peculiarly alone, untethered to anyone and anything, although Henry often reminded her that nobody can ever be truly alone when they are surrounded by stories, as she was.

Although it was sometimes undeniably daunting, she found a new confidence from having to stand on her own two feet and get on with things. Nobody was going to pick her up or rub it better. Nobody actually needed her, apart from Hemingway, and whether he needed anything other than the occasional bit of food and a bed to curl up on was a matter for debate. But that was okay, because Olivia now realized that it was far more important for her to support herself than to depend on someone else. She knew who *she* was. Without question or doubt, she knew what she wanted, and why.

Eventually the shock and devastation she'd caused by calling off the engagement and canceling the wedding dissipated. Like ink in water, everything had settled and found a new path and although it was upsetting at times, Olivia never faltered. The only lasting legacy from her five years with Jack was the chance discovery that she couldn't have children. This, above all else, broke her heart, and yet she knew she would be okay. Yes, life for her would be different now, but no less complete.

As for Jack, they'd spoken a few times, mostly civilly and mostly about practical monetary matters. Olivia had heard a rumor he was already in a relationship with someone else, which didn't surprise her. For all his showmanship, Jack was hopeless on his own. He needed the accessory of a woman on his arm as much as he needed his expensive watch. Whenever she thought about him, it was only ever with a sense of dispassionate relief that she'd had the courage to trust herself and accept the truth of their relationship. The date of their would-be wedding passed with little to mark it other than a text from Ross to say he hoped she was bathing in champagne and not hitting the gin.

Dear Ross. She thought about him often—too often, perhaps. Not only in the quieter moments when she had time to stop and think and miss his smile and the strumming of his guitar, but also in rowdy moments of excitement when she found herself wishing he was there to share it with her. That, perhaps, was when she felt most alone.

Iris wrote once a week, telling Olivia all about her new school and how nice everyone was and, as promised, Ross called for a chat every Friday evening when he'd finished writing and Olivia had locked up. He poured a glass of wine in Kerry and she poured a glass of wine in Howth and they spent half an hour or so putting the world to rights and making each other laugh. They were both still firmly of the opinion that it was best to be friends and not romantically entangled, but even so, absence did what absence does, and as the weeks and months slipped by, two hearts grew ever fonder.

As life settled down, the garden in the window began to grow again: tender stems and green shoots and tiny hopeful buds, waiting for Olivia when she went downstairs each morning. Still she couldn't explain it, and still she didn't wish to. She saw the window for what it was: a reflection of herself. It thrived when she thrived. It faltered when she faltered. Like breathing in and out, she and the shop were connected in every way it was possible to be.

But just when Olivia thought life was settling down into some sort of new normality, there was one final surprise in store.

It arrived in an envelope one amber-tinted October afternoon. Inside the envelope was a key with a label attached. It read: Number 6, Little Lane. Taking the key, Olivia stepped outside to the empty cottage beside Something Old. The key turned easily in the lock.

The interior was clear and bright. Bare white walls and dark oak floorboards. On a wall to the right hung a picture frame, inside which was a flattened coffee cup, the inscription *Live* facing outward.

She smiled and picked up a note from the desk.

"The sun shines for you he said the day we were lying among the rhododendrons on Howth head in the grey tweed suit and his straw hat the day I got him to propose to me . . ."
See, I read it. Nice try, Kavanagh. Nice try! R xx

Another envelope on the desk was addressed to her. Opening it, she read the letter inside.

Dear Olivia,

Welcome to your new shop! I've been working on this for a while but couldn't say anything because I wasn't sure what—if anything—would come of it, but finally everything is confirmed.

When my nephew was going through your grandfather's paperwork, he discovered the original deeds to the cottages on Little Lane. It has come to light that Something Old and the cottage beside it are legally considered to be one property. They were originally built as one cottage—Number 5—which was divided into two smaller properties in the late 1800s. It is all rather complicated and no surprise that the detail was missed when your grandfather leased his part of the property.

Nora Plunkett's husband was the last shopkeeper in cottage 6, and, as you know, it has been vacant since he passed away several years ago. I suspect this was as much to do with Nora grieving for her husband as it was to do with not being overly fond of your grandfather. In any event, and without getting into too much detail about ground rent and lapsed leases, it was Cormac's all the time—and now it is yours. I know you will make it something very special indeed.

Warmest wishes—and congratulations.
Henry Blake

PS The picture and the note are a welcome gift from Ross. He said you would understand. He also tidied the place up a bit. He's a very pleasant young man.

The wind whistled down the chimney breast, bringing with it the distant refrain of a familiar song. Olivia's heart danced as she looked around the empty shop. She already knew exactly what she was going to do with it.

SOMETHING NEW OFFICIALLY opened on a breezy November afternoon. With the advice and help of Henry and his nephew, the bookshop finances were much healthier and Olivia managed to furnish (albeit sparsely) and stock the new shop. Nora had been surprisingly civil about it all, and had even given Olivia a lovely oak bookcase her husband had made, which was still in the empty shop. She'd said it was nice to know a little bit of him would always be there and that she'd been silly keeping the place empty all these years.

"I just couldn't bear to see anyone else in *his* shop," she explained. "But I suppose life goes on . . ."

Olivia said she understood and felt the same way about Pappy and Something Old.

It was a truce, of sorts.

The sign arrived just in time for the opening: the same lettering as Something Old, the same slightly wonky perfection as Olivia hung it deliberately lopsided.

She was delighted with the small gathering of friends who came to wish her well with her new venture: other shop owners, regular customers, Mrs. Joyce, the ladies from the St. Vincent de Paul, the nurses from St. Bridget's. Even the solicitor and the accountant came. And of course, Henry and Hemingway. Nora Plunkett made a brief appearance, during which she pointed out that the window frames needed painting, before wishing Olivia all the best with the shop. But it was the addition of Ross and Iris that made the occasion perfect.

Olivia's occasional weekend trips to Kerry had become increasingly regular. Henry was happy to take charge at the shop as Olivia willed the miles to pass faster so she could get to Ross sooner. They walked on the hills with Iris during the day, and drank good wine beside the fire at night. Sometimes they opened a second bottle, and it was always a good idea.

Olivia smiled as they stood side by side across the street from the two shops.

Something Old.

Something New.

A breath in, and a breath out.

"When do you have to go back?" she asked.

"Tomorrow."

"So soon?" It was always going to be too soon.

"Here. I got you something." He handed Olivia a silver photo frame. "A good-luck gift, and to replace the one the cat broke." Hemingway had knocked the photo frame over the previous week while Olivia was on the phone with Ross. She'd only mentioned it in passing and was touched that he'd remembered. "I know it meant a lot to you," he added.

Olivia took the gift, and as she did she reached for Ross's hand, wrapping her fingers around his. Pieces of a puzzle that fit together perfectly.

THE BELL JINGLED brightly above the door of Something Old as Olivia stepped inside. The old silver picture frame sat on the desk, the glass cracked across Frances's face where Hemingway had knocked it over. She turned it over, carefully loosening the clasps at the back. They were stiff and unyielding, having not been moved for such a long time. She broke two nails before resorting to scissors to prize the rusted clasps apart.

When the clasps finally relented, Olivia lifted off the black backing of the frame, then a layer of thin cardboard, beneath which was a lock of red hair and several fragile fragments of paper, which she placed on the desk, fitting them together piece by piece: the faintest hint of lavender, emerald, and blue, the tip of a wing, the edge of a dress. She smiled as she recognized the fairy cutouts from the photograph of Frances and the fairies. How clever of her great-grandmother Ellen to have kept them hidden here. Olivia thought how much she would have liked to meet her. She had a feeling they would have got along very well.

She turned her focus back to the picture frame then, lifting out a small photograph concealed behind the one of Frances. It was an unusual image, but Olivia recognized the waterfall, the beck, the backdrop of trees and ferns. Half a dozen dots of blurred light patterned the image, wispy strands of something misty and peculiar. She ran her fingertips over them lightly as a broad grin spread across her lips. It was the photograph Nana had described. She had remembered it correctly, after all.

With great care, Olivia placed everything into the new frame, exactly as it had been in the original. With everything in order, she pushed the clasps shut and stood the frame on the desk. Frances smiled back at her. Her secrets would always be safe.

The photograph often attracted comment and conversation, and as Olivia discovered, comment and conversation were what ultimately sold books. When people asked her if the fairies were real, she asked them what *they* thought. With only a few exceptions, most people chose to believe they were. Whether fairies were real or not, Olivia liked to believe in the possibility. As Pappy always said, possibility is where all the best stories begin.

From the very beginning, as far back as her great-grandmother Ellen, Olivia's story hadn't been conventional or easy, but each of the women in her life had kept turning the page, living another chapter, forming the provenance that she would, one day, inherit. Where once she had dreaded what lay ahead, Olivia now relished the prospect of filling the empty page. Hers was a narrative she would write in her own words, in her own time. She would be the mapmaker, the storyteller, the dreamer of dreams.

On brighter Sundays, when the two shops were closed, she loved to climb to the top of Howth Head and admire the view, and sometimes, when the wind blew in the right direction, she would catch it: a faint whisper at first and then louder. The refrain of a song her mammy used to sing to her, wildly operatic and wonderfully silly. She would close her eyes and listen, the golden autumn sun warm against her cheeks as she thought about the determined, inquisitive little girl she'd once been and the determined, optimistic woman she'd become.

She had always been there, watching, waiting.

To find her, all she'd had to do was believe in her.

THE END

Acknowledgments

•

I'm always a little conflicted when I write my acknowledgments—excited to be a step closer to the book meeting readers, but sad to say good-bye. It's a bit like turning the lights on at the end of a great party when everyone has to leave. But leave I must, and I'll try to be brief with my thanks. Brief-ish.

Firstly, to Damien, Max, and Sam. I know I go a bit crazy when I write, but, well, you're stuck with me, so thank you for understanding and keeping me sane! And to all my family, thank you for tolerating my writerly nonsense and for all your support. Special thanks to my father-in-law, Joe, who tells unsuspecting strangers about my books on his holidays.

Writing a book can be a lonely process but no writer writes alone. It is a huge team effort and I'm so grateful to everyone involved, especially my amazing editors, Lucia Macro and Kate Bradley, who see the potential in a story before I see it myself and who make my words make sense. I adore working with you both.

Huge thanks to the following teams of wonder-people. In the U.S., my publisher Liate Stehlik, Molly Waxman, Jennifer

Hart, Michelle Podberezniak, Carolyn Coons, and all at William Morrow. In the UK, our esteemed leader Charlie Redmayne, my publisher Kate Elton, Kimberly Young, Charlotte Brabbin, Emile Chambeyron, and all at HarperFiction. In Ireland, the inimitable Tony Purdue, Mary Byrne, and Ann Marie Dolan—thank you for everything, especially the Espresso Martinis!

To my wonderful agent, Michelle Brower, who continues to amaze me with her passion, business sense, baking skills, and calm advice. Thank you for taking me with you (I would have clamped my hands around your ankles if you hadn't, which could have been awkward).

So many friends—in real life and online—cheer me on through every page of every book. You are too numerous to thank individually, but you know who you are and I hope you also know how much I appreciate your kindness. Special thanks to Paul Keogh for legal property advice, Ruth Francis Long for taking me through the intricacies of rare books, Heather Webb and Sheena Lambert for early reads and good advice (Heather, I'll see you in Paris! x), Catherine Ryan Howard for her B&B service and making me laugh most days, and to my Harpergals, Carmel Harrington and Fionnuala Kearney, it's such a pleasure to share this journey (and the parties!) with you both. Thanks also to everyone at the stunning Tyrone Guthrie Centre, Annaghmakerrig for providing the perfect writing sanctuary for a few days (and thanks to Miss Worby for not haunting me *too* much).

To all the hardworking book bloggers, booksellers, and of course, you, the reader . . . thank you for your amazing support. Please don't stop!! I must also mention my writing heroes, who inspire me every day and some of whom I was fortunate to meet while I was writing this book (my particular apologies to Tracy Chevalier for being a mumbling star-struck fool in your presence).

Finally, my sincere thanks to Christine Lynch for inviting me into her home and her family, and for being so gracious with her time and her support for this book, all of which I'm so grateful for. And to Frances, Elsie, and the fairies. Thank you for bringing a little bit of magic into the world. It seems to me that we could do with an awful lot more.

About the author

About the book

Read on

P.S.

Insights,
Interviews
& More . . .

*

Meet Hazel Gaynor

Deasy Photographic

HAZEL GAYNOR is the *New York Times* and *USA Today* bestselling author of *A Memory of Violets* and *The Girl Who Came Home*, for which she received the 2015 Romantic Novelists' Association Historical Romantic Novel of the Year award. Her third novel, *The Girl from The Savoy*, was an *Irish Times* and *Globe & Mail Canada* bestseller, and was shortlisted for the 2016 Bord Gáis Energy Irish Book Awards Popular Fiction Book of the Year.

Hazel was selected by the U.S. *Library Journal* as one of Ten Big Breakout Authors for 2015, and her work has been translated into several languages.

Originally from Yorkshire, England, Hazel now lives in Ireland. ❧

Hazel's "Notes on a Fairy Tale"

THE COTTINGLEY SECRET is my fourth novel and, perhaps more than any other, the one I was always meant to write.

On a June afternoon in 2015, I was brainstorming ideas for my next book with my agent. I had several possibilities that all excited me, but it was a line in an e-mail from her that gave me goose bumps: "Have you ever thought of doing something around the Cottingley fairies?" I still have that e-mail, and my response: "OMG. I adore the Cottingley fairies! How did you know?!!!!!" I included the iconic image of Frances and the fairy ring with my reply.

The funny thing is, I'd saved a link to information about the Cottingley Fairies in my Ideas folder years previously, and in 2013 attended a writing workshop in Dublin with author Katharine McMahon, who used the photograph of Frances and the fairies as a writing prompt. I was the only person in the group who recognized it. I wanted to know more about that little girl and the story surrounding the famous photograph.

But the most astonishing part of my coming to write this book was yet to happen.

After searching online for information about the Cottingley photographs, and particularly about Frances and Elsie, I sent an e-mail requesting a copy of a book called *Reflections of the Cottingley Fairies: Frances Griffiths in Her Own* ▶

Hazel's "Notes on a Fairy Tale" *(continued)*

Words. The reply that came back floored me. "Hi Hazel, I published my mother Frances Griffith's autobiography privately in 2009 . . ." I had unwittingly stumbled across Frances's daughter, and what's more, she lived in Belfast, only a two-hour drive from my home. It was an unbelievable coincidence.

I first met Christine Lynch at her home in September 2015. We spent hours together, talking about Frances and Christine's memories of her mother. She told me about the book Frances had always wanted to write to tell her side of the story. I told her about my ideas for my novel, which she liked. We kept in touch over the following months as my story began to take shape. We swapped family news and photos. We met again. And again.

Getting to know Christine, and with exclusive access to Frances's abandoned writings, I felt a wonderful sense of connection to that young girl in the black-and-white photograph. As I read more about the events that unfolded between 1917 and 1921, what also struck me was how the residents of Cottingley would have been caught up in all the talk of fairies, and this got me wondering: What if someone saw the girls taking the photographs? What if there were others in Cottingley who also believed in fairies? It was these questions, and the generational connection between Christine and Frances, that led to the creation of my fictional characters Ellen, Martha, and Olivia. Through these characters and my imagined connection between them and Frances, I was able to look at the events in Cottingley from another point of view, as well as from the firsthand perspective of Frances and her immediate family.

Ellen Hogan became my link between this secretive sepia-tinted past and the present. The idea of family secrets and treasured mementos passing down through generations fascinates me, and through Olivia and her Nana Martha, I wanted to explore how the photograph of Frances and the fairies might become that key to unlocking the past, a way for Olivia to find her own truths as she accepts how little time she has to capture her family's history. My grandma turned ninety-seven as I wrote *The Cottingley Secret*. I love talking to her about the past and discovering my family history, and the possible secrets hidden within it. We all have them, after all.

Writing Frances's story was an amazing experience. She has sat beside me on my desk for nearly two years now, that enigmatic smile watching me, making sure I do her story justice. That such an innocent prank should have become part of national British folklore is testament to the girls themselves. At a time when England mourned for those lost in the horrors of the Great War, Frances and Elsie inadvertently gave people something positive to cling to. In their fairy photographs, they offered hope and something quite magical. It is, perhaps, no great wonder that being rooted in such turbulent times, the photographs and the story associated with them took on such an everlasting life of their own.

When I visited the Cottingley collection at Brotherton Library at Leeds University, I was amazed by the sheer volume of correspondence about the photographs, and how quickly the story spread following the publication of Conan Doyle's *Strand Magazine* articles. When you see the scale and tone of these letters—most of which confirm the photographs as being entirely genuine—it is not difficult to understand why the girls kept quiet. The story took on a life of its own until it must have become impossible to even think about telling the truth. As Elsie said in an interview following her confession, "The joke was to last two hours, and it has lasted 70 years." Letters from Edward Gardner to both Frances and Elsie in November 1920 must have been alarming to say the least. "I send just this line at once as the *Strand* is out today and I am already getting numerous enquiries about the fairies. . . . It is just possible you may be found out and an attempt made to interview you despite my endeavour to protect you and yours from discovery. . . ."

And of course, amid all the fuss surrounding the photographs, Frances knew that she really *had* seen things at the beck, and her belief in that never wavered. As was reported in the *Times* in July 1986, beneath the headline "Fairy Lady Dies with Her Secret," "The girl who photographed fairies 70 years ago in a Yorkshire dell died last week insisting to the end that one of her pictures was genuine. . . . In her half-finished autobiography, she insists that the last photograph taken at Conan Doyle's behest in 1920 and titled Fairy Bower, showed real fairies." ▶

Hazel's "Notes on a Fairy Tale" *(continued)*

There is still hope among Frances's family that this fifth image will be analyzed with modern technology to determine once and for all what it shows. As for my suggestion that there is a sixth photograph, this is purely speculation on my part, and yet there is a line in Marjorie Thompson's book *Seeing Fairies* that refers to her "remarkable efforts to confirm the rumour of a sixth Cottingley photograph. . . ." It is also suggested that a number of the marked glass plates given to the girls by Conan Doyle and Gardner were never accounted for. So, who knows?

The Cottingley Secret is also, in part, a love letter to bookshops. Although entirely fictitious, Something Old was inspired by a lovely little bookshop in Cavan town, in Ireland, called Blackbird Books. I was so sorry to hear that the shop closed shortly before I finished writing this book. All bookshops—but especially independently owned ones—are very special places. We often take them for granted, but we always miss them when they're gone. If you have a bookshop near you, please please support it. Buy books there for your family and friends and for your children's friends. Heck, buy books for yourself!

Like the very best fairy tales, the story of the Cottingley fairy photographs endures and changes a little in each retelling, and with 2017 marking the centenary of the first two photographs, I am sure a new generation will discover these iconic images for the first time. As Frances said in a letter to Gardner in December 1920, "Thank you very much for the £5 which I received yesterday. I am very pleased that the photos have given pleasure to somebody." I don't suppose she could ever have imagined that her photographs would still be enchanting us a century after they were first taken.

Perhaps the final words on the matter are best expressed by a British TV documentary from 1975: "Elsie and Frances have lived happily ever after, and today, sixty years on, the mystery of the fairies they saw here at Cottingley remains delightfully unresolved. Some people believe in it implicitly. Others say it's nonsense. But the lovely thing about this fairy story is that no one can ever be quite sure. Good night."

The Cottingley Fairy Photos

"Frances and the Fairy Ring" (1917)
The first photograph, taken by Elsie. This was labeled "Alice and the Fairies" in Conan Doyle's first *Strand Magazine* article. ▸

"Elsie and the Gnome" (1917)

The second photograph, taken by Frances. This was labeled "Iris and the Dancing Gnome" in Conan Doyle's first *Strand Magazine* article.

"Frances and the Leaping Fairy" (1920)

The third photograph, taken by Elsie. This was labeled "Alice and the Leaping Fairy" in Conan Doyle's second *Strand Magazine* article.

"Elsie Presented with Flowers" (1920)

The fourth photograph, taken by Frances. This was labeled "Iris with Fairy Carrying a Bunch of Harebells" in Conan Doyle's second *Strand Magazine* article.

"The Fairy Bower" (1920)

The fifth photograph. This wasn't printed in the *Strand Magazine* articles, but became the focus of much speculation, even as to which of the girls took it. ᴄ✕

Note from
Christine Lynch

I TOTALLY BELIEVE my mother Frances when she said she saw fairies in the late days of the First World War. From an early age, Frances could "hear" people's thoughts and had to "close her mind" to stop others from "reading" her own thoughts. She took it for granted that everyone was the same. Frances was not a daydreamer like Elsie. As she said herself, she was a very practical person with no imagination at all.

In the spring of 1917, she was a newcomer to England and the village of Cottingley, a bright, intelligent little girl of nine years of age who had just won a scholarship to Bingley Grammar School. Returning from school in the late afternoon, she would run down to the beck at the end of the garden, and it was here she spent endless hours listening to the sound of water as it trickled over the rocks, sitting on an overhanging branch of a willow tree, absorbed in the atmosphere of the glen. Her secret life of seeing fairies began. It doesn't take much imagination on our part to understand that these were the right conditions for someone like Frances to see this rare form of life, and on a daily basis too.

I truly believe Frances saw fairies over the summers of 1917, 1918, and 1920. Although the first four of the five Cottingley photos were faked, I am certain the fifth and final photograph—what Conan Doyle called "The Fairy Bower"—was genuine and would like to see a full investigation into this photograph. With today's advanced technology, who knows what might be revealed from an in-depth examination of the original glass plate? With enhancement, the wings seen at the top of the grasses could reveal the fairies to whom they belong. The faint, partially emerging figure to the right could reveal the full image of a fairy. I myself have seen the hand of the beautiful fairy on the left of the glass plate enlarged to the extent that I could see the lines between her little fingers. Perhaps even more figures could be found in the grasses when work is done on the plate. Who ▶

Note from Christine Lynch *(continued)*

knows? What a challenge for someone with imagination!

I was delighted when Hazel contacted me to talk about the book she was planning to write on the Cottingley fairy story—in time for the hundredth anniversary of those seminal events—and I look forward to sharing it with my family. ◠

Christine Lynch
Belfast, December 2016

Reading Group Questions

1. Were you aware of the Cottingley fairy photographs before reading *The Cottingley Secret*? If so, what surprised you most in learning more about the events that unfolded? If not, what is your reaction to the story?

2. Frances and Elsie developed a very close friendship. How did their relationship influence the decision to fake the fairy photographs?

3. Ellen Hogan's belief that her daughter was taken by the fairies was inspired by the W. B. Yeats poem "The Stolen Child." What are your favorite fairy tales or poems?

4. The possibility of fairy life captured a nation's imagination in the early 1900s. Are we still as fascinated in the possibility now? If so, why do you think that is?

5. Arthur Conan Doyle's *Strand Magazine* articles were pivotal in making the Cottingley photographs public knowledge. What is your reaction to how he and Edward Gardner dealt with the girls and their family?

6. The girls had several opportunities to confess to the trick they played on their parents. Do you think they ▶

should have told the truth, or were they justified in keeping this a secret?

7. Olivia feels disconnected from her family's past, and it is only through discovering Frances's story and reading about her great-grandmother that she begins to understand her family history. Do you talk to your older relatives about the past? What events and memories do they enjoy talking about, and what do they find it difficult to talk about?

8. Olivia is at a pivotal point in her life when she inherits Something Old. How did you respond to her relationship with Jack and Ross, and her decision to call off the wedding?

9. *The Cottingley Secret* is partly a love letter to bookshops, and Something Old is depicted as a magical place. What is your favorite bookshop to visit, and why?

10. Inscriptions in books are mentioned several times in *The Cottingley Secret*. Do you inscribe books you give as gifts? Do you have a favorite inscription in a book you have received?

11. Olivia and Frances become connected by their dreams of Aisling, the mysterious little flowers, and the garden that grows in the window of Something Old that reflects these dreams and Olivia's state of mind. Do you think it is

possible for reality and imagination to become blurred in this way?

12. Even after it was admitted that the first four photographs were faked, Frances always maintained that the fifth photograph was genuine and that she really did see fairies at Cottingley beck. What is your response to that?

13. Frances and Elsie kept their secret for seventy years. Why do you think Elsie eventually confessed? Was she right to do so?

14. There are still many places in Ireland where fairy folklore is alive and well, with fairy forts shown great respect and the community refusing to build on them or affect them in any way. Do you believe in fairies? ∾

Further Reading

IF YOU WOULD LIKE to read more widely about the Cottingley fairies, or fairy sightings or fairy tales in general, the following might be helpful, as they were to me during my research.

Reflections on the Cottingley Fairies: Frances Griffiths in Her Own Words (Frances Griffiths & Christine Lynch)
Seeing Fairies (Marjorie T. Johnson)
The Coming of the Fairies: The Cottingley Incident (Sir Arthur Conan Doyle)
The Case of the Cottingley Fairies (Joe Cooper)
The Book of Fairy and Folk Tales of Ireland (W.B. Yeats)
Fairy Tales of Ireland (Sinéad de Valera)

The full Cottingley archive is held in Special Collections at the Brotherton Library, University of Leeds, England, and can be viewed by appointment.
Older children (10+) may find Mary Losure's book *The Fairy Ring: Or Elsie and Frances Fool the World* an interesting account of the Cottingley events, and for younger children the Cicely Mary Barker Flower Fairies books are wonderful. *Peter Pan* (J.M. Barrie) and *The Water Babies* (Charles Kinglsey) are also mentioned in *The Cottingley Secret*. ◡